The
DRAGON
RELICS
Book Three of the
ARLON PROPHECIES
RANDY
MCWILSON
with CHASE MCWILSON

Moving Images
Publications
Cape Girardeau, Missouri

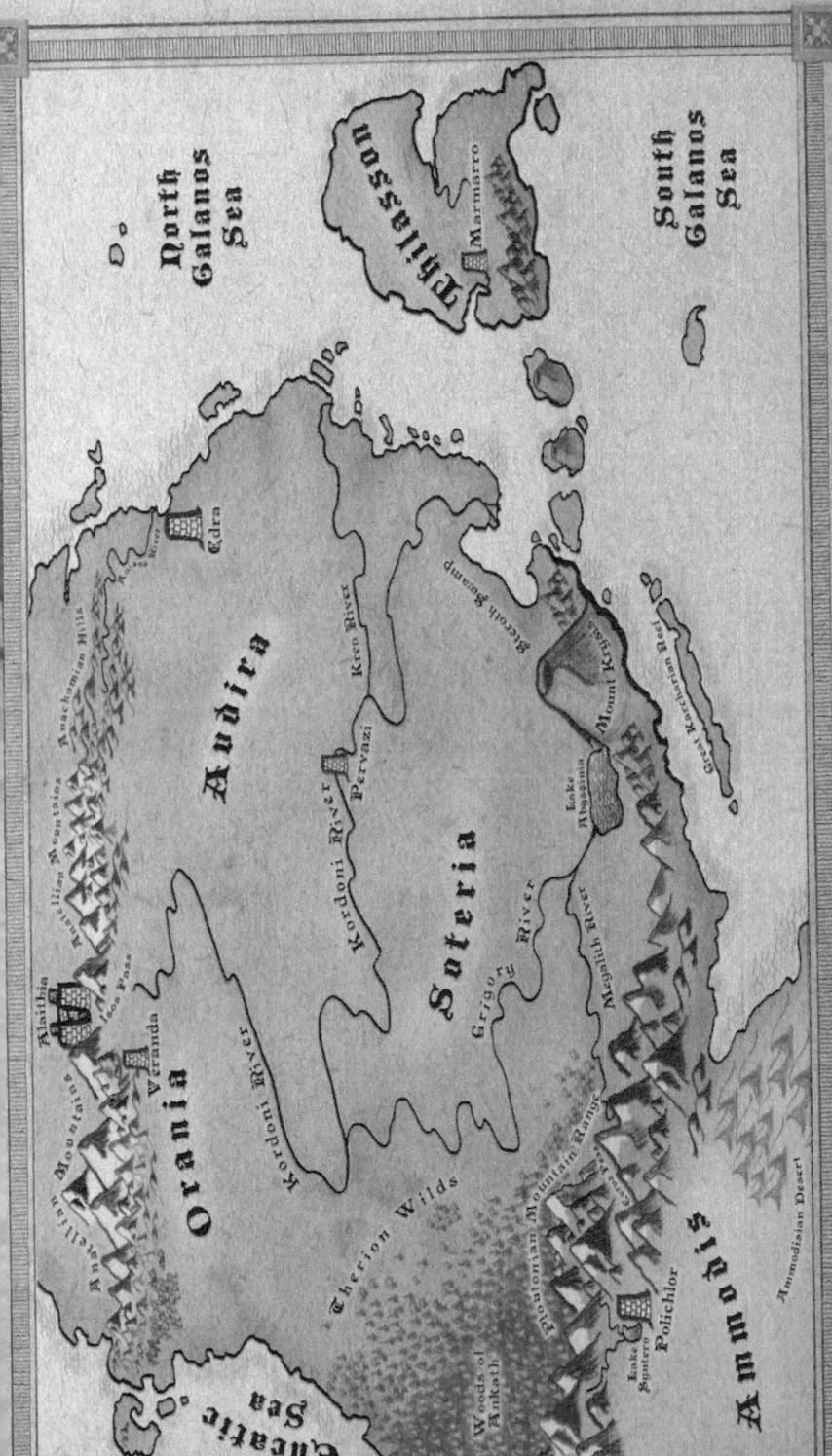

The Dragon Relics

Published by Moving Images Publications
Cape Girardeau, Missouri
www.MovingImagesPublications.com
www.RandyMcWilson.com

ISBN-13: 978-0-9977917-3-0

Dedicated to

Dr. Ravi Zacharias

*For harnessing a rare beauty in language
to convey timeless truths to our generation.*

To the Reader:

This is Book Three of a four book series.
If you have not read **Book One: The Dragon
Offering**, and **Book Two: The Dragon Wrath**, I
would encourage you to do so before reading
Book Three: The Dragon Relics.

The characters and events flow between all four
books to form a much larger overall story that
requires reading this series in the proper order.

Thank you and enjoy!
Randy McWilson

The glassy blue of the endless ocean would have been beautiful, except he was starved to near insanity while drifting aimlessly on a haphazard mass of shattered boat timbers that had riddled his sunburned arms and legs with countless splinters. But, as the mesmerizing waves floated him in and out of consciousness, he realized that even a miserable raft was better than no raft at all.

He had lost count of the days.

Each had blurred into the next.

A shadowy cluster of cruel yet efficient sharks had devoured those who had managed to survive the accident, and the next day they returned to feast on those who hadn't.

Somehow…he survived.

He was alone.

He had longed for relief from the constant heat (wishing for even a single cloud), but nighttime provided his only truly dependable shade. Terrifying and fleeting images raced through his crazed mind. He remembered flashes of the fierce storm. The violent pitching of the ship.

The fire on his face.

The water.

The waves.

And death.

So much death.

Death. That word stuck with him. Indeed, it had been his mission. But he never made it to the island. As far as he knew, the young Dunamai was still alive. He had failed.

The delirious remnants of a man struggled to raise his blistered face and squinted out at the watery horizon that had persistently mocked him. An unrelenting sun blinded his stinging eyes with a thousand shifting reflections. But today something was different.

A dark shape?

He lapsed into unconsciousness. Then revived. The puzzling shape was larger. Closer.

A...ship?

He passed out yet again. What happened next was jumbled and quite indistinguishable from a bizarre dream. He heard splashes and felt strong hands grasping his arms, his legs. It seemed that he was rolled over. And swaying. Lots of swaying.

What's…going…on?

His confusion was growing. He sensed the rise and fall of the largest waves, but yet he couldn't feel the water itself. His trembling fingers scratched along, expecting to find long planks of soggy wood, yet they clutched only cloth. Soft, dry cloth. The survivor cracked his tired eyes open until they resembled not much more than a pair of thin slits. There was light…but it was gentle and warm. Definitely not hot. And no reflections.

He dared to open them wider.

Walls?

A window?

The room was tiny, barely housing his narrow bed and a small table and chair. An ornately carved door to his right creaked open, its hinges protesting the whole way. A dark, cloaked figure (sporting a fearful mask) entered and quickly turned to shut it behind him.

Oh, no. A Sevasti!

The bedridden man's heart threatened to pound right out of his exhausted chest.

Do they know? Did they find out about my mission and the Dunamai? What will they do to me?

The hooded visitor reached up and removed his mask without making a sound. A kind, bearded face stared down with a somewhat satisfied smile.

"By all accounts, you should have perished in the deep. It would appear that the favor of the Zho shines upon you, my blessed friend."

My…friend?

He doesn't know who I am?!

The Sevasti dragged the chair closer to the bed and plopped onto it. With great care, he pulled the sheets back and studied his patient from head to toe. "It is my sincerest hope…that you *feel* better than you *look*."

"I—I've had…better days," he whispered.

"And, in the will of the Zho, you shall have better days yet again. I am Darr'mere." The kind stranger tenderly lowered the sheet back down. "I believe that you will find Alaithia to be a pleasant place of recuperation."

Alaithia?

Did he just say Alaithia?

"Wh—where am I?"

Darr'mere smiled broadly and stroked his ruddy beard. "*Safe.* Safe is where you are." He paused then slapped his right hand against the wood slats adorning the wall. "You, my friend, are safely aboard the *Splendid Endeavor*. She's a fine Avdirian vessel. The captain tells us that we're about a day's sailing from reaching port.

We snatched you from the ocean about three days past. Near the Isle of Hope."

Darr'mere leaned sideways and picked up a piece of fresh bread and offered it to him. "Take this, but in small portions. Now…once we make it ashore, it is a few weeks' travel westward to Alaithia. Our capable physicians there will tend to your wounds, especially that dreadful burn on your face."

The bewildered patient nodded before devouring the soft, delicious morsel. Darr'mere offered him a cold cup of water.

"What is your name, son?"

The injured man swallowed hard and snuck in a round of small sips. "My name?" he whispered, struggling to buy a little time to come up with a convincing lie. "My name? My name…is…*Gremlor*."

But that was over three thousand years ago.

He wanted to pinch himself.

Everywhere he strolled along the stone hallways and everywhere he wandered among the massive outdoor courtyards, Arlon's grin was infectious among every Sevasti who passed by him. He had completely abandoned any attempt to hide his huge smile.

He glanced in perpetual wonder at the sharp peaks that towered above Alaithia like patient, ancient guardians. Arlon brought his stroll to a gradual stop and rested his left hand on a cold marble ledge. He turned his gaze towards a series of terraced lower levels and the fearful chasm that opened up beyond them. His mother's vivid stories had thrilled nearly every waking moment of his childhood, but now he would have his own tales to thrill her with one day.

I can't wait to tell you about everything I've seen, mother. From the Therion, to the city behind the waterfall, to fields of glowing blue flowers. He smiled and glanced around. *To...this.*

A deep, comforting, and familiar voice interrupted the quiet awe of the moment. "This particular view never loses its luster, my boy." Kash drew alongside him and took a deep breath. "Even after thousands of years, I still find myself quite taken with it."

Arlon nodded. It was still hard to believe that the aged captive he had been imprisoned with inside of a rolling cage a few months back was actually a resident of Alaithia. And Kash was not just any Sevasti. Arlon had discovered that his mentor was one of the leading elders.

"Of course, there have been some changes." Kash gestured down and to the left. "That courtyard is fairly new. It was built, oh...only about two hundred years ago."

"*Only* two hundred years?" Arlon chuckled.

Kash folded his arms. "Sorry, my boy. It is an unfortunate consequence of living at Alaithia. Time becomes rather...trivial, I suppose." He paused and just stared up and down at Arlon with a growing grin.

"Why are you looking at me like that?" the boy asked.

Kash released a small chuckle. "I was just thinking about how proud I am of you. And of your adventures…your accomplishments. I couldn't be more pleased."

"Well, it wasn't just me. Without Trilyra and Mogg, we would never have made it."

"Yes, but you—*you*—kept them together. Anyone can get people to fight, but it is a rare soul who get people to *unite*. By the will of the Zho, you found a way to keep your friends together, and then to get them here, to safety. Within these walls."

Arlon looked away. "Not all of them."

Kash moved closer and grabbed the boy's left arm tenderly. "Even the greatest of victories are tainted with the sorrows of loss. In any respects, you must know and believe, the boy's misfortune was not your fault. It was not of your doing."

A single tear formed and hurried down Arlon's hot face. "But I saw it before. The Rone showed me that Hort would be taken. And I didn't stop it."

"My dear boy, the Rone showed you the *future*, it revealed what would happen. Rone visions are always of the future. A thousand kings leading a thousand armies could not change that." He paused and patted Arlon's arm. "But, enough of such things…how is your shoulder? Are you feeling well enough for a guided tour?"

Arlon winced as he cautiously rubbed the wounded area with his left hand. "It's…uh, still pretty tender. But, it doesn't really ache or burn like it did when I first got here. And I still have to sleep on my left side."

"You have only been under our care for just over a week, my boy. It will be some time before it fully heals. At least five or six months. If ever. But I would say that your progress thus far is nothing short of a miracle, thank the Zho. In any respects, it's a miracle that I have only witnessed once before."

Arlon's face drained of all expression, and he stared off into the distance. "What you really mean to say is that I shouldn't even be here. I shouldn't even be alive. I was bitten by a *Dragon*."

"Who knows," a voice echoed out from behind them. "Maybe *Arlon*, the famous Dunamai of Soteria, ended up killing that freaky Dragon."

They both whirled around as Paymer and Mae'Lee waltzed up.

"Think about it," Paymer continued while rolling a gold coin through his freckled fingers. "Maybe your Soterian blood is poisonous to a

Dragon." He raised his eyebrows before letting out a few hearty laughs.

Mae'Lee's face scrunched up, and she playfully punched Paymer in the shoulder. "Do we have to talk about that dreadful Dragon on such a lovely day?"

"Sorry, your Highness," he replied, wagging a finger over at Arlon. "But he brought it up first. I heard him."

Arlon squinted. *Mae'Lee probably didn't hear me. I was facing away from them.*

Kash locked eyes with her and spoke a bit louder than normal. "It appears that your hearing is much improved, Princess. That gives this old man great joy!"

She came to a stop and nodded. "Well, yes, it is much better, thank you. I still have trouble with certain sounds, especially some kinds of music. And when I talk, my own voice still sounds…odd. Almost muffled."

"Our remedies have enjoyed great success in healing injuries, but I was a bit skeptical regarding their effectiveness on your…*unique* condition. By the will of the Zho, perhaps all will be perfectly restored," Kash replied. He looked around. "May I ask, where is your Endochorian friend? The Assembly will convene soon."

Paymer kept his voice down. "He, uh, he is still in his room, sir. He has been kinda quiet lately. I think he is...well...*heartbroken* over the loss of Tempest."

"Tempest?"

"His, uh, *horse*, sir. I know it sounds strange, but they were very close. Like family."

Kash nodded. "Ah, yes. His *two-headed* horse. Is that right?"

"Yes, sir," Paymer answered. "That beast was a sight to see."

"We had heard rumors for years."

"Oh, Tempest is no rumor," Paymer replied as he hunkered across the low wall, studying the courtyard below. "But we lost him. During our last Dragon attack."

"Better to lose one's horse rather than one's *life*," Kash observed. "Even a two-headed horse."

Paymer flipped around and reclined against the wall. "I'm not so sure that the powerful Vish'tar of the Kla'aven Mage would agree. And, uh, someone did lose their life."

"Yes. Yes, I know. A most tragic loss, to be sure. But the Assembly has requested that *all* of you be present at our solemn convocation today. There are urgent matters to discuss. Matters that need to be addressed. Dangerous days are ahead. For all kingdoms and all peoples. We even harbor a fair share of unrest here in Alaithia. There is considerable disagreement about the prophecy."

"Who exactly will be at this council?" Paymer inquired.

"It is the Assembly, the chief governing body at Alaithia. Twenty-four Sevasti elders. They want to speak with you. And I must insist, your Therion friend needs to attend."

Arlon waved his hand. "Don't worry. I'll get him. I, uh, I will make sure that Mogg is there." He gestured off into the distance, across the gorge. "But what about her? Can she come?"

Kash squinted. "I imagine that you are referring to the Ammodisian girl?"

"*Trilyra*," Paymer noted. "She's saved our lives. More than once. And here we are, all safe and sound inside this fortress...and she's out there. Alone. Doesn't seem right."

Kash fidgeted in place, but he couldn't seem to escape the penetrating eyes locked on him. He gathered up the edges of his robe and started to hasten away. "Come. The Assembly will be seated within the hour, and I want to show you something first. I promise all of you that it will be well worth it."

No one else budged. "We're not moving until we get an answer," Paymer objected (probably a little harsher than he meant to). "At least, *I'm* not." He cleared his throat before softening his tone. "*Sir*."

"When Mae'Lee was on the verge of death, we took her to the Twin Witches," Arlon explained. "One of them warned us about Trilyra. The crazy old woman said that she was a liar. Does that have anything to do with it?"

Kash seemed intrigued. "You have met the Magici Dyad?" he asked. "At the splitting of the rivers in Gilmoth?"

Arlon nodded. "We met both of them. Shendollyn and Sister. I don't think I've ever met two people from the same area that were more different."

Kash fought back a strange chuckle. "On the contrary, young Dunamai, I doubt that you've met two people that were more *alike*."

"What?"

"Think back…did you ever see them together?" Kash inquired.

Arlon looked at the others. Most of them shook their heads. Mae'Lee just shrugged. "Uh, well…no," Arlon responded. "We met Shendollyn at—"

"You met Shendollyn at *night*," Kash interrupted. "And the old, odd woman, who babbled on and on senselessly…you saw her only in the *day*."

Arlon squinted in confusion. "How could you possibly know all that?"

"They are not the Twin Witches of Gilmoth, my boy," Kash declared. "Rather, she is just Shendollyn. They…are her."

"*They* are *her*? Wait, what? Am I the only one that is confused?" Paymer asked.

"You're not alone," Arlon admitted.

"Thanks, pal."

Kash folded his arms and stared off into the distance. "Her curious condition is the result of an ancient blessing, or as some say…an ancient *curse*. Many, many centuries past." He pointed at the sky. "Each night, at the setting of the sun, the woman Shendollyn returns to the same beauty and youthfulness she possessed at the time of her blessing." He looked back at them. "And each morning, she returns to the ravages of her true age. She will continue to grow older and feebler as the years pass. But it is said that death itself is denied her. Until the end of the Age of Dragons. Or so the legends go, but who can speak with any certainty of such things?"

Arlon's jaw dropped open. "So Sister and Shendollyn are the same person?"

"As the Kray would say," Kash began, bringing his hands together. "It is *well-spoken*. But now, come. We have much to see and little time to see it." He started to move.

"Wait…you still haven't answered our question, sir," Paymer declared delicately. "About Trilyra."

Kash froze in mid-step but didn't turn around. "Our decision stands firm," he replied flatly. "The young woman…will remain *outside* Alaithia."

"But why?" Mae'Lee begged. "What has she done? Or what do you *think* she's done? I've asked, but no one will tell me anything."

The revered Sevasti pivoted around, stroking his beard lightly as he collected his thoughts for several seconds.
"Because…she…*lied*," Kash began.

"Her twin brother…was *not* the Dunamai of Ammodis."

The stone corridors seemed to grow ever-narrower with each successive doorway and every sudden sharp corner. The stifling stench of smoke trailed overhead from Kash's torch to the last Dunamai following behind him in single file.

"Where are we going?" Arlon called out from the back of the line as his voice reverberated into the dark distance. He struggled to see around Mogg's broad shoulders.

"Here in Alaithia…we have a saying about patience," Kash announced.

The group turned another corner and passed through yet another doorway.

"Well?" Arlon said as it closed behind him. "I'm still waiting."

"Oh that," Kash chuckled. "Yes, well, we do not share that particular saying about patience with anyone until they have been here at least a hundred years."

Arlon sighed. "A hundred years? Very funny."

Paymer looked back. "You gotta admit, pal...that was pretty good."

"Just what we need," Arlon groaned. "A Sevasti with a sense of humor."

Kash slowed as the hall widened, and they approached an impressive door with a series of broad metal hinges. A ribbon of bright, white light escaped through the narrow gap below it and lit up the dust swirling around their feet. Kash passed his torch back to Paymer as he fished something out of the folds in his cloak.

"Now," the old man said, inserting a key into the lock. "You might want to step back." He yanked on the handle, and the massive door gradually swung outward. "And you might want to shield your eyes."

It was too late.

The stone corridor flooded with warm, moist air and a brilliant blast of light, temporarily blinding his surprised guests. They probably couldn't tell, but he gestured for them to step inside. "Move along," he encouraged. "I want to show you something."

From the back end of the slowly shuffling line, Arlon thought he detected the sound of rippling water. And then he distinctly heard Mae'Lee gasp.

"Oh my," she said.

"Incredible," Paymer declared.

"By the Red Leaf," Mogg mumbled.

Kash came up behind Arlon and gently nudged him forward. The boy's eyes finally adjusted to the intense blaze that was streaming down from above as he stepped into a spacious room where the air felt and smelled a bit like summer.

And that's when he saw it.

"Behold!" Kash boomed, stepping out in front of them with his arms spread wide. "The Cardidendron!"

Arlon was both speechless and yet irresistibly compelled to speak. "It's...beautiful. Wonderful."

The thick and gnarled tree rose to a height of at least twenty-five feet out of a plot of dark soil in the center of the humid chamber. Its long and irregular branches were heavily laden with enormous leaves (most of them the size of dinner plates), all shining in a brilliant and captivating shade of deep crimson. Several leaves were scattered along the ground, but they all appeared just as fresh and vibrant as the rest.

Arlon's eyes drifted above as he studied the ornate, vaulted ceiling. Beams of warm sunlight poured down through a thick glass skylight surrounded by a wonderfully detailed mosaic depicting a massive waterfall.

Wait! he thought. *I've seen this tree before! I know I have.*

But where?

Where?

Arlon clutched his necklace. *Of course! The vision I had at the Rone. The huge tree with the red leaves. But…is this the same tree I saw in my vision?*

Mogg had dropped to one knee in an attitude of reverence, and Paymer stepped closer and tapped on one of the leaves. "What did you call this?"

Kash smiled again. "The Cardidendron, my Oranian friend."

Mae'Lee pointed. "Those leaves…on the ground. They look just as lovely as the rest. How long have they been laying there?"

Kash waltzed over and grabbed one from the dirt. He rolled the stem between his fingers, twirling the leaf round and round. "One day…or a hundred years. It doesn't matter, your Highness."

The Princess frowned. "What do you mean it doesn't matter?"

Kash approached her and dangled it before her eyes. "The leaves of the Cardidendron do not wither; they do not fade. This leaf will remain as soft, and as rich in color, for hundreds—even *thousands*—of years." The old man reached overhead and plucked another leaf from a low hanging branch. "And by tomorrow morning, another leaf, just as large and just as red, will be in this one's place." He laid it across her delicate palm.

"We've seen a leaf like this before," she replied.

"Oh?"

Mae'Lee gestured off to her right. "Arlon found one in the ruins of an ancient city. It looked just like this. And just as red."

"Tar'tain," Mogg declared.

"Yes…in Tar'tain," Mae'Lee repeated. "It was a dreadful place."

"A forbidden city. A cursed place," Mogg mumbled, spreading his hands out wide. "It is an ill thought."

Kash seemed quite intrigued and shot a quick glance over at Arlon. "You found a leaf of the Cardidendron? In Tar'tain?"

The boy nodded.

"The Endochorian capital," Kash noted. "Most interesting," he whispered. "Most interesting."

"What happened to the Endochorians?" Arlon inquired. "King Leandros told me about a crime or something. What is their connection to the Therion? Or is there a connection to the Therion?" He caught himself. "I mean…the Kray?"

Kash turned away and strolled over to a narrow creek that Arlon hadn't really noticed before. "That dark story of the Great Treachery will have to wait, my boy, for another time. But come, all of you. Let me show you some of the wonders of our engineering."

Seconds later they were all crowded around as Kash knelt beside the gurgling, steamy stream. "There are an abundance of natural springs that flow out of the mountains surrounding Alaithia. We capture some of this pure water." He paused and pointed off to their left. "And then it passes through a coil of metal pipes in a room just beyond that far wall. Those pipes are heated by a perpetual fire that we have maintained for many thousands of years. There is a layer of rocks sitting on a metal mesh just below the pipes. And below the rocks is the fire. The rocks absorb the flames' heat and then radiate that heat more evenly along the pipes. And if the fire gets low, the rocks continue to heat the water until the flames build back up again. Those who are responsible for such things are called Fire Keepers."

He smiled as a wistful look spread across his face. "As a matter of fact, when I first arrived at Alaithia, my first official duty was to help maintain the hot water for the Cardidendron. I was a Fire Keeper. But after a few months, I secretly began calling it the *Sweat Station*." He wiped his forehead. "The heat can be unbearable at times."

Paymer cleared his throat. "How, uh, how long have you been here at Alaithia? If I may ask? Sir."

Kash caressed his beard. "That's yet *another* story for yet another time, young Dunamai." He stood up slowly and stared at the artificial creek. "The hot water serves at least three purposes. First, it obviously provides water for the Cardidendron there. Secondly, it helps to regulate the temperature in this chamber. Winters at Alaithia can be brutally cold, but the Cardidendron needs a much milder climate. And finally, some of the heated water is tapped for cooking and cleaning and bathing and so forth. It's quite a clever arrangement, in any respect." He looked up. "Oh yes, and the glass ceiling above. That portal allows for plenty of light. The glass is beveled on top to capture sunlight even when it is low on the horizon and then directs it down to the tree."

"Fascinating," Paymer muttered.

Kash raised his eyebrows and rocked back on his heels a bit. "Not bad for a bunch of mysterious scribes who sit around and discuss the ancient prophecies, wouldn't you say?"

Arlon folded his arms. "You know…like Paymer said, it really is fascinating. But what is it? I mean, why is it here? Why are you taking such great care of it? Was the tree here first, or was Alaithia here first?"

Mogg looked almost offended and Kash grabbed Arlon by his good shoulder. "Always the inquisitive young man, aren't you? The Dunamai of a thousand questions. *Why* is it here? Is that what you asked, my boy? *Why* are we taking care of the Cardidendron?!"

Arlon felt a rebuke coming. "Uh, yeah. But lemme guess…it's yet *another* story for yet *another* time?"

Kash brushed past them all and placed his right hand firmly against the tree. "Because the Cardidendron is *life*. It is *healing*. It is…many things. In any respects, if it were not for the leaves of this precious gift from the Zho, then I would not be here. And *you* would not be here, our Dragon-bitten friend. We take care of it, my boy because the Cardidendron takes care of us."

"Well, I think it's just wonderful, thank you!" Mae'Lee exclaimed. "I would love to have such a tree in our palace back in Edra!"

"I'm sorry, Princess," Kash said with a forced grin. "But there are two and *only two* Cardidendron trees in the entire world."

"Oh," she replied, slightly dejected. "Where is the other?"

He kept his voice louder than usual. "Trust me, Princess, when I say that I am not being evasive, but the excellent answer to that excellent question will have to wait for another time."

He pushed away from the tree and headed back for the door.

"But come…the Assembly is waiting for us."

Kash's cloaked form rose from his heavy wooden chair, and the murmuring room fell eerily silent, interrupted only by the irregular flickering of the torches scattered around. "The prophecy is truth, my brothers," he bellowed out.

A chorus of monotone voices echoed off the stone walls and floors back to him. "*And truth is our guide.*"

From his vantage point with the other Dunamai, Arlon strained to see and hear everything that transpired. He studied the massive circular table in the center of the chamber and the twenty-four solemn faces equally spaced around it. He recognized Kash and Gremlor but none of the others. The surface of the metal-rimmed, rough-hewn wooden table was basically empty, with the exception of five thick books and a single, small, curved horn.

Kash raised the ornately-carved instrument to his lips, offered three rapid blasts, and lowered it. "The Assembly has been convened." He offered a small glance to his left. "Brother Falsparr, may the Chronicle of the Assembly reflect that all members are accounted for."

An elder, three seats over, cracked open the largest of the leather-bound books and made a careful notation. He made eye contact once again. "It has been recorded, Brother K'Kashmalon."

Arlon perked up.

Wait…what? K'Kashmalon?

K'Kashmalon?

Paymer leaned into Arlon's ear. "I thought his name was *Kash*."

Arlon paused. "Maybe K'Kashmalon is a, uh, a title or something," he whispered. "Maybe Kash is a nickname."

Mae'Lee's face contorted in disappointment. "I wish they would speak up," she mumbled. "I can barely hear anything."

Arlon patted her arm tenderly.

"Brothers of the Assembly," Kash continued, "the extraordinary circumstances of our present gathering is without precedent in the Chronicles of the Sevasti. Not since the Great Division following the overthrow of King Kyros the Cruel has the world faced so great a challenge." He gestured towards the Dunamai, who were off to his right. "In any respects, not once in all the millennia that our sacred fellowship has endured, has this council witnessed the presence of four of the Chosen Children in this hallowed hall."

Wow, Arlon thought. *I knew that Kash was a good talker, but he sounds so…official.*

So impressive.

Almost like a king.

I wonder what other surprises he holds.

"And not since the Treaty of the Five Kings, brokered in this selfsame chamber, has a more urgent convocation been assembled for both wise deliberation and prudent courses of action. Perhaps a more worthy and weighty matter has never visited this Assembly."

Another wrinkled elder, with grey wisps of hair resembling tiny bushes popping up over each ear, rose to his feet from the opposite end of the table. "Keep us not in suspense, our brother. What weighty matter has led to the urgency of our gathering?" He returned to his seat.

Kash pursed his lips and squinted. "Whereas I would normally be inclined to reveal that answer…if it pleases the Assembly, I propose that Arlon, the Chosen Child of the Kingdom of Soteria, be allowed to address this council instead."

Arlon straightened up. *What did he say?!*

His heart suddenly pounded, and he was fairly certain it skipped several beats. His chest tightened like a noose.

Me address the council?

Did Kash just nominate me to talk?

Paymer elbowed him with a huge grin. "Did you know about this?" he whispered.

Arlon couldn't speak, he just shook his worried head.

Kash scanned the crowd. "Are there any among us who would protest such an appeal?" He hesitated for several seconds.

A red-headed elder with rosy cheeks and a well-trimmed beard slapped his hand on the table. "I have no argument with allowing the Chosen Child of Soteria to speak. No argument indeed." He paused and motioned towards the Dunamai. "But I am questioning the wisdom of allowing a representative of the murderous Endochorians to sit in these honorable chambers. The curse still covers he and his people as a dark and loathsome blanket."

Kash nodded and rested his fingertips on the table. "Your concern, Brother Tollkermere, is well-founded, and I suspect that you are not altogether alone in your reservations."

A few other heads nodded.

"But," Kash continued, "the present distress is a curse and a plague covering all kingdoms and peoples. Surely the traitorous indiscretions of the past do not disqualify the Vish'tar of the Kla'aven Mage from having a valid voice in such matters!"

Gremlor rose up. Arlon couldn't help but stare at the huge scars that surrounded the left side of the Sevasti's solemn face.

Is that a battle wound? He wondered.

Or maybe a burn scar?

"Let us well remember, my brothers," Gremlor began, "that we must operate within the boundaries of our oath and no further. It is not within the power of this council to go beyond that which either the scriptures or the Dread Guardians have pronounced. The unspeakable evil of the Endochorians has truly been visited upon them in their denial to partake in the Doro Drakon, and their misfortune to have become a fractured and barbaric people." He paused and made careful eye contact with all those around him. "Neither the curse nor the scriptures provide sufficient reason to exclude any of the Chosen Children this day, regardless of their ignoble heritage."

Arlon glanced to his right. Mogg was unflinching, staring at the stone floor in total silence.

Brother Tollkermere stroked his chin a few times and nodded. "Brother Gremlor, your wisdom and insight are sound. May the record reflect that I withdraw my previous concern."

Gremlor looked around expectantly before slowly returning to his seat. Kash studied his audience. "Are there any others among us who wish to voice their grievances or opposition?" He paused. "Then let the Chronicle reflect that the Assembly recognizes Arlon, Chosen Child of the Kingdom of Soteria, to make his case." Kash stretched his robed arm out towards Arlon as the elder lowered himself into his seat. "Come, child."

Paymer reached around and pushed firmly on his nervous friend's back. "Go on," he whispered. "Say something smart. Like you did to Mogg and the Therion elders. Or at least, just don't *embarrass* us and get us kicked out. I like the food here." He winked.

But Arlon never saw it.

He might not have even heard him.

Arlon's head started spinning and the boy felt like throwing up and passing out. To make matters worse, every Sevasti head had turned and every Sevasti eye had locked on him in curious expectation.

"Please, son," Gremlor offered warmly with a quick wave of his hand. "Please come forward and share all that is within your troubled heart. Few outside of our order have been considered for such a privilege. Fewer still have been selected."

Arlon tried to lift himself out of his chair, but his body seemed to be frozen in place. Mogg leaned forward and reached across Mae'Lee's lap to grab Arlon's forearm.

"It is time to speak with the Northern Elders," he urged. "For the Vice…for the Kray."

Mae'Lee's brown eyes welled up with trembling tears as she turned and stared at Arlon. "For…*Pelias*. For *Hort*."

Her miserable reminder triggered something down deep. *For Pelias*, he thought. *Yes…and for Hort*.

Arlon swallowed hard and finally found the courage (or foolishness) to rise up.

"Remember…don't embarrass us," Paymer muttered, leaning forward. "And if you need me, I'll be right back here…thanking the Zho that I'm not right up *there* with you."

Arlon rolled his terrified eyes. "Uh, thanks."

"Now…go say something smart, pal."

Kash relaxed against the cushion of his high-backed chair and grinned as Arlon inched towards the Assembly. "Please, Arlon…stand by me," he beckoned. "And speak clearly. Do not be afraid."

The boy's mind raced with a thousand things to say and yet not even a single good way to say any of them. As he thought back, his encounter with the Therion elders had felt much easier, at least he had the bargaining power of the mysterious Red Leaf. But here before the Sevasti, he had precious little to offer and even less expectation of receiving anything in return.

He reached the spot beside Kash and stiffened like a statue.

"Speak," Kash whispered discreetly. "Tell them what you shared with me."

Arlon swallowed and took a strained breath. "On, uh, on behalf of myself and my fellow Dunamai...I thank you for this...privilege of speaking before this...assembly today."

Paymer slid over into Arlon's vacated seat. "Not too bad a start," he whispered to Mae'Lee through cupped hands.

Arlon inhaled again and did a quick survey of the two-dozen faces around him. A few were smiling. Most weren't.

"We, uh, we have come to Alaithia seeking your protection."

"Protection from what?" a raspy voice called out from somewhere on his right. He didn't see who it was.

"Well, sir...my fellow Dunamai and I are being hunted. Hunted by...the *Order*."

A good deal of surprised murmuring broke out. Arlon didn't know what to do or say. Gremlor raised his arms. "Calm yourselves. The young man speaks the truth, my brothers. Hear him."

Arlon cleared his trembling throat as the chamber settled down. "After the Dragon Offering, and the destruction and all, we were all warned to flee. To flee to Alaithia for protection. Someone told us that the Order wanted to kill all of the Dunamai."

More murmuring.

Kash rose up quickly and stood right beside him. "This intervention was of my doing, my brothers. Once I gained knowledge of this wicked plot, I dispatched a messenger to rouse the Chosen Children, and to encourage them to seek the protection of our walls."

Another elder from the opposite side slapped the table. "A simple request for asylum seems a poor reason to gather the Assembly. It is certainly not the urgent matter we were led to believe that this would be, Brother K'Kashmalon."

A few more voices chanted in agreement.

Kash waved his arm. "You are indeed correct, Brother Ranmalon. But asylum is not the urgent matter presented before us today. The Chosen Child of Soteria has yet to make his case." He patted Arlon on the arm and sat down. "Continue, my boy."

The room fell silent.

Arlon swallowed. "Many have, uh, many have blamed the Dunamai for the...*unusual* behavior of the seventh Dragon. Many have said that we are at fault for his cursing of all kingdoms and all peoples. I do not know if that is true. I pray it is not." He paused and stared over at his friends. "But...if we have somehow caused this misery, then I ask you—*we* ask you—to help us to relieve it. To stop it."

"What do you mean by this?" another unfamiliar voice cried out.

Arlon glanced down briefly at Kash. The old sage nodded ever so subtly.

"Well, sir, what I mean is...is that, we need you—your collective wisdom—to help find a way to stop him."

"Stop him?!" another voice hollered out in disbelief. "Stop a Dread Guardian?"

"Yes, sir. Stop him. We need to find a way to...*kill* Terras Telos."

The room instantly exploded into a deafening mix of harsh laughter, muffled shouting, wild arm waving and repeated fist pounding. Arlon couldn't decipher what most of them were grumbling, but the word *'impossible'* was impossible to miss. For several seconds, he felt completely humiliated and totally alone. He wanted to run out and never look back.

Kash grabbed his sleeve. "Arlon! Look at me. Don't worry...I knew this would happen."

"Then *why* did you have me stand up here and make a fool of myself?!"

"Just wait...patience. Patience, my boy. This council is not over yet."

After the commotion began to subside, another elder rose up and slammed the table with his fist. "*How dare you!* How dare you stand before this gathering and call into question the truth of the scriptures! The prophecy is truth!"

"And truth is our guide," several irritated voices echoed in unison.

Arlon panicked. "I, uh, I am sorry, sir. But…I don't understand how—"

The enraged elder wagged a finger at him. "*Hold your tongue!* The scriptures are clear on this matter!" He turned and pointed off to his right. "Bring me the Book of Consummation."

Elder Falsparr picked up one of the large, leather-bound volumes and delivered it to him in haste.

"Here you are, Brother Kratton."

The angered elder opened the cover and scanned through several pages. "Listen, Arlon…Chosen *Child* of Soteria!" the man demanded. "Listen well to the scripture. From the Book of Consummation, Reading Fourteen: '*As he was from the beginning, so shall the same be at the last. Their power, no mortal shall vanquish.*'" He flipped through a few more pages and located another passage. "From Reading Eleven. '*And when the days of the Sixth Dread Guardian are fulfilled, the last will come, full of wisdom and might, and reigning without end.*'" The man shut the book and glared over at Arlon. "The scripture of truth declares that no mortal man can kill a Dread Guardian. And even if it were possible, foolish *child*, Reading Eleven confirms that his reign will be without end. Terras Telos is an immortal creature!"

Another elder raised up. "And do not forget this passage, Brother Kratton, also from the Book of Consummation: '*And he shall come, the last, born of cruelty. And all shall know his power which shall endure through timeless ages.*'"

Kratton nodded and pointed at Arlon. "Do you not hear the truth of the scriptures? Even the very words of your disgraceful request are an offense and sacrilege to every member of this body." He looked around with anger growing in his eyes. "It is my opinion that this Assembly be dismissed at once before further blasphemy is allowed to fall from this child's unlearned lips."

A quick round of approving chants erupted and more than a few of the Sevasti elders rose up in disgust. More shouting. More fist pounding.

Kash jumped to his feet and raised his voice. "*Brothers!* My brothers! Calm yourselves! Listen to my words."

"Why should we listen to your words?" one hollered back. "We have already heard the words of the prophecy!"

Kash slammed his own fist down on the table, knocking over the horn and catching several of the elders off guard. "The prophecy is true," he shouted out. "The prophecy is true. But only when understood *correctly*."

The murmuring died down.

Some returned to their seats.

A defiant Kratton remained standing. "What are you saying?!"

Kash took a deep breath. "What I am saying, my brother, is that we must not imagine that we have understood all things perfectly and completely." Kash hesitated, obviously measuring his words. "Our interpretation of a perfect scripture may be imperfect...*flawed. Incomplete.*"

The veins on the side of Kratton's reddening neck began to bulge. "I just quoted the scripture," he yelled. "I cannot imagine how such clear passages could be misunderstood or twisted, my erring brother."

Kash folded his arms and grinned. "Correction, my brother. You quoted only a *part* of the scripture. Is there a reason that you left out the last part of Reading Fourteen? Was that deliberate? Was that intentional?"

"This is clearly outrageous," Kratton fired back.

"I will quote the passage once again, in its fullness," Kash announced. "'*As he was from the beginning, so shall the same be at the last. Their power, none mortal shall vanquish.*'" Kash paused. "And the end of that scripture states: '*Dread against Dread, or suffer misery without end.*' The Book of Consummation, Reading Fourteen, lines forty-one and forty-two. I believe that my quote is quite correct. You may verify my accuracy if you like." Kash pointed. "The book is still before you."

Kratton frowned. "I know the passage."

Arlon straightened up. *'Dread against dread'? Dragon against Dragon? Two Dragons?*

Something stirred within him. A memory.

My Rone vision, he mused. *There were two Dragons. And a volcano.*

Kash wasn't finished. "Then you must also know, my brother, that there is perhaps more that we do not quite fully understand. It clearly states *'Dread against Dread, or suffer miseries without end.'* Notice that these unending miseries are *optional*…not unavoidable. It says *'or suffer'* not *'will suffer.'* We must read *every* word, not just those that agree with our position. "

A few heads nodded.

Kash continued, "And, as all of this esteemed body are well aware, that famous passage *'And he shall come, the last, born of cruelty. And all shall know his power which shall endure through timeless ages.'* That scripture has been the subject of intense debate down through the years. Some believe it is not speaking of a Dread Guardian." He paused. "Some have considered that this may be referring to a man, a coming king. A king whose rule shall not end."

"The Age of Mankind died with that tyrant, King Kyros!" Kratton countered fiercely.

"The Age of the Dread Guardians shall have no end. Your private interpretations are hardly worth considering. Few scholars among us would agree with your fanciful delusions."

"How can you reconcile the prophecy?" Kash retorted with a fire building in his eyes. "The Book of Consummation clearly reveals that the final age will be an eternal blessing and not a curse, yet Terras Telos has brought nothing but a curse to all kingdoms?"

Kratton appeared at a loss for words. He started to sit down. "This changes nothing," he rebutted coldly.

"On the contrary," Gremlor declared, pushing his seat back and rising to his feet. "This changes *everything*." He shoved his right hand into his cloak and withdrew a small, rolled document. "I beseech each of you to consider that small phrase…'*Dread against Dread*.' While much has been written and discussed over the ages about the verses before it, and even the lines following it, we must admit that precious little is understood about that curious phrase itself. What does the scripture of truth mean in such a declaration that has puzzled even the most devoted among our ranks?"

Kash nodded and dropped back down.

Arlon took advantage of the tense situation and quietly retreated to the relative safety of the other Dunamai. He hoped no one would notice.

"Welcome back. This is getting freaky," Paymer whispered.

Arlon didn't reply.

"'*Dread against Dread,*'" Gremlor repeated. "What can it mean?" He stared down at the document in his hand as he began to unravel it. "Perhaps this can shed some light on this difficult passage." A strange expression washed across his disfigured face. "It was just over fifteen hundred years ago. In Edra…and her surrounding townships. A tragic business. All know of it. But only a handful of you were there."

"The Second Great Purge," a voice said.

"Ah, yes," Gremlor replied. "Yes. The Second Great Purge."

"Wow," Paymer mumbled with excitement. "Did you hear that? Some of these guys are over a thousand years old!"

"With all due respect to you, Brother Gremlor," Kratton piped up, "but what does an ancient attempt to wipe out the remaining vestiges of the Order have to do with—"

"With all due respect to *you*, brother," Gremlor forcefully interrupted, "if you would let me finish, then perhaps all those present could judge the merits of what I am about to reveal."

Kratton held his peace (but he didn't look too happy about it).

"If memory serves me, well above two hundred members of that despicable and dangerous cult were ferreted out and apprehended over a space of four days. And all were speedily executed less than two days later."

"Two hundred and *sixteen* souls," Kash added.

"Yes," Gremlor replied. "Thank you, Brother K'Kashmalon. Two hundred and *sixteen* adherents of the Order perished for their unforgivable trespass. We had hoped to capture the Apex, their perverse leader, but somehow that monster slipped through our fingers. But…justice at the edge of the sword was not the *only* benefit of that dark but necessary inquisition. Out of that investigation, we discovered hundreds, perhaps thousands, of documents pertaining to that vile creed. As is our custom, most of those heretical writings were rightly delivered to the flame."

He stared back at the paper in his hand. "But there was a small collection of more pertinent and also yet more *cryptic* information that was permitted to survive in our archives for future study." He hoisted the document aloft and shook it lightly. "And here in my hand today is one of those surviving manuscripts."

Kratton couldn't seem to contain himself. "I still fail to see how—"

"And in this manuscript," Gremlor fairly shouted, ignoring him, "is a most curious passage; a passage that did not bear serious consideration until after the treachery, and perhaps *endless* cruelty of the seventh Dread

Guardian, became a grim reality." He stared at the parchment and pulled it closer. "The Order often engages in short bits of peculiar poetry, and this excerpt is no different. It reads:

> *'With tooth, with scale, with claw.*
> *Hallowed remnants of those long dead.*
> *Gather them each,*
> *Gather them all.*
> *Mortal poison for the immortal Dread.'"*

Arlon hunched forward with growing interest. Paymer tried to keep his voice down. "Now that is some freaky poetry. Gives me the chills, pal."

Mae'Lee's frustration was obvious. "It's dreadful. I'm only hearing about half of this," she complained. "And the half I'm hearing doesn't sound very good at all. What's going on?"

Arlon leaned back and locked eyes with her. "Hope," he said. "*Hope* is what's going on."

"Brother K'Kashmalon…you told us that this meeting was unprecedented," Kratton said. "And now…I am beginning to agree. A thorough search of the Chronicle may prove otherwise, but I do not believe that a Sevasti has ever dared to utter the corrupting and deceptive messages of the Order in this chamber."

Kash placed his hands on the table and stood up. "Unusual circumstances dictate unusual *methods*, my brother. When faced with a threat that endangers all peoples in every kingdom, one must consider every option, from every angle...even from those perspectives that we may not feel comfortable indulging."

Gremlor jumped in. "The Order is an accursed cult, Brother Kratton, but that does not necessitate that their every utterance is bereft of truth. Many of the greatest lies hold a seed of truth at their heart."

Kratton fairly launched back up and thrust his finger out towards the Dunamai. "We are wading into treacherous waters...I refuse to discuss this matter further until *they* are put out of this Assembly."

Another elder rose up. "I concur with Brother Kratton."

Paymer dug a coin out of his pocket and shuffled it through his tense, sweaty fingers. "This isn't looking or sounding too good."

Kash peered over at Gremlor with a worried look. Three additional elders stood and joined the angry dissention. Seconds later...two more.

"What's going on?" Mae'Lee asked, leaning close to Arlon's face. "What happened to *hope*?"

Several Sevasti elders ratcheted up the already stressful situation with aggressive shouting.

Arlon clutched her hand and gave it a squeeze. "I...I don't know."

More bitter shouting followed.

Moments later the meeting crumbled into pure chaos.

And the Dunamai were quickly escorted out and the doors closed.

"How much longer will they be in there?" Mae'Lee moaned, shifting her weight on the heavy wooden bench. "We've been sitting out here for over an hour!"

Arlon stood up and began pacing (for at least the third time). "Well, I'm sure it is pretty difficult to get twenty-four stubborn men to agree...about anything."

Paymer arched back with his hands over his head. "I bet they agree on one thing," he said, cracking his knuckles. "I bet they agree to throw us out of Alaithia by tomorrow morning, pal."

"It is an ill thought," Mogg declared, spreading his arms out. "We must trust the wisdom and generosity of the Northern Elders."

Paymer fought back a grin and kept his voice low as a small cluster of younger Sevasti passed by in the hall. "I don't mean to shatter your image of the great Northern Elders, Mogg, but, uh, there's a good chance that a lot of those men in that room are very *uncomfortable* with your presence here."

Arlon rubbed his chin. "It was very strange, wasn't it?"

Mae'Lee looked up at him. "What do you mean?"

"To listen to them; to hear the things they talk about. Like the Second Great Purge…and King Kyros and all that. To us, those things are just legends, or maybe made up stories." He pointed at the door. "But to them…those things are part of their history. Some of them lived it."

Paymer rolled his eyes. "Okay, listen pal…maybe some of them were there for the purge, but you'd have to be a little messed up in the head if you think that any of those bearded freaks actually knew King Kyros." He glanced around at each of them. "Think about it, they would have to be over five thousand years old. That's crazy. Even for a Sevasti. No way."

CLUNNNKKK!

Everyone nearly jumped as the massive chamber door's lock popped and its hinges creaked before it swung steadily outward. A handful of murmuring elders rushed out, scattering in haste in various directions.

None of them seemed to be very pleased.

And not one of them even acknowledged the Dunamai.

"Well then," Paymer whispered. "This *continues* to not look very good."

"Don't rush to conclusions," Arlon urged. "Let's wait for Kash."

"You mean *K'Kashmalon*?" Paymer smirked.

They didn't wait long.

Less than a minute later, Gremlor and Kash exited the chamber and briefly shared an intense, private exchange. Gremlor nodded before disappearing down the hall, his fast footfalls echoing the entire way. Kash plastered a forced smile and approached the Dunamai.

"Come. Follow me," he urged. "We have much to discuss. And much to plan."

The modest space was roughly square and sparsely furnished. A narrow bed (adorned with a messy pile of blue sheets) occupied the wall opposite the entrance, and a stone bathtub filled the corner to the right just beyond the headboard. A desk, covered with documents and trinkets, sat along the wall off to their far right, flanked by a pair of tall, overloaded bookshelves. And all of it surrounded a cluster of four fire pits in the center of the chamber.

"Welcome to my little private corner of Alaithia," Kash beamed as he shut and locked the door securely behind them.

The others came to a stop, but Arlon wandered about examining everything, especially the curious diamond-shaped arrangement of fire pits crowded in the center of the dwelling. Each was constructed from a single black metal bowl, and the entire layout was perched atop a bricked slab about knee high. A dark metal shroud hung down from the arched ceiling directly over them.

"Do you like them?" Kash called out. "Those are fire pits, my boy. They are for my Vision Fires. And sometimes just for heat on an intolerably cold day." He pointed up. "And that contraption above helps to vent the smoke. Usually." He smiled.

Mae'Lee squinted. "Vision Fire? What's that?"

Kash chuckled. "What is a Vision Fire? My dear Princess, surely you must know by now. You've created at least two of them on your journey to our fortress."

"*The freaky blue fire!*" Paymer exclaimed.

Kash folded his arms and raised his bushy eyebrows. "I have never heard it described in quite those terms, but *yes*…your particular Vision Fires have been blue. But they can be a great many shades and hues."

"Oh, *that* fire," Mae'Lee mumbled. "The blue fire."

"In my defense, I only saw the first one," Arlon offered with a slight shrug. "In the cave. Before Mogg kinda ran in and…ended it."

"Ended it?!" Paymer roared. "He stomped it out like a wild team of horses!" Paymer thrashed his legs around, acting out the scene. "Blue sparks went flying everywhere. Like fireworks."

"I feared that it was a tool of the enemy," Mogg explained firmly.

Kash strolled towards him. "Don't judge the Vish'tar too harshly. Your Therion friend is more right than he knows. We have heard scattered reports of the Order using Vision Fires to communicate. In any respects, a Vision Fire can be a wonderful tool, but it can also be a most dangerous liability. Anyone standing before a Vision Fire can see *who* you are, *where* you are, and hear everything that you are saying. With varying degrees of clarity."

Mae'Lee locked eyes with Kash. "Wait…so that was *you?*" she inquired. "That was *you* talking to us through the round fire thing?" She pointed at one of the fire pits. "You were actually right here…talking to us out there? In the cavern and by the Firebridge?"

The Sevasti elder nodded with a reassuring stare before grabbing his desk chair and sliding it before one of the pits. "My dear

Princess, I was actually right about...*here.*" He plopped down. "Both times."

"Freaky," Paymer muttered.

"Incredible," Arlon whispered, holding onto each and every syllable.

"It is one of the many, many things that I will share with you and endeavor to teach you about," Kash said in great haste, jumping up and relocating his desk chair over by the bed. "You have many challenges and dangers ahead. I do not envy your difficult task." His kind eyes reddened somewhat. "To many...it would seem *impossible*, but you have shown great courage and great strength. All of you. And by the will of the Zho, perhaps you shall overcome."

The long locks of Mogg's dark hair swayed as his head rocked up and down. "And none can resist His will."

"Indeed," Kash replied. "Indeed. But now," he waved his arm as he sat down. "Please, please...sit yourselves on the bed. Thousands of years have passed before my eyes, and yet now, *time* is not in our favor."

Arlon glanced over at him.

Thousands of years?

How old are you, Kash?

One by one, each scurried into place, and the edge of the bed became quite crowded.

Arlon half grinned. The whole spectacle reminded him of countless encounters with his mother as he sat in his room, clutching his pillow, while she entertained with incredible stories of powerful people, fascinating places, and ancient events. He glanced up at the only window in the room.

"I wish Trilyra could be here," he mumbled.

"The Ammodisian warrior?" Kash asked.

Arlon nodded.

Paymer ran his freckled fingers through his red hair. "Earlier you said she lied. And that her twin brother wasn't a Dunamai."

Kash hesitated and sucked in a deep breath. "She *did*…and he *wasn't*. It was a tragic deception, doomed to fail. Unfortunately, the Sevasti did not learn the truth of it until it was too late. The boy's death was…most regrettable."

"What happened?" Arlon asked.

A prolonged and uncomfortable pause followed.

"The Chosen Child of the Kingdom of Ammodis, Pelias—*the real Pelias*—died several years ago. A sickness of some kind," Kash explained. "At least that's what we were told."

Paymer's face contorted. "Huh?"

"So, then…the Pelias that we met, that was not the *real* Pelias?" Mae'Lee asked.

"No, your Highness. He was not. He was a substitute. A fake Dunamai, as it were. But none of us knew. At the time."

"But the *Dragon* knew," Arlon muttered in sudden realization. "That's why he, uh, he killed him. I remember what he said. The Dragon said that only a Chosen Child may approach him."

"Unfortunately, that is correct," Kash responded gravely.

Huge tears welled up in Mae'Lee's heartbroken eyes. "Poor Pelias," she sobbed. "He...he probably knew that something dreadful could happen...and yet he was still there. He still did his duty."

Kash squinted. "He might not have had much of a choice. King Mandibar of Ammodis is not known for his generosity nor his mercy, child. He is ruthless. In any respects, he no doubt threatened to kill Pelias' family if the boy did not carry out the foolish scheme to fulfillment." The old man patted her arm and lifted her chin. "Now, I do not wish to seem cold or indifferent regarding your deceased friend, your Highness, but we have much more to discuss. Right now, your *future* is much more important than our *past*."

Paymer cleared his throat. "You know, sir, a person doesn't have to be as wise as a Sevasti to see that the meeting tonight didn't seem to go too well."

Kash's expression shifted from somewhat anxious to simmering anger. "Dogmatic fools, the lot of them! They can hold endless debates about the slightest of matters, and yet overlook a sizable truth displayed right before them! A mountain of evidence is overthrown by suspicions no larger than a grain of sand—"

THUD! THUD! THUD!

Everyone flinched as three dull raps resounded at the door. Kash wasted no time scurrying over and unlocking it. Brother Gremlor, clutching a large bag, squeezed through in a huge rush the moment it opened.

"Did anyone see you?" Kash asked discreetly.

Gremlor shook his head. "No."

Kash locked the door. "Did you find them?"

"I found *most* of them," the new arrival muttered, patting the bag.

"Let's pray that it is sufficient. Please, brother, take my chair," Kash offered as he gestured towards the seat. "I will recline here by the fire pits."

Both elders sat down as Gremlor dug around inside the satchel and fished out a small stack of papers. He delivered them to Kash.

"If I may ask…what happened after we were…made to leave the room?" Mae'Lee ventured politely.

"A maddening display of stubborn ignorance is what happened, daughter of Leandros," Gremlor replied in a huff. "Brother

K'Kashmalon and I underestimated the various obstinate factions in the Assembly."

"Are they going to help us?" Arlon asked, his eyes flitting back and forth between the two men.

"*They* are not," Kash replied. "But *we* are."

"As much as we can," Gremlor added. "But we do not have much time. You must be gone by first light tomorrow morning."

Paymer shook his head. "I knew it! I told you guys they'd throw us out of here!"

"On the contrary, young Dunamai," Gremlor retorted, "*they* want you to stay." He paused and pointed at Kash. "*We* want you to leave."

"Oh, okay," Paymer mumbled. "Wait…what?" He shot a hopelessly confused glance over at Arlon.

Arlon just shrugged in return.

"The Assembly voted to hold you here until messengers from Alaithia could be dispatched to notify your home kingdoms," Kash explained. "Their plan is to send out four fast riders on horseback at dawn. Once delegations from your lands arrive back here, then the Assembly would authorize your release. They do not trust you to leave, shall we say, *unchaperoned*."

"We would be…*prisoners* of the Sevasti?" Mae'Lee asked.

Kash's forehead wrinkled. "Certainly that is not a term they would ever choose, your Highness. In any respects, you would be treated very well and—"

"But still, we would be prisoners," Paymer affirmed.

Kash squinted. "Yes. In the sense that you could not come and go as you wish."

"Sounds like the old days before the Dragon Offering," Arlon grumbled as he leaned back against the wall. "Trapped once again inside stone fences. I spent seventeen years of my life like that. I couldn't wait to get out."

"But needless to say, returning you to your respective lands is a most dangerous proposition," Gremlor added. "We have received word that the Order has infiltrated the security forces of many, if not all, of your kingdoms. There is a great likelihood that you would depart Alaithia a few weeks from now…and then be lost. Kidnapped. Killed."

"But…by the will of the Zho, we are not going to wait for that possible future to befall any of you," Kash insisted. "We have devised a plan. To help you escape. And then…" He lowered his voice to a harsh whisper. "To help you *kill* the final Dread Guardian."

"So, there is a way to kill the Dragon?" Paymer whispered back.

Both Sevasti elders nodded slowly with somber stares. Gremlor hunched forward. "It is no coincidence, our young friends, that the scripture of truth and the writings of the Order agree concerning the possible *mortal* fate of the final Dread Guardian."

"But I was always taught that no mortal could kill a Dragon," Mae'Lee protested.

"That is indeed correct, Princess," Kash replied. "Only *'Dread against Dread'*…only a Dragon may kill a Dragon."

Mae'Lee's cute face scrunched up. "But Terras Telos is the last and final Dragon, right? Where would we find *another* Dragon to kill the *only* Dragon?" She looked around. "That doesn't make sense. Does it?"

Mogg's head shot up suddenly. "But a weapon fashioned of a Dragon could destroy a Dragon."

Kash smiled and brought his hands together in the custom of the Kray. "It is well-spoken," he said with a subtle bow.

"Wait…Dragons make weapons?" Paymer asked.

"Not quite," Gremlor countered. "But a weapon fashioned from the remains of Dragons would have the potential to dispatch a Dragon."

"What exactly did that poem say that you read earlier?" Arlon inquired.

Gremlor pulled out the ancient rolled page and handed it to him. Arlon unfurled it with caution as Gremlor pointed. "It is right here, my son."

Arlon cleared his throat.

"'With tooth, with scale, with claw.
Hallowed remnants of those long dead.
Gather them each,
Gather them all.
Mortal poison for the immortal Dread.'"

"We have to make a poison?" Paymer asked.

Gremlor rubbed his chin. "It indicates a very specific poison, young Dunamai. A lethal concoction of Dread Guardian remains to harm a Dread Guardian."

Arlon lowered the document. "So, we would need to find something, some kind of remains from one of the other Dragons. Like it says...a scale, or claw, or something."

"Not just a single relic, my boy," Kash corrected. "But a relic from *each* of the previous six Dread Guardians. '*Gather them each, gather them all*,' it says. You would need *six* relics."

Arlon's eyes grew wide. "Hold on! What about pieces of their *Rones*?! Surely we can collect a piece of each of the six Dragon Rones without too much trouble." He reached into his shirt and hoisted his necklace. "I mean...I have one right here!"

Gremlor seemed quite interested at first but then pursed his lips. "If only that were true, my optimistic friend. But the writing is very specific, it mentions *'remnants of those long dead.'* And it also speaks very clearly of tooth and scale and claw. No mention of the Rone of a Dread Guardian."

Paymer's eyebrows shot up. "I've heard that Dragon bones have some amazing properties."

"Let me guess," Mae'Lee began with a smug smile. "If you touch metal to them, it will turn to gold?"

He looked disappointed. "You, uh, you already knew that?"

"*Everybody* knows that," she replied with a wink.

Paymer cleared his throat. "So, we need to find out where the Dragon's all died?"

Kash nodded.

Arlon's excited expression collapsed. "But, then there's no hope," he sighed while glancing over at Kash. "When we were together in the slave cart, you told me that no one knows where any of the Dragon's remains are. You said that a dying Dragon hides its final resting place."

Kash grimaced. "Well, my boy, you see—"

"Though he may be very wise," Gremlor interrupted, "my Sevasti brother is not always entirely correct."

Every eye turned to Gremlor's scarred face.

"There are rumors, legends you might say, concerning the whereabouts of some of their remains." He shifted his weight. "It is said that the Order has located a few of them and even make pilgrimages to these holy sites."

Paymer grew quite interested. "Do you know any of these legends?"

"I must confess that I find it somewhat ironic that the Chosen Child of Orania has put forth this question," Gremlor responded.

Paymer squinted. "Why's that?"

"Because one of the most well-known legends speaks of a Dragon dying in the snowy mountains of Orania," Kash replied with a smile. "It is said that his massive form can still be seen as a dark shadow within its ancient, icy slopes."

"But there are hundreds of mountains in Orania," Paymer protested. "The Anatellians stretch from the coast in the West all the way into northern Avdira. It would take a lifetime to search them all." He glanced up at the faces of the two Sevasti elders staring back at him. "Well, I mean…the lifetime of a *regular* person. You know…like me."

"Indeed," Kash said.

"Then it's hopeless," Mae'Lee mumbled.

Arlon felt compelled to close his eyes. Something disturbed him, something way down deep. A feeling. A knowing. A prodding. *Hold on,* he thought. *A Dragon. In the snow. In the mountains.*

Why does that sound familiar?
His mind's eye raced.
A shadow. In the ice.
But where did I hear this?
He paused.
Wait...I didn't hear this. I...saw this.
I saw this. Yes, I did see it!
In the Rone vision! My first Rone vision!

"I've seen the place," Arlon blurted out, pretty much unintentionally.

Everyone grew quiet as they turned and glared at him.

"I, uh, I've seen it," he repeated. "I have."

"Seen what?" Gremlor inquired.

"The Dragon," he replied. "A *dead* Dragon. In the snow and ice." He nodded towards Kash. "Like you said, kind of like a dark shadow down in the ice."

"Where did you see this, my boy?" Kash asked.

"When I was at Mt. Krysis. At the Rone. I touched it and I had a vision."

"He did," Paymer noted. "Knocked him right to the ground. It was freaky."

Kash leaned closer and closer to Arlon with each and every word.
"What...did...you...*see*?"

"I, uh, I saw mountains. *Three* mountains. And the one in the middle was much bigger than the other two." He traced the outlines of the mountains in the air with his hand. "It was way taller."

Kash and Gremlor exchanged intrigued glances.

Arlon closed his eyes again. "And there, in the snow and ice…just below the biggest mountain…was the Dragon. Buried in the ice. It was just a dark shape. A dark shadow." He opened his eyes slowly. "I saw it."

"Are you sure?" Gremlor asked.

"Well, I'm sure that's what I saw."

"Three mountains? Middle one far taller?" Kash pressed.

"Yes. It was a lot taller."

Gremlor rose up with a widening grin and began pacing. He looked back at Mae'Lee. "You see, your Highness…it is *not* hopeless. We now know the exact location of the remains of one of the Dread Guardians."

"Hold on," Paymer said, his voice building with excitement. "Three mountains? Three peaks close together. The Valley of the Three Peaks?!"

Kash also stood up. "That is correct. Mount Kephali is the center, taller peak. Ancient legends say that the other two mountains descended from Kephali's loins."

Paymer jumped to his feet. "That's in Orania!"

"Indeed it is," Kash said as he wandered over to his desk and dug out a map. He studied it.

"And better yet…it is only a four-day journey by horse from Alaithia. Weather permitting, of course. It can be nasty this time of year in the higher elevations."

"But even if we find it," Mae'Lee began, "that's only one. We need six. Are there any clues to help us find the others?"

A strange grin washed over Gremlor's face. "Actually, your Highness, you only need to find *five* relics."

She looked puzzled. "Five?"

Kash glanced up from his map. "Yes, five." He gestured at Gremlor. "Show them."

"Show us what?" Arlon asked.

Gremlor reached deep within his large, burlap sack and pulled out a curious object. The square item was covered in thin, translucent, silver ovals that almost resembled the smooth petals of a huge flower. He grabbed one end and pried it apart. The device unfolded at the center into a larger rectangle about three feet high.

"It looks like some kind of a shield," Paymer said.

"That is because it *is* a shield," Kash responded quickly. "But not like any shield any of you have ever seen. Or any of your parents, or grandparents. Or anyone outside of Alaithia for the last thousand years."

Gremlor handed it to Paymer and pulled another folded shield out of his bag. "These are the only two ever made."

Paymer placed his hand through the inner strap and raised the shield up and down quickly. "Wow! It is so light. Amazing!"

"Light as leather and tougher than iron," Gremlor announced as he tossed the second one over to Arlon. Arlon undid the small latch and opened it up.

Mae'Lee and Mogg ran their hands along the intriguing surface. "What are they made of?" she asked.

"Those silvery scales are called Pyros," Gremlor replied. "They are from the inner lining of a Dread Guardian's throat and mouth. We believe they protect the beast from being burned by the heat of its own fiery breath."

Arlon was mesmerized by the peculiar craftsmanship. "Where did you get these?"

"Another story, for another time," Kash mumbled.

"I knew he was gonna say that," Paymer smirked as he played with a golden coin. "I did."

"Did you bring the collection?" Kash asked.

Gremlor nodded and dug around inside the satchel. He withdrew a folded, white cloth that was bundled with a pair of thin leather straps. He loosed the strands and carefully opened it. All four of the Dunamai gathered around as he laid it across his empty chair. Three rough stones came into view.

"Those are Rone pieces!" Mae'Lee cried out joyfully. "Lovely! Just lovely!"

Gremlor couldn't resist smiling. "You are correct, your Highness. These are from the Rones of the second, fourth, and sixth Dread Guardians," he explained, pointing to each of them in turn.

Kash strolled over to Arlon. "If I could see your necklace?"

"Oh, yes, absolutely," Arlon mumbled as he reached around his neck and pulled it over his head. "Here you go."

"Thank you, my boy," Kash almost whispered as he laid it ever so carefully beside the others. "And there you have it, a Rone from the first Dread Guardian." He glanced over at Gremlor. "I believe it is finally time to test the legend. After all these years."

Gremlor's face beamed, as thrilled as a child expecting to open a large gift. "It is," he replied in quiet awe.

"What do you mean, '*test the legend*'?" Paymer asked.

Kash folded his arms. "Many thousands of years ago, during the First Great Purge of the Order, we discovered a very interesting document. It has since been lost, but it seemed to indicate something…incredible. Something mystical. There is a passage in the prophecy of truth which is very similar."

"What?" Paymer asked. "What did it say?"

Kash took the shield from Paymer and laid it across his own arms, with the Pyros facing up. "Arlon," Kash called out. "Would you please pick up each of the Rone fragments and lay them on top of the shield? One at a time. And slowly."

"Uh, sure," the boy replied. "Is something going to happen?"

"Just oblige this curious old man," Kash replied with a wink.

Arlon snagged his Rone necklace and laid it across the shield. He looked up.

"Now the next one, please," Kash instructed. "Don't stop."

Arlon carefully placed the second fragment beside the first. Kash nodded. The boy bent down and grabbed the third piece and started to set it on the shield.

"Look!" Mae'Lee cried out, pointing.

The instant the beautiful stone touched the shield, it began pulsing with a radiant light and emitted a shrill but pleasant pitch. Gremlor and Kash patted each other on the back.

Arlon jerked his hand away and the light and sound both faded quickly.

"Please, Arlon," Kash encouraged. "Simply place your finger back on the Rone. It is safe, I can assure you."

As the boy did, the spectacular show returned without delay.

"What an odd sound!" Paymer exclaimed.

Mae'Lee wrinkled her forehead. "Are you really hearing something?" Paymer nodded at her. "Because I can't hear it," she moaned.

"It's kind of like a long bird tweet," he explained.

She collected a fistful of her long, black hair and held it to the side as she leaned her ear just above the Rone.

"Do you hear it now?" Arlon asked.

She raised up with a sigh. "Nothing."

"That's okay," he reassured her. "But you can still see the light. Isn't that amazing?"

"It is lovely."

Gremlor moved closer. "And so the legends are true."

"What does this mean?" Paymer asked.

Gremlor pointed at the glowing stone. "It means, young Dunamai, that these shields were made from the Pyros of Terras Schema. That fragment is a piece of the Rone from the fourth Dread Guardian."

Arlon squinted and rubbed his chin. "So, the legend said that a Rone would react if it ever touches any of the remains of its own Dragon?"

"Almost, my boy," Kash replied. "You forgot to mention the *third* ingredient of that legendary recipe…a Chosen Child. This will only occur if a *Dunamai* touches the Rone while it touches any of the remains of a Dread Guardian. Remove your finger."

Arlon raised his hand away and the rock returned to normal.

Gremlor pushed his cloak sleeve back and placed his own finger against the Rone.

Nothing.

"I may be a Sevasti, but I am not a Dunamai. Now," Gremlor said, "your Highness…please touch the stone."

Mae'Lee lifted her arm and placed a trembling finger against the fragment which immediately responded with its brilliant display. She jumped up and down on the bed, almost knocking Paymer off.

"And if there were ever any doubt about the status of our Therion friend," Kash began. "Mogg, Vish'tar of the Kla'aven Mage, would you please do us the honor of touching the stone?"

Mogg stepped closer and laid his index finger atop the irregularly-shaped relic. It began glowing and sang out its steady pitch. "By the Red Leaf," he muttered.

"My turn," Paymer teased as he playfully shoved Mogg's hand aside. He touched a Rone.

Nothing happened.

Paymer's shocked eyebrows shot up and Mae'Lee's stunned mouth dropped open.

"What in the world?!" Paymer gasped in horror.

Kash and Gremlor glanced at each other.

"Calm down," Arlon urged with a forced smile. He pointed just to the left of Paymer's hand. "Uh…wrong stone, *pal.*"

Paymer's freckled face instantly flushed red with embarrassment. "Oh, yeah. Sorry." He moved his finger over and tapped the proper piece. It lit up along with his relieved face. "Okay, that's better! Much, *much* better!"

"Since the scales on the shield are from the fourth Dragon," Arlon began, "now, we just need five more relics. Right?"

"That's right," Paymer chimed in. "And now we know for sure where one of the other Dragons is buried. In the mountains. Less than a few days from here. So that would be two freaky finds in under one week. No problem."

"Perhaps," Kash muttered. "Perhaps not."

"K'Kashmalon's reservation is warranted," Gremlor agreed. "It could be that the remains of Terras Schema, the fourth Dread Guardian, are buried in the ice."

"Oh," Mae'Lee moaned. "So these scales right here could be from the Dragon that Arlon saw buried up in the mountains?"

Kash nodded. "Indeed. In any respects, unless my mathematics have failed me, there appears to be only a one in six chance of that being the case, Princess."

Paymer scratched his head. "So you're saying that even if we get there and somehow dig into the ice and get some part of that dead Dragon, we might not even need it? We might already have it, right here? And we would *still* need five more?"

"That is a possibility, young Dunamai," Gremlor responded.

The room fell silent for several seconds.

"But, there's no way to know…to be *sure*," Arlon said. "So we have to go into the mountains."

"What about *after* that?" Mae'Lee inquired with a bit of despair in her voice.

Kash handed the shield to Arlon and strolled back towards his desk. "The situation is not as hopeless as it now seems, Princess." He rummaged through a pile of papers and did a bit of organizing. "Over the millennia, the Sevasti have collected many documents and have encountered many tales concerning the final resting places of the Dread Guardians. Some of it may be true, all of it may be false, but who knows about such things?" He turned back towards them, carrying a handful of materials. "Here are maps and legends and testimonies to guide your journeys. Study them well." He locked eyes with Mogg. "One of the legends centers around a cave in the lands of the Kray. I believe it is in the southern reaches of your lands."

Mogg raised his head slightly. "I know of this story."

Arlon leaned forward and peered over at him. "Really?"

"It is well-spoken," Mogg replied. "All children are taught this story. It is in the lands of the Kla'aven Wins'orr."

"Take these," Kash urged.

Paymer grabbed the awkward stash of documents from the Sevasti's hand.

Kash snapped his fingers. "Oh, yes! And this." He reached beside one of the fire pits and snatched a tiny clay jar. He dangled it in the air by its leather strap. "You will need this."

"Is it food?" Paymer asked. "Cause if it is, it won't last long around this group. Have you seen Mae'Lee eat?" He winked at her.

"No, no, no, my young friend. This is far more important than physical sustenance."

"Does it hold crushed up red leaves from the Cardidendron tree?" Mae'Lee ventured.

"A worthy guess, Princess," Kash replied. "But, no. No leaves here. This is *powder*." He swirled his free hand in the air above the metal pit. "Powder to make a Vision Fire." He gestured towards Arlon. "I imagine that the supply in your necklace is running low."

Arlon frowned. "I think it's empty."

"A Vision Fire is the only way that you will be able to speak with us after tomorrow morning," Gremlor cautioned. His voice grew quite serious. "Once you leave Alaithia, you will be fugitives. Hunted by the Order, hated by the Dragon, and under the official condemnation of Alaithia."

"Oh, yeah," Paymer quipped, "and don't forget to add '*and blamed by our kingdoms for the disaster at the Dragon Offering*' to our growing list of problems and enemies."

"Once again, it just sounds so hopeless," Mae'Lee grumbled as her shoulders drooped.

Kash laid his comforting hand upon her. "On the contrary, Princess. Remember…it was *hopeless* that you would be able to avoid capture and reach Alaithia. But yet…here you are. It was *hopeless* that you yourself would survive the ravages of the Walking Fever." He raised his hand and pointed at her. "Yet…here you are, on the mend. It was *hopeless* that Arlon would recover from the fatal jaws of a Dragon. And yet, he sits here before us. Alive. And well. Mostly." He smiled at her and then at each of them. "It would appear that the blessing of the Zho shines mightily upon this small band of unlikely companions. You have all encountered insurmountable odds and yet have overcome. Such is far beyond the realm of coincidence or mere good fortune. This speaks of the design and purposes of organized destiny."

"It all sounds so big and impressive when you say it like that," Paymer observed. "But I can tell you that the last few weeks have felt more like accident and…and *chaos* rather than any sort of design or destiny or whatever."

"So says every sailor whose ship is tossed across the unforgiving ocean by unpredictable winds," Gremlor rebutted. "But once they anchor in some unknown harbor and discover the wealth of some unknown land, then they look back and see the good and guiding hand that led them through each and every storm. Trust me, I know."

He raised his right hand and drew their attention to his own somewhat disfigured face. "You see these? Some see only scars. But I see something more. I see a reminder…I see the evidence of a good and guiding hand that led me—under extreme and difficult circumstances—to where I am today. I was lost at sea, but only so that I would be found." He paused.

"Lemme guess," Arlon said. "That is another story—"

"Yes, for another time," Gremlor replied with a warm smile. He dug out a pile of bright, white blankets. "But now, you must be prepared."

Paymer squinted. "Prepare us for what?"

A somber look overtook Kash's typically-kind face as he handed them the blankets.

"For your possible *escape*, young Dunamai."

The distant and echoing wail jarred her from a fairly deep sleep as she rested a stone's toss from the edge of the frightful chasm.

BUUUUUUWWWHHHAAAAHH!

A groggy Trilyra had heard that unforgettably ominous horn once before. Its mournful tone had resonated out just over a week earlier, under much more desperate circumstances. She sat up quickly and stared out across the gorge. The first hints of a clear dawn had laced the towering peaks guarding Alaithia with shifting gold and was just beginning to accent the upper levels of the sprawling stone fortress itself. Scores of men in dark robes were scrambling about.

Oh, she realized. *It looks like they're opening the Firebridge!*

Maybe they're finally going to let me into this cursed place!

A series of loud pops followed by a continuous grinding rumble confirmed her suspicion. The long and fascinating process of opening the massive, folding bridge had begun.

Trilyra stretched twice before climbing to her feet and dusting herself off. She glanced over to her right as she pulled a few tangled strands of hair out of her ear-chain. The smoldering remains of her cooking fire ejected a thin white trail into the crisp, still morning air. The nights had been chilly, but not too cold. She was very thankful that it hadn't rained much beyond a few sprinkles, since her options for any type of real cover from the elements weren't too promising.

I wonder if Arlon is alright? she mused.

Maybe they're opening up the bridge to tell me that he died.

Wait, no, no, no. She literally shook her head as she debated within herself.

Stop that! I am not going to think like that.

But another disturbing thought raced by before she could silence it:

And why shouldn't Arlon die?

My brother died.

No, no…stop this! Time to get busy.

Trilyra straightened her belongings and rolled up her bed before tossing the charred, bony remnants of her last few meals over the nearby cliff. She had only made a modest dent in the liberal food supply the Sevasti had provided a week earlier and her stack of firewood was far from being depleted. They may have kept her outside, but they still had treated her with that bit of surprising generosity. Trilyra grabbed her bow and quiver and slung them over her shoulder before securing her sword to her hip.

The initial section of the Firebridge swung out and locked in place (still swaying a bit) as a contingent of Sevasti pole bearers hurried out to assist with the next phase of the well-rehearsed operation.

The long days of Trilyra's temporary exile on this side of the canyon had been uneventful, even boring…a far cry from the danger and commotion of the weeks leading up to their desperate arrival. Several shattered and mutilated logs were scattered about, having suffered the fury of hours and hours of her unrelenting sword practice. Trilyra had even embarked on a fair bit of travel, exploring the jagged reaches of the gorge in either direction. The elevated landscape was treeless and desolate for the most part, but she felt it was still beautiful in its own rugged way. To her it was certainly more interesting than the vast, uninhabited regions of her own desert kingdom (with the small exception of the oasis of Polichlor. She loved the lakeside capital and the lush green blanket of well-manicured grasses and hedges that adorned it).

She took a small drink from the water barrel and glanced up at the progress of the Sevasti workers. The second section of the Firebridge had just completed its noisy and labored pivot. The fascinating final stage was in motion.

The whole experience of being excluded from the others had been incredibly lonely.

Her thoughts and dreams had been constantly of her brother. The brutal and horrifying murder of her twin tormented the isolated girl at irregular intervals. Without anyone (or anything else) to distract her, it was nearly impossible to avoid the painful memories that haunted her.

After the bridge opens, it'll be nice to talk to a real person, she thought with growing anticipation.

I wonder how the Princess is doing?

I bet my bow Paymer's been up to his usual tricks.

And Mogg is probably still…

Mogg.

She smiled for the first time in a long time. It felt good.

The crunch of the last leg of the Firebridge scraping against the rocky soil snapped her away from her excited, jumbled thoughts. Just like before, several of the Sevasti exited the transom before forming a pair of silent, orderly lines. The rest of the workers jogged back towards Alaithia.

The Firebridge was completely clear. Trilyra looked for any activity.

That's odd, she thought. *I don't see anybody headed this way. What's going on?*

Just then…movement in the distance.

Wait…I see…um…horses?

One…two…three…three…no, wait…four.

Four horses. And riders.

The Dunamai?

Oh…wait…those don't look like our horses.

And dark robes?

Definitely not the Dunamai.

Her hopeful heart sank.

Moments later the convoy of man and beast trotted along the Firebridge in a tight formation. Trilyra's momentary elated expectation waned.

They are wearing Sevasti masks.

This doesn't look good.

I doubt they're coming on horseback just to let me in.

The first three masked riders galloped off the bridge and raced past the double row of Sevasti in a furious stampede into the southern distance.

Yep, she thought. *They're leaving.*

And in a hurry.

No one seemed to even notice her.

And…I'm not going anywhere.

The fourth rider exited the Firebridge and yanked his steed hard to the right, sending a couple of the Sevasti workers clambering to get out of hooves' and harm's way.

Trilyra's eyebrows shot up.

What's this?!

The horse trotted up beside her, and the rider shot out a strong arm. "Get on!" a muffled voice yelled.

"What's going on?" she asked, a little startled.

He grabbed her hand and the masked-figure leaned down. "Get on the horse, *Woman of the South!*"

A huge grin broke out across her face. "So good to see—"

But, before she could finish, he yanked the surprised girl onto his horse, and they stormed off down the long, sloping hill.

The sun rose steadily across all five of their sweating backs. And after two hours of uninterrupted riding, their team of exhausted horses deserved a much-needed break. Mogg signaled the others trailing behind him before bringing his animal to a gradual stop alongside a shallow, fast-moving mountain stream that gurgled across a colorful variety of smooth, rounded stones.

Trilyra immediately hopped down and threw her hands in the air. "Would someone care to tell me what's going on?!" she fairly yelled.

"I'm sorry," Mae'Lee called out as her own horse trotted up. "I didn't hear all of that."

A stunned Trilyra put her hand over her mouth. "Your Highness! You're…you're *talking*. And hearing?!"

The Princess dismounted quickly and led her horse over to the cool waters. "*Talking* much better than *hearing*," she admitted. "But it does seem to be getting a little better every day." The two girls exchanged warm hugs.

"Yeah, she can hear," Paymer chimed in, as he and Arlon rode up, side by side. "So be careful what you say. If you want to make fun of her, just whisper kinda high-pitched. *Like this*."

"I still heard that," Mae'Lee scowled.

Paymer slid out of his saddle and hit the dirt with a thud. "*Good*."

"And Arlon!" Trilyra shouted while Mogg and Paymer helped their injured friend down to the ground. "You're alive!"

Arlon's face grimaced, but he managed to plaster a weak smile. "Don't believe everything you see," he said before winking. "It's a clever illusion."

She strolled over and stared at his shoulder. "How are you feeling?"

"At the moment," he winced, "pretty horrible. Every bounce on that horse feels like a hot knife being jabbed into my arm."

"But you're alive! You've survived a Dragon's bite. I didn't think that was possible."

"Apparently it's happened *twice* in the last several thousand years," Paymer quipped. "So, if you think about it, he's really not all that special."

Mae'Lee put her hands on her hips. "Oh, he's pretty special, thank you."

Arlon's face flushed.

Their horses wasted no time in trotting up to the stream.

Trilyra pulled Mae'Lee aside. "Look, uh, your Highness," she began rather awkwardly. "I…I don't know if you remember very much about what happened after we left Mogg's waterfall city…but, umm, I said some really hateful and terrible things."

Mae'Lee blushed and nodded. "I really don't remember much, but Arlon and Paymer told me about it a few days ago." She locked a tearful stare with Trilyra and clasped her friend's hand. "And I am fairly certain that it is *I* who needs to beg *your* forgiveness."

Trilyra's eyes also began to water, and she brushed away a tiny tear. "Believe it or not," she chuckled, "I, uh, I was ready to shoot you." More tears ran down. "I had an arrow on the string."

Mae'Lee also couldn't help but giggle as they half-hugged again. "You probably should have shot me. I'm sure I deserved it! They said I was pretty dreadful."

"Oh, you were, Princess," Paymer smirked as he walked by. "Plenty dreadful. And hateful." He looked back over his shoulder. "But still cute. Dreadful, hateful *and* cute. A nice little collection of traits. Perfect for a spoiled princess."

"Thank you, Paymer," she said. "I think."

Trilyra wiped her own wet cheeks and stepped back. "So, what happened at Alaithia?" she asked, obviously searching each of their faces for answers. "Why did we have to ride out of there like a frantic pack of guilty thieves? The Sevasti didn't look like they were expecting that."

"That's because they weren't," Paymer replied.

"We, uh, we *escaped*," Arlon added.

Mae'Lee joined in. "Basically…we were prisoners."

"But, wait…I don't get it," Trilyra muttered. "If you were prisoners, then why did they open the Firebridge for you to leave?"

"Because they didn't really know it was us," Arlon explained. He pointed at their animals. "Those four horses were supposed to carry four messengers to each of our four kingdoms. They wanted to hold us at Alaithia until delegations could arrive to transport us back home."

"Like I said," Mae'Lee quipped. "*Prisoners*."

Trilyra squinted and began nodding. "So—"

"So we kinda *traded places* with those messengers," Paymer interrupted. "They just didn't know we traded. Those freaky Sevasti masks really helped."

Mae'Lee bit her bottom lip. "And we had a little…*help* on the inside."

"We had a *lot* of help on the inside," Paymer corrected.

Trilyra squinted and twirled her single ear-chain. "I'm sure it all makes sense somehow. So, what's the plan?" she asked, adjusting her bow.

Mogg pointed at the ground. "We need to collect as much grass and straw as we can carry."

It took only a moment for everyone to turn their puzzled heads and stare at him.

"Our horses will need food…in the high country," he explained. "I doubt that they will eat the snow. Roll it into bundles and fasten it with rope."

"Oh, right," Paymer piped up. "Good thinking."

Trilyra wasn't satisfied. "*High country?* So, where are we going? What're we doing?"

"Well, thanks to our little ruse back at Alaithia, we probably have enough provisions for a few days, and enough golden Royals to buy whatever we need," Paymer replied. "And we have enough cloaks and gloves and so forth. So I think that the first thing we need to do is to find a town and get us another horse."

"I think we've crossed over into your kingdom now, Paymer," Mae'Lee noted. "You should probably handle that little endeavor once we find a village. Our whole group is too…*conspicuous*." She pointed at her bare arms.

"None of us have those...*lovely* tattoos such as you have. We don't look very Oranian."

"I agree," Arlon piped up.

"Okay, get another horse," Trilyra repeated. "A horse for me. And then what? What's the bigger plan? Where are we really going?"

"I'm not sure you're gonna like it," Paymer commented. "Being from the desert."

"What's that mean?" she asked.

Arlon stepped closer. "Do you like snow? And cold and all that?"

"Maybe. Where are we going?"

Everyone grew quiet and exchanged uncomfortable glances. Mogg peered over at her as the cool breeze rippled his long, dark hair across his tanned face. He finally broke the tense silence. "We are headed north into the mountains. And then, by the Red Leaf, we will find what we need."

She squinted. "And what do we need?"

The Therion's frigid stare seemed to cut right through her.

"What we need to kill the Dragon."

A thick line of healthy pines bordered by a steep incline of jagged, shattered granite was all that met the eye from most any direction.

But beyond all appearances, the tree-shrouded mountain face on the northern slopes of the Ploutonian Range held a much deeper secret. Several secrets, in fact.

For many, many years.

It was impossible to tell if the old man, perched silently atop a large, flat boulder, was forcefully concentrating or merely fast asleep. His bony, motionless head faced the setting sun; its dying rays carving deep shadows into the angular folds of skin that undeniably proclaimed his great age. This faithful servant of the Order had outlived all of his children, and their children, and even all of their great, great grandchildren.

Many of the younger Dragon worshipers had strong suspicions that he was the Apex, the mysterious pinnacle of their forbidden cult. But the elders gathered deep within the hidden mountain cave, they knew better.

The focused old man sensed the stealthy arrival of a messenger, a young man who approached him from behind with no more noise than a soft breeze.

"Is there a problem?" the wrinkled elder mumbled, his eyes still clamped tightly shut.

"Lord Dyrden," the boy said, trembling. "My apologies. But, the Vision Fire has been kindled. The Master has summoned you."

Dyrden cracked his eyes open.

The Master, his mind repeated with a growing resentment. *Now that Terras Telos has come…very soon we will see who will be the Master.*

"I will be in," he declared. "Make all things ready."

He had seen his Master's murky form dozens and dozens of times through the flickering red flames of the circular portal over the years. But every time, it felt like the *first* time.

Terrifying. Unsettling.

Dyrden longed for the opportunity to meet the Apex in person, but that day had never come.

"Are we alone?" the Master's deep voice called out, a bit muffled as it reverberated off the painted stone walls of the ornately decorated room.

Dyrden knelt before the Vision Fire on a plush pillow and took a deep breath. "We are alone."

"A great opportunity has presented itself. We must act quickly."

Dyrden's head bowed slightly. "Your servant awaits, my Lord."

"Take the Rone fragments to the Mediator. By their power, he must summon the Dread Guardian, may he live forever."

Dyrden's trepidation was obvious. "Bring Terras Telos *here?!*"

"Indeed. The Mediator must convey to his Majesty the importance of making haste to the Valley of the Three Peaks."

"The mountains of Orania, my Lord?"

"Yes."

Dyrden seemed puzzled. "To the…*cold*?"

"His visit shall be short."

"But…why?"

"There he will find the remaining Dunamai."

"Are you certain, my Master?"

"They sought refuge at Alaithia eight days past. They now travel to Orania, seeking relics. Terras Telos must find them…and kill them." The dark, blurry visage was silent for a moment. "His wrath burns against them with a powerful vengeance. Perhaps his Majesty will finally accept an offering. *Our* offering. Of their blood. It will be the Age of the Order at last."

Dyrden squinted and nodded. "If it can be done, it will be done. Is there anything else, my Master?"

The dark apparition seemed to lean closer within the glowing portal. "Yes. One last thing. The Chosen Child of Soteria has something I wish to have back…" He paused.

"…Ask his Majesty to search through the boy's ashes and bring me what remains of his Rone necklace."

Tiny paintings of tiny mountains capped with snow could hardly compete with actually seeing majestic mountains blanketed in brilliant white from horizon to horizon.

This...this is magnificent! Arlon observed with a steady smile as he rode on and on and climbed ever higher. He and his horse had been urged to take the lead hours earlier as the quiet convoy wound their way through the thinning trees and steepening slopes. Irregular and dirty patches of snow began to appear in the shadows of large boulders and cling to the sides of deep ravines as the temperature plummeted.

In the desperate days leading up to their arrival to the Firebridge, the group had witnessed a remote, hazy view of the Anatellian Range far off to their north. And even during their short stay in Alaithia the icy summits still felt unreachable, but now it seemed like each jagged and snow-covered peak was finally within their grasp.

There was little doubt that they would be trudging through a white, wintery blanket by sundown.

Arlon's gaze drifted from the beautiful scene ahead as he took a brief moment to glance back. Trilyra followed not quite five yards behind him atop her muscular new steed (purchased two days earlier in a riverside Oranian town). The Princess was third in line with Paymer trotting alongside her (more or less), and Mogg kept his distance, his eyes ever-watchful. Though their Therion friend always seemed content and focused, Arlon knew that the loss of Tempest was a horrific wound that would always remain tender.

And that reminded him of another loss.

Arlon spun back around and sighed.

To see his friends was a comforting sight, but Hort's painful absence weighed heavily on the boy's mind. He couldn't decide which was worse: the constant memory of Hort's terrified form getting carried away by the Dragon, or the guilt of knowing ahead of time that the tragedy was going to happen.

His distracted thoughts drowned out the sound of Trilyra's sudden approach. "Getting close?" she called out.

A startled Arlon flinched and blinked several times. "Oh, uh…yeah. Yeah."

"I didn't mean to make you jump," she replied through a slight giggle.

"Oh, you didn't." He pointed at the ground. "I think my, uh, my horse stumbled on a rock."

Trilyra rolled her eyes at him before wiping a few blowing strands of blonde hair out of her face. "Oh, sure. I hate when that happens." She faced forward and squinted. "So, I take it those are the mountains we're looking for?"

He nodded. "According to the map Kash gave us."

"*And* your vision. Don't forget about that." She paused and stared for a while. "Did it look like that?"

"Did *what* look like *what*?"

"Your vision," she replied firmly, wagging her fingers forward. "Did your vision look like those three mountains up ahead?"

Arlon studied the scene. "It's hard to be sure," he admitted before looking skyward. "I was way…*way* up there."

Arlon didn't notice the tiny tears that were welling up inside of her reddening eyes, but he did notice the awkward pause. He glanced over.

"What's wrong?"

Trilyra blinked hard. "I...was just...thinking," she began. "You were *'way, way up there,'* and...uh," her voice cracked. "And, I, I shouldn't be way, way down *here*."

"What does that mean?"

She played with the reins. "I think you know. I think everyone knows. I *know* they know."

"Everyone knows what?"

"You don't even have to say it. I can see it in your eyes. Everyone's eyes. The Sevasti must've told you." Her tears started streaming down. "The truth...about...Pelias."

He struggled with a comforting reply. "They...did...tell us." Arlon's panicked mind raced. "But listen, no matter what happened, we all know how brave your brother was. We—"

"They said they'd kill us all if we said anything," she sobbed and snorted. "Our mother. Our father. All of us." Trilyra attempted to dry her face with the back of her trembling right hand. It didn't work. "But...in the end, I guess it didn't really matter. My brother still died. And who knows if my parents are even still alive. And who knows if *any* of us will make it out of all this alive."

Arlon paused and collected his thoughts.

"What was his name?" he asked respectfully.

Her furrowed eyebrows shot up. "*Pelias'* real name?"

Arlon nodded respectfully.

"It was…Treygon," she whispered, brushing away a fresh round of tears. "Treygon. I was actually older, you know." Trilyra shoved a grin through a nervous laugh. "About five minutes older. And, uh, I never let him forget it."

"I know that I've said it before, but I am so sorry. I can't even imagine losing someone that close to me. The only family I have is my mother. And…if you think about it," he looked down. "When Pelias—*when your brother*—died, I lost the closest thing I had ever had to a friend. When I arrived at the Karaval, just before the Offering, he was so kind. So friendly. He took me right in." Arlon blinked away a tear or two. "I really wish I had known him better. He must've been a really wonderful person."

Trilyra's head was bobbing and her ear-chain wobbled helplessly. "Wonderful? I suppose. And funny. He loved to play practical jokes. As the precious Dunamai of Ammodis, he had plenty of time to think of very devious little plots."

"Was he a trained warrior, like you?"

"*Warrior?*" she roared. "Oh, no, no, no. I bet my bow that his soft hands never even held a real knife. No…swordplay was considered *unsafe* for a Dunamai, even a fake one, I guess. His only dangerous skill was his sharp tongue. And it did get him into trouble. All the time." She paused and stared down. "We used to swim together. And race across—"

"*Swim?*" Arlon interrupted. "In the desert?"

Trilyra rolled her eyes and sighed. "We happen to have a lot of very beautiful streams and lakes in my kingdom," she replied. "It's not all desolate sand and sun, you know."

"I guess I had never pictured any of that in Ammodis. No offense." Arlon fought hard to hold back a mischievous grin. "Woman of the South."

She squinted and released a nasty look before holding her head high. "Careful there, Soterian boy. I doubt that any other capital in the Five Kingdoms could rival the beauty and majesty of Polichlor. Mandibar may be greedy and selfish, but he does it with great style. The architecture and landscaping in the city are unrivalled...so I've been told."

"Well," he began, "I've traveled here and there, and I've been to Edra. I would have to admit that it's more beautiful than my own capital back home. The Avdirians have gorgeous marble buildings...with bright, colorful banners blowing in the breeze, and then there's the huge palace." His eyes grew wide as vivid memories flooded in. "We have the Citadel in Pervazi, and it sits above the river, but Leandros' palace actually overlooks the ocean! It's really something."

"You've never seen Polichlor," she countered. "Our capital spreads out along the shore of the crystal-clear waters of Lake Syntero. The desert turns into wonderful green lawns and hedges and forests, with the towering peaks of the Ploutonians framing it all in the north. Mandibar's royal residence actually sits on an island near the middle of the lake." She raised her left hand slowly, as if to trace something in the air. "It rises like a crown right out of the water. I bet my bow that it's prettier than whatever Leandros has in Avdira."

"You might be right. But the ocean is amazing."

"You've never seen Lake Syntero."

Arlon glanced over and smiled at her as a gentle breeze tickled his skin. "Maybe one day."

Not quite a stone's toss away, Mae'Lee studied their playful conversation with concerned interest. But, before long, she forced herself to look away.

———————————————

Beautiful brown horse legs became dark, soggy messes, soaked with filthy splashes from the slush kicked up as their hooves plodded dutifully uphill. The ground was nearly all white now, and the snow was getting noticeably deeper. Mogg had retaken the lead hours before, and Arlon had gradually floated to the rear of the quiet pack as shifting rays from the lowering sun played a rhythmic peek-a-boo through the thinning forest.

He was fascinated with the thin wisps, rising like smoke, as his own warm breath greeted the frigid mountain air. Arlon fished out and donned a pair of woven gloves and pulled his cloak ever-tighter around his neck. He was immediately grateful that Kash and Gremlor had the foresight to provide warmer clothing, not just maps and money and myths.

Let's hope they're right about all this, he sighed within himself.

Mogg kicked his steed and bolted the last few slushy yards to gain the rim of a steep ridge in their path. He halted his horse before waving his right arm excitedly towards the others, beckoning them to join him.

Paymer dashed ahead and quickly drew alongside, as Arlon waited for the ladies to master the difficult slope. He saw Mogg raise his arm and point, just as a chilling breeze began blowing into their faces.

"This is the valley?"

Paymer brushed his ruffled, red hair back and folded his freckled arms. "Well, even if it isn't, it still might be one of the most beautiful sights this Oranian has ever seen. And I've seen quite a few."

"Lovely!" Mae'Lee exclaimed, clapping her gloved-hands together which made an oddly-muffled sound. "Unspeakably lovely!"

Arlon and his horse finally plopped onto the narrow plateau and halted. The Princess was right.

"Oh, my," he exhaled.

An enormous bowl of pristine snow sank down in front of them before rising up to meet the sheer, rugged crags of a trio of peaks arranged in perfect fashion along the horizon. A splay of warm rays from the west bathed the upper levels of the white wonderland in deepening amber shades as it accented the harsh, gray faces of the mountains with golden highlights. A powerful northern wind seemed to cascade down from the massive summit before them, kicking up shifting, smoky rivers of white that rolled along the surface of the spectacular vista.

"The Valley of the Three Peaks," Arlon announced, as flitting memories in his mind's eye confirmed what his physical ones were gawking at.

Trilyra looked over towards him. "This is what you saw? In your vision?"

Everyone glanced over.

He nodded. "It is."

Mae'Lee's face scrunched up. "I know that the sun is low...but...I'm afraid that I do not see any dreadful remains of a Dragon in that valley. Nothing but lovely, white snow. It's wonderful."

Arlon didn't seem bothered in the slightest. "Oh, don't worry. He's out there, your Highness."

"You mean *under there*," Paymer interjected. "Under the snow. *A lot* of snow. And probably ice, too. Who knows how deep?"

Mogg positioned himself before the group. "It will be night soon. And with this wind, it will be a very cold night. We must seek out shelter and gather firewood."

"Sounds like a good plan," Paymer replied. "Plus, I'm hungry."

"*Hungry?*" Trilyra smirked. "I've seen you sneaking quite a few bites out of your pack."

A more-than-guilty look washed over his surprised face. "Wait, no…see…I was just *sampling* the supplies. You know, making sure that the Sevasti had given us fresh food. We wouldn't want anyone getting sick from spoiled meat or something. We've been traveling for several days now." He held his arms out defensively. "I was just thinking of others."

Trilyra pulled her cloak tighter as stiff, cold gusts slammed into them. "Well," she chuckled, "then you were thinking of others *a lot* today."

"Paymer," Mogg called out sharply, disrupting their little bit of fun. "I will ride towards the setting sun." He pointed in the opposite direction. "You will ride that way. We will seek shelter." He stared at the others. "Build a fire and wait here for our return."

Arlon watched in silence as Mogg galloped off and eventually disappeared behind a jumbled protrusion of granite boulders in the west. Before long, Paymer was out of sight to the east, as well.

No one noticed the menacing shadow with enormous wings gliding in and out of the clouds to their south.

He hadn't heard that voice in a long time.

And it woke him up.

Immediately.

Arlon stretched before pushing himself off the hard floor of the damp cavern into a sitting position (more or less) and squinted into the daylight streaming in from the distant mouth of the cave. There was a silhouetted figure approaching him.

A woman?

In a dress?

He glanced at the jumbled assortment of sleeping bodies strewn around the smoldering remains of their campfire. Paymer was flat on his back, snoring intermittently, as usual. Through the shifting trails of smoke, he could see that

Mogg was face down, with a sword still loosely in his grasp. The ladies, off to his left, were both buried under layers of blankets.

The mystery woman drew closer.

Arlon started to reach for Paymer's ankle.

"Wait…don't wake them," a sweet, comforting, and very familiar voice called out.

Arlon jumped up. "*Mother?*"

He couldn't tell for sure, but it looked like she was placing a finger across her lips.

"Shhhh."

A rush of emotion warmed his chilled frame as Arlon scrambled to his feet. He bumped into Paymer in his haste to get to her. The snoring Oranian made a few unintelligible gurglings and rolled over.

"Careful, my precious son," she scolded with a growing smile. "No need to hurry."

Mother!

The moist gravel crunched beneath his feet as Arlon quickly closed the rocky gap between them. "What are you doing here?" he asked, almost out of breath. "How did you find us?"

She threw her arms out and pulled him close, swaying from side to side, savoring the moment. Chara swept his blond hair out of the way and kissed his forehead with a tenderness that had waited for far too long. "So many questions," she whispered. The weeping woman leaned back and gazed at him. "Though he is growing up and growing wise, yet my Arlon, the very heart of my heart, is still a little boy whose favorite toys are questions."

"But *how*—?!"

A soft, delicate finger came across his excited lips.

"K'Kashmalon," she replied with a solemn stare.

Her simple answer only served to open up a thousand more complicated questions. Arlon clutched her hand and slowly lowered it from his face. "But why are you here? You shouldn't be here."

Her voice was dripping with pain as she looked away. "You say that, as if *I* am the one out of place."

He paused. "What?"

Chara spun back around. "It is *you*, my precious and only son. *You* are the one who is out of place." She glanced all around at the dark cavern. "You shouldn't be here."

His tortured mind raced. "But, but...mother. I have to be here. I have —"

Chara clutched his hand and leaned towards him with a visible rage he had never before seen in her hazel eyes. "*No*. No. You did the only thing you *had* to do, my son. You did the one thing that you were raised to do, the one thing that was expected of you. You fulfilled your duties to your kingdom as our Dunamai."

"The Dragon Offering," he whispered as his head drooped.

"Yes," she confirmed with a fresh round of tears. "The Offering. And now, *I need you*. I need you to fulfill your duties to me. As a son. As my only son." She hesitated. "Life has been harder than you know since you ran away from me. Very...hard."

"But I didn't run away from —"

"You can call it whatever you wish, my son, but to a mother's heart, you have abandoned the very one who loves you more than you can ever hope to know." Chara took a few quiet steps and studied the sleeping bodies around the campfire. "You have abandoned me, and surrounded yourself with...strangers." She pointed at Mogg. "Even wild and dangerous strangers." Her hand gestured towards Trilyra. "And liars." She glanced back at him. "Who knows what any of their motives are?"

"But, but these are my *friends*, mother. We have been through so much together. And we are on an important—"

"So," she interrupted coldly, "you have made your decision. Your so-called friends of only a few months over your own family. Over your own mother!"

He fought to keep from crying. "Why are you saying this?"

Mae'Lee pushed her blanket back and stretched with a large yawn, but didn't wake up.

Chara glared at her and folded her arms. "Perhaps it isn't friends that keeps you here...that keeps you away from me." She carefully picked her way over and knelt beside Mae'Lee. "Perhaps the reason you have left the most important woman in your life, is for the love of another woman in your life." Chara began brushing Mae'Lee's long, dark hair out of her peaceful face. "She is beautiful."

"But, no, listen...mother," Arlon stumbled, as he tried his best to hold his voice down. "It's not like that, I...I—"

Chara's face scrunched up. "You don't think the Princess is beautiful?"

His head bobbed from side to side. "Well, she is...you know, what you said, but—"

"You're blushing," Chara observed as she rose back up with a growing smile. "And you're almost stuttering. Is this love, my son?"

"What? *Love?* What're you—"

She stepped closer. "You know what I mean. Of course, who wouldn't want to marry into a royal family?"

"Um, *marry?!* Uh...that's quite a stretch. Why are we talking about marriage?"

Her grin continued to expand. "A fabulously wealthy royal family."

"Well, um, look, this is not really the time...or, or the place," he responded in desperation. "We have a...a mission. There is something I have to do. For…for you, and for everyone. Not just for our kingdom, but for all kingdoms."

Her smile transformed into scorn. "You already did what you were called to do! And now it is time to come home. This mess…this *misery* that has come upon us all, it is a matter for kings and conquerors…not for…children."

"Mother, please try to understand…I have to do this."

Chara darted over and clutched his left shoulder. "Even if it costs you your life?!"

He could no longer restrain his tears. "Yes."

She shook him. "Even if it takes you away from me?!"

He clamped his weeping eyes shut. "I…I'm sorry."

Chara squeezed harder and shook him over and over. "Don't you love me, my son?! Arlon?!"

He tried to answer.

The shaking continued.

"Arlon?!"

He felt strange.

"Arlon!"

The voice was familiar, yet different.

"Arlon!"

He snapped his eyes open. As they gradually adjusted, he made out the forms of

Trilyra and Mae'Lee hovering over him with concerned faces.

"Are you alright, Arlon?" the Princess asked as she released his left arm.

"Uh, what?" he replied, struggling to sit up.

"You were babbling," Trilyra snickered. "It sounded pretty serious."

Mae'Lee bent down and tenderly wiped his wet cheek. "And you were crying. Was it another bad dream?"

Trilyra squinted. "Was it a *Dreadwood* kind of a bad dream?"

Arlon rubbed his eyes and stretched his back. "Uh, well...sort of, I guess. I don't know...it was good...and bad."

Mae'Lee's big brown eyes locked onto him. "I thought I heard you say something about marriage. And love."

He looked away and jumped to his feet. "Uh, well, it was a dream. We all have them." Arlon straightened his outfit. "Most of them...you know, don't make much sense. Just a bunch of random...whatevers."

"You hungry?" Trilyra asked. "Paymer fried us something...meaty."

"I think it's bacon, pal," Paymer piped up, between mouthfuls. "Same stuff we had yesterday. I think it's mountain goat. The Sevasti had a lot of them back in Alaithia. Tasty little critters, I'll give 'em that."

Mae'Lee snatched Arlon's left hand and yanked. "Come on," she urged with some excitement.

"Uh…okay. Where are we going?"

"To see a big, lovely pile of snow."

"It's pretty freaky," Paymer quipped.

Arlon frowned as they headed around a sharp bend. "But…didn't we see plenty of snow all day yesterday?"

"This is kind of…special," she said.

Once again, the Princess was right.

They neared the glowing opening of the cave entrance, but something looked odd. It was bright, but not quite bright enough.

What?

A white wall?

"Isn't it something?" she said, jogging ahead. "Mogg was the first one to see it this morning. He dug a small tunnel. It will take some work to make it big enough to get the horses out."

Arlon caught up with her and admired the enormous wall of snow. The pile stretched beyond the rough, rocky ceiling fifteen feet overhead. "This is amazing," he admitted, scooping a large, white handful. "But how?"

"The wind," she replied, donning a pair of gloves. "Remember how strong it was last night?"

He raised his eyebrows. "How could I forget? It sounded like a thousand wolves howling. Maybe *two* thousand."

"Trilyra said it blew all night long. It must have piled up the snow." Mae'Lee trotted towards the left side of the barricaded cave entrance and motioned for him to follow. "Come on…it's a most lovely day outside. Not a cloud in the sky."

Once again, the Princess was right.

"You gotta plan, Mr. Valley Vision man?" Paymer teased as he plopped down onto a sizable rock, wiping his hot sweat away with his ice-encrusted gloves.

Arlon finished dragging yet another blanket-load of freshly dug snow from their widening tunnel, before squinting in the bright morning sun.

"The plan?" he replied, taking a deep but unsatisfying breath. The thin, mountain air constantly reminded him how high they were, and the throbbing wound in his right shoulder continually reminded him how lucky he was. "Uh, well…the plan is to find the dead Dragon." He dumped the blanket and pointed towards the center of the valley. "Out there. Somewhere."

Paymer bit his bottom lip. "There's a lot of 'out there'…*out there*, pal."

"I know."

Trilyra barreled out through the hastily-carved exit and rested her hands on her hips. "Sitting down *again*, Paymer? This tunnel isn't going to dig itself."

He rolled his eyes. "Well, we would've already been done with this little project if everyone would've listened to my original plan."

Arlon peeked over at him. "What was your original plan?"

"He wanted to melt a tunnel," Trilyra answered with a healthy dose of obvious skepticism.

"*Melt* a tunnel?"

"It would work," Paymer protested, rising up. "It's smart. Build a big fire and let the heat melt the snow. But, I guess everyone else wanted to use their muscles, instead of my brain."

Arlon's brow furrowed. "You know, Paymer, I'm not really sure that—"

"*What's that?!*" Trilyra yelled, jabbing her left arm skyward and drawing out a sword with her right.

Arlon dropped back and did his best to follow her line of sight. "What's *what*?"

"I just saw something flying overhead. It was dark…and big. Maybe we should—"

"There it is!" Arlon hollered. "I see it."

Paymer saw it too, and grinned.

"Freaky," he quipped. "I told you those birds were native to the highlands of my kingdom."

"Bloodfeather Falcon?" Arlon ventured.

"Blood...*tip* Falcon," Paymer corrected. "And a really big one at that. Incredible."

Trilyra released a tremendous sigh. "Thank goodness. I thought that maybe it was...the Dragon."

"Oh, don't worry. We're okay...we're safe way up here," Arlon assured.

Paymer raised his hand to shield his gaze from the sun's morning rays as he studied the massive bird's movements. "If only we could see the valley the way that Bloodtip sees it from way up high. We could probably find that Dragon carcass in no time."

Trilyra slapped Paymer on the shoulder with the flat of her drawn sword. "Well, our friend from Soteria has already seen it from way up high. I'll bet my bow he'll find it."

A burning question washed over Paymer's whole face as he locked eyes with Arlon. "What'd you mean by that?"

"By what?"

"What you said about us being *safe* up here."

"It's true."

"Um...I don't understand. Help me out."

"Dread Guardians dread cold and snow." Arlon paused with a homesick smile. "So I've been told."

"I hope you're right," Trilyra whispered as she slid her blade back into its sheath.

Arlon cleared his throat. "Just remember this: '*Snowy cold lacing mountains white, forbids the terrible Dragon's flight.*'"

"Hey," a sweet, new voice echoed through the tunnel. "I'm happy to say that I actually heard that just now…and I'm also pretty sure that I've heard that cute little rhyme before." Mae'Lee burst out into the sunlight wrapped in a thick cloak, with Mogg trailing close behind. "And if I remember right," she announced, tapping Arlon on the chest, "you heard that rhyme from your mother."

Paymer's eyebrows shot up. "Your mother?"

Arlon directed his gaze across the treeless valley and up at the mighty mountains. "My mother is a very wise woman. Did you all know that much of the greatest wisdom in all the Five Kingdoms is preserved in simple poetry?"

Mogg seemed unimpressed. "We do not need poetry…or wisdom." He also glared out at the blinding white of the frozen landscape that sprawled out before them. "We need relics. Dragon relics."

"It's a dreadfully large valley," the Princess observed, sounding more than a little discouraged. "Where do we even start?"

Trilyra and Paymer glanced silently over at Arlon, leading to an uncomfortably long lull in the conversation. Paymer cleared his throat twice (and much, much louder the second time).

"Well," Arlon began, taking the hint. "In my Rone vision, the dark shadow that I saw beneath the snow and ice was…" He paused before loosely gesturing. "It was…up there. Not quite in the middle…just slightly west of it."

Mogg studied the terrain. "We will need the horses," he declared.

Paymer rubbed his chin and squinted. "Oh, I don't know about using the horses," he countered. "I took a little stroll earlier, and that is almost like pure ice out there. It looks like the wind blew most of the loose snow last night." He pointed back towards the cave. "That's why we had to dig ourselves a little escape hole this morning."

Arlon ventured out several yards and examined the slippery conditions. "Uh, I think I agree with Paymer on this one." He stomped his foot several times and almost fell. "There's no way the horses could navigate on this ice. It'll be tough enough for us."

Mogg nodded reluctantly and peered along the massive, elongated granite outcrop that was responsible for their overnight accommodations. "Then we will ride our horses north along this ridge, as far as the conditions will allow. After that we will pursue the Dragon relics on foot."

"And…when we find it," Trilyra asked, "how do we get it out of the snow and ice?"

"We only need one small piece," Arlon answered. "Just one relic."

"That still doesn't answer my question," she retorted. "What are we going to do, stay there and wait for the spring thaw?" she smiled.

"I hate to be the one to tell you this, but there is no spring thaw this high up," Paymer corrected. "Every day is winter in the high Anatellians."

Mogg clutched his sword and rammed its tip into the frozen ground. "We dig the relics out."

Paymer faced away from the others and kept his voice low.

"If the relics are even here."

He had never imagined that the high mountain air could be so warm, or that the blazing mountain sun could be so bright. For just a moment, Arlon stole a glance back over his shoulder across the expanse of shimmering ice. Their tired horses, tethered to a pile of boulders, had long since faded into the glare of the unseen distance.

The weary group fanned out into a long line with Arlon dead center, doing their best to cover as much territory as possible in the (more than) difficult conditions. The lonely search continued for hours…with nothing to show for it, except for punishing headaches caused by the thin mountain air.

"Kinda freaky, isn't it, pal?" Paymer called out from over twenty yards away.

"Freaky?" Arlon hollered back.

"To be so hot," the redhead replied, pointing at his sweat, "and yet," he stomped on the smooth, frozen ground, "and yet…to be so cold."

Arlon resumed his forward progress and continued scanning the glassy glacial valley for any hint of an ancient, buried beast. "Indeed," he mumbled. "Indeed it is freaky, my friend."

The exhausted Soterian sucked in a deep breath.

It didn't help much.

Freaky, he thought.

Yes, Paymer…it's freaky that we're out here.

He plodded along.

It's freaky that any of these people would believe that I could help them find a dead Dragon.

He squinted and blinked several times, trying to erase the bright white blotches that plagued his vision.

And…it's freaky to think that we could find a way to kill a Dread Guardian.

The blinding combination of reflected sunlight and Arlon's thick cloud of dark questions masked Mogg's gradual approach from the north.

"The day is far spent," Mogg declared once he was in earshot. The long-haired, Therion Dunamai drew closer and a frustrated Arlon waited for him. "It would be an ill thought to travel back to the cavern in the night. We should return back."

Return back.

Arlon bristled at the thought.

Return back.

And with nothing to show for it.

Maybe my mother was right.

He sighed.

Maybe I don't belong here.

"Does the *Vice* agree?" a smiling Mogg pressed, straining to catch his breath. "We should return back soon?"

Arlon nodded and brought his hands together, Kray-style. "It is well-spoken," he replied with a forced grin. "Let's round up the others, we—"

That's all he got out.

At first…a high-pitched, sizzling sound.

Then, a dark blur in the sky.

A fraction of a second later…

A sickening explosion.

SHHHHHHHRRRAAAAKKKKTTTT!

A blast of blood. Of hair.

And huge chunks of bone.

The force of the violent impact flung Arlon and Mogg backward, skidding them across a sea of red-splattered ice. A stunned Arlon, covered with pieces of warm, shredded flesh and tufts of hair, rolled onto his side, struggling to get answers.

A bloody saddle sailed past him, spinning wildly out of control.

"What happened?!" Mogg shouted.

"It was…a…horse."

"*A horse?!*"

Arlon stared into the sky. "It fell…from way up there."

Mogg wiped the blood away that was trickling into his eyes before glancing upward. "What madness is this?!"

One by one, the others noticed and all began clambering to reach the horrific scene.

Arlon rushed to his unstable feet and pointed at a dark blur, high in the sky, which was growing larger by the moment. "*Dragon!*" he screamed.

Paymer tried to look up as he fairly skated across the bluish ice. "What do we do?!" he yelled. "What do we do?"

Arlon scrambled over to Mogg and yanked him off the ground. "What do we do? We *RUN!*"

The three young men dashed through the bloody remains and headed due west as a horrific, squealing roar echoed down from overhead.

"Where is Mae'Lee?!" Arlon yelled, his head swerving in every direction.

"There!" Paymer hollered, pointing off to their right. "There! She's coming!"

Arlon shifted his course a bit north to intercept the Princess. "Run Mae'Lee!" he screamed. "*Run!*"

Another wave of ear-piercing wails rained down upon them, just before a blast of liquid fire slammed into the ice several yards ahead of Mogg and Paymer. The terrified young men tumbled to the ground in a frantic attempt to avoid sliding into the red-hot jet of lethal heat. A huge, hissing wall of thick steam erupted from the frozen ground as the Dragon's primal rage met hardened layers of ancient ice. As the rivers of fire flowed downhill and gradually cooled, they carved deep, uneven ridges into the glacier and filled the sky with a blinding fog.

Arlon finally reached Mae'Lee and grabbed the frightened girl's arm, doing his best to remain on his feet as they bolted into certain doom.

There was nowhere to hide.

He knew it was just a matter of time.

"We can't make it!" the Princess cried out. "We're going to die!"

He squeezed her hand even tighter as his shoulder throbbed afresh. "*NO!* We're not going to die!" he hollered back, shaking his sweating head. "We've been in worse situations than this! *Come on!*"

Not quite fifty yards to the south, Trilyra already had a shaking arrow loaded on her bow as she darted towards their horses. Through the confusion of the rising veil of steam, she could just barely make out the others.

A second, larger torrent of blistering liquid fire plummeted from the sky, splashing and splattering all across the unforgiving landscape. From pits and pools and heated rivulets, blasts of steam shot up from the ground with volcanic force.

The Dragon—no doubt blinded by the gathering fog unleashed in his own fiery fury— sailed overhead and careened erratically from side to side, showering the white world below with volley after volley of punishing wrath. As his hopeless victims scrambled for imaginary safety, the enraged roars of Terras Telos saturated the air and shook the ground like rolls of powerful thunder.

"It issss timmme to dieeee," the Dragon taunted repeatedly into the tormented minds of each of the Dunamai. "Yesssss…..deathhhh comessss."

Paymer glanced right just in time to witness Mogg lose his footing and crumple hard, face first, onto the ice, before sliding out of control and down into a steamy crevasse. Paymer sought desperately to maneuver north to assist his fallen friend, but a sizzling stream of fresh Dragon fire flooded between them, destroying any chance for intervention.

"*Mogg!*" he shouted, over and over.

If there was a reply, he couldn't pick it out above the roaring of the Dragon, the hissing of the steam, and the extreme pounding of his own panicked heart. Paymer instinctively continued west, using the lowering sun as his guide in the on-going confusion. He caught a few fleeting glimpses of Trilyra ahead of him, once as she fired off a salvo of arrows, but then lost sight of her again. He silently prayed that the deadly-accurate Ammodisian had brought at least some measure of pain to their winged enemy.

Paymer ran and ran, pushing forward even though he felt like his deprived and burning lungs would burst inside his heaving chest. With his red hair soaked with sweat and his thick pants dripping with melting ice, he ran...completely unaware that the furious aerial assault had ended long before.

He strained his eyes, gazing into the distance.

A dark shape was moving.

Near an outcropping of low, rounded rocks.

He drew closer.

It was Trilyra.

But something was wrong.

The unmoving shapes...weren't rocks.

"Oh my," he mumbled, coming to a traumatized stop. The snow at his feet had been stained with several streams of blood draining from the slaughtered carcasses of their other four horses. There was no evidence of fire, but plenty of evidence of the Dragon's savagery involving teeth and talons.

"He's a monster," Trilyra muttered. "I can't wait for the day that I can fire a poison arrow right down his cursed throat!"

Paymer spun around and squinted back out across the valley. "Any sign of the others?"

She shook her head. "Honestly…I figured that Mogg would get here first."

Paymer looked down at the ground and bit his lip. "I, uh…I don't think…"

She folded her arms and stepped closer. "You don't think *what?*"

He kicked at the snow, struggling to talk. "I don't think…that…Mogg, that he…made it."

Trilyra's eyebrows raised slowly, and she just froze in place. "*Oh.*"

"Wait a minute," he said as a grin began to form. "Wait. A. Minute." Paymer jogged out several yards. "I think I see something. Coming this way."

She trotted up alongside him. He was right. "Now I see it," she replied. "Or *them.*"

"It's a them," he agreed.

"All three?"

"Uh, no…just two."

"That looks like…the Princess," Trilyra observed. "And Arlon?"

"It is."

"Any sign of Mogg?"

Paymer scanned the long, white horizon. "Nothing." He paused. "Yet."

———————————————————

One uneventful hour later, four exhausted friends began the long, quiet, and miserable trek back to the cave.

The campfire blazed to life easy enough, but none of its flickering amber flames could break the solemn chill that had followed each of them as they had staggered back into the cavern. All four sat in the silence of bitter anguish mixed with utter exhaustion. Their shifting shadows which danced playfully along the stone walls seemed to mock the paralyzing heaviness that plagued each of their hearts.

Arlon toyed with the burnt edges of his cloak.

What have I done?

He was afraid to make even the briefest of eye contact with anyone, so he stared into the center of the fire. Every time his eyes closed, he felt as if he would collapse under the weight of blame that crushed down upon his shoulders.

'*You're not supposed to be here,*' his mother's voice echoed through his sorrow. '*You're not supposed to be here…*'

Arlon's head hung low.

I…think you're right, Mother.

This has been a mistake…I've made a horrible mistake.

His earlier dream flooded into his mind. He saw her pointing at Mogg with grief in her eyes. '*You have abandoned me, and surrounded yourself with strangers.*'

It felt like she was still standing right there before him. *It started with Hort, Mother…and now…another one of those strangers is dead.*

A tear worked its way down his cheek.

Another…friend…is dead.

"What do we do now?" a new voice called out.

Above the distractions of his own inner turmoil, Arlon detected a young girl sobbing. He recognized that whimpering.

It was Mae'Lee.

His eyes cracked back open. Through the flames, he watched her dab her soft cheeks with her sleeves. She looked so beautiful…and yet so terrible.

"Did you hear me?" Paymer said.

Arlon swung his tired head to the left. "Uh, sorry, what?"

"I said, what're we gonna do?"

"I…don't know."

Trilyra tossed a small branch into the fire. "Well, we didn't get any relics," she said in disgust. "We didn't even *see* any relics. We got nothing. And we paid for it dearly. In blood."

Paymer grabbed his knees and pulled them close. "Maybe you…interpreted your vision wrong?"

Arlon just stared at him.

Paymer squinted. "I mean…we did *see* a Dragon. It tried to kill us. *Again*. And we saw the snowy valley. Maybe that's what your —"

"No!" Arlon snapped. "No." He took a deep breath and tried to relax. "No. I saw the remains of a Dragon *in* the ice, buried. I'm sure. It wasn't the same thing."

"Hey…sorry, pal. I'm just trying to make sense of it all."

"I…uh, yeah…I'm sorry, too." Arlon bit his bottom lip. "I'm not so sure we can make sense of it all. This is all wrong. Everything is just wrong."

"We didn't even go back," Mae'Lee sobbed. "We didn't even try to go back and help him."

"We already talked about this, Princess," Trilyra replied firmly. "Remember? We all agreed that it was too dangerous to send anyone back out there." She paused. "And there just wasn't time. We barely made it back here before it was pitch black outside."

"But what if he was just injured?" Mae'Lee complained as her tears flowed once again. "Then he'll just lay there and slowly freeze to death. All alone. It's a dreadful thought! Just dreadful."

"Then, uh, then we'll just have to believe that he...that he died *quickly*," Trilyra responded. "Painlessly."

"I don't know how we can go on without him," Paymer said.

"Even if he were still...*with us*," Trilyra began, "we don't have any horses. And we are a long way from anywhere."

"Our options are...slim," Paymer mourned.

"Slim?" Trilyra countered with a nervous chuckle. "How about *none*? We can't stay here, or we'll starve to death...or *freeze* to death. We can't go home, because the cursed Order will most likely be waiting there." She collected her thoughts. "We certainly can't go back to Alaithia, after what you guys pulled back there when we left. And, probably anywhere else we go, the Dragon will hunt us down."

"I just wanna go home," Mae'Lee mumbled, her lips quivering. "I want to go home to my father."

"I don't think we have homes anymore, Princess," Trilyra rebutted. "Do you really think that anyone wants us now?"

"My mother wants me," Arlon muttered (before he could really stop himself).

Paymer shot him a hard glance. "I, uh, I don't have a mother…anymore."

Arlon scolded himself. *Terrible choice of words. Terrible. And at a terrible time.* "Sorry, Paymer. Really," he replied. "I didn't mean anything by it."

"I bet you didn't," Paymer smirked.

"Look! I said I was sorry," Arlon continued. "I'm sorry that I brought all of you here, and I'm sorry that it has come to this. I'm sorry about everything."

"That's real nice and all," Trilyra said. "But all the *sorry* one Soterian Dunamai can muster isn't going to get any of us out of this. We've got some hard choices to make. And not a lot of time to make them."

Paymer rose to his feet slowly and strolled over to Arlon before plopping back down. "Look, pal, I, uh, I was wrong to come at you like that." He patted Arlon's good shoulder before rubbing his own face. "I just think that we're all exhausted. And nobody acts right when they're real tired. I know I don't." Paymer made eye contact with the girls. "I think we all need to get some rest. We will think clearer in the morning."

Mae'Lee stood up. "I agree."

Arlon looked over at Paymer. "Who'll stand first watch?"

Trilyra gathered some blankets and began preparing her bed. "The shape we're in, I doubt any of us could do much even if there was a problem. I say we all sleep, and the first one to wake up...they can take the first watch."

"Sounds good to me," Paymer agreed.

"Just keep your weapons close," she said.

Arlon collapsed onto his left side and grabbed some nearby blankets.

Oh well, he said to himself. *It's too cold for a Dragon. We won't have any visitors this night.*

He, of course, was completely wrong.

The pale-blue moonslight that trickled in through the cavern's snow tunnel wavered somewhat. It was a subtle shift, but a shift nonetheless. Then…it happened again.

Something—or *someone*—was moving outside the entrance.

Shifting light patterns grew more distinct as a dark figure stole its way along the icy corridor into the cave. The stealthy visitor picked its path carefully, making about as much noise as a black shadow drifting along the damp, rocky floor. The few sounds that it made were easily masked by the popping embers of the dying fire nearby.

The unknown arrival crept around the corner, its dark cloak scarcely accented by the rich, warm glow of the campfire's pulsating red coals.

It drew closer.

Then slowed.

The visitor appeared to be studying the cave's four sleeping occupants before finally closing in on Arlon. There was motion under its cloak. A shiny, metal object appeared, flashing red in the firelight.

A sword.

The faceless figure came to a silent stop beside Arlon and lowered the tip of its weapon just above his chest. With a sudden, curious motion, it slapped the flat edge against the boy's shoulder.

Arlon didn't budge.

It repeated the odd maneuver, but considerably harder.

An unconscious Arlon reached across and scratched his upper arm. The figure hit him once again and bent down.

"*Wake…up,*" it whispered harshly.

Arlon's arms shot out as he stretched hard, before beginning to blink.

The visitor laid his sword on the ground and shook the boy. "*Wake up.*"

A quite disoriented Arlon finally managed to keep his eyes open as he strained to discern anything in the dim, red glow. The dark figure hunkered towards his face.

"It is me," he announced.

What?! Arlon thought. *It can't be.*

"Is everyone without harm?" the visitor inquired, shivering noticeably.

Arlon quickly sat up, his pulse racing. "*Mogg!* You're...you're...alive!" He looked around at the other sleeping bodies. "Or, am I just having another dream?!"

The figure sat down next to him and kept his voice low. "The Vice, dreaming about the Kray?" He spread his hands out. "By the Red Leaf, that is an ill thought."

Arlon could hardly restrain himself as he threw his arms around Mogg and hugged him. "I can't...I can't believe it! We thought, you know, that you were—"

"*Dead?*"

"Yeah, that. But...you're not! Oh, my! I need to wake up the others!"

Mogg snagged an armload of branches and stoked the dwindling fire as Arlon made his way around for a series of reluctant awakenings. But, one by one, groggy irritation transformed into giddy joy.

"It's a miracle, a big, freaky miracle!" Paymer exclaimed. "Are you hungry?" He rushed over to nab some food. "We have a saying about that here in Orania: '*He who spends all night hiking for miles in the cold and snow will probably be really hungry when they get back to their cave.*'" He handed him several hunks of meat and two healthy slices of bread. "I bet you're starved, my friend. Take this. I'll go get a cup of snow and melt it so you can have a nice, cool drink!"

"Thank you, Paymer."

Arlon grimaced with a skeptical smile as Paymer jogged around the corner and vanished. "Once again, a very *convenient* Oranian proverb."

"Oh, lots more where that came from, pal," the response came echoing back.

Arlon's eyebrows shot up. "I can't wait."

Trilyra just stared at the new arrival as her reddening eyes began to flood. A few ravenous bites later, Mogg finally glanced up at her.

"Tears of joy...or tears of sorrow, Woman of the South?"

She sucked in a deep breath and wiped her cheeks during a long, thoughtful pause. "Uh...joy."

He squinted and bobbed his head, which made his long, black hair sway back and forth. "Good," he said. "Joy is good."

"Yeah," she began. "I'm pretty sure they are tears of joy. *Relief*, actually."

"Oh?"

She folded her arms. "Yeah, I, uh, I was worried that the miserable burden of keeping all these Dunamai misfits safe was going to fall on me." She winked at him, and they exchanged quick smiles. Trilyra offered a firm pat on his shoulder. "Welcome back." Her voice cracked.

Arlon threw a blanket over Mogg's shoulders and then studied Mae'Lee's weeping face. "You're pretty quiet over there, Princess. You have anything to say to our special guest?"

It was more than obvious that her intense sobbing prevented Mae'Lee from uttering even a single word.

Paymer rounded the bend with a metal cup packed with snow just as Arlon leaned close to Mogg's ear. "You should know, oh mighty Vish'tar of the Kla'aven Mage," he whispered, "that she was horribly worried about you. Probably didn't sleep a wink all night. An *Avdirian* princess worrying about a *Therion* Vish'tar…imagine that."

Mae'Lee strolled up and swallowed hard. "I, I went to sleep…with a broken heart," she managed to eke out. "But now…now, I am awake with a heart restored."

Mogg nodded with a fresh grin. "I am burned in a few places, but I am alive by the will of the Zho."

"And I, for one, am glad that no one can resist His will…and I am fairly certain that all the rest of us also have burned skin or clothes." Paymer set the cup down on a soot-coated, flat rock near the fire and plopped down beside him. "So, what happened? Why are you just now getting here?"

It took Mogg a moment to swallow a mouthful of bread. "In my haste during the attack, I fell to the frozen ground and slid into a long ravine. I recall nothing else until I awoke just as night was beginning to fall. I then traveled here by moonslight."

"Must've hit your head," Arlon surmised.

"Knocked out for sure," Paymer added.

Mae'Lee cleared her throat. "This is all so wonderful! I feel so much better now. I do believe that hope is returning."

Trilyra didn't seem as enthused. "You can *feel* and *believe* all you want, Princess," she began, "but, in a very real sense, our pitiful predicament hasn't really changed."

Mae'Lee's face scrunched up. "What?"

"Think about it." Trilyra dropped down beside Arlon and sat on some blankets. "Mogg is back…and that is worth celebrating, for sure. But, we still haven't found any Dragon remains, and we're still fugitives. Fugitives without a real home. And fugitives who have to keep looking over our shoulders for a cursed Dragon that is bent on seeing us all burn." She sighed. "So, tonight we celebrate, and yet tomorrow we mourn. And the next day. And the next, as well."

Mogg leaned forward to make eye contact with her as he set his food down. "In some of your statements…you are mistaken."

She hesitated with a puzzled look. "Uh, *no*…no, I'm not. Everything I said was true. We are fugitives. The Dragon wants us all to die. And we don't have much to celebrate."

"That is not all that you said," Mogg replied with a strange smile.

Trilyra was visibly frustrated and her eyes flitted back and forth. "I don't know what you're getting at here. Where am I wrong?"

He raised his jet-black eyebrows. "You said that we have not discovered any remains of a Dragon."

"And…uh, look around. We haven't."

Mae'Lee agreed. "I dread admitting it, but she's right. We didn't find anything. Sorry, Mogg."

"Maybe *you* have not," he countered. "But I have."

Arlon gripped Mogg's shoulder and hunkered towards him. "*You have?!*"

Mogg's hands came together. "It is well-spoken."

"You actually found the Dragon down in the ice?" a fascinated Paymer inquired. "*Really?*"

"I swear by the Red Leaf, I am speaking the truth."

"But when?" Arlon pressed. "Where?!"

"It happened very quickly," Mogg explained as he stood up, recalling the incident. "As I slid into the ravine, I saw a dark figure entombed below me."

"Freaky," Paymer mumbled.

"And the reason we couldn't see the remains before the attack," Arlon added, nodding slowly, "it's because they were too deep."

"Oh, I get it," Paymer said. "But the Dragon's fire melted away the top layers of ice. And those cuts almost exposed the dead Dragon."

"When I awoke," Mogg continued, "the light was far too dim to see the body again. But, before I sought to return here to the cavern, I used my long knife to mark the location. My blade is sticking up out of the ice."

"That's pretty smart," Trilyra offered with a wink. "For a Kray, that is."

Mogg took his sword and dragged it in the soil. "And then I placed long scratches in the ice as I traveled back. It was not easy. The frozen ground is as stone. But these should help us return to the relics."

"Better than a map!" Paymer erupted.

Mogg slid his sword into its sheath. "There is a large pile of rocks to the north that I built to mark the end of my path. Then we must follow the scratches to the east. Once we find my blade, the relics will be near, if it is the will of the Zho."

Trilyra rubbed her chin. "Do you have any idea of how deep the Dragon is buried in the ice?"

"It is there," Mogg answered. "But the depth I do not know."

"Maybe it's very shallow," Mae'Lee said.

"Shallow or deep, both are a real problem," Trilyra muttered. "Like you said, Mogg...the ice out there is hard as a rock. Even if we only needed to dig down a foot or so, we don't have the proper tools to excavate it. "

Mogg bent down to get a drink from the metal cup that Paymer had brought him, but not before some of the melted snow spilled out and sizzled on the hot stone below. Paymer seemed captivated by the tiny trail of steam that vanished an instant later.

Mogg took a small sip. "It would be a most difficult task. Swords and blades will be almost useless."

"You mean, difficult like digging a tunnel out of this cave?" Paymer asked as he stood up.

"That was *snow*, Paymer. Loose snow," Trilyra countered. "But he is talking about ice. Totally different. I bet my bow that our ten-foot tunnel of snow was much easier to dig than busting through even one-foot of rock-hard ice."

Paymer glanced over at the pair of shields that the Sevasti had given them. He folded his freckled arms and grinned. "Maybe. Maybe not."

"Listen, Paymer...I think Trilyra is right," Arlon added.

"I know I'm right," she said. "We don't have the tools."

Paymer stepped over and took Mogg's cup out of his hands. "We don't need tools," he began. "Watch this." He knelt to the ground and carefully poured the cup's contents onto the rim of heated rocks surrounding the campfire. The water immediately flared up into a hissing cloud of steam.

He smiled.

Trilyra didn't. "And…?"

"*And*, don't you get it?"

She wagged her head. "Not really."

He glanced at the rest of them. "Anyone else get it?"

Blank stares.

Paymer pointed. "We just need fire, and rocks."

Arlon looked confused. "So, we're still talking about getting to the Dragon relics, right?"

"Of course."

"And you think we can do it with…fire?"

"And rocks," Paymer beamed. "Once you heat up a rock, it stays hot for a long time."

Arlon squinted. "So fire and rocks?"

"You bet, pal."

Mogg took a stab at interpreting the puzzling plan. "You wish to put rocks on the ice above the remains of the Dread Guardian?"

"It is well-spoken," Paymer replied, bringing his hands together.

Mogg nodded very subtly. "And then you wish to…*build a fire* above the rocks…"

"So that the hot rocks would melt down into the ice," Mae'Lee added.

"No…and *yes*. I guess, sort of," Paymer corrected awkwardly. "And we'll need those shields Kash gave us. Oh, and those thick white blankets would probably come in real handy."

Trilyra pointed at the rim of stones. "Wait a minute…making steam out of liquid water and melting rock-hard ice are two different things."

"I agree. The rocks would have to be way, way, way hotter than these rocks," Arlon complained.

Paymer's head bobbed. "I agree. And they will be."

"But…how do we build a fire that dreadfully hot?" Mae'Lee requested.

"*We* don't," he said.

"Okay, now I'm totally lost," Trilyra admitted as she twiddled her ear-chain. "And I'm also totally too tired for games. So tell us, what are you talking about?! Where do we get fire that hot?"

"It's simple. Don't you see?" Paymer replied, pointing up.

"We get it…from the Dragon."

Chapter 14

The plan was inelegant.

Beyond improbable.

And deadly dangerous.

Trilyra was thankful for the brilliant moonslight, but the intermittent clouds made their lonely trek across the ice less than ideal, and it made tracking down Mogg's ice scratches next to impossible. The unending bleak landscape meant that the only thing that seemed to move was the smoky trails of her own chilled breath.

"Are you still back there?" she called out over her right shoulder.

"It is well-spoken," came the delayed reply.

He has to be getting tired, she thought. *I'm tired, and I'm not even carrying a heavy load.*

She smiled and kept moving forward. "Do you need me to carry the rocks?"

A longer pause.

"It is an ill thought."

"Just asking," she hollered as she readjusted the bundle of firewood hanging at her side wrapped in a large white blanket.

The two of them had discovered the remains of their horses and Mogg's tell-tale pile of rocks over two hours earlier, then turned steadily eastward. The subtle purple and crimson glow that was beginning to stretch out along the gray horizon was a most welcome sight to the shivering traveler. The rising sun would not only elevate the frigid temperatures, but she felt that it might raise her discouraged mood as well.

I hope it's not much further.

Trilyra did her best to wiggle her toes.

I can't feel my feet.

It had been her idea to stay in the lead.

Mogg had volunteered to carry both of the heavy bags of rocks, one slung over each shoulder, as well as a satchel packed with extra clothes and an assortment of horse bones. They both knew that this necessary burden would slow his response time considerably in the event of a surprise assault.

Trilyra kept one eye on the ground and the other to the sky at all times, with her bow and quiver close at hand. If Arlon's prediction was right, the extremely cold air prevented the

Dragon from attacking them at night, but she stayed watchful nonetheless. Her distracted mind drifted between all sorts of fears, questions, and possibilities.

A lot of things can go wrong with this crazy mission, she pondered. *Too many things.*

That cursed Dragon might be gone.

And if the Dragon is gone, then no fire.

And if no fire, then no Dragon relics.

She smiled and shook her head.

I must be insane.

I am actually hoping that I can get a Dragon to attack me! How did it all come to this?

She clenched her teeth.

Stay focused. This is the only path to revenge.

The first amber flashes of the dawn finally burst forth in the distance just as Trilyra discovered the first evidence of the furious and fiery assault that had brutally disfigured the once smooth valley floor. Jagged pits and long, wide gouges began littering the ground like a strange mess of frozen pools and rivers.

Even if the Dragon shows up, this probably won't end well. Either of us, or both of us, could die.

The sun eventually broke free of the ragged horizon and bathed the valley in a crisp, golden glow. She snuck a quick glance behind her. The distorted form of her extended shadow stretched all the way back to Mogg, and then some. He trudged along dutifully, his own dark silhouette trailing behind as well.

Her thoughts returned to the miserable pain that had paralyzed her heart only one day earlier.

I thought I had lost you once already, Mogg. I don't think I could handle it again.

She pulled in a deep, cold breath and did her best to concentrate on something else. Anything else. It didn't work.

Why did I have to meet you?

You're such a…uh…a demanding, yes — demanding — and moody person. Oh, and difficult! So closed off and difficult.

I wish that I didn't —

An instantaneous flash of light caught her by surprise. The flare was very brief and much brighter than the annoying reflections of the orange sun glinting off of the icy surface.

What was that?

It happened a second time.

She picked her way carefully down into one razor-sharp ice gouge and then back up again.

More flashes.

Oh! It's the blade! Mogg's blade!

She spun around and waved her arms wildly. "We found it! We found it!"

Mogg lowered the final rock into place, just slightly uphill from the dark and frightful outstretched Dragon foreleg entombed in an icy grave beneath their feet. The remainder of its massive frame faded into blurry obscurity, merging with the frozen, bluish glacier below them.

"How far down do you think those claws are?" Trilyra inquired as she hunched over for a better view in the early morning light.

"It is difficult to tell," Mogg admitted. "If it is the remains of a very large Dragon, then it could be deep."

"Makes sense," she said. "I hadn't thought about that."

"And water—even frozen water—can deceive one concerning distance. Have you ever crossed a stream that, at first, seemed to be shallow?"

She bobbed her head and smiled. "Many times. Once, I actually went all the way under, including my horse."

An odd grin spread across his rugged face as he looked away. "I have done this as well. With Tempest."

Oh, no, she thought.

Tempest.

Time to change the subject.

"Do, uh, do you think the Dragon will come?" she asked.

He glanced into the clear sky and squinted. "I do not know, but I believe that it is the will of the Zho."

She stood up and unpacked their shields, laying them across a large, white blanket. "Well, uh, is there anything we can do to *help* His will a little?"

He nodded. "We can build a fire."

"Great idea." Trilyra stepped towards her sling of firewood. "As the flames warm us up, maybe the smoke will get the Dragon's attention."

"It is well-spoken."

She stacked the branches atop the rocks. "So, do you worry about your people back home? In Lamillar?"

He unpacked a pile of clothing and laid a variety of horse bones next to it, before staring down at her. "Only when I am awake." Mogg grinned, but in a thoughtful way. "The Kla'aven are the sacred responsibility of the Vish'tar."

"Sorry, that was a dumb question." She packed several strips of dry cloth around the branches. "It must've been very hard for you to leave them."

"That is also well-spoken." He squatted down directly across from her and studied Trilyra's eyes. "And how about you, Woman of the South?"

"What? Was it hard for me to leave?"

He nodded (but just barely). His dark brown eyes seemed to pierce right through her.

"Well, no," she answered, peering down. "It wasn't really all that hard. Not really."

"Your mother, your father…they still live?"

She struck the flint a half-dozen times with a small blade and showered the tinder with a barrage of sparks. "Uh, yes…both of my parents are still alive. At least, they were when I started out on this crazy journey."

A tiny, yet growing, cloud of smoke signaled hope of fire building success. She blew on it and fanned the smoldering heap, before plopping down on a blanket. "Let's dream a little," she said. "Now, let's say that we somehow find all these *almost-impossible-to-find* relics, and then we also somehow find a way to kill that *almost-impossible-to-kill* Dragon. What then?"

He adjusted a few of the sticks and poked around as the fresh, green wood popped and cracked, somewhat reluctant to ignite. "Once the beast is dead…our peoples will be safe. Both the Kray and the Vice."

"I understand that," she responded. "But what about us? You? Me? Arlon? Paymer? And the Princess?"

"We will go back to our peoples."

She folded her arms and stared into the smoke.

He glanced over at her. "Do you not wish to return to your people?"

"Maybe." Trilyra took a moment and scanned the skies for danger. "Honestly? I don't know."

"You fear that things will not be the same without your brother," Mogg observed.

"*Nothing* will ever be the same without my brother," she erupted. "Nothing."

"I am sorry...Trilyra."

Trilyra?

Did he just use my name?

"Oh...it's not your fault," she replied, tossing a twig into the blaze. "It's no one's fault, except maybe for the House of Mandibar."

"He is the Vish'tar of the Kla'aven Ammodis?"

"I suppose. *Vish'tar* Mandibar. That kind of rhymes. It sounds nice, but trust me...he isn't nice." She locked eyes with him. "He is not well-liked in my kingdom. Or his cursed son, who will be on the throne very soon."

"Perhaps someone will challenge him."

Her eyebrows shot straight up. "Well, that may be the way the Kray do things, but down in my kingdom, it's a bit different. We have a royal family. A royal line."

"No battle?"

"No battle. Just blood."

"*Blood?*"

"Oh, sorry," she said. "I meant *family*. The children of a king or queen usually go on to become king or queen." A new thought hit her.

"Unless there is a war. Then anything is possible. That's probably true in all of our kingdoms. The *Vice* kingdoms."

"War comes to the Kray, as well."

Trilyra pulled her cloak tighter before suspending her chilled palms over the modest fire. "So, who will be the Vish'tar of the Kla'aven Mage after you one day? Your son?"

He blushed (and she was fairly certain that she had never seen him blush). "It is an ill thought," he responded quickly. "I do not have a son."

She fought back a smile. "I know that. I meant, when you get back to your people. After all this cursed mess."

He fumbled in his words as Trilyra leaned forward, toying with her ear-chain. "Do you plan on ever having a family? A wife? Children?"

Mogg jumped up and drew his sword with muscles bristling as a crazed look overtook him.

Trilyra scrambled back and slipped sidewise on the ice. "Hey, look, Mogg…I'm sorry, I didn't really mean—"

He lunged for the shields and tossed one over at her.

"He is coming!"

They only had a handful of seconds to prepare.

The wide, jagged form of the beast accelerated towards them from the west like a waking nightmare in a cloudless sky. Trilyra wavered between an intense desire to flee and a paralyzing terror that froze her in place.

"Grab the clothes! And your sword!" Mogg hollered as he snatched an armload of bones and laid them out on the ice several feet away.

Trilyra snapped to action and haphazardly scattered an assortment of cloaks and belts on top of the horses' remains. They both tossed their swords onto the curious piles. Mogg spun around, snagged one of the white blankets and covered all of it. Trilyra shook her head.

This is crazy.

I hope it works.

They hurried back towards the campfire as her heart felt like it would burst at any moment.

"Wait!" she cried out. "I almost forgot!"

Trilyra reached up with shaking hands and detached her ear-chain, then tossed it onto the blanket.

"Keep the shields down until the very last instant!" Mogg commanded while they scrambled over to the second large white blanket positioned alongside the campfire. He wadded up the sheet and tucked it under his arm.

Trilyra swallowed hard.

An odd silence enveloped them.

There was no roar.

No piercing scream.

But she knew the assault was coming.

Both of them glanced up just in time to see a mesmerizing ball of light and fire billowing directly at them. The enormity of the growing, turbulent, swirling blast obscured any sight of the fearsome creature lurking directly behind it.

"*NOW!*" Mogg yelled as they knelt down, yanked up their large shields, and braced for the lethal impact.

Trilyra expected that it would be ferocious.

Unfortunately, the Dragon's rage did not disappoint.

An intense shockwave of searing heat rippled past a fraction of a second before the fiery storm engulfed them. Trilyra struggled and strained to remain on her feet as the force of the blast pummeled her shield like a violent gust of scorching wind. A thundering roar rumbled and cracked the ice all around them while the deafening hiss of a thick wall of steam billowed up into the sky.

In a flash, the world transformed into a blinding white mist in every possible direction. With a single fluid motion, Mogg grabbed Trilyra's arm, yanked her to the ground, and tossed the white blanket over both of their shivering bodies. She felt yet another blistering surge roll over them and the unforgettable wail of an enraged Dragon sailing overhead.

Then...silence.

(Except for the rhythmic pounding of her own throbbing heart blended with the fading sizzle of ice being vaporized.)

Trilyra dared to crack her eyes open, and as they adjusted to the dim, diffused light beneath the blanket, she could make out the messy black locks on the back of Mogg's head.

"Is it gone?" she whispered.

He pivoted his head around until they were nearly nose to nose. "It is an ill thought," he mouthed in a breathy reply.

She couldn't help but stare at the Dunamai birthmark that dominated the left half of his tanned face. She had never seen one this close. She had never seen *him* this close.

A new sound.

What's that?

Whsh.

Whoosh.

Flapping. Dragon's wings.

Whooshhh.

It's close.

WHOOSHH. WHOOOOSHHH.

Very close.

BOOOOM!

Too close.

CRAAAAACKKK!

The frozen ground shuddered and shattered from a sudden, massive impact that she couldn't see, but one that she couldn't help but feel. There wasn't a single doubt in her fear-stricken mind that the beast had just collided with the ground less than ten yards away. Mogg slid his left arm up and cautiously lifted the edge of the blanket with just two of his fingers. Trilyra raised her head off the ice a fraction of an inch and adjusted it until she could see through the tiny, white sliver of a window into the outside world.

A dark, hulking figure rippled through the jets of steam that blurred her view like a series of thin waterfalls. The Dragon moved about, unfolding its long neck like a hideous snake while probing at the ground. Trilyra was fairly certain that she could hear the jets of breath passing in and out of its wide, flaring nostrils. With its powerful forelegs, the monster snatched both swords out of the smoldering ashes and displayed them in the air as a pair of shiny trophies.

The mighty beast reared back, unfurled its wings and split the frigid morning air with a thundering roar of murderous victory. Trilyra fought the urge to protect her ears from the piercing wail that often haunted her dreams. A few seconds later, the satisfied Dragon flung the weapons aside and bolted straight up and out of sight.

WHOOOSHHHH.

WHOOSHH.

WHSHH.

She spun her head around and locked eyes with Mogg as he withdrew his hand from the edge of the blanket and laid a single finger across his lips. Trilyra nodded before closing her eyes, straining to listen. A crisp and peaceful stillness had settled, once again, to the desolate scene. She glanced back at him after a long pause.

"*It…is…gone*," she whispered (with just a hint of a question lingering about).

"It is well-spoken," he replied quietly and quite a bit more confidently.

Mogg reached out and peeled back the white sheet just to the edge of their heads. Their eyes squinted before flitting about desperately as they both scanned the skies for any sign of their winged enemy.

Good, she thought, breathing out a sigh of overdue relief while venturing to pull the sheet down lower.

All clear.

A few light taps on her shoulder almost made her jump. A more-than-tense Trilyra looked over at Mogg, who was wide-eyed and gesturing off to their left.

"Dragon," he muttered in pure disbelief.

Trilyra grabbed the sheet, yanked it back over her head, and clamped her eyes shut again.

More light tapping on her shoulder.

"*What?*" she whispered.

Mogg jerked the blanket back.

"Dragon."

She refused to open her eyes. "I heard it the first time."

His strong hands clutched her head and gently pivoted it around. "You may have *heard*, Woman of the South, but you failed to *see*."

"What?"

"Open…your…eyes."

She did. One at a time.

Mogg was right.

A Dragon was right in front of her.

But it had been dead for thousands of years.

"It was there? Just sticking up out of the ice!?" Paymer's face was beaming in the bright, fitful glow of the cave campfire.

"It was." Trilyra nodded with a controlled grin. She raised her arm straight up and curved her fingers as if in a loose, painful grip. "Like this." Her demonstration cast an ominous shadow on the rock wall that arched up behind her.

"Freaky," Paymer whispered before staring hard over at her. "Hey...where is your ear-chain?"

Trilyra blushed. "It perished in the attack". She gestured towards Mogg. "My traveling companion planned an amazing deception. He fooled the Dragon into thinking that he had burned us alive. We used cow bones and clothing and other items."

Paymer raised his eyebrows. "I guess it worked."

"Here we are."

Mae'Lee's face was all scrunched and contorted. "Did it...*smell?*"

Trilyra was caught off-guard. "Sorry, what? Did *what* smell?"

"The...you know...the Dragon remains coming up out of the ice."

Trilyra broke out into a full smile. "Even if it did, Princess," she replied, "I wouldn't have noticed. I've been so cold, I don't think my poor nose will work again until the spring."

Arlon glanced first at her and then over at Mogg. "So, are either of you going to show us the prize?"

Mogg stuck his hand under the layers of his cloak and fished out something rolled in a dark cloth. He deposited it into Arlon's hand as everyone gathered close.

"It's pretty heavy," Arlon observed.

"It's pretty big," Trilyra replied.

With trembling fingers, he peeled away the crude wrapping, as the others pushed in even closer with anticipation. The final bit of cloth gave way, revealing an enormous, curved talon, every bit as long as Arlon's entire hand. The thick base was roughly broken, but the tip still retained a lethal sharpness.

"Oh, my," Mae'Lee exclaimed. "What a dreadfully hideous sight."

"Hideous?" Paymer countered. "It's...amazing. Was it difficult to break off?"

Trilyra nodded. "The foreleg was as hard as a stone sticking out of the ground."

Paymer was giddy with joy. "So, my idea with the rocks and the fire, it worked right?"

Trilyra patted his shoulder. "Arlon is holding the obvious answer to your question."

"Freaky."

Arlon hoisted the relic closer and turned it over. "It looks fresh. As if it was taken from a living Dragon."

"The ice," Mogg responded. "Perhaps the ice preserved the remains?"

"Maybe dead Dragons don't decay?" the Princess added (without much confidence).

"Some very interesting ideas," Arlon commented as he hurried over to a leather satchel. "But now, for the most important question." He dug out a pouch and returned. "Trilyra, if you would open your hand, and Mogg...would you bring us that shield over there?"

They both quickly complied and he emptied the little bag's stony contents into Trilyra's outstretched palm.

"Ah, the Rone test," Paymer whispered with reverence.

"Rone test?" Trilyra asked.

"Yeah," he responded. "Remember when we told you about the weird lights and sounds when a Rone touches a relic?"

"Oh…that."

Arlon nodded before selecting one of the fragments. "Now, let's see if all this hard work and danger was for nothing." He held the piece against the Pyros lining the shield. As everyone expected, it immediately lit up and generated a pleasant pitch.

Mae'Lee leaned closer and smiled. "Wait! I can hear something. I can hear it!"

Trilyra's eyebrows shot up. "Oh, wow. Now that…is really…something."

"Told you," Paymer whispered with a gentle jab of his elbow.

"It sounds very lovely," Mae'Lee said.

Arlon removed the Rone piece and hovered it over the ancient Dragon claw in his hand. "Well, Princess, let's hope and pray that none of us will hear—*or see*—anything *lovely* when these two meet."

Arlon sucked in a deep breath and froze for a moment, keeping the piece suspended just above the relic.

"Come on," Trilyra urged. "It isn't going to jump up and bite you."

Arlon exhaled with a nervous laugh. "I, I know, but…"

"But *what?*" she asked.

He hesitated momentarily before stretching his arms out and offering both items to Mogg. "I think that *you* should be the one to do the test. You two risked your life to get this, so I think this moment belongs to you."

Paymer grinned. "Great idea."

"Well, just hurry," Mae'Lee implored. "The suspense is giving me goosebumps!"

After several seconds of exchanging glances with all those around (most of them nodding), Mogg finally accepted the proposal silently. Arlon transferred the relic to his friend's left hand and the Rone fragment to the other.

Paymer bit his bottom lip. "Here's hoping for *nothing*."

"So we don't want anything to happen, right?" Trilyra asked.

Arlon bobbed his head. "Right."

Mogg lowered the stone towards the huge talon.

Everyone hunched closer and closer.

The fragment made contact.

"Nothing!" Arlon yelled, almost hopping up and down. "*Yes!* Nothing!"

"Whew!" Paymer mumbled.

"Wonderful!" Mae'Lee exclaimed.

Mogg tapped the two items together repeatedly. "It is well-spoken," he observed.

"So that proves what?" Trilyra inquired.

Arlon selected another Rone fragment. "That proves that the remains buried in the ice are *not* Terras Schema. The fourth Dread Guardian."

"So, which Dragon is it then?"

"Let's find out," Arlon replied as he lowered the stone onto the remains.

Paymer craned his neck. "Nothing."

"Is that a good thing?" Trilyra asked.

"That was a part of the Rone of the sixth Dread Guardian," Arlon explained as he traded the piece with the third and last fragment. "And now…here is a part of the Rone of Terras Kratos."

"The *second* Dread Guardian?" Paymer piped up.

"That is correct, my friend," Arlon replied. He tapped the dark stone against the talon.

An immediate flash of light made Mae'Lee's fascinated face glow with delight. "Lovely!" She glanced over at Arlon with hopeful eyes. "So now we have two. Two different relics. This claw and those Pyros-scale things."

"Two out of six," Arlon answered.

"A good start," Paymer noted.

"But a long way to go," Trilyra mourned.

Mogg held up the talon and studied it in the flickering firelight. "But, just as this…we will find them. If it is the will of the Zho."

Arlon squinted. "And let's hope that none can resist His will."

At times during their travels, spirits had been lower (and enthusiasm had been harder to find), but after nearly two difficult days of plodding through waist-high snow banks and enduring bone-chilling breezes, smiles had dwindled into an uncommon sight.

Arlon shook his legs vigorously, kicking clump after clump of gnarled snow and ice that constantly collected onto the leather surrounding his numbed feet. He glanced back at the others straggling behind. The mountainous terrain had certainly been tough enough on horseback, but now he feared that the Oranian highlands would turn out to be both beautiful and deadly for all of them.

That Dragon might've already killed us, he pondered. *Without our horses, we probably won't make it out of these mountains alive.*

Despite their misery, he was thankful that they had eaten well. Trilyra's bow and Mogg's unparalleled hunting skills had landed a nice selection of wild game along the way. The pair had guaranteed that hunger would not be a distraction in their pursuit of shelter, supplies, and fresh horses.

I just don't remember traveling through this much snow, Arlon lamented as he trudged along. *It must've stormed at these lower elevations the whole time we were searching for that relic.*

The exhausted boy couldn't help but sigh while gazing at the endless, frozen sea of white and trees stretching out before them. But after hours of an unchanging landscape, something in the distance moved. It was a small, subtle shift, and Arlon blinked hard a half-dozen times to clear his vision.

It happened again.

Then…nothing.

Come on, Arlon. It was just the wind kicking up the snow. Stop being so jumpy.

He yanked his cloak tighter around his neck.

It might've been better to die quickly, in one big blast of heat from that Dragon, than to suffer a slow death out here in this cold!

It was a foolish thought.

He struggled to reason it away.

But the morbid idea (like an annoying fly), would escape for a few minutes before returning to unsettle him again and again.

No, he argued within himself. *No. Kash was right. We have survived against all probability. We made it to Alaithia. We found the dead Dragon. We have the relic.*

He rubbed his shivering arms.

We will succeed.

In spite of his misery, the cold air had numbed the typical burning pain that plagued his wounded shoulder.

We must succeed.

A dark and solitary form, soaring overhead nabbed his startled attention. He glanced skyward as his heart throbbed out of control within an instant.

Dragon?!

Arlon squinted, releasing a relieved breath.

Falcon. Another Bloodtip.

A strange look overtook his stinging eyes and reddening cheeks.

I wish it were the Dragon, he mused while kicking at an icy clump of snow.

At least we would have some fire.

Some heat.

The falcon curiously followed the discouraged convoy, circling lower in long and graceful arcs set against a brilliant blue sky. Arlon studied the familiar pattern with growing interest.

I've seen birds fly like this before, he recalled. *Vultures. Vultures circling above something.*

Something...dead.

Interest gave way to concern.

Or...something...about to be dead.

The massive bird of prey swooped lower.

Arlon stole a tense glance back over his shoulder. Trilyra already had an arrow leveled on her bowstring (but somehow it didn't give him much real comfort). Mogg was obviously at a heightened state of readiness with his right hand on his blade. Mae'Lee was pointing up. Paymer hadn't noticed anything yet.

And that's right when the attack came.

The falcon darted upwards before tucking both wings in tightly and plummeting directly down at them like a dark, deadly missile.

"Watch out!" Arlon yelled, reaching for his sword.

WHHHSSHHHHHH.

An arrow sizzled through the clear sky and narrowly missed the plunging attacker. Arlon raised his blade and braced for the imminent assault. The falcon whisked downward and then slammed into the snow a few yards in front of him before thrashing about in a mad rampage, filled with ear-piercing shrieks and wails.

What?!

Is it injured?

But Trilyra's arrow missed!

A thin column of white rose up out of the snow and carried the thrashing bird several feet off the ground.

What??? What is happening?!

WHHHSSSSSSHHHTT!

Another arrow whistled by inches above his left shoulder, lodging firmly into the side of the mysterious white column, which began contorting as if a giant rope in the wind. The Bloodtip Falcon continued to unleash a terrible fury, tearing into its writhing opponent with unbridled ferocity. Rivers of (what appeared to be) red blood began seeping from the deep gashes carved by the falcon's long, razor-sharp talons.

Moving like a dark blur against a bright backdrop, Trilyra scrambled past Arlon with her gleaming sword brandished high. "*Snow Serpent!*" she screamed. "*Attack!*"

Snow Serpent?!

That thing…is a…snake?!

The horrific answer to his question arrived before he had even finished his thought, as a gaping red mouth bordered by rows of long, slender teeth opened up in the snow several feet in front of him. The snake's head shot upward, and Arlon caught a glimpse of its terrifying eyes, embedded like a pair of black, lifeless slits in a shiny mass of white scales. The boy lunged back and clumsily swung his sword around in a desperate maneuver, barely grazing the nostrils of the enraged serpent before he tripped and fell to the snow.

Trilyra jumped straight up, then brought her swift sword crashing down onto the creature's backside with a loud warrior's cry. An instant later, Mogg rammed his own blade deep into the throat of the wiggling monster as he struggled to stay out of reach of its flailing jaws. The Bloodtip Falcon continued tearing away at the serpent's flesh with repeated lashes from both talons and beak, seemingly unaffected by the violent actions of its human counterparts only yards away.

Mae'Lee and Paymer rushed up behind Arlon and knelt beside him.

"Are you alright?" an out-of-breath Princess demanded as he sat up while she checked him over for injuries.

"Yeah, yeah," Arlon struggled to reply. "I'm fine."

Paymer seemed skeptical. "You sure, pal? From back there it looked like that thing got you for sure!"

"It missed. Barely."

"*Watch out!*" Mogg warned.

Paymer grabbed both Arlon and the Princess and jerked them over a few feet just as the wide jaws of the serpent crashed beside them into the snow. Trilyra straddled the beast and began hacking away with the force of a lumberjack and the speed of a skilled fighter. Splotches of deep red blood splattered across her arms and littered the broken face of the once-pristine snow.

Paymer drew out his sword, advanced forward, and started swinging wildly himself. The serpent brought its sharp, heavy tail around and slammed him face-first into the snow with a sickening thud.

"Paymer!" Mae'Lee screamed. "Paymer!"

She started to bolt towards his motionless form when Arlon grabbed her arm and yanked back.

"Mae'Lee! No!"

The bloodied snake arched its battered head and recoiled for what would surely be its final strike. Its black eyes shifted from Paymer and locked onto Arlon and the Princess. The boy shoved Mae'Lee behind him before raising his own sword in defense.

You said that you didn't want to freeze to death, Arlon, he thought. *Instead of a Dragon, it looks like you're gonna die at the teeth of a serpent.*

And then, three different things all happened at once.

The snake thrust its head forward.

Mogg dove through the air.

Mae'Lee screamed.

There was a momentary flash as the waning sunlight glinted from the surface of Mogg's accelerating sword. His swift and powerful blow collided with the creature in mid-strike.

SHHHWWWAAACKKKK!

The Therion's blade passed cleanly through the monster's neck, severing its head, which plummeted down and tumbled to a bloody stop. The Princess took a quick look at the gruesome sight and immediately vomited all over the snow. Arlon spun around and did his best to comfort her.

"Paymer!" Trilyra yelled, scrambling to reach her fallen friend. She clutched the end of the serpent's tail (which was still writhing and contorting in various waves across Paymer's back) and hefted it aside, then plopped onto the frozen ground beside the boy.

"Hey, now," she begged, patting his shoulder and rolling him over. "Talk to me, Paymer. Come on. Come on."

Mogg rushed alongside as the Bloodtip Falcon screeched twice and then took back to the air. "Is the young man breathing?" he asked.

Trilyra hunched forward and hovered her ear above his mouth. "Yes, he's breathing."

Mogg looked him up and down. "The young man does not appear to be injured."

Trilyra clutched Paymer's shoulders and shook him vigorously. "Come on…you red-headed, freckled-faced, little spoiled Dunamai! Wake up!" She used her teeth to rip off her glove before slapping him right across the face with her bare palm. *"Wake up!"*

Mogg winced and stared at the growing red patch that appeared on Paymer's cheek. "But *now*, the young man appears to be injured."

Trilyra glared at him. "Funny," she mumbled. "Very funny."

Arlon handed the Princess a small rag to wipe her mouth before glancing over at the others. "Is Paymer alright?"

"He *was*," Mogg smiled. "But the warrior Woman of the South is seeking to remedy that."

"Sometimes," Trilyra grumbled through gritted teeth, "sometimes…you have to hurt someone…to *help* someone."

She whacked his face once again and Paymer's surprised eyes immediately shot open. The disoriented boy clambered to his feet and spun around frantically. "Snow Serpent!" he yelled. "Snow Serpent!"

"Calm down, my friend," Arlon urged as he strolled up, pointing at the creature's decapitated head now partially submerged in a slushy pool of blood. "I think you mean *dead* Snow Serpent."

"Oh…my," Paymer whispered.

"Do you feel alright?"

Paymer pulled off a glove and traced his own cheeks with a light touch. "My face is kinda burning, but…other than that, I'm just cold. And tired."

"As we all are," Arlon agreed.

Paymer stuck his trembling right hand out and studied it. "It's funny…I don't know if it's shaking because I'm scared or because I'm cold."

"Well, I'm scared *and* cold," Mae'Lee complained.

Paymer took a few steps and squatted beside the grisly remains of the snake's head. "Growing up in Orania, I had always heard about these things, but…uh. Wow. This thing is almost as big as a bear's head."

"And the body is as thick as a small tree," Trilyra added.

"I won't be able to sleep for weeks," Mae'Lee said, folding her arms. "If ever."

Paymer dared to reach out and feel the tips of the snake's countless teeth. "I thought you said you had seen an Anatellian Snow Serpent before?"

"I have," she replied. "But there is a big difference between seeing them from high above in a show at the palace, and being attacked by one with nowhere to run!"

He grinned. "I can't argue with you there, Princess."

"Plus, the creatures I saw back in Edra weren't even half as big as that dreadful...*thing*."

Mogg picked up the tip of the tail and sliced it off with a quick blow from his sword. He pulled the chunk of pinkish meat closer and smelled it. "Is it...safe to eat?"

Paymer rose up. "Uh, yeah. Actually, it is."

"I was afraid you were going to say that," Mae'Lee mumbled.

"I've seen Snow Serpent meat being sold in the marketplace. There was even some back at the Karaval. It's pretty expensive. I've never tried it."

Trilyra joined Mogg and pulled her gloves back on. "Well, I guess the two of us won't be needing to hunt for food for a while. I wonder what it tastes like?"

"Snow Serpent," Paymer teased.

She shot him a dirty look and held her hand up. "Don't tempt me to slap you again."

"*Again?*" He rubbed his cheeks. "Wait a minute...is that why my face hurts?"

"Let's just say that I'm surprised you have any skin left, my friend," Arlon chuckled. "She hit you pretty hard. More than once. I think she was enjoying it."

Paymer glared at her playfully. "Is that right?"

She shrugged. "It worked, didn't it?"

"I suppose."

"And yes," she said.

Paymer squinted. "Yes? Yes *what?*"

She paused. "Yes…I enjoyed it."

He started to reply when Arlon thrust his hand out and pointed due south. "Look!"

Mae'Lee almost jumped behind him. "Is it another snake?!"

"Well, it is long and white," he responded. "But it's not a Snow Serpent."

"It's smoke," Paymer said. "I see it." He paused and gestured to the right. "And look…there's more, just to the west a bit."

"People," Trilyra muttered with just a hint of a smile.

"Yep," Paymer said. "And, here in Orania, we have a saying about that."

Arlon rolled his eyes. "Here it comes."

Paymer took a deep breath. "It goes something like: '*Smoke in the sky means there's fire on the ground which means there's probably people and towns and fresh horses for sale for people who have been traveling for days.*'"

Trilyra sighed.

"How's our money situation?" Paymer asked.

"Kash and Gremlor took very good care of us in that respect," Arlon answered. "We have enough gold Royals to supply horses for a small army."

"We're all going to need some fresh clothing," Trilyra noted. "And shoes."

Mae'Lee brought her hands together. "All I can think about is a long, lovely hot bath. I just want to soak for hours and hours." She bit her bottom lip. "Oh, and some nice, fresh fruit."

"We can't risk being seen by too many people," Trilyra countered. "I don't think a royal hot bath is in our immediate future, Princess."

"We could use the Sevasti masks," Mae'Lee offered.

"That's pretty risky," Trilyra replied.

"I hate to admit it, but Trilyra is right," Arlon said. "If we need anything, we should send Paymer, alone. Just like before. Mogg's Dunamai mark on his face would attract too much unwanted attention, and my lack of Oranian tattoos would probably do the same. So, as for right now, we need horses."

"What we need right now is a *plan*," Paymer added. "And horses."

"I would just be glad to get out of these mountains," Mae'Lee grumbled. "I'm tired and sore, and I'm ready to get to dry, warm ground. That's a good plan."

Trilyra nodded. "Paymer's right. We need to start thinking about what's next." She glanced at Arlon. "Have you had any other *interesting* visions, lately?"

He shook his head.

"Visions?" Paymer snapped his freckled fingers. "Hey…maybe we should make a *Vision Fire*." His excitement grew with each and every word. "We could get some Sevasti advice."

Trilyra's face contorted. "Vision Fire?"

Paymer leaned towards her. "Ask me later."

"No," Arlon replied. "Kash and Gremlor already gave us all that they had and told us all that they knew." He patted a satchel hanging off of his left shoulder. "Once we make camp tonight, we should probably start reading through the documents and maps in here."

Trilyra looked stunned. "Do you honestly think that the five of us are somehow going to understand something in the next few days that hundreds and hundreds of Sevasti haven't figured out in thousands of years?"

"If it is the will of the Zho," Mogg muttered.

It was quiet for a moment.

"We might have to find the…Order," Paymer ventured.

"Excuse me?" Trilyra replied.

He raised his eyebrows. "Well, Gremlor said that the Order knows something about where some of the Dragon remains are."

"Maybe I did slap you too hard!" she exclaimed. "That may be the worst idea I have ever heard." Trilyra rested her hands on her hips.

"So, you're proposing that we actually try and find the ruthless murderers that are actually trying to find and murder us?!"

"It, uh, it sounded a lot smarter in my head," Paymer replied. "Sorry."

"Don't be sorry," Arlon said. "It might actually come to that. We might have to work out some kind of deal with the Order."

"I don't believe this!" Trilyra complained. "I think this cursed cold air is freezing your Dunamai brains! Are you two even listening to yourselves?!"

Arlon cleared his throat and struggled for a response. "I'm just saying that it's a possibility."

"Well then, count me out," she rebutted. "I don't want any part of that little mission. Now, when it comes to killing the Dragon, I'll be the first in line, but don't ask me to deal with those vicious people." She glared at Mae'Lee and pointed at the snake's head. "You think that the Snow Serpent's gonna give you nightmares? That's nothing compared to the horror stories I've heard about the Order."

"We've all heard the stories," Paymer said.

"Then you *all* should know better than to even think about any contact with those monsters!"

"I only said it was a possibility," Arlon added.

"Not for this girl," she said.

"Forget about the dreadful Order," Mae'Lee intervened. "What else can we do?"

"Maybe we could go to Veranda," Paymer ventured. "We're only a few days away. We might find some information there. It's a huge city and we—"

"No way," Trilyra rebutted. "You are far too well-known in your own capital."

"She's right," Arlon said.

"Oh, I know," Paymer mourned. "I was just hoping to, you know, maybe sneak in a small visit with my little brother." He stared at the ground. "I'm all he has, you know. He's probably worrying himself into a knot about me."

Mae'Lee put her arm around him and laid a comforting head on his shoulder. "I know how you feel, Paymer. I miss my family terribly, too. But, soon this will all be over, and you will be reunited."

"I hope."

There was a bit of awkward silence.

Arlon looked up thoughtfully. "Mogg...back in Kash's chamber, you said something about a place you knew."

Mogg nodded with a deep sigh. "It is well-spoken. It is a story that all the children of the Kray are told. It speaks of a dying Dragon, and a cave."

"That sounds promising," Paymer mumbled.

"It is an old story. It is a story that is used to teach our children lessons. Lessons about danger."

"Well, we must be really desperate," Trilyra groaned. "We go from ideas about meeting with bloodthirsty killers to placing our hope in bedtime stories for babies."

"Many legends have a seed of truth in them," Arlon countered. "I'm sure Kray legends are no different."

"Show me a map," Mogg said.

Arlon yanked off his gloves and searched inside the satchel for several seconds. "Any particular kind of map?" he asked, looking up.

"A map with all lands."

Arlon thumbed through a small collection of parchments. He drew one out and Mae'Lee helped him hold it open. Arlon hunted for a spot in the Kingdom of Orania, and he pointed at it. "I believe…that right now…we…are…right about…here."

Everyone gathered close while Mogg removed his gloves and studied the map for a while. He slid his finger down the page and traced a small circle in the forests just north of the Ploutonian Range. "The legend speaks of a cave where the forest meets the mountain. It is here."

"Where is *'here'*?" Paymer asked.

Arlon pulled the document closer and tried to keep his cold hands from shaking it too much. "It is in the forest…the Woods of Ankath.

In the southwestern Therion lands. Close to the Encatic Sea. Sort of."

"That's just beyond the northern border of my kingdom," Trilyra noted.

"The Kla'aven Wins'orr," Mogg explained.

Arlon glanced up. "Does the Vish'tar of the Kla'aven Mage have...*good dealings*...with Kla'aven Wins-whatever?"

Mogg hesitated. "Wins'orr. We are not at war."

Arlon nodded slightly. "So, uh, does that mean that you are friends? Friendly?"

"We are not at war," he reaffirmed.

"Are they...dangerous?" Mae'Lee inquired.

"All the Kray can fight."

"Yes, we are very aware of that," Arlon said. "But...are they as bad as...the Skree?"

Paymer locked eyes with Mogg. "You know, those raiding savages from the Kray that killed my father for no reason and kidnapped my mother and dragged her away screaming the whole way? That Skree. Are they anything at all like them?"

Everyone froze.

Arlon's mind panicked.

Oh no, this could get bad, he thought.

Real bad. Real quick.

Paymer continued staring.

"They are not as the Kla'aven Skree," Mogg answered at the tail end of a thoughtful pause. "But, to trust them…is an ill thought." Another pause. "My friend."

Paymer finally looked away.

"Um, well, good," Arlon mumbled. "That is good to know. Good information." He caught Trilyra's attention. "*Right?*"

She cleared her throat. "Oh, yes. Right. Good. Really good information. Very helpful."

"How far is that from here?" Mae'Lee asked.

Arlon examined the map and slid his finger south. "So…hmmm…there is no easy way to get there. To avoid the Skree, we would…either have to follow the river south…and then head west. Or…" He reset his finger to their estimated location and then traced it to his left. "Or…go due west through southern Orania until we hit the sea and then ride south along the coast. Then, head back east a bit in the Woods of Ankath. Probably about the same distance either way."

Mae'Lee's brown eyes brightened. "That way sounds nice, thank you. I love the sea. The breezes are lovely and—"

"It is an ill thought," Mogg interrupted.

"Something wrong?" Arlon asked.

"The Kla'aven Skree have strong villages near the sea. And much people."

Arlon nodded. "Well, okay, then. It looks like our only choice is to go back the way we came to Alaithia. South along the Kordoni River then west."

"Is there any chance that we could take a little diversion, pal?" Paymer asked.

Arlon glanced up. "Where do you want to go?"

"We could visit Shendollyn. The Witch at Gilmoth."

"The witch? Wait a minute," Trilyra protested. "You're not talking about going back to that crazy old woman, are you?!"

"She could help us. She is very wise," Paymer said.

"*Wise?!*" Trilyra blurted out. "She talks to sticks! And to people that aren't even there. Now, the other one...she wasn't too bad, at least what I saw of her. Which wasn't much."

Paymer frowned. "The '*other one*'? There was no other one."

Trilyra returned his frown. "What do you mean? I'm talking about the other woman. The younger one in the pretty dress. She was there that night."

"Yes," Paymer replied. "Shendollyn."

"And," she held up a pair of fingers, "the crazy lady who talks to sticks. That makes *two*."

"*Also* Shendollyn," he announced, raising a single finger.

Trilyra's eyes flitted around the group. "Are we all talking about the same two people? And the same kind of mathematics?"

Paymer squinted at her. "We are talking about the same *one* person."

"You are talking nonsense, my freckled friend."

Mae'Lee shrugged. "Truthfully, I don't remember most of that. It comes and goes, like the memory of a dream."

"It's a long story," Arlon half-snickered. "I'll explain it later, Trilyra. I promise. It's weird."

"Freaky weird," Paymer agreed. "Anyway, I was thinking that maybe Shendollyn could tell us something about the other Dragon relics."

"But that was in the middle of Skree country," Trilyra warned. "The only reason we risked traveling there was to save our royal companion here. We didn't really have much of a choice, remember?"

Arlon nodded. "She's right. I don't think we should risk it, Paymer. The Sevasti felt that the Kray legend had merit. I think we should trust their judgment."

"That sounds reasonable enough to me," Mae'Lee said. "But I would like to meet her one day. To properly thank her."

"Fair enough," Paymer conceded after a few moments. "But I have a better plan on how to get to the Woods of Ankath. Faster."

"Let me guess...you want to take a boat down the river?" Arlon surmised.

Paymer's eyes grew wide and he pointed at the western edge of the map. "I do want to take a boat, pal. A great big boat..."

"...but not down the river."

It was obvious that the massive, ivy-encrusted wall was ancient. The deteriorating stone boundary carved an unending path across the fertile lowlands and crowned the rolling green hills as a formidable reminder of a tangible fear that spanned hundreds of miles and at least as many generations. Over the uneventful two and a half weeks they had followed its meandering course to the west, Paymer had entertained them with elaborate (and highly questionable) tales of Oranian bravery and Therion savagery.

With the irregular exception of a handful of token military outposts along the crumbling barrier, they had managed to avoid compromising interaction with most of the region's inhabitants. Their strategy had been both bold and effective: at the first hint of a patrol or fort, everyone but Paymer immediately donned a Sevasti mask. When stopped by the authorities (which only happened twice) Paymer claimed to be a local guide hired to escort an Alaithian delegation all the way to the coast. That plausible cover story—plus a few gold Royals for good measure—had enabled them to navigate hassle-free to Orania's largest seaside city.

"Welcome to Port Final," he beamed as they crested a bushy ridge overlooking the bustling town. Magnificent ships with towering masts and curling sails caught the first rays of the morning sun as it broke upon the wide harbor, and hundreds of boats of various sizes and shapes lined the docks that littered the hectic shoreline.

"It's just lovely!" Mae'Lee exclaimed while peering out across the glimmering sea. She took a long, deep breath, obviously enjoying the gentle, salty breeze. "I almost feel at home."

"Careful there, Princess," Trilyra cautioned. "None of us can afford to get too comfortable here."

"Oh, relax, Trilyra," Arlon countered with a warm smile. "This is a port city. There will be people from all over gathered here. Merchants and travelers and traders, you name it. From different kingdoms. We will blend right in."

Trilyra pointed at Mogg. "Uh, *he* won't."

"She's got a point," Paymer said. "No one could miss seeing that mark."

"I will wear the mask of the Northern Elders," Mogg replied.

"And it looks good on you," Paymer teased. "It really does."

"Well, this is a really pretty view, and I wouldn't mind staying here all morning," Trilyra began, glancing at each of them. "But, what's the plan?"

Arlon gestured towards the harbor. "Hopefully, we're going to get passage south on one of those big boats."

"Of course we're going to get on a big boat," she huffed in reply. "But what's the *plan?*"

"I'm sorry, I guess I don't get what you're asking."

She seemed beyond frustrated. "What's the plan? How are we going to be on the boat? As one big group? As individuals? As what? What's the story?"

Paymer fidgeted with a coin, rolling it through his fingers. "Now that's a good question."

She grew considerably louder. "We're gonna be in close quarters, with a lot of people, on a ship, out on the water with nowhere to go, for a long time. That's a risky situation many times over."

Arlon and Mae'Lee stared at Paymer. He shrugged. "Don't look at me, guys. Getting a boat to sail down the coast was my idea. Someone else needs to come up with this whole plan-thing. But whatever we do, Mogg needs to be a little less...*Therion*-like. Oranians have had a bad history there, as you know."

Mogg folded his muscular arms. "We should not remain as one group."

Arlon squinted. "Care to explain?"

"If we remain as one, then when trouble comes...it would be trouble for all."

Trilyra was impressed. "That's an excellent strategic observation. If I understand it right, if we break up into at least *two* groups, then if one has problems, the other might be able to fix the problem."

"I like the sound of that," Mae'Lee chimed in.

"It makes sense," Arlon responded. "And we will all need fake names."

"Definitely. And since Mogg has to wear the Sevasti mask anyway," Trilyra offered, "then maybe we should continue the whole *Alaithian delegation* story...for one of the groups."

Paymer frowned. "No offense, ladies, but I don't think that either of you should try to impersonate a Sevasti on this part of the trip. You were able to keep your distance from the Oranian soldiers, but everyone will be too close on a boat." He rolled his coin. "Someone will catch on that you are not a couple of old men."

"Paymer's exactly right," Trilyra replied. "That's an unnecessary risk."

"Well, if we continue as the Sevasti delegation," Arlon wondered out loud, "then where is this delegation going? What's their story?"

"They would most likely be traveling down to Ammodis," Trilyra replied. "Probably to the port at Leemont. I bet my bow that a good portion of these larger ships are headed there, like you said—hauling passengers and items for trade. I've heard that most of the marble in my capital is imported from Orania." She studied the wagons filled with goods headed along the narrow streets towards the coastline. "It was probably loaded here."

"We do have the finest marble," Paymer boasted before winking at Mae'Lee. "And the finest men."

"On the contrary, the finest marble in the Five Kingdoms is mined from the quarries in Thilasson," Trilyra retorted. "But it's too expensive. Even for Mandibar." She paused. "Now, as to the question of whether or not Orania has the finest *men*…I will let you know. If I ever meet any."

"That hurts," he whimpered, flicking his coin into the air with one hand and catching it in the other.

"Good."

Arlon rolled his eyes. "Okay, now that we have figured out who has the best marble, we still need to figure out who has the best plan."

"I vote for the idea of a Sevasti delegation traveling to Ammodis," Mae'Lee said with her hand up. "That is, if we are voting."

"I was your Oranian escort to Port Final," Paymer reminded them as he carefully concealed the gold Royal in his fist. He made a few wild gestures before opening his empty palm with a satisfied smile. "I think Trilyra is the natural choice as our Ammodisian guide."

Arlon massaged his chin before folding his arms. "Now that's an interesting idea. I like it. Seems plausible."

"Thanks. Glad you like it, pal."

"But...I do have one big problem," Arlon commented. "That leaves Mae'Lee all alone. She would be the only person in the second group. If we got into trouble, that would be asking too much for the Princess to rescue all of us. One helping four isn't a good ratio."

"But, she won't be alone," Trilyra declared with a devious smile.

"She won't?"

Trilyra shook her head. "No. She will be traveling with her new, young husband."

Arlon and Paymer traded brief, puzzled glances. Paymer dared to raise his hand. "Um, so the Princess is somehow going to get married...to a total stranger? In the next day or so?"

"Wrong again, *twice*," she replied. "She already *is* married. And we all know her husband very well."

"I am?" Mae'Lee asked. "*You do?*"

Arlon shrugged his shoulders. "Well, I have no idea."

"You should," Trilyra replied.

"Why?"

A wide grin spread across her face as she brushed long strands of blonde hair out of her eyes. "Because, Arlon…it's you."

Arlon stared down into the mostly-empty satchel. His disappointed eyes told the tale. "This is all you got for them?" His hands rummaged through the mixture of coins. "This is barely half of what we bought them for!"

Paymer's face flushed. "Listen, pal! I did the best I could! Horses are cheap around here. I was lucky to get that much."

Arlon couldn't hide his disbelief as he looked around at the shops in the busy marketplace. "You've been gone for probably three hours. And this is what you bring back?" His eyebrows shot up as he leaned closer. "Are you sure that maybe you didn't spend some of the money along the way?"

"Do what?" Paymer stammered.

"You heard me."

"Wait…where's you-know-who and the girls?"

"The girls are getting new clothes and other supplies," he responded firmly. "And our Sevasti companion is staying out of public sight until we sail. Now, answer my question."

"Well, there…uh…there were, some, uh…*traveling* expenses."

"Traveling expenses?"

Paymer nodded rapidly. "You know, like food—"

"Food?" Arlon reached into the satchel and grabbed a handful of silver coins. "That couldn't have been more than a few fractions."

Paymer swallowed. "And, uh, drink. It's rather hot today, you know. I got thirsty. A few times."

"And drink? Well, let's see…" Arlon dropped the silver and dug out a few bronze pieces. "That might have cost you two or three clinks, maybe five at the most."

Several people sauntered by on the brick-lined street guiding a cart overloaded with an assortment of fruits. Paymer snagged an apple and quickly flipped them a few bronze pieces.

Arlon waited for the cart to pass. "So, food and drink. Anything else?"

Paymer pursed his lips. "Well, and…uh, *protection*."

"Protection?" Arlon replied. "Oh, this sounds good. Tell me more, please."

"It's a, uh, a dangerous world out there," Paymer began. He leaned in close to Arlon's ear. "And we are wanted people. There's people after us," he whispered.

Arlon folded his arms. "Oh really? You don't say."

Paymer backed away slowly. "Oh, yes. Absolutely. And so…I…*obtained* something that would help all of us in our present distress."

"Obtained something? You mean *bought something*, right?"

"Well, yes, of course. I didn't have much to trade for it."

Arlon waited and tapped his foot. "So, are you ever going to show me this protection you've obtained?"

Paymer's eyes glistened with excitement. "Oh, you're in for a rare treat. She's a real beauty, pal."

"An *expensive* beauty."

Paymer frowned. "Hey…you can't put a price on quality craftsmanship. It's worth its weight in gold."

"Obviously," Arlon smirked, patting the satchel. "And, um…I'm still waiting. And our boat leaves soon."

"Oh, so you found a boat? What does it look like?"

"I did find a boat. And can we please stay on subject?" Arlon insisted. "You suddenly seem to be having a little difficulty with that simple task."

"And the subject was?"

"The *high cost* of protection."

"Oh, yes." Paymer peeled back the edge of his cloak. "I hope you're ready. It is a weapon worthy of our…*quest*."

"So, it's a weapon?"

Paymer was beaming. "But not just *any* weapon. It's a weapon worthy of a king. Get ready." In a long, slow, and fluid motion, he slid a magnificent sword out of the sheath hanging at his side. The center of the shiny blade was meticulously engraved with tightly-packed Oranian symbols, and the leather-wrapped hilt was topped with a silver and gold cross guard, each finely worked.

"It's layered steel," Paymer explained with a sense of reverence as he handed the impressive weapon over to Arlon. He pointed at the hilt. "And that, my friend, is real gold. Oranian gold. The finest."

The sunlight flashed across the sword's mirror-like surface, and Arlon caught a glimpse of his own reflection. He hefted it up and down a bit. "It's heavy," he said with a growing grin.

"It is," Paymer agreed. "But, go ahead…swing it around."

Arlon retreated back a few steps and whisked the blade through the air in wide arcs. "Wow…that's…nice." He held it vertical and examined the craftsmanship.

Paymer drew alongside. "Told you she was a beauty. And did you feel it? Perfect balance."

"Who's a beauty?" a female voice called out from off to their right.

Paymer leaned back and looked over at the girls. "I only see two beauties in this whole town. And they are both walking towards me right now."

Trilyra ignored his flattery and gravitated straight to the weapon with wide, adoring eyes. "Where. Did. You. Get. That?" she asked.

Paymer reached over and peeled it away from Arlon with considerable difficulty. "*I* found it, thank you."

"He did a bit more than just finding it," Arlon added. "He bought it."

Paymer flattened the blade and delivered it to her, hilt first, with a subtle bow. "For your inspection."

"It is quite lovely," Mae'Lee said. "It reminds me of a sword my father has. Except, his has red leather on the handle. And there's a small lion, right at the end."

"It was expensive," Arlon noted. "I'm still trying to find out *how* expensive."

"Who cares how much a treasure like this costs?" Trilyra gasped before stepping into the street and slicing it through the air. "A blade like this is worth its weight in pure gold."

Arlon cleared his throat and patted the satchel once again. "You're probably more right than you know."

"She said it was worth it," Paymer replied under his breath.

"Did you find us a ship, my handsome husband?" Mae'Lee inquired with a coy smile as she set her bags down.

Arlon blushed before pointing down the street towards the center of the harbor. "It's the big one. With the green band around it. Dear."

"Oh, my," she exhaled. "That is a big ship."

"They call her the *Graceful Galleon*. She's Oranian. And she sails at sundown. Captain's name is Theele."

Trilyra lowered the sword and peered down the length of it with only one eye. "Where is it headed?"

"Ammodis."

"Leemont?"

He nodded. "With fair weather, we'll make port there in seven or eight days. And then, we can get a fresh set of horses and head east to Wins'orr lands."

She balanced the blade straight up in the center of her right palm. "What is the fare?"

"Six Royals each for you ladies. Eight for the men."

Paymer's freckled-face scrunched up. "Why the difference?"

"They said that men eat more."

"Speaking of food," Mae'Lee said, "did anyone take some to Mogg?"

"Already done, my beloved," Arlon replied. "And I gave him a pouch loaded with Royals."

"Did you lovely ladies find us plenty of clothing?" Paymer asked.

Trilyra returned the sword to his waiting hands. "We did. And I bought a few dozen new arrows. Has everyone settled on a new name yet?"

"I don't need a new name," Paymer boasted as he slid the sword back into its sheath. "Sevasti don't give out their names. It's part of the whole mysteriousness of their ways. We just have to remember to call each other '*my brother*' and '*the prophecy is truth*' and '*truth shall be our guide*.'"

"And don't say *freaky*," Trilyra cautioned.

"When do I ever say that?"

"Only every other sentence or so."

Paymer paused. "I do?"

Arlon's head bobbed up and down.

So did Mae'Lee's.

"Well, okay, then," Paymer replied. "From this moment on, until we reach our new port, *freaky* shall be stricken from my mouth."

"Good luck with that, my friend," Arlon snickered.

"Well, Paymer, you may be a nameless Sevasti, but I am now Kallyndra, your guide," Trilyra announced, keeping her voice low. "That name belonged to my best friend in Polichlor." She gestured towards the Princess. "And this recently married young lady is...Polina."

Arlon squinted before folding his arms. "Po-li-na. Polina," he rehearsed. "It kinda fits. It's nice."

"And who might you be, sir?" Trilyra asked.

"I, too, have chosen a name of a friend." Arlon's eyes glistened quickly before beginning to flare red. "I wanted to honor a friend. A friend from...*Ammodis*."

Trilyra froze. "Pelias?" she whispered.

"Pelias," he nodded.

Paymer patted him on the back and encouraged Mae'Lee to scoot closer. "That's a nice gesture, pal. It really is." He stepped back and looked them up and down. "So, now we have our happy couple, Pelias and Polina...what a good looking pair you are. From heart to heart to home!"

"From where to where to what?" Mae'Lee asked.

"From heart to heart to home," he repeated. "It's an old Oranian saying. We use it at weddings. I guess it's supposed to mean something about two people becoming one family."

Mae'Lee hugged Arlon's left arm. "From heart to heart to home. It sounds lovely!"

Trilyra picked up most of their bags. "I've got a better one…how about '*from Orania to Ammodis to more Dragon relics*'?" She pivoted about and started down the brick-lined road. "Paymer, go fetch your Sevasti brother…."

"…It's time to sail."

"In all my years, living beside the ocean," Mae'Lee whispered, "this is the first time that I have ever seen a sunset over the sea. And it is beyond wonderful." She leaned against the polished rail as the steady, warm breezes from the northwest wrapped playful locks of her long, dark hair all around her gentle features. "That seems odd, doesn't it?"

Arlon rested his elbows on the ledge and squinted into the crimson-golden glow that crowned the flat horizon. His cheeks took on a rich, warm hue. "Not odd at all…it is my first as well."

She raised to her tippy-toes and stared down at the whitewater frothing along the sides of the creaking vessel. "It seems that we have shared many first things together."

He hesitated as a young deckhand passed by. "And not all of them were…as pleasant as this view."

"Pleasant?" a man's gravelly voice interrupted. "Such a view merits a far greater title than merely *pleasant*, my boy."

Arlon straightened up and spun to his right. An older man, with sun-ripened skin laced with tattoos and a thick beard, strolled up carrying a metal cup.

"Soft cloth is *pleasant*," the new arrival noted after taking a quick sip. "A sweet tune is *pleasant*. But this…" He gestured to the west with his mug. "This…this is…majestic. I never tire of it."

Mae'Lee slid closer to Arlon and patted his hand. "My…*husband* is a man of simple words," she said.

The newcomer lowered his mug to the rail and studied her. "My, my…yet another majestic sight. I pray that your husband does not consider you as merely *pleasant*."

Arlon cleared his throat. "I, uh, was…I was comparing the sunset to her beauty." He pointed off to the horizon. "That is pleasant." He gazed down into her brown eyes. "But that…that is…truly beautiful."

"Ah-ha-ha," the man laughed and roared from way down deep. "Now that, my boy, is an

answer borne of wisdom far beyond your years."
He stole another drink. "Well played. Well
played! And well-spoken!"

Mae'Lee glanced back towards the sunset.
"What lies beyond the sea?" she asked.

The man seemed surprised. "Beyond the
sea?" he chuckled. "To the west?"

She nodded innocently.

"Well, lassie, there's nothing beyond the
sea," he replied.

She cocked her head. "*Nothing?* You mean
that the sea goes on and on?"

He set his mug on the rail with a serious
stare. "Oh, no, no, no. Gracious me, there is an
end. Legend has it that there is an edge to the sea.
An edge, but no shore."

"An edge without a shore?" Arlon
muttered. "You mean like a wall?"

"I mean an *edge*," the newcomer insisted
with a deep, breathy reply.

Mae'Lee was intrigued. "So, what holds
the water back?"

The man turned to face her. "Some say
that *nothing* holds her back. They say that the sea
is bounded by a waterfall."

Arlon glanced west. "The edge of the sea
is a waterfall?"

"So say the legends." The friendly stranger
thrust out his stubby hand. "I am Korridge. Of
Verdana. Or, at least, close enough."

Arlon returned the gesture. "And, uh, I am Pelias. Pelias of…Soteria." He stepped back. "And this is my wife. Polina."

"Soteria?" Korridge replied in disbelief. "Gracious me…a long way from home for such a young pair."

"We're, we are headed to Ammodis. We just want to make a fresh start."

"A fresh start?" he chuckled. "In the desert kingdom?"

Arlon stared at Mae'Lee and took her hand. "Our parents…they…didn't…*approve* of our…love."

"Ah, runaways, then."

"Pretty much."

"You got folks out looking for you?"

Arlon swallowed hard. "You have no idea."

Korridge took a long drink with his head thrown back and wiped the white foam from his curly beard. "Well, I've made my fair share trading with them, but, truth be known, even if every last grain of sand in those dunes was gold, I still wouldn't live in Mandibar's kingdom."

"We've heard that Lake Syntero is beautiful," Arlon offered with a forced smile. He did his best to act natural. "We hope to live near there."

"Well, then…you best hope that the desert sand *is* gold, my boy! Syntero…that's the king's private pond. Only the royal family, the wealthy, or the well-connected can afford to live in those parts. And no offense if I'm speaking out of place, but neither of you appears to be wealthy, well-connected, or royalty."

Arlon fought back a tiny smile as he glanced over at the Princess. "We are just...*simple* people," he replied. "Wanting to lead simple lives."

Korridge raised his mug and smiled broadly as he walked away. "Well, in that noble endeavor, I wish success to the both of you." They watched him disappear around a corner.

Arlon released Mae'Lee's hand and repositioned himself along the support. "Was I very convincing?" he asked quietly, staring off at the horizon's fast-fading colors.

Her face scrunched up with an odd sort of smile. "That depends," she replied.

A few children hurried past, followed by another chasing after them.

"Depends? On what?"

She leaned her left side against the rail and folded her arms. "That depends on *who* you were trying to convince, thank you."

"Who?" He glanced over at her. "Don't you remember the big, older fellow with a beard and a mug?" He pointed off to his right. "He was standing right there, just a few seconds ago. Him."

"Oh," she sighed before pivoting around and setting her elbows on the wooden support. Once again the fitful breezes toyed with her long hair.

Arlon's gaze returned to the sea. A pair of long, slate-gray clouds laced with purple highlights were attempting to veil the sinking sun as a smattering of stars became the first of many to peek through the darkening sky.

"Did you mean any of it?" the Princess prodded as the playful children scurried back by a second time, giggling the whole way.

He paused. "I, uh, I'm not really sure what you mean by that. I was just trying to, you know, stick to the story that we all agreed on."

"Oh," she mumbled. "So then you didn't mean what you said about me?"

He kept his voice low and avoided making eye contact. "Well, I called you my wife…and obviously that's not true. And I said that our parents didn't approve of—"

"I wasn't talking about that part," she countered.

His mind raced. "I, I'm sorry then. I guess I don't know what—"

Mae'Lee rolled to the side and fixed her eyes on him. "You said that I was…beautiful." She continued staring. "Did you mean it? Do you think I'm beautiful?"

He suddenly had the urge to run, yet his legs felt like two chunks of heavy iron welded to the deck. "Beautiful? Well, listen, I...uh—"

"I'll tell you what's *beautiful*," a new voice called out from just beyond Mae'Lee. "The bed in my cabin. It has thick sheets and a big, soft pillow. That is the very definition of beautiful."

They both whirled about and saw that Trilyra was relaxing against the rail about five feet away. "And it has been a long, long time since I have slept in a real bed," she noted while gazing out over the sea. "Actually, the last time I had anything close to a real bed was on another boat. On the river headed upstream to Alaithia. Now please...quit staring at me," she urged with a quiet firmness. "We don't know each other, remember?"

They both looked away instantly. Arlon checked to make sure no one was close enough to hear them.

"How is everything with...the...uh, the boys?" he asked.

"They're fine. Their room is next to mine."

"They should probably just stay out of sight the whole trip."

Trilyra tried to brush the hair out of her face. It didn't help. "That is going to be a little difficult," she replied. "Already."

"Why's that?"

She scanned the area. "Because, our host, good old Captain Theele, has invited them to dine with him and his officers tomorrow evening. As special guests."

"Oh, no," Mae'Lee gasped.

"Oh, yes. And better yet…he insisted that I join them as well."

Arlon thought about that for a few moments. "Well, just stay low. Don't do anything to attract undue attention to yourself."

Trilyra wandered off. "Don't worry. They won't even know I'm there."

Paymer took a deep breath.

It had been a long time since his nose had been treated with such a rich diversity of tantalizing and mouthwatering aromas. His eyes flitted back and forth between steaming meats and buttered breads and fruits and vegetables of every size, shape, and brilliant color—and all exquisitely prepared in a distinctly Oranian fashion. Nearly a dozen of the crew and a handful of other special guests lined the long, rectangular table which sat in the middle of a modest, but not quite cramped, dining area.

Paymer took a sip from his cup through the mouth hole in his oversized Sevasti mask (an awkward maneuver which required most of the evening to master just right).

Ah, he relished inwardly with a satisfied smile. *Blooddrake juice. It's been awhile.*

Wait…what did Arlon call it back at the Karaval?

He lowered the cup and studied its crimson contents. *Blood juice. No. No. Everybody else calls it that.*

Bloo-juice. No. That wasn't it.

Bloo-joo. Yep. Bloo-joo.

It's a shame he couldn't be here for this.

He took another quick drink and peeked over towards the towering figure in a deep blue jacket that sat at the head of the table off to his left.

Captain Theele, sir…I think I'm gonna really like sailing on your ship.

He continued looking around and taking it all in. There were lots of controlled smiles and chatter, but no one seemed to be eating. A frustrated Paymer leaned to the right towards Mogg.

"What are we waiting for? This is even a better spread than we had back in Alaithia!" he whispered (probably a bit louder than he meant to, but it was hard to tell, since the Sevasti masks and hoods made everything sound funny).

Mogg was silent, but Trilyra hunched forward and gestured towards their left. "Our host," she whispered with some urgency. "*Look!*"

Paymer straightened up and saw that the Captain was now standing at the head of the table with a cup outstretched in his tattooed right hand.

"Honored guests and faithful crew," he announced with a clear, commanding voice which Paymer thought befitted a man of his responsibilities. "May the Zho bless our voyage with strong winds and calm seas...and may good health and good success rest upon all those aboard the *Graceful Galleon*."

Nearly two dozen other cups were immediately raised into the air with broad smiles all around the room. "*The blessings of the Zho*," several voices echoed back, in staggered unison. It was a traditional Oranian response, but Paymer and Mogg held their peace.

Captain Theele nodded with approval before lowering his own mug and staring over at the three of them. "Before we partake, I would like to say that it is an honor to host your Sevasti delegation on this portion of your journey to Ammodis. The blessings of the Zho upon your travels."

More mugs shot up, and more voices chanted back "*The blessings of the Zho*." Paymer and Mogg both offered a subtle nod or two.

"Now, please," the Captain urged as he dropped down into his ornately carved, high-backed chair. "Please. Everyone. Enjoy the hospitality of the *Graceful Galleon*. Eat!"

Paymer pressed up against Mogg as the room burst into activity and casual conversation. "The Captain doesn't have to tell me twice!"

In less than a minute, he had snagged more than his fair share of sliced meats, seasoned potatoes, and no less than four different varieties of breads. The hungry young man was on the verge of spearing a few pieces of fruit with one of his long forks when Mogg laid a firm left hand on Paymer's right arm.

"Show *restraint* and *dignity*, my fellow Northern Elder brother," Mogg muttered.

Paymer withdrew his fork. "It is well-spoken."

The Captain cleared his throat and set his fork down. "My lords," he called out, peering in their direction. "I cannot help but notice by the tenderness of your hands and the height of your stature, that surely you must be considered, shall we say, *uncommonly young* as members of your ancient calling."

Paymer froze.

Trilyra looked like she was trying hard to *not* look like she was bothered by the troubling observation.

Mogg set his own fork down and dabbed his lips with a cloth napkin through the confines of his mask. "The halls of Alaithia are home to those of many ages among the many peoples of the Five Kingdoms, Captain Theele."

Whoa, great answer, Paymer thought. *Wish I would've said it.*

"Of course," Mogg continued in a flat, monotone delivery, "time and age mean very little within our ranks."

The Captain smiled, "Ah, yes...I have heard much of the, shall we say, *mysterious timelessness* of the Sevasti." He paused and squinted. "It is true, my lords, that some who dwell at Alaithia are many thousands of years in age?"

The room fell completely silent.

Mogg hesitated. "We do not speak openly of such things."

The Captain blushed. "Forgive me, my lords. Of course." He dabbed the corners of his own mouth. "But I do find it curious that the House of Mandibar would send a young female all the way to Alaithia as your guide back to their court." He hunkered forward, resting his elbows on the table while staring at Trilyra with an obvious skepticism. "Most curious, indeed."

Paymer tensed up even further.

Oh, boy. What do we say to that?

"Have you never heard of the Tar'deel?" Mogg inquired (without the slightest hint of concern).

"Tar'deel?" the Captain repeated before shaking his head. "I cannot say that I have, my lord."

"The warrior women of the court guard," Mogg answered firmly.

"Warrior *women?*" one of the officers chuckled. "Surely our Sevasti friend intended that in jest. We cannot—"

Captain Theele silenced the man with the mere wave of his left hand in conjunction with a quick hard stare. "Interesting. Tell us more of these warrior women," the Captain implored.

Mogg placed both hands on the table and rose up. "I will not tell you, Captain Theele...I would rather *show* you." He glanced to his right at Trilyra. "Kallyndra? Would you please stand?"

She set her drink down and rose up.

Mogg glanced back. "Captain, would you choose your finest fighter among your men?"

A wave of controlled laughter rippled through the officers. Theele smiled and pointed across the table. "That is an easy request, my lord. *Hollard!* Please stand."

Paymer watched with increasing horror as a hulking figure rose up from the far side. The dark-headed brute sported broad shoulders and was at least a foot taller than Trilyra.

Oh, my! Paymer thought in horror.

She's in trouble.

This is probably not a great idea.

Mogg motioned off to the right. "Take up your knife and stand near there."

Hollard looked over at the Captain who nodded and gestured for him to comply. The oversized sailor sauntered over to the corner as his crewmates slapped him on the back with a few snickers.

"My lords," the Captain intervened as a few others donned nervous looks. "I think we can see that this is an unfair contest at best. Perhaps we can arrange a more convenient time and manner for your emissary to display her physical prowess?"

Mogg disregarded the Captain's offer. "Kallyndra, please step back and relieve this man of his weapon. Without harming him."

A huge grin broke out across Hollard's wide face. "I don't know about *taking* my knife," he said, dangling it in the air. "But if you get closer, I might just *give* you my kiss." He pursed his lips and flitted his eyebrows at Trilyra.

His friends exploded into laughter, including the Captain who couldn't refrain from chuckling (though he tried to conceal it behind his napkin).

But it didn't matter.

It was over in less than four seconds.

Trilyra lunged forward, jumped onto an empty chair, and launched into the air. Her legs wrapped around his thick neck as she twisted about, flinging the startled man violently to the floor squarely on his back. There was not much more than a blur as she snatched his blade and brought it up under his chin while straddling his heaving chest.

The room was beyond speechless.

Paymer was stunned.

Wow. Wow.

Something deep inside him found the scene a little too familiar.

Wait…I've seen this before!

Yeah, that was almost exactly like that freaky move she did to Mogg back in waterfall city. Well done, Trilyra. Well done, my friend.

The Captain immediately shot up out of his chair and brought his hands together in a quick round of enthusiastic clapping. Others joined him and the dining room was spontaneously filled with amused chatter and excited pointing. Trilyra flung the knife away with a fast flick of the wrist and offered Hollard a quick hand to his feet. He refused, before returning to his seat, red-faced and silent.

Another one of the officers raised his hand. "Young lady," he ventured. "I presume you are an Ammodisian by birth?"

"I am," she answered with a nod.

"But then, I am confused," he admitted, making an arc under his chin with his thumb. "I have never met one from your kingdom who did not wear an ear-chain."

Paymer tensed up yet again.

Oh, great. Now this.

She paused. "I…lost it."

The amused man kept on. "Where?"

She narrowed her eyes and raised her hands as if squeezing something directly in front of her. "I used it…to strangle a man."

The shocked dinner party grew quiet again.

"Uh, may I ask…*why* you strangled the poor soul?" he inquired timidly.

She glared at him without a single blink. "Because he *asked* too many questions."

His eyebrows shot up, and his friends roared while slapping him on the shoulders.

"No more questions, young lady," he chuckled with both hands raised in playful protest coupled with a traumatized smile. "No more. I promise. I promise!"

Paymer released a pent-up sigh and smiled inside of his mask. *Well, that little scene might go a long way to helping us out.*

He relaxed enough to take a juicy bite of roast pork.

I bet no one else will dare to bother us on the rest of this trip.

It was a dangerously foolish thing to think.

The rocky ground beneath Arlon's unstable feet shifted. It was a very odd sort of shift. A drastic shift. A puzzled expression was all he could muster as he glanced at the dark forest floor and fought to maintain his balance.

CREEEEAAAAAAKKKKKKKK.

The immense trees all about him swayed and popped and protested under the strain of the heaving ground. Branches collided with branches far overhead, showering him with fragments of splintered wood and bits of tattered leaves as he himself was thrown from side to side.

And then…the violent rocking tossed him over a cliff.

Arlon fell.

And fell.

And slammed face-first into the floor, snapping him awake in his darkened cabin. A scared voice called out to him from somewhere on the other side of the room.

"What's going on, Arlon?!"

CCRRRREEEEEAAAAAAKKKKKKK.

He slid along the wood planks and grabbed (what felt like) the door frame.

"I don't know, Mae'Lee," he replied, fighting desperately to get to his feet. An eerie howling roared in the distance, making the hairs stand up all along the back of his terrified neck.

"Why is the ship rocking like this?!" she asked. "I'm scared."

CCRRREEEEEAAAAAAAKKKKKKKKKK.

"So am I," he mumbled.

KAAAAABBBOOOOOOOOOMMM!

Paymer jerked up from a deep sleep and threw his legs over the edge of his narrow bed. "What was that?!" he yelled breathlessly as Mogg struggled to maintain his own balance while lighting a lantern.

"It is a storm," Mogg replied. "A very bad storm."

CCRRRREEEEEAAAAAAAKKKKKKKK.

Paymer tried to steady himself against the nearest wall as the ship bobbed and rolled. "You, uh, you don't think that it's a…you know…*sea monster* or something? You think that Snow Serpent was bad? I've heard stories about—"

KAAABOOOOOOOOOMMMMMM!

"That is an ill thought," Mogg replied the instant the echoes died away. "Unless monsters cause the wind and waves and thunder." He blew lightly on the emerging flame as the crimson glow painted his concerned face in flickering shades of deep red. "It is a *storm*." He transferred the lantern over to Paymer's trembling hands. "Hold this."

Mogg threw his cloak on and snatched his Sevasti mask.

Paymer's face contorted. "What're you doing?"

"The same thing that you must do," came the reply as Mogg grabbed the lantern once again. "Get dressed. The crew may need our help."

Paymer rose up with considerable hesitation and gathered his outfit. "But...I don't know anything about *ships*...or *sailing* or any of that."

Mogg donned his mask just as the reeling vessel sent him crashing into his nervous friend. He raised the swinging lantern between their faces and leaned closer. "Then you can pray and beseech the Zho that we survive."

The horrific chaos playing out on the deck was almost beyond description. As Mogg fought to climb the last bit of stairs and plunge out into the confusion (with Paymer close behind), a blast of ferocious wind nearly toppled them both back through the slippery entry. Wave after wave of torrential sheets of stinging rain pummeled the two as deckhands raced by them in every direction for what appeared to be a vain effort to lower the sails while securing the rigging.

Blinding flashes of lightning fractured the cloudy sky in jagged arcs, as peals of thunder first shattered through the howling wind before booming on and on and on into the dark distance.

Paymer held onto his soppy hood and tried to get close to Mogg's ear. "I…I don't think…this…is a…good idea," he yelled.

Three frantic members of the ship's crew hustled by and another attempted to scramble up a twisting rope ladder that beat against the main mast. Paymer shielded his eyes and glanced overhead through his uncomfortable mask. As the lightning flashed, he could see that the merciless winds had torn the lower corner of the topsail and the others bulged and rippled violently.

They'll be ripped to shreds, he feared. *And then we won't be sailing anywhere!*

SHHHHRRRAABOOOOOOOMMM!

Wow! That was close! Too close.

"My lords!" a voice called out, getting louder. "My lords!"

A hand clutched Paymer's shoulder, and he spun around.

"Captain!"

"My lords," the experienced seaman hollered through cupped hands. "It is too dangerous out here! Please, return to your cabin! My men know what to do. I beg you."

"What about...the little boat?" Paymer yelled.

"The tender? It wouldn't last ten seconds in these blasted swells," Theele responded. "Now, I beg you, return to your cabin!"

Paymer nodded and the Captain rushed off into the intermittent darkness.

KAAABBOOOOOOMMMMM!

"I told you that...we should be...inside," Paymer screamed as he grabbed the wet wood rail to avoid sliding once again. "We need...to listen to...the Captain!"

He was right.

And late.

Within seconds, two stout ropes snapped in quick succession and crumpled onto the deck several feet away as a long, dark form accelerated towards them.

"Watch out!" someone yelled out (just barely above the howling gale).

Paymer ducked and covered his head.

Mogg didn't.

THHHWWUUMMMPPP!

A broken boom swung free of the mast and slammed squarely into Mogg's chest, sending him sprawling across the deck. A frantic Paymer paused for a moment before daring to rise up and scan the area for his fallen friend.

He didn't see him.

But he saw something else during a long, brilliant blast of lightning.

Oh no…

Paymer did his best to rush over and grab the object as it slid across the swaying deck.

His Sevasti mask.

Another flash.

FLAASHHHH-KAAAAABBBBBOOOOOOOM!

The bright explosion compelled him to hunker down, but Paymer forced himself to whirl around. Another pair of quick flashes revealed Mogg, plastered flat on his back, not quite twenty feet away…and a member of the crew leaning over him.

Oh no…

As the battered ship continued to rock like an enormous, creaking pendulum, Paymer took advantage of the downhill slope and raced to his friend's aid.

"Is he okay?" Paymer yelled, dropping down beside him.

"He's breathing," the lanky crewman hollered back into his ear. "I think."

Paymer quickly lowered the mask over Mogg's face and glanced up as the pounding rain stung his own eyes. "I will take care of my brother. Thank you."

The young deckhand nodded and patted Paymer on the shoulder, then scurried towards a handful of others clustered around the main mast. Mogg began coughing before blinking several times and rubbing his chest.

Paymer arched closer. "Don't move, pal," he instructed. "I'm gonna get Trilyra and then we'll carry you back to our cabin so you can recover."

If Mogg had heard any of it, it didn't show.

Paymer pulled his cloak tighter and stood up with his chilled back to the punishing wind.

That is…if we all live through this.

Mae'Lee clamped her eyes shut and buried her face in his arms. "When is this dreadful storm going to end?" she moaned. "It's been like this for hours!"

Arlon sat there in the weak light of their small lamp and struggled for a reassuring response. "Well, now…that's, that's a *good* thing," he replied.

She wiped her nose and glanced up. "What?"

"That's a good thing," he said through a forced grin. "That means we are still afloat. Ships are made to rock back and forth. Rocking is a good thing. Sinking is a bad thing."

KAAABBOOOOOOOOOOOMMMMM

She clenched tighter. "But it sounds so scary. It sounds like the world is ending."

He patted the beautiful black locks of her head. "It's…just…*noise*. That's all. And sound can't hurt us. It will pass." He paused. "No storm lasts forever."

"What if this one does?"

"It won't," he affirmed. "It can't. I promise."

Arlon gently raised her trembling chin and stared into a pair of brown eyes paralyzed with fear. "We have a mission…a job to do, remember?" He glanced away with a confident smile. "This little storm can blow and shake this boat all it wants…but it can't stop that."

"Are you sure?"

KAAABBOOOOOOOOM!

"Absolutely," he responded calmly. "Plus, all this thunder kinda reminds me of the night that we first met."

She sat up a bit.

"Do you remember?" he asked.

"You…you were chained…to a bench," she said as a slow, cautious smile broke out across her tense face. "You looked so…pitiful."

He smiled back at her. "I guess I haven't really changed much, then."

"Oh, a lot has changed since then," she said, still shuddering.

"I would say that we have changed places," Arlon observed.

"What? How so?"

He stared into the lamp, collecting his thoughts as the creaking ship continued to sway. "Well, on the night we first met...I was the miserable one, and you tried to console me. And now—tonight—*you* are miserable and *I* am consoling you."

Mae'Lee rubbed her eyes. "I guess we're even, then."

Arlon leaned back with a stunned look. "Whoa...wait a minute, your mistaken *Highness-ness*. We're not even close to being even."

"We're not?"

He folded his arms. "Nope. Unless the skin on your pretty royal back is covered in gashes from a long, leather whip after being accused of stealing your own property while serving as a slave after being kidnapped and thrown in a cart like a worthless dog."

She squinted while biting her bottom lip. "Oh, yeah. I forgot about all that. That was pretty...bad. Sorry. I can't even imagine how dreadful that must've been."

"*But*…in your defense," he continued, "you did help me recover on the way to Karaval. And your royal cart was a lot nicer than the slave cart. So, maybe that does make us even."

The boat rumbled from another deep blast of the storm's lessening fury. She grabbed his arm, before slowly releasing it. "We've been through so many things. And we've been to so many places. The Karaval…it seems like a very long, long time ago." The Princess sighed as a trickle of tears rolled down her face. "And home…it seems like a very long, long way away."

"You're right," he replied as the boat's swaying began to subside. "We are far from home. All of us are. But if being surrounded by those who love you is being home…" Arlon reached up and dried her cheeks with a tender brush of his finger. "Then you, Mae'Lee…are home."

He unrolled the ancient map and set his mug and a handful of gold Royals on opposite ends to anchor the curling edges. His weathered finger traced a route along the smeared ink outline of the coast and tapped several times in a few different spots.

"But where is this *Graceful Gal*?" he muttered with a furrowed brow. "Where has this storm landed us?"

Someone rapped on the door.

"Enter," he called out.

A skinny ship's mate slipped through and quickly shut the heavy door behind him. "Captain," he greeted as his voice cracked a little.

Theele didn't even bother to look up.

"What is it, Plyde?"

The young man cleared his throat and stepped closer. "Captain, sorry to bother you, sir."

"That blasted storm was a bother, Plyde," he countered. "*You*...are just an interruption."

"Yes, sir. Sorry, sir."

Theele raised his eyebrows and glared over at him. "I imagine that you are here to do more than repeatedly apologize, crewman?"

"Yes, Captain. Sorry, Captain." Plyde shuffled his feet.

"Are you here...to provide me an update on the mast repairs?"

"Uh, no, sir. I, uh, need to tell you something. Captain."

"Believe it or not, Mr. Plyde...that is the usual reason that most people visit me in the map room," Theele smirked. "To *tell* me something. Some of them are even brave enough to *ask* me something."

"Oh, yes, Captain. But I need to tell you something...*important*, sir."

"Well, now," he said. "That is different." Theele leaned away from the map table and folded his arms. "Please, tell me something *important*. Although, at this moment I cannot imagine something more important than the repair status of our mainsail or our current whereabouts."

"Yes, sir. Well, during the storm…I saw something, Captain."

"I did as well, crewman Plyde. I saw lightning, and waves, and tattered sails and damaged rigging." His voice grew both irritated and his face flared red. "And right now, all I see is a young man who is continuing to waste my precious time!"

Plyde cleared his trembling throat once again. "Sorry, Captain. I, uh, I saw the…the face of one of the Sevasti. Sir. His mask was knocked off. It was an accident."

Theele smiled and rubbed his wrinkled forehead. "While that is an *interesting* experience, Mr. Plyde, for sure…I fail to see how it warrants any further distraction of my—"

"That's not all that I saw, sir. And forgive the interruption." The deckhand stepped closer and lowered his voice considerably. He pointed at his own cheek.

"I saw something…*else*."

A voice echoed into the distance.

"Get up," it boomed.

A groggy Paymer tried his best to ignore it, cocooning himself in a thick blanket.

"Get up!" it repeated.

Something (or someone) shook his shoulder.

Paymer batted it away. "C'mon, Mogg. Let. Me. Sleep."

"I must insist," a new voice declared firmly. "Please...get up. My lord."

My lord?

Wait...I know that voice.

He reluctantly began to roll back over.

That's the voice of...

"Captain Theele said to get up!" the first voice demanded as Paymer's coverings were ripped away violently.

He dared to crack his eyes open, one at a time. An angry face was glaring down at him, flanked by four sailors brandishing knives…and Mogg already in bonds.

Without a mask.

"Good morning, my lord," Theele offered with a wide smile that was short on sincerity. "I am sorry to bother you, but after our dangerous storm last evening, I need to ensure that my special passengers are…*uninjured*."

Theele motioned his right hand, and two sailors quickly jerked Paymer off the bed and onto his feet.

"Do you have any…*bruises* that you would like to declare?" the Captain pressed. "Or, other *marks*?"

One of the sailors yanked the boy's shirt off before spinning him around. Captain Theele squinted and inched closer with growing interest. He traced a yellowed fingernail along the center of Paymer's back.

"Well, well. That's a nasty bruise, my lord. Nasty indeed." He pointed at the birthmark on Mogg's cheek. "You both must've been hit in the exact same way. Imagine that." He nodded as his men grabbed a rope and bound the boy's hands with a firm knot. "We will need to relocate both of you to more secure lodging, my lords." He motioned behind him. "Escort our famous Dunamai guests to the brig. We wouldn't want any harm to come to such valuable cargo." He playfully rubbed Paymer's red hair. "I see a wagon load of golden Royals waiting for us at the end of this crossing."

"You need to let us go, Captain!" Paymer bristled, struggling against his restraints.

"Oh, I will," his captor replied with graying eyebrows raised. "In the market. For a price. To the highest bidder. And I'm confident that the bids will be quite high among many from the Five Kingdoms."

Theele's men roughly shoved the two through the doorway and out into the sunlit hall.

"The storm may have cost us a day or two, lads," the Captain noted with a deep, satisfied chuckle while he followed behind. "But now, it has paid more than handsomely for our trouble."

"Mae'Lee!" Arlon whispered with a desperation far stronger than the volume of his voice. He dropped beside her bed and shook her shoulder gently (but not too gently). *"Mae'Lee!* You need to wake up! Wake up! Something's happened."

The Princess slid both arms out from underneath her load of blankets and stretched hard as her bloodshot eyes blinked open.

"Arlon…it was a long night." She tried to bury her face in her pillow. "Just let—"

"Keep your voice down," he urged as he scooted closer. "Listen. Something terrible has happened."

Mae'Lee rolled onto her side and faced him with a yawn. "Is the ship sinking?"

"No," he replied. "And I almost wish it was."

"What?"

"Forget it. Listen. I woke up hungry a little while ago, so I went to the galley to find something to eat."

She rolled her tired eyes. "Being hungry isn't so terrible, Arlon. To tell you the truth, I—"

"No, no, no. That's not it. Anyway, while I was on the deck, I overheard some of the crew talking." He hesitated and lowered his voice. "They said that a couple of Dunamai were being held below deck."

"What?!" Mae'Lee jumped up. "Are you sure?!"

"*Shhhh!* Keep it down. I even heard the word '*Sevasti.*'"

Her eyes flitted back and forth around the tiny cabin before flooding with tears.

"I went by their room," he continued. "No one was there. I've looked everywhere."

"Trilyra?"

"Gone, too."

She brought a trembling hand up to her worried face. "Do, uh, do you think they will be coming…to get us, as well?"

He clasped Mae'Lee's hand between his and crawled up beside her. "No, no…hey…of course not." He sat down on the edge of the bed and stared into her eyes. "I don't believe that for one second. Not one second."

He hoped that she was convinced.

That way at least one of us can avoid despair.

Paymer and Mogg flinched as the outer door to the brig burst open, allowing a harsh, rectangular beam of late-morning light to expose streams of lantern smoke and billows of wood dust that swirled in the musty air just beyond their tiny cell. Paymer squinted as a slender silhouette was shoved into the bluish pool of light, followed by three much larger (and armed) silhouettes.

Mogg straightened up on the wooden bench and leaned into him. "The Woman of the South," he whispered discreetly.

Oh no, Paymer gasped. *They got her, too.*

A fifth figure stepped into the light as the creaking door of the adjacent cell was opened and Trilyra was thrust inside.

"It was a clever ruse, I'll give you that," the Captain bellowed out as he stepped up and laid hold of the metal bars separating him from his terrified captives. "Clever, indeed. But, we had our doubts from the moment we set sail. When it came to the three of you, there were far more questions than there were blasted answers. And let's just say that the answers…didn't…smell right. But, no matter. It was a doomed venture. *Great* lies…require great *liars*." He rattled the bars and stared down at them. "And I suspect that none of you are great liars."

Paymer jumped up. "Captain! Listen to me…you must release us!"

"Must? *Must?!* The only thing I *must* do is keep you alive long enough to see how much you will fetch in Ammodis." He paused. "And…if I judge the reward too slight, I may haul you back to Orania. I'm confident that interested parties from each of the Civilized Kingdoms would travel far for that notable sale. Time is on my side, young Dunamai." His heavy boots echoed while he slowly worked his way over to the next cell. "I've even heard rumors that the Order is seeking the likes of you."

"Don't you know the prophecies?" Paymer asked. "Don't you know the penalty for any who would harm a Chosen Child?!"

Theele grew indignant. "You dare speak of penalties and harm, dear boy? It is you and your kind that has brought penalty and harm upon us, upon us all! Because of you, that blasted Dragon is wreaking havoc across our lands. So shut your mouth, or I'll have it sewn shut!"

"You will regret this!"

"A little threat from a little boy trapped in a little cage."

Mogg grabbed Paymer's cloak and pulled his furious friend back towards the bench.

"It is an ill thought," Mogg muttered.

Theele stopped and studied Trilyra. She avoided making eye contact.

"Did you examine the female?" he demanded (without breaking his penetrating stare).

"Yes, Captain," one of the sailors responded. "She does not have the mark."

"Are you certain?" He narrowed his eyes. "She is of the proper age. One of the Dunamai was a girl."

"Yes, Captain. We are certain."

Theele rested against the bars with a skeptical grin. "Well, then…except for that odd black streak in your hair, it appears that you have no mark. Just an ordinary girl. So…what is your role in this ruse, young lady? Who are you?"

She kept silent and faced the far corner.

"Remember, girl…I've seen your training," he taunted. "You are an exceptional warrior. Are we to believe that such a skilled fighter is merely a casual acquaintance of these two fugitives?" He shook the bars again. *"Who are you?!"*

She remained a silent statue.

"Very well," he mumbled, digging out his knife and brandishing it into the light. "Hold your tongue….if you cooperate, I might even let you keep it." The Captain spun around and headed out. "Tan'marr? Secure the door behind us and post a guard outside. Feed our guests once a day." He paused. "And if they give you trouble, once every other day."

"Yes, Captain."

SHHHH-KLUUNNNKKK.

The heavy, thick door slammed shut, hinges creaking the entire way, and Paymer grimaced as it latched from the outside. He waited a few seconds and then kept his voice down.

"What're we gonna do?!"

Trilyra moved closer. "Look around, Chosen Child. Our options are pretty limited.

Unless you have some kind of magic trick to help us out."

"That's not good enough!" he retorted. "There must be *something* we can do!"

"The way I read it," she smirked, "we only have two options. *One*...we try to find a way to overpower the guard when he comes in to feed us. Or *two*...we try to escape when we arrive at port during the time that they are transporting us to the market."

"I don't think I like the sound of either one of those."

"Think all you want...I bet my bow you won't be able to come up with option number *three*," she challenged.

"And I bet that your bow *would be* option number three."

She laid her head back against the rough wooden wall. "I appreciate your confidence, but...out here in the middle of the sea, my bow wouldn't be much help. Even if we escaped, where would we go?"

Paymer started to answer her two or three times, but stopped himself on each occasion. His typically optimistic smile soon vanished, and he collapsed against the back wall. "Oh, you're right."

She stared up at the low ceiling as the sound of hammers began pounding above them. "Smartest thing you've said all day. Maybe even all week."

"Do you think they've looked through all our things?"

"They probably are right about now," she replied. "Who had the relics?"

"Arlon had all those," Paymer piped up, sounding a bit relieved. "And the Rone pieces. And the maps."

She rolled her head in their general direction. "What about the shields?"

"Uh, we had one, and they had the other one."

"If we somehow get out of this cursed mess, we need to get that shield back."

"And our freaky masks, too," Paymer added.

"Forget those masks...the Pyro shields are far more valuable. Oh, and my weapons. We need those."

"You're probably right," he said. "Again."

Trilyra smiled. "Seeing the pattern yet?"

"Yeah, but don't forget about my new sword." He stuck out his hand as if he was holding and admiring the blade. "My beautiful new, shiny, expensive sword. I miss it already. Did I say shiny yet?"

Trilyra held up two fingers. "*Twice*. And don't worry about your new sword, Paymer. I'm sure that was the first shiny thing that Captain Theele added to his own personal collection of shiny things. Right after all of our shiny golden Royals."

"You just said 'shiny' three times."

"And now," she grinned. "So have you."

"Right again," he huffed.

"There is another option," Mogg muttered.

Paymer's head fell forward and he shot him a confused look. "There's what?"

"There is another option."

"As in…*another option* to get my shiny sword back?"

Mogg shook his head. "Another option to get free from these bars. By the will of the Zho."

Paymer leaned towards him. "What's the plan?"

"The plan is not a *what*," Mogg replied firmly. "The plan…is a *who*."

A smiling Mae'Lee clung adoringly to Arlon's left arm as they strolled across the main deck, enjoying the warm sunlight and the unusually crisp air. And they weren't alone.

Scores of young and old alike wandered about and gawked at the pitiful condition of the once majestic ship. In every direction, the previous night's tempest had left a visible trail of significant damage in its wake.

High above the sightseeing crowd, a handful of brave sailors scrambled about like spiders on webs of rope, attempting to mend a series of horrific gashes all along the tattered mainsails. Closer to the deck, a construction detail was hammering away at a set of braces intended to immobilize at least two different splintered booms. Other crew members were busy securing or replacing frayed and torn cables that dangled free like a hundred tassels playing in the late-morning breeze.

Arlon paused and stared over the rail beyond the small tender secured to the side of the vessel. The seas were surprisingly calm. The ship was hardly moving.

"Well, my dear," he began quietly. "I'm afraid that the *Graceful Galleon* is now the *Slothful Galleon*."

She relaxed against the rail beside him and enjoyed the sun on her face for a few quiet moments. "Well, my husband, at least the morning is pleasant."

"Pleasant?" a rough voice boomed out. "There's that word again."

They glanced to their right as a familiar face picked his way through the passing crowd.

"And there's that Soterian couple again," he observed with a hearty laugh.

Arlon plastered a huge smile. "Good morning...Kor...Korrash...Korrish?"

"*Korridge*. I was named in honor of my grandfather on my mother's side. Legend has it that he was a powerfully good cook." He proceeded to rub his expansive belly. "Whereas I...I am a powerfully good *eater*. You need both, you know."

"We can't argue with that," Arlon admitted, pulling Mae'Lee close.

"So, how are my favorite runaways?"

Oh no. Arlon's mind panicked. *He called us runaways. That's not a good word right now.* He kept his voice down. "Well, we're still a little shaken. Scary night."

"It is truly difficult to take in," Korridge began, peering out at the sky. "Last night, a storm with all the fury of a dozen Dragons. A storm that could have sent us all swimming, but now...*this*. Couldn't ask for a finer day." He spun about and pointed to the east. "See that dark outline on the horizon? That's the coast. Storm must've blown us far off course. I've sailed this route before and never seen land at this stage. Winds must've been fierce as all blazes."

"I hardly slept at all," the Princess complained. "The howling was dreadful. And the rolling was worse. My stomach still hurts."

"Dreadful? *Bah!* But…I suppose that would've been terrifying for those not well-acquainted with the treachery of the seas. Now, for an old sailor like myself, I would call last night…*exciting*."

"No offense," Arlon replied, "but we are not interested in any more *excitement* on this voyage."

"Gracious me, too late for that, lad."

"Too late?"

Korridge pivoted to face them and rested his elbow on the rail. "Did you hear the news?"

Mae'Lee squinted. "News?"

Korridge nodded carefully and crept closer. "It's been spreading all over the ship like a wild grass fire." He changed his voice to a harsh whisper. "They caught some dangerous fugitives on board. Earlier this morning."

Arlon did his very best to act surprised. "Really?" he whispered.

"Three of them."

It was Mae'Lee's turn to seem shocked. "On this boat?"

Korridge motioned towards the rear of the ship on the far side. "They're in the brig, back over there." He pointed down with a single finger. "One level lower."

The Princess gripped Arlon's arm. "Well, at least they're locked up."

"You know what else I've heard?"

Arlon bent towards him and raised his eyebrows.

Korridge glanced about and restrained his voice even further. "One of the crew told me that two of the troublemakers…are…*Dunamai*."

"Dunamai?!" Arlon whispered back. "Really? On this ship? Right now?"

Korridge nodded and stretched. "There's four of them on the run…so I've heard. They say that the Dragon up and killed the fifth one. At the Offering."

"How dreadful," Mae'Lee mumbled.

"What do you think will happen to them?" Arlon inquired.

"Captain Theele is a shrewd businessman. I've sailed with him before. Once we dock, he'll probably send the word out about his little bit of good fortune. I don't know how long it will take, but those two will probably bring enough to refresh his coffers, that's for sure. I've heard that there's more than a few folks who want to haul those traitors to justice."

Arlon frowned. "Really?"

"They must've done something terrible. The way I see it...if they weren't guilty, then why did they flee? Those pampered children have brought a lot of misery on all of us. They need to answer for it. They offended that Dragon, and now it's been burning up the farmland outside the capital. A lot of good folks have perished. Before I left Verdana a few weeks back to head for the coast, the Queen had posted a sizable reward for the Oranian Dunamai." He smiled and rubbed his face. "Truth be known, Captain Theele doesn't care much for Eudorra, but I'm sure he wouldn't mind taking her gold."

Arlon looked down at the deck and kicked a wad of seaweed. "Well, we just hope that the Dragon will leave us alone down in Ammodis."

Korridge straightened up and started to walk away. "It is a *pleasant* thought, my friends...but I wouldn't count on it. I've heard news that terrible misfortune has fallen upon Ammodis. Droughts and sickness and the like. I think all our kingdoms will suffer for a long time." He gradually blended in with the thickening crowd. "Maybe even until the end of time."

The Princess sighed as soon as he was gone. "That sounded depressing."

"He might be right," Arlon commented while sneaking a glance over the rail a final time.

"You didn't have to agree with him."

The small boat lashed to the side of the ship seemed to capture his attention. He grabbed Mae'Lee's hand and encouraged her to start moving. "Come on," he whispered. "I have a crazy idea."

"Captain?"

Theele lowered his serious gaze from checking the progress of the repairs on the main mast down to the skinny ship's mate that had just arrived to his right.

"Yes, Plyde?"

The nervous young man scooted closer and kept his voice discreet. "Sorry to bother you, Captain, but I was thinking."

"You are no bother, crewman Plyde. In fact," Theele paused as a huge smile rippled across his reddened and rough cheeks, "the last time you bothered me, it turned out to be quite valuable. So, by all means...*bother* on. Within reason."

"Thank you, Captain. Well, with all that has happened...I was thinking."

Theele waited.

And waited.

"And hopefully, Mr. Plyde, I will soon be hearing about these thoughts of yours?"

"Oh, yes, Captain. Sorry. Sir. Well, we have two of the Dunamai fugitives in the hold. Sir."

Theele folded his arms and squinted. "I think that just about everyone aboard the *Graceful Galleon* is well aware of that fact, sailor. Now...do you have any other thoughts that aren't quite so well known?"

"Yes, sir. Well, I was thinking that there were *four* Dunamai fugitives that ran away from the Karaval. Three boys and one girl."

Theele tapped his foot. "That news is *also* fairly well known, Mr. Plyde."

"Well, Captain. We have two in the hold. That means there are two more...that aren't."

"I can't argue with your impeccable accounting," Theele scoffed, looking back towards the mast. "But I can argue with the blasted need to continue with this uninformative conversation."

Plyde cleared his throat. "What I am trying to say, sir...is that, since we found two of them on the ship, then wouldn't it be safe to say that all four of them are on this ship?"

Theele froze.

His penetrating gaze drifted back and locked onto the young man.

Plyde fidgeted under the weight of his stare. "And, uh, Captain...I think that it would be a boy and a girl, sir."

"Indeed it would," the Captain muttered. "Indeed...it would."

"Do you think there's a chance they could also be aboard the *Galleon*, Captain?"

Theele pivoted about and scanned the pockets of people milling all about the deck. "Indeed they could."

"I, uh, thought so as well, sir."

Theele slapped him on the shoulder with a hearty (but controlled) laugh and pulled him to his side. "Share this with no one," he growled through just a hint of a smile. "*Not...a...word.*"

"Yes, sir," Plyde whispered. "I mean, I won't, sir."

The Captain narrowed his eyes.

"Now, listen carefully...we have work to do."

By the middle of the hot and humid afternoon, Mae'Lee's bunk resembled a colorful fruit and vegetable stand, with another basket on the floor overstuffed with breads and assorted dried meats. The cabin door barely cracked open and Arlon pushed through before closing it without delay.

"Oh, wow," he said, admiring her culinary collection. "Think we have enough?"

Her black eyebrows shot up. "Depends on how long it needs to last. Any idea?"

He set a water satchel down. "I, uh…I don't know."

She lowered her voice. "Did you find them?"

Arlon plopped onto his bed and nodded. "Guards?"

He raised a single finger.

"That should be helpful," she replied. "How about keys?"

Arlon nodded again.

"Weapons?"

He squinted before shaking his head. "At least, none that I could see."

"That could be either good or bad," she replied.

"Then I'm hoping for good."

"But we need to be ready for *bad*. Maybe even dreadfully bad."

"Then I'm hoping for dreadfully *good*," he whispered with a wink. "We need to get this all packed up and then try to get some rest." He took a deep breath. "It's gonna be a long night."

Mae'Lee frowned. "Or, a very short one."

The radiant bluish glow of the full moons had trouble penetrating into the long, narrow hallway one level below the main deck. A trio of wall-mounted lanterns provided irregular amber patches of light along the lonely, darkened corridor.

And he just stood there.

He had been standing there for hours.

Leaning against the rough wooden wall like a stone silhouette. It was boring and uneventful and dull and quiet, but he had remained dutifully at his post. But all that was about to change.

"Oh, my...I made a wrong turn, didn't I?" a sweet voice echoed out from down the hall.

The surprised young guard rolled his tired head to the left just in time to see her dainty form slip into a soft pool of light.

"I just left my cabin for a late evening snack," a very shy Mae'Lee admitted as she drew closer. "And I think I got all turned around in the dark."

"Uh, yes, ma'am," he said with a broad smile as she approached. "But that's alright, I can help you."

"Oh, thank you!" she replied, laying her soft hand on his arm. "It's such a big ship. And I've never been on a big ship before."

He blushed as he nodded. "Don't worry. You'll be fine. What is your cabin number, ma'am?"

"Thirty-seven." She cocked her head. "I think."

"Thirty-seven? You are a long way from home," he chuckled. "It's at the other side of the ship. But I can show you."

"No…no…no," she protested, rubbing his arm. "I don't want to be any trouble…especially to an important sailor like yourself."

"It's no problem, ma'am. It's why we're here." He spun her around and led Mae'Lee down the hall. "We just need to go back this way and head topside."

She hooked her arm in his. "Topside?"

"Sorry…that's what we call going up on deck."

She squeezed his arm as they passed through the final bit of warm lantern light. "I hate this dark corner," she complained. "You never know what might be waiting in the shadows."

He patted her hand. "Don't worry, ma'am, there's nothing to—"

KLUUUNNNNGGG!

The poor guard never saw Arlon or his quick swing or the long chunk of wood before it all collided with the back of his unsuspecting skull. Arlon and the Princess guided his limp body to the ground and then dragged him back towards the door to the brig.

"Nice job," he whispered.

"It was your plan."

"Yeah, but it wouldn't have worked without your special royal charm."

They leaned their unconscious victim against the wall as Arlon dug around inside the man's coat.

"Found them," he said.

"Hurry," she urged. "Before someone else sees us."

Arlon rose up and frantically fumbled with several keys in the lock before success. "Just make the guard look like he just fell asleep right there." He raised the metal bar and shoved the door open. "I'll be right back. With our friends."

"Hurry!"

He nodded.

The entry to the brig was even darker than the poorly lit hallway, and Arlon strained to see much of anything.

"*Paymer?! Mogg?!*" he called out in a gruff whisper as he pushed inward. "*Trilyra?!*"

There was a long pause.

Arlon stuck out his hands, feeling in front of him as he inched through the uncertain darkness. His fingers landed on a series of metal bars.

"Paymer!" he growled. "Trilyra! Mogg! Wake up!"

Another pause.

"Arlon?" a quiet voice whispered back.

"Paymer?!"

"Arlon!"

"It's me," he replied. "I'm here to get you guys out."

"Well, it's about time!" Trilyra's sarcastic voice resounded out.

Arlon took a deep breath as he tried different keys. "Well, good and proper rescues take time. Can you move? Are any of you in chains or anything?"

Paymer was the first to reach the bars. "No, we're free."

Mogg came in close behind. "The third option," he mumbled with satisfaction.

Arlon's eyes were finally adjusting. "What?"

"I'll explain later," Paymer said. "Did you grab my shiny sword?"

Arlon found the key and unlocked their door. "What?"

"Forget about his pretty new pig-sticker and get me outta here!" Trilyra demanded as the other two rushed out.

Arlon scooted to the right. "I'm working on it!"

"Well, work faster. I'm hungry."

"We have plenty of food," another voice responded. "And water."

"Mae'Lee!" Paymer erupted. "Are you alright?"

The Princess stood in the doorway and waved her arms. "I'm fine. I'm fine. Now come on, let's get to the boat!" she urged.

Mogg grabbed Arlon's shoulder. "Boat?"

Arlon unlocked Trilyra's cell door and threw it open. "Yes...*boat*," he replied. "And I hope you guys know how to row."

———————————————————————

Arlon ducked his head back around the corner. "Only one crewman on the main deck," he whispered to the others crouched behind him. "And he is pacing between us and our little floating escape plan."

Trilyra shoved forward. "I can take care of him."

Arlon grabbed her. "It needs to be quiet," he urged firmly.

She shrugged him off. "He won't make a sound. Does anyone have some cloth?"

Mae'Lee dug around her pockets. "Here's some."

Trilyra snatched it. "Perfect."

"Wait," Arlon whispered. "We probably need a diversion, too."

She smiled and cocked her head. "And I will take care of that, as well." Trilyra double-checked the area. "You all get on that boat and don't worry about me. I will get to you, I promise."

She bolted off across the deck.

"Trilyra!" Arlon whispered a bit late.

"That girl is crazy!" Mae'Lee whispered.

Paymer nodded. "Maybe. But she's a brave soul. I'll give her that."

"My father says that the difference between foolishness and bravery is whether or not the person survived," Mae'Lee retorted.

Paymer's eyebrows shot up. "Then let's hope that she is brave and not foolish."

Trilyra's footfalls were totally silent as she rushed up behind the sailor and jabbed the wad of cloth into his mouth before choking the wiggling man out and lowering him to the deck.

"Wow," Mae'Lee mumbled.

"Brave," Paymer replied.

Trilyra waved the group on as she dragged her unconscious victim into the shadows behind several crates nearby. She raced towards the front of the ship.

"It's now or never," Paymer urged.

"It's now! Let's go!" Arlon encouraged, rising up and leading the desperate pack across the deck. They reached the rail, and he took Mae'Lee's arm as she began to climb over. "Paymer! Follow her into the boat. Mogg and I can operate the winch and lower it down. Then we will climb down the rope."

"No!" Paymer barked. "Your shoulder can't take a long climb like that! Mogg and I will lower the boat. You and Mae'Lee get in now!"

Arlon shook his head.

"Arlon!" Mae'Lee growled. "He's right. Come on! Now!"

"Don't argue with her royal Highnessness," Paymer smirked as he and Mogg grabbed the handles on both winches and began cranking feverishly. "We will join you shortly. Now go!"

Arlon reluctantly scurried over the rail as the small boat gradually jerked and swayed towards the water.

Mae'Lee glanced up at him with terror in her eyes. "I hope Trilyra makes it."

He scooted in beside her and looked over the edge. "She'll make it."

He swallowed hard.

I hope.

"How much further?" Paymer hollered out (without really hollering).

Arlon leaned over once again and then looked up. "About ten feet," he whispered.

"How will we know where to go?" the Princess inquired. "Once we start rowing."

Arlon straightened up. "Well, we know that the *Graceful Galleon* is sailing south, more or less." He pointed straight across from them. "Which means that land is that way…to the east. I watched at sunset, and I could still see the coast. We're not that far."

"How far do you think?"

He shrugged. "Not far."

"What if they try to catch us?"

He turned to her with a big, comforting smile. "Well, my nervous young wife, we can be thankful to the Zho that the winds are very gentle tonight." He reached his hand out. "I can barely even feel a breeze. We will be fine."

"There's more than a breeze," she replied.

"We'll be fine."

With a splash and an awkward bobble, the small boat struck the water. Arlon cupped his hands around his mouth and looked up. "*We made it!*" he hollered skyward in a coarse whisper. "*Come on down!*"

Paymer and Mogg wasted no time scrambling over the side rail before scurrying down the guide ropes.

"Where is Trilyra?" Mae'Lee fretted as Mogg reached them quickly and hopped in.

"Don't worry," Arlon replied. "She said that she would meet up with us. Hurry up, Paymer!"

"This…is…not…as…easy as…Mogg…made…it…look," the redhead huffed and strained.

"Don't fall," Mae'Lee urged.

"That…is…the…plan…Princess."

Arlon and Mogg both reached up and grabbed his ankles, guiding their flailing friend down the last several feet.

"Any sign of Trilyra?" Paymer asked, quite out of breath, as he plopped into the center of the skiff with a dull thud.

Everyone scanned the length and height of the ship.

"Nothing yet," Arlon lamented.

"What do we do?" Mae'Lee asked anxiously.

Arlon shrugged. "She said that she would meet up with us."

Paymer dug out a pair of oars. "Should we take off?"

Mae'Lee jerked her hand towards the deck. "*Look!*"

Everyone glanced up. A deep orange glow played along the rails, and a wide trail of white smoke began to drift towards the rear of the massive vessel. Moments later, unintelligible screaming and yelling echoed out from above.

"Fire!" Mogg said.

Paymer's eyes grew wide. "You don't think..."

Arlon nodded. "The diversion."

"Freaky."

"Smart," Mae'Lee mumbled. "I think."

Paymer whirled his head around. "What do we do?"

Arlon squinted and gnawed on his bottom lip. "Let's wait...just a little longer."

"Oh, no!" Mae'Lee gasped.

"What now?" Paymer asked.

And then, they saw him.

Or, more importantly, he saw *them*.

A ship's mate was nearly hanging over the rail...and starting to point and yell.

"This is not good," Paymer muttered. "We need to go...*now!*"

A second crewman rushed up to the rail. A much bigger crewman. The boat wobbled and shook.

"The winches!" Arlon yelled. "They're trying to crank us back up!"

Mogg dropped to his knees and ransacked the bags and satchels. "Where is a blade?!"

Mae'Lee bent down and yanked out a sword. *"Here! Take it!"*

Mogg snatched the weapon and lunged for the first rope. "Everyone get down!" he yelled.

The nose of the small boat was already out of the water, and the whole skiff was beginning to sway.

"Hurry!" Mae'Lee screamed.

Mogg drew the sword back and swung hard.

SSSSSWWWWAAACCKK!

The rope sliced cleanly, and the front of the boat smacked back down into the sea, sending Mogg and his sword hurtling to the wooden floor. Arlon bent down and retrieved the weapon and struggled to establish stable footing.

He drew it back. "Watch out!"

SSSSWWWWAAAUUUNNNGGGG!

The sword slammed into the thick rope but immediately rebounded back, almost striking Arlon in the leg.

"Careful!" Mae'Lee hollered.

The back of the narrow boat wobbled and rose higher out of the water.

"They're trying to dump us!" Paymer yelled. "Hold on! And stay low."

Arlon settled in a firm stance and chopped at the rope again. And again.

"It's fraying!" Paymer announced. "Keep going!"

WHHHAACCKK!

WHHHAAAACCKK!

SHHHHWWTAAANNNGG!

The frazzled rope finally split and their craft splashed down hard, rocking so violently that Arlon was launched out into the water, headfirst.

"Arlon!" Mae'Lee screamed. "Where is he?!"

Paymer pointed. *"There!"*

Mogg snagged an oar and thrust it towards him. "Take this, my friend."

Arlon coughed, spitting out a mouthful of water before rubbing it out of his eyes and clutching the oar with his left hand. A few seconds later, a dark object fell from above and plunged into the sea with a tremendous splash.

"Watch out!" Paymer yelled, glancing up. "They're throwing things at us!"

Mae'Lee scooted closer to Mogg. "Pull him in," she said. "Pull him in. Careful."

Paymer dropped to his knees to assist hauling their waterlogged friend back aboard. "Did you lose your sword, pal?"

Arlon struggled to raise his right hand and the long sword came into view, trailing behind. Mogg grabbed him and started to lift.

"Watch that right shoulder," Mae'Lee cautioned.

"I'm okay," Arlon replied as he slithered over the edge and flopped in like a huge fish. "I'm okay. Where's Trilyra?"

"Look out!" Paymer yelled, hurling himself over Mae'Lee and throwing his arms over his own head.

KKEERRRSSPPLLAAASSSHHHHH!

A second projectile narrowly missed the nose of the boat and bobbed back to the surface.

"We've got to get away from the ship!" Paymer demanded. "Now!"

"What about Trilyra?!" the Princess countered.

"If we don't get away, then she won't have anything—*or anyone*—to come back to."

"What?" Mae'Lee's face scrunched up. "That doesn't make any sense!"

Arlon crawled onto a bench. "I, I hate to admit it," he shivered. "B-but he's right."

"Whoa!" Paymer exclaimed. "When Trilyra gets back, and if we survive this mess…would you mind repeating that to her?"

KKEERRRSSPPLLAAASSSHHHHH!

"G-get us out of here!" Arlon commanded.

Mogg and Paymer shuffled to opposite sides before shoving their oars into the water and pulling back hard. Arlon watched in horror as their small craft drifted closer to the *Galleon*.

"Wrong way!" he yelled. "We need to go *away* from the ship!" He jabbed his finger to the west. "That way!"

"How do you steer this freaky thing?" Paymer hollered out in frustration.

Mae'Lee frantically pointed at Mogg. "Row harder on the right side!" she explained. "You steer using the oars! Like the reins on a horse."

"I hate to tell you, but this is a bit harder than riding a horse, Princess," Paymer quipped as he flailed away with his oar.

"Watch out!" Arlon yelled, ducking down.

KKEERRRSSPPLLAAASSSHHHHH!

A huge explosion of whitewater erupted straight up and came crashing down, soaking all four of them and most of their supplies.

Paymer wiped his terrified face and blinked several times. "That was too close!"

Arlon glanced back. "We need more distance!"

"We're working on it!"

"Work faster!"

Paymer squinted. "Now you're starting to sound like—"

"*Trilyra!*" Mae'Lee screamed. "Look there!"

Everyone followed the path of her excited hand way up to the deck. She was right. Trilyra's silhouetted form was in a full sprint along the rail, backlit by a spectacular wall of orange fire and broiling billows of white and gray smoke.

"Wow," Paymer muttered. "Now that's what I call a diversion."

Trilyra banked left and disappeared into the madness.

Paymer frowned. "Wait…where'd she go?"

"Don't worry," Arlon replied. "Keep rowing. I'm sure she has a plan."

He was right.

A few tense seconds later, Mae'Lee thrust her hand out again. "*There!*"

Trilyra seemed to launch straight towards them through the smoke and fire before plunging over the rail. At first, she rapidly plummeted towards the water but then suddenly swung out in their direction.

"Look at that!" Paymer yelled through a wide grin. "She's on a rope!"

Trilyra reached the full end of her swing and plunged into the water a stone's toss from their tiny boat.

"Come on!" Paymer urged, waving his arms. "Come on! Swim!"

"Don't just stand there, Paymer!" Mae'Lee objected. "Stick out an oar!"

He hunched over and stretched it out as far as he could. "I'm on it. Calm down."

Arlon glanced up from the crimson and orange reflection rippling across the gentle waves. "Wow. Look at that. The whole main sail is on fire."

"It's beautiful and dreadful. All at the same time," Mae'Lee observed. "I hope none of them gets hurt."

Scores of people were now crowding the rails, and dozens of ropes and buckets were being slung overboard in a noisy and desperate bid to quench the expanding blaze. Trilyra finally reached the skiff, and Paymer and Arlon hauled her aboard.

"That was really something," Mae'Lee said to her.

Paymer offered a sloppy pat on her soaked back. "That may have been the freakiest thing I have ever seen!"

Trilyra hunkered over with her hands on her legs, struggling to catch her breath. "Glad…y-you…liked…it."

Arlon knelt down and smiled at her. "That was brilliant. And courageous. And incredible. And…just…*yeah!* Wow!"

Her eyes met Mogg's through the steady drips of water falling from her drenched hair.

"By the Red Leaf, that was well done, Woman of the South." He brought his hands together along with a subtle bow and even more subtle smile.

"Th-thank you, m-mighty Vish'tar."

"You know that we weren't trying to leave you," Arlon said. "We had to—"

"Y-yeah, I know. Y-you had to get away f-from those crates. It was a good call. I w-would've done…the…same."

She slowly straightened up and pivoted back around towards the fiery ship. Her eyebrows shot up. "It looks like…that sh-ship…is in trouble."

"Actually," Arlon chuckled, "I think that the *Graceful Galleon* is a lot safer now…now that Trilyra of Ammodis is *here* and not *there*."

She nodded with satisfaction as the amber light from the distant inferno highlighted all of their stunned faces. "You're probably right."

"Nice little diversion," Paymer noted as he sat down and returned to rowing.

"Rather...a wise *strategy*," Mogg corrected, plunging his oar into the water to match Paymer's rhythm. "First, the fire distracted our enemies from our escape. And second—"

"And *second*," Arlon interrupted, "by destroying their sail, you slowed them down!"

"So they won't be able to chase us," Mae'Lee added.

"That was the plan."

Paymer looked up. "A great plan."

She shot him a fast glance. "Actually, this was all Arlon's plan. I just...*improvised* at the end."

"Wait a minute," Arlon protested, holding his hands up. "If you remember, this was all Mogg's idea. He's the one who said that we should split up on the ship. So, he had the perfect plan."

"Well, I wouldn't call it *perfect*," Paymer countered.

Mae'Lee folded her arms. "Uh, excuse me? We all just escaped from a ship full of dreadful people who wanted to harm us, and now we have our own boat, and food, and water...and we have each other. So, that sounds pretty perfect to me."

Paymer shrugged. "We are missing someone."

Mae'Lee paused and brushed the hair out of her concerned face. "Oh, you mean…Hort."

Paymer sighed. "No, I wasn't talking about him."

"Then *who* are you talking about?" she pressed.

He held up his oar and admired it.

"We don't have Royal."

Mae'Lee traded glances with Arlon. "We don't have *who?*" she asked.

"Royal."

"You mean our Royals?" Arlon asked. "Our gold Royals? Because I have—"

"No," Paymer insisted. "I mean *my* Royal."

They all stared at each other.

Even Mogg looked bewildered.

"So, who is this Royal?" Arlon asked again. "You aren't talking about the Princess, I take it?"

Paymer shoved his oar back into the water. "It's not a *who*, it's a *what*."

"I am totally confused," Mae'Lee admitted.

"I'm right there with you," Arlon agreed.

"Oh…it doesn't matter," Paymer balked. "It's gone. It's okay."

Trilyra reached under her wet cloak. "Perhaps our heartbroken friend is speaking about this!" In a grand gesture, she drew out a long, glimmering sword and held it aloft. A mixture of pale moonslight and deep orange flames danced across its mirrored surface.

"Royal!" Paymer squealed. "You found my new shiny sword!"

Trilyra lowered the impressive weapon and delivered it to him, handle first. "You're lucky," she said. "I found it right next to my bow."

Arlon was shocked. "You…*named* your sword?"

"Of course." Paymer pulled it close, relishing every little detail. "All great swords have names. We have a saying about naming swords in Orania."

"Oh, no…here it comes," Trilyra moaned.

Paymer took a deep breath. "It's something like '*Great swords are given great names by great people after great events*.'" He paused. "I think I might've missed another *great* in there somewhere."

Trilyra looked rather disappointed. "Wait…that's it?"

He continued to study the weapon's craftsmanship. "Yep. Something wrong?"

"Oh, I don't know," she replied, unslinging her bow from her shoulder. "It's just that your little proverbs are usually longer. A lot longer."

"And usually way more convenient," Arlon jabbed.

Paymer's face contorted. "Really?" He shrugged with a smile. "I hadn't noticed."

Trilyra finally sat down. "So, where'd you get the name?"

"Well," he began, "since this little beauty set me back quite a few coins...I named it *Royal*."

"I think it's a lovely name," Mae'Lee said.

"And coming from a royal, that's royally nice," Paymer replied as Mogg returned to rowing.

Trilyra looked around. "So, I see...two swords...and...my bow, which is probably now ruined. What else is in our inventory?"

Arlon bent down and dug out another blade. "*Three* swords. And somewhere else in this soaked mess, there are two knives. And...plenty of food—"

"Now *wet*," Paymer quipped.

"Yes, Paymer, plenty of food...*now wet*. And drinking water, and our documents and maps—"

"Now *wet*."

Arlon frowned. "Probably. And our Rone fragments. And our Dragon claw."

"And two shields?" Trilyra asked.

"*One* shield," Arlon corrected. "And, uh, *zero* Sevasti masks. Unless you've got them hidden under your cloak somewhere?"

"I saw them," she admitted. "But I decided against snatching them. Weapons were more important."

Paymer leaned back. "I agree."

"How about money?" she asked. "We're gonna need horses whenever we get to wherever we're going."

Arlon squinted and stared at the floor. "We should have enough. If we need more…we could probably sell a sword I know."

Paymer picked up Royal and brought it close to his mouth. "Relax, sweetheart. That silly Dunamai from Soteria didn't mean it."

"So, I know that every time we make a big escape, I seem to ask the same thing, but where are we going? What are we going to do?" Trilyra looked around. "And I hate to break it to you, but I don't think this little boat is meant for sea travel."

"You're right, it's not," Mae'Lee said. "We call them tenders back in Edra. They are used to ferry people and supplies once the bigger ships make harbor. I used to see them every day from the palace."

"Well, this little tender won't be ferrying anything or anyone if we have a storm like last night," Trilyra declared. "Do we have any idea of where we are?"

Arlon pointed over her head. "That way is east. We were close enough that I could see the coast at sunset. I think that we should all take turns rowing and head for land. Two can row, three can sleep."

Trilyra nodded as she squeezed water out of her cloak. "Sounds like a plan."

Mae'Lee looked worried. "How long until sunrise?"

Arlon scanned the skies. "Probably seven or eight hours, I guess."

The Princess seemed even more worried. "But, without the sun, how will we stay on course? What if we just row around in circles all night?"

A wide grin broke out on Arlon's face, and he leaned closer to her as he pointed into the sky. "You see that group of really bright stars…right there? There are seven of them. Three in a line, up and down, and then four more just above those?"

"Oh, yes," she said, nodding. "I see them."

"That, is the constellation Omada-Proto."

"My mother called those the *tree stars*," she said. "Because it reminded her of a tree."

Arlon nodded. "I guess it does."

"One of those is my uncle," Paymer noted. "On my mother's side. I, uh, I know that sounds weird. Just ask me later…carry on, pal."

Arlon raised his eyebrows. "Okay, then." He traced his finger lower in the sky. "And now, Mae'Lee, if you will follow those three stars, the trunk of the tree, down to the horizon…that way will be east. More or less."

"Always?"

"Always."

Paymer raised his dripping oar out of the water and aimed it at the constellation. "To my uncle's tree!" he announced.

Arlon smiled.

"Yes, Paymer…to your uncle's tree."

He didn't want to open his eyes.

It led to bad things.

Being awake meant rowing.

And rowing meant…*aching*.

Every muscle (from the waist up) burned with unyielding and insufferable pain. For some on the boat, it even hurt to breathe. A night and a day and yet another night of rowing left Arlon, and all the others, supremely exhausted and sore beyond measure.

And so he lay still on the cold, uncomfortable wood bench with a rolled up, damp cloak as a miserable pillow. Even the fresh sunlight kissing his cheeks failed to cheer him much.

It is morning at sea.

Again.

But something was wrong.

Something was missing.

Arlon kept his eyes shut and listened.

It was quiet. Too quiet.

No splashing.

Wait, he thought. *Nobody is rowing?*

The boat felt perfectly still.

Could it be…we made it?!

Arlon jerked up (which the sudden pain made him instantly regret) and glanced about to find more questions than answers.

He was in the boat.

But nobody else was, except for a single rower with his back to Arlon. And he wasn't rowing; he just sat there in a dark cloak with his hood up.

Arlon's heart raced. "Where is everybody?"

"They…took them," the rower replied.

That voice…that's not Paymer. Or Mogg.

I know that voice.

It can't be.

Arlon inched his trembling hand closer to his sword. "*Who* took them?" he asked.

"The same ones…who left me here."

Arlon's fingertips reached the cold steel of his blade. He did his best to retrieve it without making any sound louder than the gentle lapping of the morning waves against the hull. He tried to buy a little more time. "And…who…left you…here?"

The rower spun around and peeled his hood back. Arlon instantly recognized that round face, that shaved hair on the sides, that shy smile.

It can't be!

"*Hort!*" he exclaimed before he could stop himself. "Hort?"

"Hello, Arlon."

"Hort?"

"It's me."

"You're…*alive?*"

Hort released a sigh. "I hope you're not…disappointed."

Arlon tried to blink away the tears that began to drown his eyes. "No, no," he whispered, his voice cracking. "No. I…I just…can't believe it. I…saw you. I saw—"

"*The Dragon?*" Hort interjected, setting his oar down. "You watched the Dragon carrying me away?"

Arlon nodded.

"You knew," Hort said. "Didn't you?"

"Knew what?"

Hort stared down as his own hot tears started to form. "You knew it was going to happen. Didn't you?"

Arlon lowered his sword discreetly. "I, uh, I saw…a vision. That's all…just a vision."

The teardrops were collecting on the tip of Hort's plump nose and dripping onto his lap. "I...know."

Arlon scanned the area. There was no land, just endless sky and endless ocean. And now, endless questions.

"Where is everyone else?" he asked.

"They took them."

"Who?"

Hort's bloodshot eyes looked up. "The people we've been running from."

"Who?"

"*The Order*."

Arlon's mind raced. His heart pounded louder and louder. "The...Order?!" He whirled around, panic-stricken. "*How? When?!*"

"While you were sleeping. They took them, and returned...me."

No! The Princess! Paymer. Mogg...

"Except Trilyra," Hort continued quietly. His trembling voice grew distant and heavy. "They, uh, they threw her overboard. I couldn't stop them."

Arlon jumped up and searched the water in every direction. *Trilyra!*

"They knew that she wasn't...you know...one of us." He glanced up at Arlon. "You can sit down...you won't find her. It was hours ago. She's...gone."

With a reluctant sigh, Arlon returned to his seat. The burden of Hort's terrible revelations made his aching chest feel like lead as he sat in the silence of grief. But the silence didn't last long. A faint sound drifted across the waves. A familiar sound.

What was that?

Hort nodded with a pained, troubled smile. "You need to know something."

What is that sound?

He found it difficult to speak. "What, uh, what do I need to know, Hort?"

"The truth."

It sounds like…flapping?

Sails? A ship?

Arlon wrestled against the flurry of emotions that boiled inside. "The truth about what?"

"The truth about Pelias."

More flapping. And a rushing sound.

Arlon gritted his teeth. "Oh, that…well, I already—"

"No. You don't."

"Look…Trilyra already told—"

"No!" Hort rose up with a cold stare. "Even she doesn't truly know."

"What are you talking—"

The source of the sound finally came into view.

The Dragon!

But it was far too late.

Hort slowly closed his sorrowful eyes. "Don't forget us."

The dark, angular form of the menacing beast soared low over the ocean waves. It approached with stealth and speed as it flew up behind Hort and snatched the boy out of the boat with its powerful forelegs. With a mighty burst of wind and a horrific roar that rumbled like rolling thunder, Terras Telos bolted straight up into the clear sky with its helpless prey. Arlon exploded into more tears and reached out his hands.

"Hort!" he cried. "*Hort!*"

"We know you hurt," Trilyra called out over her shoulder. "All of us hurt. My cursed right arm feels like it's gonna crack and fall off."

Arlon blinked hard in a shocked state of disbelief. Trilyra and Mogg, mostly silhouetted by the warm sunrise, were facing away from him with oars in hand. Paymer was passed out at the back of the skiff under two makeshift blankets, and the Princess was sleeping (in a most uncomfortable position) along the bench off to his left with a folded pair of trousers tucked beneath her head.

"I can't believe you're up already," Trilyra remarked, as the morning glow highlighted the wispy edges of her blonde hair. "You've only slept a few hours."

"You're...you're here," Arlon muttered, allowing himself to smile just a bit. "You're all...here."

"Of course we're here," Trilyra replied dismissively. "And better yet...we're almost *there*." She pointed ahead with her oar and his squinting eyes followed.

Trees! Hills!

As he rose up to take in the comforting view, Arlon did his best to shake off the chilling memory of his recent dream. Unfortunately, his success was limited. One word kept bothering him.

Dream.

Dream?

That didn't feel like a dream.

He bent down and gently rubbed Mae'Lee's shoulder.

Dream...or...or...vision?

"Wake up, your Highness," he whispered before shifting around and lobbing a half-eaten apple at Paymer's head. "Get up, pal."

The Princess yawned sweetly, and an incoherent stream of gurgling sounds drifted from Paymer's lips.

"It's time to get up, you two," Arlon insisted. "We made it to the coast."

Three oversized rabbits dropped between Arlon and Paymer, and they both glanced up from their roaring beach campfire on the edge of the sandy woodlands.

"There," Trilyra announced victoriously. "I've done my job this morning. Now, have you two done yours?"

Mae'Lee was busy spreading their soaked satchels and wet clothing on a sturdy framework of sticks nearby. "They seem to think so," she replied.

Trilyra set her bow down and winced as she massaged her right arm. "Where's Mogg?"

"Out scouting the landscape," Paymer responded. "Looking for enemies and such."

"I hunted out into the forest quite a ways. I didn't see anyone."

"That's good," Paymer said before lowering his voice. "The less Therion savages we meet, the better."

Arlon selected a rolled parchment and spread it out, securing the corners with several rocks. He placed his index finger on the map and motioned for her to look. "To answer your question…six days ago, we sailed from here…Port Final. In Orania."

"That's old news," she smirked.

He slid his finger down the document. "And then we sailed south for three days."

"And then the big, bad storm," Trilyra added.

Mae'Lee shot her a look. "Don't remind me of that dreadful storm."

Arlon nodded and stopped tracing his finger. "And then the big, bad thing that the Princess doesn't want us to talk about," he whispered playfully. "And, on the fourth day, while the Sevasti delegation and their Ammodisian guide were enjoying the wonderful comforts of your new rooms in the brig—"

"Comforts?!" Paymer interjected. "That place smelled like a wagon-load of stale goat droppings."

"While you all were in jail," Arlon continued without missing a beat, "the ship didn't make much progress. The crew spent most of that day fixing the damage."

"I heard their freaky hammers," Paymer said, playing with a pair of gold coins. "It sounded like huge woodpeckers. I couldn't sleep. And Mogg snores. Sometimes. When he's real tired."

Arlon traced his map-finger to the right. "The night of the fourth day, we escaped and started rowing to the east."

Mae'Lee smiled and glanced skyward. "Towards my mother's tree stars."

"And we rowed and rowed," Paymer added. He shoved the coins into the palm of his right hand before concealing them in his fist. He tapped it on Arlon's head and opened his fingers. The coins were gone. "And I can prove that we rowed and rowed…I've got the blisters to show for it. I sure wish I could make those disappear."

"And we rowed east on the fifth day, and all last night," Arlon said, tapping his finger along the coast. "And we ended up, probably…right around…*here*. On the sixth day." He straightened up and gestured beyond Trilyra to the south. "See those mountains in the distance? Unless this map is incomplete, that should be the northwestern edge of the Plou—"

"*Ploutonians*," Trilyra said. "You know that I lived in the foothills of that mountain range, right? I saw those mountains every day. Every single day."

"Well, yeah, but Ammodis is on the *southern* side of the Ploutonians. And Polichlor is much further east."

"I know where my own capital is. I just want to know where *we* are."

"We are in danger, Woman of the South," Mogg announced quite abruptly, sneaking up behind her. "That is where we are."

Paymer flinched, trading glances with those near him. "Whoa! Did anyone else see that? He just appeared out of nowhere."

Mogg bent down and nabbed one of the rabbits by its long ears. "As will the Kray of these woods, Paymer. So keep a sharp watch."

"You gotta teach me that trick," Paymer implored.

Mogg pulled out a knife, plunged it beneath the rabbit's neck and sliced down through the abdomen.

Arlon refused to look, preferring to stare out at the gentle rhythm of the incoming waves. "How, uh, how do we avoid meeting them as we travel to this legendary cave-place, or whatever?"

With a quick motion of his skilled hands, Mogg ripped the rabbit's hide from its bloody, plump body. (Even though Arlon didn't see it, the sound alone was unnerving.) "Avoiding Kla'aven Wins'orr is an ill thought. They have guidance that we need. And by the Red Leaf, I tell you, we will meet them." Mogg wrenched the creature's head off and pitched it into the fire.

"The only doubt which remains," he muttered, "is *when*."

In a word, the woods were...unusual.

They were *unusually* thick and had grown unmistakably thicker, especially since just after midday. Their stout, level branches were *unusually* high from the spongy mat of dead pine needles that blanketed the dense soil below. And finally, they were *unusually* quiet.

It was the unusual silence that fascinated Arlon the most as they navigated the forest in a southeasterly direction; a mysterious and dangerous forest that he had visited a hundred times in a child's vivid imagination. He held back a grin and shook his head.

Mother, you wouldn't believe where I am today. I am in the wilds, following one of the wild men of the western reaches. He took a deep breath and plodded along behind Mogg. Arlon pictured his mother journeying beside him sporting her favorite blue dress and wearing her kindest smile.

Actually, Mother...you wouldn't believe a lot of things that have happened of late. And it will probably be a long, long time before I can tell you the half of it.

He blinked away the threat of tears.

I've had to do things that I'm not proud of...I admit that freely. But I pray that the passing of time will judge me in a better light. And I hope, above all else, that you will be proud of me.

"You alright up there?" Paymer's concerned voice called out above the muffled crunching of dry pine needles and tiny sticks.

Arlon didn't try to hide anything. "Just, uh, just thinking about back home. About my mother, that's all."

Paymer upped his pace and drew alongside with an encouraging grin. "And that's okay, pal. I think about my little brother and my mother all the time, too. I know I don't talk much about her, but I do think about her. A lot."

Arlon glanced over and patted his shoulder. "And you know what? I just know that your mother is out there, somewhere, and she's thinking about you all the time, too."

Paymer's comforting expression instantly fell. "No. I gave up on that kind of thinking a long time ago. That kind of hope doesn't help make things better…it just seems to make the hurt last longer."

"I understand, but it doesn't matter if we hope or hurt…what is true is still true no matter how we feel. And if your mother is out there, then she's probably thinking about you as often as she can."

Paymer sighed. "You're right, I guess. But it's been a long time."

"Time doesn't change what's true."

"And you're probably right *again*. That's twice. Wanna go for three times?"

Arlon chuckled. "Maybe. Is there a prize?"

"How about…no more Oranian proverbs for a whole week?"

"Now that, my friend, is very tempting."

Paymer narrowed his eyes while tilting his head to the side. "Back home, we have a saying about temptation."

"Very funny."

The tired group crested a small ridge, and the forest floor began sloping downhill, allowing for a more leisurely pace. Arlon was glad for the small break.

He glanced back at Paymer. "So, tell me, what's your mother's name?"

"Vyssini."

Arlon's face lit up. "Like the star?"

Paymer bobbed his head. "Just like the star. My grandfather loved to study the sky." His freckled face blushed somewhat. "Would you believe that he named all eight of his children after stars and such?"

"Eight? Really? I don't think I ever met anyone who was named after a star."

Paymer pulled his new sword out of the sheath and carefully practiced a few moves. "Yeah, it's kinda freaky. Sometimes at night I'll look up and say, '*well, hello to you, Uncle Rowda, and Uncle Branduda*' and '*good evening, Aunts Lelini and Pheryshini and Gaellini and Harth'mar.*'"

Arlon counted on his fingers and then rechecked his math. "Uh, that's only seven."

Paymer pointed Royal straight up and balanced it in his left palm. "Oh, sorry…yes, and *Aunt Ulth'mar*. But she died before I was born." He grabbed the hilt. "I never met her."

"Well, to be honest," Arlon began, "I think I only know where three of those stars are."

"And to be honest, I will never forget where any of them are," Paymer responded. "Except for Aunt Ulth'mar. Anytime our family was together, my mom's kin would each take me outside and remind me where their particular star was." He grinned. "If I would point out their star without being shown, some of them would even give me money or some other treat."

Arlon was glad to see his friend's mood improve. "Sounds like some great memories."

"Yeah, there have been some." Paymer looked away and almost laughed. "Even some really great memories. But…then…" His voice tapered off.

"But then…you remember what happened to your parents."

Paymer looked down. "Uh, yeah. Especially my father."

"I am so sorry," Arlon said, not much above a whisper. "It's hard for me to imagine what that must feel like."

Paymer kicked at the ground. "Oh, I don't know. You might have it worse than me."

Arlon turned his head. "How so?"

"Well, what's worse…knowing that your father is dead, or not knowing who he is, and not knowing if he's alive or dead?"

That caught Arlon a little off guard. Paymer noticed.

"Hey, look pal. If that was inappropriate or if I—"

Arlon shook his head. "No, it's fine. You're just saying out loud the kinda things that I keep saying inside my head. All the time."

"Nobody wants to hear the things I have rolling around inside my head, pal," Paymer joked as he practiced jabbing with his sword.

"I think the answer is…I really don't know."

"Don't know what?"

"The question you asked me," Arlon replied. "About which is worse."

"Oh."

"They're both painful…but in different ways, I guess. It's hard to compare." Arlon hesitated. "Not to sound too depressing, but for you…there is a grave somewhere that you can visit. But for me…I, uh, I don't even know if there is a grave, or if there is one …I don't know who's in it."

Paymer exhaled long and low. "That's…"

"Yeah."

"Whoa."

The two walked side by side in mutual silence for a while. Mogg hurried, taking full advantage of the sloping terrain, and each had to adjust their pace to match his. Trilyra, keeping watch at the back of the pack, grabbed her bow and scanned the woods from side to side.

"Do you really think there's a grave?" Paymer inquired respectfully. "You know, earlier you told me to keep the hope alive that my mother is still out there…somewhere. How about you? Do you think your father is still out there, somewhere? Alive?"

Arlon stared long and hard at the huge trees that lined their path. "Most of my heart says…*yes*. Yes, my father is alive."

"But most of your head is not quite so sure."

Arlon squinted at him with a flat smile. "That's probably a good way to put it."

"I'm right there with you, pal."

The two friends bumped shoulders.

"I wish you guys would talk louder," Mae'Lee grumbled from a few yards back. "I've only been able to hear a few phrases every now and then. It's difficult to eavesdrop when your hearing isn't what it should be."

Paymer slowed down and allowed her to catch up. "Actually, your Highnessness, we were just having a fascinating discussion about your loveliness and charm." He held up his sword. "This, this may be Royal, but you, Princess, are a royal *beauty*."

Mae'Lee blushed and patted his arm. "Paymer, you must grow a new freckle every time you lie."

He looked dejected. "Whoa...I was being totally serious. That hurt!"

Mae'Lee shook her head and pointed down. "The only thing that *hurts* is my feet. It's been awhile since we've walked all day like this." She kept her voice down. "I think our Therion guide is forgetting that we are not horses. These bags are getting—"

Mogg immediately raised his right arm and brought the convoy to an awkward, sluggish stop. Arlon glanced at the others, but all he found was a variety of confused shrugs. Trilyra placed an arrow on her bowstring and swiveled around.

"What's wrong, Mogg?" Arlon asked. "Why are—"

"Lay the sword…on the ground," Mogg insisted firmly.

Paymer took a few steps forward. "Why?"

Mogg pivoted around with a deadly serious stare. "*Now.*"

"Okay. Alright." He bent down. "There. My shiny new sword is on the ground."

Mogg wasn't finished. He glared at Trilyra. "And your bow."

She seemed even more reluctant than Paymer but held her peace. Mogg gestured towards the ground.

"Your…bow," he repeated. "Slowly."

She complied. Slowly.

Mae'Lee leaned into Arlon's ear. "What's going on?"

"By the Red Leaf!" Mogg suddenly cried out, bringing himself around very methodically. "May peace reign between us."

"Who is he talking to?" she whispered.

"I have no idea," Arlon whispered back. "And I hope we don't find out."

Mogg ventured a few steps away from the others. "You have no enemy among the Kla'aven Mage." He paused before bringing his hands together directly over his chest. "I have come seeking only provision."

Paymer looked frantically in every direction (even up). "I think he must've hit his head when he fell during the storm," he mumbled.

Arlon's eyebrows shot up and he pointed. "Look again, Paymer."

He did.

"Oh...freaky."

At first, it almost seemed like the dark brown bark of the thick trees was somehow shifting. Then, long thin branches appeared. Almost a dozen branches. The shifting bark shifted away from the trees. And they stood there.

"The Therion," Mae'Lee gasped.

Arlon was awestruck. "The Kla'aven Wins'orr."

Paymer appeared terrified and flitted his eyes about. "They...are...all...around...us...pal."

"Yes...and...they...have...big...spears," Arlon noted through gritted teeth and a forced smile. "So...don't...move...pal."

Mogg leaned forward slightly. "May peace reign between Kla'aven Wins'orr and Kla'aven Mage."

"You speak as the Kray," a voice boomed out (Arlon couldn't tell which one it was), "but you appear as the Vice. And among the Vice. And the Vice are the enemies of all the Kla'aven."

"Please, my brothers. I appeal for an audience," Mogg implored without sacrificing his dignity.

Arlon detected a little movement off to their left. One of the men, clad in long brown furs and a dark painted face, approached, javelin in hand.

"And who makes this appeal?" the warrior asked, drawing near.

Mogg turned to confront him. "The Vish'tar of the Kla'aven Mage."

The warrior came to a stop and could not hide his surprise. "By the Red Leaf," he mumbled. "It is the Mark of Power." He offered a reverent bow. "I am Gollmarr, of the Kla'aven Wins'orr."

Mogg stepped closer and placed his right hand just above the man's heart. "May peace reign between us."

The warrior narrowed his skeptical eyes, first at him and then at Arlon and the others, before returning the formal gesture. "Your enemies are my enemies, my brother."

"We have come seeking provision. And our cause is just."

Gollmarr lowered his arm. "Your cause may be just. But you walk among the enemies of the Kray."

Mogg lowered his hand as well. "It is an ill thought. I walk among those of the Mark of Power." He motioned towards them. "Please, my friends. Reveal that which needs to be seen."

Paymer handed his satchels to Arlon, and Mae'Lee set her shield and bags on the ground. They both displayed their birthmarks. The Therion warriors all pressed closer.

"By the Red Leaf," Gollmarr murmured. He whisked around and waved his arm. "Bring the horses!" He glanced back at Mogg. "I will bear you safely to Lycera."

The elegant, black-haired woman paced within the colorful chamber, a round room furnished with a variety of colorful tapestries suspended from the center of the arched ceiling and swooping down to meet the curved walls. By her manner (and the attitude of those attending to her) she seemed to be of some importance. "*The Mark of Power?!*" she inquired with urgency to the warrior presented before her. "Are you certain?"

Gollmarr brought his hands together. "It is well-spoken, our Kiffar. It is Mogg, Vish'tar of the Kla'aven Mage."

She relocated behind a cluster of three older men seated near her. "And he has come, on foot, within our borders? Accompanied by the Vice?"

Gollmarr nodded. "There are four Vice within his party, Kiffar Lycera. Three have the Mark of Power."

"This is a most dangerous and grievous matter," one of the elders cautioned.

"I fear that they may be spies," another warned. "Perhaps an alliance of our enemies seeking to discover our weaknesses?"

Lycera continued meandering across the room before stopping by the door. "Your concerns are noted, my brothers, but this council is adjourned. I must hold a private consultation."

"But, Kiffar—"

"Adjourned," she insisted. "Gollmarr will remain."

The feeble trio rose and trudged out, murmuring and bickering and casting disapproving glances the entire way. Lycera smiled at them before closing the thick door and folded her arms with a curious look in her eyes.

They were alone.

"Why have they come?" she asked.

"The Vish'tar claimed that they needed provisions."

"In what direction did you discover them?"

"They were traveling south, my Kiffar. A half-day's ride from the sea."

Lycera circled him in a slow, wide arc. "A most...*unusual* path for any Kray of the Kla'aven Mage," she deliberated. "To proceed along the western sea, yet not along the eastern borders? Most unusual. And lightly armed? With no horses?"

"It is well-spoken."

"And adorned in the fashion of the Vice?"

"It is also well-spoken, my Kiffar. Even the Vish'tar."

She shook her head. "Contrary to the fears of my short-sighted advisors, these are clearly not spies. I do not sense deception…I sense…great *desperation.*"

Gollmarr took in a deep breath. "And I sense great wisdom in your words, my Kiffar."

A strange smile matched a strange resolve rising in her voice. "I sense…a great…*opportunity.* An opportunity for Lycera, Kiffar of Kohmmitain, to expand her influence in the Kla'aven Wins'orr."

His confusion was more than obvious. "I fail to understand."

She finished her thoughtful circling and lowered herself into a tall, narrow chair. "A gift of mercy…an alliance forges, Gollmarr. And an alliance forged is a path to power. And, as I rise…others loyal will rise with me. I will seek a Mei'bia."

He brought his hands together. "It is well-spoken."

"It is time. Bring them before me."

Arlon detected sounds.

Twigs popping, feet shuffling.

A group was approaching.

"Someone's coming," Paymer whispered.

"A *few* someones," Arlon replied under his breath.

"What did you say?" Mae'Lee grumbled. "It's bad enough to wear these blindfolds, but when you're having hearing problems, it's positively dreadful!"

"Don't worry, Princess," Trilyra assured quietly. "There's not much to hear. Yet."

"Actually, I'm beginning to appreciate these sacks over our heads," Paymer joked. "I am really enjoying this wonderful shade of black."

"Just like you, pal," Arlon chuckled. "Always looking on the bright side."

Paymer took a few hard sniffs. "And, I am really enjoying this wonderful aroma of rotting potatoes. It's quite stimulating and—"

His words turned to gurgling and spitting sounds. "Oh, freaky. I think…I just swallowed a dead bug."

"Hey, Paymer?"

"Yeah, Arlon?"

"It's probably not too terribly smart to spit inside of a bag that is on your head."

"Yeah…my face…just…found that out."

Arlon sensed a hand on his shoulder a fraction of a second before the brilliant afternoon light blinded his unprepared eyes. He still couldn't see that much, but the air was much improved.

"The Kiffar of Kohmmitain will consider your request," Gollmarr's somewhat-familiar voice announced.

A pair of rough hands began patting up and down Arlon's clothing as his vision readjusted.

"You will appear before the Kiffar...unarmed."

"Oh my," Mae'Lee gasped. "Would you look at that."

Paymer followed her upward gaze and his jaw sprung free. "Whoa." An instant later he put his hand below Arlon's chin and applied pressure. "Look, pal."

Arlon's blinking eyes traveled up the side of the nearest tree trunk, past the first few layers of broad branches, and stopped.

What?

What could that be?

It reminded him of a rough-hewn floor, only upside down (and well over a hundred feet above the ground).

"What is it?" Mae'Lee whispered.

Paymer whirled about and scanned the immense structure. "It's like a ceiling. A huge, freaky ceiling. It goes on and on."

"A ceiling, in the forest?" Trilyra added. "For protection?"

Mogg pointed with a smile. "A pol'kyll."

Paymer squinted. "A pole keel?"

"The sky dwellings of the Kla'aven Mage."

Arlon was beyond fascinated. "Wait...are you saying that there's a *city* up there? On top of that...thing?"

Gollmarr strode over to him and brought his gloved hands together. "It is well-spoken." With a quick motion of his arm, several warriors assembled and guided their stunned guests onto a platform inside of a sturdy, wooden cage.

Arlon admired the series of heavy ropes that connected them to the mysterious Therion village far overhead. Mae'Lee clutched his arm as their crate rumbled and jerked before rising steadily higher and higher.

"I have never liked heights," she admitted.

"Don't worry...these ropes are plenty strong," he assured her.

Paymer leaned towards a tense-looking Trilyra. "Wrong's wrong?" he whispered. "Do the heights bother you, too?"

She glared straight ahead as an impressive corral, filled with dozens of horses, stretched out below them. "*Cages*, Paymer. Cages bother me. Especially when I'm inside one without any weapons."

"Oh, come on! This is great!" he countered, soaking in the dizzying sight straight down through the bars. "And I like the view."

Arlon stared overhead, struggling to hold back a giddy smile. "Well, Paymer, I think that's about to get a lot better."

Trilyra took a deep breath. "Or, a whole lot worse."

BBBUUUUUUUAAAAAAHHHHHH!

A long, mournful horn blast wailed into the distance as the cage finally passed through a gap in the wooden canopy and back into the blaze of the late day sun before settling to a shuddering stop.

Paymer looked around in wonder before leaning towards Arlon. "Whoa, you were right, pal. Very right."

Mae'Lee released his arm. "I have never even imagined that there would be a place such as this!"

Arlon tried to take it all in. *Mother,* he thought, *I wish you could be here to see this. I considered Mogg's city to be incredible, but this is truly amazing.*

Gollmarr opened the gate and led them out into the bustling walkways. The short convoy wound their way towards a brightly painted, multicolored round building near the center of the sprawling platform, now filled with hundreds of Therion inhabitants engaged in innumerable activities (and plenty of gawkers who froze in mid-step as the Vice strolled by). Arlon lost count of the smaller round structures that dotted the surreal landscape, most which he figured to be houses.

A few of the enormous trees continued rising above the elevated city. But most of the giants of the forest had either been sawed even with the smooth floor, or lobbed off several feet above it and converted into cylindrical storage bins or hollowed out as sturdy water tanks.

"Look!" Mae'Lee encouraged, gesturing off to their far left. "Gardens and farmland!"

Paymer did and shook his head. "Farms…in a city in the sky!"

Huge tracts (of what Arlon assumed to be barley and corn) lined the edges of Kohmmitain, and each cluster of the Therion's round huts appeared to share a sizable garden, and even a smattering of fruit trees every now and then. And chickens. Lots of chickens.

Gollmarr and a handful of warriors finished guiding the party to the middle of the village before opening the door to the meeting hall.

"The Kiffar awaits you," he beckoned.

Trilyra didn't look too happy as she peered through the dark doorway. "Another cage," she whispered. "A prison."

"I don't think they wish us any harm," Arlon muttered quietly. "They could have easily killed all of us long before now."

"Not if I would have kept my bow," she grumbled.

"Come on," he said, trying his best to smile. "It's not like we have anywhere to run."

"May peace reign between us," Lycera declared in earnest, rising from her seat as the captives were shuffled in. "I greet you on behalf of the Kla'aven Wins'orr."

Mogg came to a standstill and brought his hands together. "Your enemies are my enemies, noble Kiffar."

Arlon surveyed the half-dozen contorted and viciously skeptical faces that flanked their seemingly gracious host. He couldn't shake the feeling that—if any of those men had anything to say about it—their chances of finding assistance were about as high as Trilyra's spirits at the moment.

And the odds of being killed…much higher.

Lycera stepped forward. "It is an honor to stand before those graced with the Mark of Power."

All eyes turned to Mogg.

"It is a greater honor," he said, "to stand before those who have shown grace and mercy to strangers in need."

She appeared to be struggling with an appropriate response. "It is only right to ask, what business has brought the Vish'tar of the Kla'aven Mage, along with the Vice, into our lands?"

"By the Red Leaf, a matter of great urgency, noble Kiffar," he replied with grave solemnity. "A matter which made this journey…a *necessary* trespass."

Lycera commenced a thoughtful pace. "There are many…even many in this chamber…who harbor concerns about your true intentions."

He spread his hands out as wide as possible. "It is an ill thought. Our intentions are just. We have only three requests." Mogg took a brief moment to stare at Arlon and the others. "According to the wisdom given us by the Northern Elders."

A stunned gasp rippled through the Therion meeting hall. Even Lycera halted. "You have spoken with the Northern Elders?"

Mogg brought his hands together as the murmuring subsided.

A visibly shaken Lycera returned to her seat. "And what are your three requests, honorable Vish'tar?"

"We request safe passage through your lands as peace reigns between us," he began. "We also request suitable horses with provisions for our long journey." He paused.

Lycera arched forward as her dark eyes narrowed. She nodded. "I swear by the Red Leaf, these things you shall have in abundance. What is your third request?"

"*Information*, noble Kiffar. Guidance."

She squinted even further as a fair amount of quiet murmuring broke out among her disgruntled companions. "And what is the nature of this information you seek?"

Mogg approached with cautious expectation and locked unblinking eyes with her.

"For this, Kiffar...we speak...*alone.*"

Mae'Lee yanked left on the reins.

Twice.

Her horse didn't seem to care. Twice.

"I, uh, hate to complain," she called out to the others riding ahead of her.

"The royal princess of Avdira complaining? Really?" Trilyra couldn't resist sneaking in a playful jab from the back of the pack. "What's changed?"

"I think my horse is broken, thank you very much."

"Of course, it's broken," Paymer hollered over his shoulder with a lighthearted smile. "Or you wouldn't be able to ride on it, Princess."

Mae'Lee sighed. "No, Paymer, not broken...but *broken*. Like, it's not working right."

"I agree with her," Arlon replied quickly. "These Kray-trained horses are a bit more stubborn than our last ones. Or even the ones before that. Mine really knows how to get its own way. And that way isn't usually *my* way."

"Sounds like another stubborn creature of the Kray I know," Trilyra almost shouted. "One with dark hair and only two legs."

Arlon thought about holding back a chuckle, but he let it slip out naturally. It felt good to smile and laugh once again. After a tense afternoon and a mostly-sleepless night under the uncertain hospitality of the Kla'aven Wins'orr, he knew that they all needed to release a little pressure.

But he also knew that different and dangerous pressures were surely lurking not too far behind. Or ahead.

The day had been quiet and uneventful for the most part. They had spotted another ancient, vine-encrusted set of crumbling ruins off to the east, but decided to leave it as unexplored for now.

"How did you get it, Mogg?" Paymer asked as they reached a stony stream at the bottom of a shallow ravine. The stubborn horses seemed quite eager to suddenly be led to the cool water. "How did you get directions to this Dragon's cave place?"

"*Potential* Dragon cave," Trilyra corrected as she dismounted. She stooped to fill her water satchel and splashed a little in her own face as well. "Remember, it's probably just a children's story."

"You can call it whatever you want," Arlon barked back. "But unless you've got a better plan, it is our best bet."

"Betting is for gamblers," she replied.

Mogg tethered his powerful steed and crunched through the wet, rounded rocks right up to her. "It is a lesson given to our children," he said as their eyes met. "But to many of the Kray, it is not only a lesson. To many, it preserves a tale of our past."

"What tale?" Mae'Lee asked, stretching her legs. "Would you mind sharing it with us?"

Trilyra raised her eyebrows. "It'll be easy, just pretend we're silly little children."

"I'm always ready for a good story," Arlon countered. "It'll make me feel like I'm back home in Soteria."

Paymer cupped a handful of water and dumped it on his own head. "And if it's a good enough story, I might be able to make a new Oranian proverb out of it!"

"The Kray also have such sayings, my friend," Mogg said. "And some arising from this very tale."

Mae'Lee was growing impatient. "And will you *please* share the story with us?"

Mogg knelt beside the creek and sipped water from his palm. "It is an old tale. Among the oldest of those preserved by the Kray. It is said that a great Dragon had reached the end of his long years. The beast collapsed, deep within the forests of Wins'orr. The dying Dragon was sought out by a foolish people, who came to hunt it with javelins. And swords. And dogs."

"Did they get it?" Arlon asked.

Mogg shook his head. "The Dragon crawled away, seeking refuge in a cave, a cave inhabited by scorpions at the base of the mountains. None dared pursue it into the darkness, but instead released their animals."

Arlon leaned forward. "Did they get it?"

Mogg glared at him. "A pack of dogs entered the cave. The foolish people waited. A bright light appeared. And then, one beast came out...a beast of terror...the Mal'korr." His eyes grew wide. "It seemed as a range wolf, but with the girth of a bear, possessing a scorpion's tail and a scorpion's sting."

"Oh, my," Mae'Lee gasped.

"Now that's freaky," Paymer whispered. "I mean *really* freaky."

Trilyra yawned. "Sounds made up to me."

"Our elders have said that the dying Dragon's last sorcery turned their animals into an eternal guardian of the cave. On that same day, the Mal'korr killed all those who sought the

Dragon, save for one young man, who returned to his village with gashes on his arms and legs."

"And I guess we just have to take that one young man's word for it," Trilyra grumbled. "Come on, isn't it more likely that he made it all up? Or maybe *none* of it is true…it's a just a story you tell little kids to keep them from going into dark caves. Just to scare them."

"Trilyra! Let him finish." Arlon insisted.

Mogg took a deep breath. "And since that day, it has killed all those who have ever foolishly sought to enter the cave. The area is forbidden to the Kray. None have trespassed that cursed region in many, many, many generations of my people."

Arlon cleared his throat while glancing over at Trilyra. "So, uh, you have anything to say now about this *silly little children's bedtime story*?"

She folded her arms. "Let's see…we have Mogg, a *young Kray man*, telling us a story that he heard when he was a little Kray boy. Even if some of it is true, you know how legends can take one little event and turn it into some huge deal!"

"We have a saying about that," Paymer began.

Everyone instantly shot him a serious glance.

"And," he said, looking around. "I…will…keep it to myself."

"The Sevasti thought that there might be some truth to it," Mae'Lee said.

Trilyra sighed. "Which proves absolutely nothing, Princess. Nothing."

Arlon glanced over at Mogg. "What was the name of the creature?"

"The Mal'korr."

"And this Mal'korr…it's kind of like a wolf, but the size of a big bear?"

"Don't forget about the scorpion's tail," Paymer added, placing his arm behind his back and striking at the air just overhead.

Mae'Lee shivered and rubbed her arms. "It sounds positively dreadful."

"It sounds positively fake," Trilyra grumbled.

Arlon ignored her. "And this scorpion-wolf creature, can it be killed?"

"The Kray do not know."

"You know…you never did answer my question, Mogg," Paymer noted.

"What question is that, my friend?"

"How did you get the Kaffer lady back at the tree-city place to give you directions?"

Mogg grinned. "The *Kiffar* was persuaded by a Mei'bia."

Paymer's face scrunched up somewhat. "A Mei'bia?"

"It is an…*agreement*. A promise between the Kray."

"What did you promise to her?"

"It was a Mei'bia of peace. Peace between Kla'aven Mage and Kla'aven Wins'orr."

Arlon looked puzzled. "But, I thought you said that you were already at peace?"

"This Mei'bia is more than just peace," Mogg replied. "It is a Mei'bia of alliance. May their enemies be my enemies."

"Oh," Arlon nodded. "Well, that makes sense. Is she powerful in her Kla'aven?"

"As the Vice would say…*no*, she is not. But she will use this agreement to seek it."

"Whoa!" Paymer exclaimed. "Wait, did Mogg just say '*no*'?"

"*Yes*. Yes…I did," Mogg replied with a strange smile.

Paymer was beside himself. "What is happening here? That was freaky! He just said *no* and *yes*. I heard him. You all heard him!"

Arlon chuckled and brought his hands together. "It is well-spoken, Paymer of the Kla'aven Orania…a Vice who bears the Mark of Power."

"And tattoos," Mae'Lee quipped with a cute grin. "Don't forget about those. Oh, and freckles. Lots and lots of freckles."

Trilyra didn't look too happy as she ambled towards her horse. "Really? You guys are excited about Mogg saying *yes* and *no*? How about we get excited if *yes, he's right,* or *no, he's not wrong* about this Dragon cave situation?"

"How far is the cave?" Arlon inquired.

Mogg stood up and glanced south. "Three days."

Arlon rose as well and glared at Trilyra. "Then in three days we will see if this is just a bedtime story…or something a lot more dangerous."

Paymer glanced up. "But, uh, we want dangerous. *Right?*"

Arlon nodded.

"Let's go."

Chapter 26

Paymer squinted, straining to see above the huge trees. "They're not as pretty as ours," he said.

Arlon gently kicked his horse and drew closer. "What are you mumbling about up here?"

"The mountains," Paymer replied, pointing off with his free hand. "The Anatellians back in Orania look much nicer. And taller."

"Oh, that again."

"Uh, correction," Trilyra bellowed out. "Kyrochalla is the highest mountain, freckle boy. Anywhere. And it's in the Ploutonians."

"You can't prove that," Paymer blurted.

"Don't need to. Everyone knows it's the highest."

"I'm pretty sure she's right," Arlon admitted.

"Are you really taking her side?"

"Is anyone else as tired as I am about this silly argument?" Mae'Lee asked. "Taller. Snowier. Prettier. That's all we've heard about the last three days."

"It's his fault," Trilyra muttered. "I was gonna let it go."

Paymer spun around in the saddle and jabbed his finger into his own chest. "My fault? You're the one who keeps stirring the pot of controversy, Woman of the South."

"You know," she growled through clenched teeth, "you're starting to make me regret that I went back to get your stupid sword."

"Oh really? Well, you're starting to make me regret—"

"Ever since we left tree city," Arlon interjected, "you two have been bickering about mountains. How about we just enjoy this wonderful view? In silence. Beautiful, sweet silence."

Mae'Lee straightened up. "Silence? Sounds like a lovely idea."

"It's still her fault," Paymer grumbled.

Arlon just shook his head.

A rattled Trilyra leaned to the side in her saddle and looked past them. "Something seems to have caught the attention of our Kray leader."

She was right. Mogg quickly dismounted from his horse and strolled towards an overgrown rocky patch on the east side of the southerly trail.

"Something wrong?" Arlon called out.

Mogg climbed onto the pile of moss and root encrusted stones, meandering through tufts of tall, dry grass which jutted up through the cracks. "Actually...something *right*," he replied.

"Is it water?" Paymer asked. "Like a spring? I'm thirsty!"

Mogg shook his head. "Not *water*. A *warning*, my friend."

"What?"

Arlon hopped off his horse and led it closer to the rocky rubble. "What do you mean?"

Mogg picked his way carefully along the weathered boulders before pointing down. "This is a warning pile."

Trilyra brought her horse to a stop and glanced about. "It just looks like a bunch of rocks to me."

"Well then, Trilyra of the Prettier Mountains," Paymer began, "just take another look around. Do you see any other big rocks nearby besides these?"

"Paymer's right," Arlon said. "This isn't natural. Someone put these here. And by the looks of it, a very long, long time ago."

"It was placed here by the Kray," Mogg commented. "In a narrow, triangular shape."

"Like the point of an arrow," Arlon said.

"Like the point of a *javelin*," Mogg countered.

"Sorry, yes, a javelin."

"A javelin? Pointing at what?" Mae'Lee asked.

Mogg turned his attention towards the mountains. "Pointing at danger. This is a warning for all those traveling. Warning all to stop here. To continue further invites harm."

Paymer squinted. "Harm. Danger. Warnings. So, all that's a good thing, right?"

Mae'Lee couldn't hide her concern. "A good thing and a bad thing."

Arlon stooped low and selected a fractured chunk of weathered granite. He turned it over and over in his hand. "Looks like someone went to a lot of trouble just to warn people about a children's story."

Trilyra looked away. "It's still just a bunch of rocks."

He tossed the stone. "You don't look as confident as you sound."

Mogg shielded his face from the sunlight overhead while squinting up. "The day is not yet half-spent. I say we move forward."

"You say that like we have a choice," mourned the Princess. "But we don't have much of a choice, do we?"

Arlon locked onto her brown eyes and took a deep breath. "No." He sighed. "Not if we want to make things right, and stop the Dragon."

She dropped her head. "I know. I guess that wasn't really me…that was just *hope* asking."

"That's okay," Arlon responded with a smile. "My mother always says that *'hope gives light in our darkness and strength in our weakness.'*"

"I like that," Paymer piped up. "I'm gonna remember that one. I will, uh, change it a little, of course."

"It's a lovely saying, but right now I don't think I have that much hope," she admitted.

"It only takes a little," Arlon offered with a wink.

"So, tell me, Mogg," Paymer said, swallowing hard. "How close do you think we are to that bear-scorpion thing?"

An expressionless Mogg returned to his horse and immediately retrieved a javelin.

Paymer's eyebrows shot up. "Well, okay, then." He grabbed his own gleaming sword and clutched it at his side. "We are *that* close."

Silence.

And danger.

Arlon found it strange how often those two seemed to mingle…especially in the weeks since they had fled the Karaval.

Not that their trek was entirely quiet. The sloping forest floor had become a broken patchwork of flat, grayish granite surrounded by dark stretches of hard soil, all accented with brown streams of dead pine needles collecting in the cracks. The rhythmic clomping of the horse's hooves provided a mesmerizing percussion that eased his nerves somewhat, but he still couldn't help flinching with every sudden flutter of a bird or any quick movements his nervous eyes imagined on either side (and they imagined quite a few).

Even though he had felt the jagged jaws of a Dragon and witnessed the terror of a Snow Serpent, the prospect of an ancient creature equipped with a lethal tail crashing through the trees with murder in its beastly heart terrified Arlon in surprising ways. But he pressed on. And though he would never admit it, he secretly harbored a growing desire that Trilyra was right.

A bedtime story is certainly much better than a nightmare of a monster, he thought.

Mogg jutted his right hand up and brought his own horse to a silent standstill just before topping a low ridge rimmed with a sporadic mess of craggy bushes. Paymer and Arlon relayed the familiar signal to the girls trailing them, and one-by-one they eased to a tense stop. Trilyra instantly snagged an arrow and brought her bow into battle position. Her squinting eyes raced in every direction.

"I didn't think bedtime stories were so dangerous," Arlon whispered back as he grabbed his sword.

"I'm not worried about bedtime stories," she growled without even looking at him. "I'm worried about running into a savage pack of Therion warriors like my delegation did on our way to the Karaval."

He fought back a big grin. "Oh, I see. Well, that's a nice story."

"If you had been there," she retorted quietly, "I bet my bow you wouldn't be wearing that little smirk. Trust me."

Mogg clambered up the slope, all the while keeping his muscular body plastered against the rocky soil. It was obvious that he was intently studying something in the distance through the cover of a tight cluster of shrubs. Moments later he slid down in a cascade of falling dirt before scurrying back towards his expectant friends. Mogg patted his dusty hands across his dustier garment.

"What did you see?" Paymer whispered.

"A cave," Mogg replied. "It matches the description given to me by the Kiffar."

Arlon glanced at Trilyra. "So the cave is real," he muttered.

"Of course there is a cave," she huffed, rolling her bluish-green eyes. "We're in the mountains. There's probably thousands of caves." She paused and pointed up. "And it might be a good idea to start looking for a big and dry one, it'll be dark soon. And those clouds in the west are getting lower. And thicker."

"And I hate getting wet, thank you," Mae'Lee sighed. "Especially while sitting on a wet horse."

"And nothing smells worse than a wet horse," Paymer added quietly.

"Does the cave look big enough for us and our horses?" Trilyra inquired.

Mogg's serious expression turned grave. "It is large enough, but according to what I have seen, it would be most unwise to venture within."

Paymer hunched forward and squinted. "Why? What else did you see?" His voice trembled somewhat. "Did you see the bear-stinger thing?"

Mogg turned and locked eyes with him. "Bones. That is what I saw, my friend. I saw many piles of bones."

"Oh, uh…that's nice. Piles of dead things."

Mae'Lee rubbed her arms. "Let's hope that we don't become one of those piles."

Mogg glanced back over his shoulder. "It would appear that we have found the cave. And the Mal'korr."

"Lots of animals eat other animals," Trilyra replied. "Probably most of them. We're in the mountains...I bet my bow it's a bear. Or a family of bears."

Arlon rubbed his chin and stared up into the branches of a few nearby trees. "Well, there is one way to find out. Mogg, did you say that the Kiffar gave you some of that Kray sleeping powder?"

_____

Paymer struggled to get comfortable, but the rough bark and frequent twigs seemed to be making things difficult. "Arlon!" he whispered harshly. "Do you think I've climbed high enough?"

Arlon and Mae'Lee both glanced over from their perch atop a broad branch in a neighboring pine. Arlon nodded. "Sure. There's no way a huge creature could reach you way up there. You're safe."

Paymer didn't seem convinced. "What about its tail? And its freaky stinger?! Could it reach way up here?"

"Trust me, pal. You're in no danger. I mean, unless you fall and land on your head. Or I guess you could die slowly and painfully if you get a life-threatening splinter." Arlon winked.

"Very funny."

The Princess watched with growing concern as Mogg and Trilyra approached the mysterious cavern carrying a large clump of fresh, bloody meat. The pair set it on the ground quietly, and Trilyra stood guard while Mogg seasoned the bait with a pouch full of powder.

"Do you really think it will work?" Mae'Lee whispered.

"That freaky stuff knocked all of us out," Paymer replied. "Remember?"

"Barely," she mumbled.

Arlon glanced back at her. "Mogg said he's seen that powder knock out everything from horses to bears." He smiled with confidence. "If there's a creature in there, it'll put it out."

"What if it doesn't?"

"It will."

"I hope you're right."

"I am."

He looked away. *I hope, Mae'Lee. I really hope.*

"Do you think our horses are safe?"

He nodded. "They'll be fine. They're pretty far back."

With careful and silent steps, Mogg and Trilyra retreated from their work, keeping watchful eyes on the cave's dark entrance and vigilant hands on their weapons.

"What now?" Mae'Lee asked. "Do we just sit and wait?"

"I, uh, I think that they also have a plan about that," Arlon responded. "Just watch."

The brave pair far below scurried to the base of the closest tree, and each selected a handful of fist-sized rocks. Trilyra nodded over at Mogg, and they both hurled their stones at the mouth of the cave and then unleashed a volley of yelps and screams that echoed eerily into the distance.

Mae'Lee flinched and grabbed Arlon's arm. "I, I wasn't quite ready for that!"

Without a moment's delay, Mogg and Trilyra scrambled up into the tree and continued to saturate the late-afternoon air with terrifying shrieks while ascending higher and higher.

"I don't know what's more dreadful," the Princess complained, "thinking about that terrible creature or hearing those terrible sounds!"

"I know what you mean."

Before long, Mogg reached a comfortable position and Trilyra braced herself at the junction of a couple of broad branches with an arrow readied on her bow. They each made a final yelp or two and then stopped.

Everyone strained to listen.

The forest grew unusually still.

Even the afternoon breeze died away.

Nothing moved.

Then…a sound.

Or a feeling.

Arlon perked up.

What was that?!

Arlon laid his hand on his chest.

It must've been my heartbeat.

He was wrong.

Mae'Lee hunched forward, keeping a firm grip on his arm. "Do you hear that?" she asked.

It began somewhat like a far-off moan. A deep and mournful rumbling. Arlon clamped his trembling eyes shut and concentrated harder. The unsettling roar was growing louder, and it was certainly emanating from the direction of the cave.

Mae'Lee buried her face into his back. "I'm scared."

He detected scraping and snorting.

Whatever it was…it had to be huge.

"That's alright, Princess," he said, patting her arm. "I am, too."

"*Look!*" Paymer almost shouted, thrusting out his finger.

They saw it.

"Wh-what is that?" Mae'Lee quivered.

A sharp, thin figure emerged from the center of the darkness, bobbing and swaying in gentle arcs from left to right.

"Is that another giant snake?" she asked.

"No," Arlon countered. "It's not a snake."

"Then what is it?"

"That's…the…stinger!" Paymer shouted as he frantically scrambled up to the next branch.

The elongated nose of the beast appeared next, its black nostrils flaring in rhythm with the foreboding hum of its own labored breath. Its frightful head was truly massive (easily larger than a wooden barrel) followed by a dark, hulking frame that Arlon estimated to be the size and weight of two plow-horses. The creature crawled along on four stubby legs with long, vicious nails crowning each thick foot.

Paymer was shaking. "It's the—"

"Mal'korr," Arlon whispered in awe.

Mae'Lee shoved her head in his back a second time. "Oh! I can't look!"

Trilyra yanked back on her bowstring and released an arrow which sizzled through the air before slamming into the beast's right side. The Mal'korr erupted in a horrific wail before clamping on the end of the protruding arrow with its jaws and quickly ripping it out of its hairy, scaly flesh.

She fired another.

The second round glanced off the side of the scorpion-like tail and tumbled to the dirt. The Mal'korr whipped its stinger back and forth, striking wildly in various directions. She grabbed a third arrow, but Mogg stood up and apparently cautioned her to wait.

"Why did he do that?" Paymer whispered in confusion.

Arlon paused for a moment and pondered the situation. "I'm not sure…maybe he wants the Mal'korr to take the bait, rather than being worried about defending itself."

Paymer acted like he was firing a bow. "Uh, she made it a little late for that, don't you think, pal?"

Arlon half-nodded and half-shrugged.

Mae'Lee peeked over his shoulder.

"Look!" she urged. "It might be working."

In slower and slower arcs, the beast's frantic tail motions began to subside as it lumbered in the general direction of the irresistible bloody treat.

Paymer straightened up. "Here it goes."

The Princess squeezed Arlon's arm. "I hope this works," she said.

"We'll know in a few seconds," he replied.

"And if it doesn't?"

"Well," he offered with a forced smile, "then I hope you like living up in this tree."

The Mal'korr came to a snorting stop several feet away from the bait and swung its tail around before jutting it out over its head. With methodical precision, the beast lowered the enormous stinger until it hovered just above the meat.

A sudden chill shot through Arlon, as he imagined himself lying flat on his back with the monster's tail inches from his chest.

I am never leaving this branch, he told himself.

In not much more than a blur, the creature plunged the sharp tip into the meat three times in rapid succession. The Mal'korr hesitated for the briefest of moments before racing up and devouring the mess, filling the air with disgusting snorts and splattering blood all across the ground.

Mae'Lee shuddered with excitement. "It ate it!"

Arlon squinted. "It shouldn't be long then."

It wasn't.

The first thing they noticed was that the creature's terrifying tail started to bobble and droop. The dazed Mal'korr's head swayed from side to side as it careened about in a drunk circle, etching a deep trench in the soil with its immobilized stinger dragging behind.

"It's working!" an excited Mae'Lee whispered with a huge grin. "It's working!"

Its front legs gave way first, plunging the beast face-first into the ground leading it to erupt with a mournful wail. The Mal'korr's huge body convulsed violently, but it was only a matter of time. Finally falling silent, the monster rolled over onto one side, thrashed its hind legs a bit more…and then went completely still.

Mae'Lee almost jumped up. "*We did it!*"

In her jubilation, she slapped Arlon on his injured shoulder. He jerked back and couldn't help but yell a little.

"*YEOWWWWW!*"

"Oh! I am so sorry!" she cried out, her brown eyes reddening up a bit. "I got carried away…I didn't mean to hurt—"

He held his hand up and winced. "It's…it's okay. I understand. It's a big moment. Things happen."

Paymer stretched and breathed a sigh of relief. "So, what do we do now?"

Arlon gestured towards the others. "I think that maybe we should wait on them."

Mogg and Trilyra had already scurried back down to the surface and were cautiously approaching the slumbering beast, weapons at the ready.

Paymer cupped his hands around his mouth. "*Hey!* Do you want us to come down?"

Trilyra raised her arm and shook her hand silently.

"Told you," Arlon smirked.

"Just checking, pal. But trust me…I'm happy to stay right here."

The Princess sat back against the tree. "That makes *two* of us."

Mogg reached the head of the Mal'korr first and fished out a small leather pouch. He tiptoed up to its flaring snout and gently poured another healthy dose directly into both nostrils.

"That thing's gonna sleep for a week," Paymer chuckled.

Arlon's face scrunched up. "If it's lucky. But I…uh, I don't think they plan on letting it wake up." He slowly drew his finger across his neck.

Paymer's eyes went wide. "Oh…the *long, long* sleep."

"Mmmm-hmmm," Arlon nodded.

Mae'Lee looked into her lap as Mogg approached the beast's midsection with a long javelin. "Oh, dear…I don't want to watch."

Trilyra stood back with an arrow readied on her bowstring while Mogg took up a strong stance with both hands on his sharp weapon. He reared it back and then jammed it into the beast's chest with his full weight coupled with a loud warrior's cry.

"HEEEEYAAAAHHHHH!"

The javelin penetrated deep into its side, and the monster immediately roared in agony, flailing all four legs as its body contorted in sudden pain. Mogg caught the full brunt of the reaction and was tossed a dozen yards through the air as the creature's tail whipped around and slammed squarely into his chest.

Trilyra ducked down and dropped her bow, replacing it with a sword just as the stinger swung around for a lethal second pass. The writhing Mal'korr struggled to its unstable feet and stamped about, but Trilyra lunged beneath its hairy belly and rolled to the opposite side in a tumbling cloud of dust.

Paymer jutted out his arm. "Uh-oh…Mogg's in trouble! He's not moving!"

"Come on," Arlon urged. "Roll over and get up. *Get up!*"

There was little doubt that the enraged Mal'korr had noticed its fallen assailant and was straining hard against the effects of the powder to reach him. By all appearances, Mogg was either unconscious or dead and plastered face-down in the rocky dirt.

A frantic Trilyra screamed and waved her hands wildly to attract the attention of the beast, but to no effect. It lumbered towards its easy prey. Arlon's heart raced. He knew that, even if Mogg wasn't dead, he would be shortly. Trilyra lunged at the Mal'korr, hacking at its neck with her blade. The creature roared in anguish but plodded forward.

She raised the sword overhead and plunged it in deep with the force of both hands. A fearsome wail echoed off the rocks and the beast took aim at her with its unsteady tail. She jumped sideways just in time to avoid a fatal strike as the stinger whisked past, ejected a stream of dark purple venom that stained the ground.

"Why won't that thing die?!" Paymer cried out.

"Maybe we can't kill it," Arlon mourned.

"Don't say that!" Mae'Lee replied.

Trilyra raced over and yanked out her bloody sword an instant before the scorpion-stinger whirled by again. In a desperate and dangerous move, she threw her arms around the tail and the Mal'korr easily swung her off the ground. Her sword went tumbling through the air, but she managed to keep her grip long enough to arc around and land firmly on the monster's back.

"What is she doing?!" Paymer yelled.

Arlon shook his head. "Surviving."

The Mal'korr paused and unleashed a fearful volley of quick strikes at his unwelcome stowaway, soaking its own hairy, scaly back with repeated jets of dark venom.

Paymer rubbed his arms. "They are both going to die."

"Stop saying that!" Mae'Lee yelled.

Trilyra struggled to keep her balance as the creature raised its tail high above for a killing strike.

Paymer stared down. "I can't watch."

The Mal'korr began its lightning-fast assault, plunging its stinger directly at her defenseless head. Trilyra bolted to the side, allowing the stinger, once again pulsing with venom, to plunge into the creature's own back. Seizing the opportunity, she threw her full weight on the tail and held it down. The enraged Mal'korr reared back like a bucking horse and flung her away, unleashing a sickening wail that

made the Princess cover her ears and cower in
fear.

"Did you see that?!" Arlon hollered.

Paymer didn't dare look up. "I told you, I
can't watch."

"No," Arlon continued. "No, the
Mal'korr...she made it sting itself!"

"What?"

"Trilyra made it sting itself. Right in the
back. And something's happening. Look!"

Paymer and the Princess both snuck
reluctant peeks.

Trilyra and Mogg were both sprawled out
on the ground (over fifty feet apart), but the
gurgling and injured Mal'korr was flipped over
on its back, its head thrashing about.

"I think it's dying!" Arlon said.

Paymer frowned. "Maybe it's just the
powder."

"No, I don't think so. This looks different."

One by one, each leg of the Mal'korr shook
to a deathly stillness as the scorpion-tail first
waved, then wiggled, and finally collapsed across
the ground like a falling, crumbling log.

"It's dead! It's dead!" Arlon yelled,
scrambling to climb down.

"Arlon, wait!" the Princess urged. "Are
you sure it's safe?"

He dropped down to another branch and
glanced back up. "Stay here."

"Whoa there, pal," Paymer scolded. "Wait up. I'm coming with you!"

By the time they reached the bottom, Trilyra had managed to crawl up to one knee and dust herself off. "Don't worry about me," she announced as they rushed up. "I'm fine, more or less. Check on Mogg."

It looked bad.

Their Kray leader hadn't moved an inch.

"Please tell me he's breathing," Paymer muttered as Arlon dropped beside their fallen friend and carefully rolled him over.

Arlon hunkered close to his face. "He's…alive! He's breathing!" He looked around with a huge grin. "He's breathing!"

Paymer knelt as well and lightly tapped his face. "Hey, Mogg? Mogg? Wake up." He paused. "Wake up, or that Woman of the South is gonna get all the glory for this big day!"

Trilyra rose to her trembling feet and whirled about, wiping the sweat off her flushed face. "Has anyone seen my sword?"

Arlon pointed off to his right. "It's over there, on the other side of the…uh, dead Mal'korr."

She squinted. "Are you sure it's dead?"

"Uh, well…no, not really sure. But I think so."

"*Think so* and *know so* are about as different as life and death, my young Soterian friend." She made her cautious way up to its head and stared at its nostrils. "But...it appears that this time, you are correct." She placed her hands on her hips. "What you see before you is one rather dead Mal'korr."

Arlon couldn't resist one more jab. "That's the biggest, scariest, *hairiest* children's story that I've ever seen."

Trilyra sauntered over to her blade and snatched it up. "My dear Arlon," she began, wiping off the sword, "if you wish to see another day, and, uh, *not* become your own little children's story, then I suggest that you never speak of that again." She glared at him. "Ever. As in...not ever again. Understand?"

He squinted. "Speak of what again?"

She nodded and ambled towards the Mal'korr's tail. "That's what I thought. You may be stubborn, but you are a fast learner."

"How is Mogg?" another female voice called out, getting closer with every word.

Paymer glanced off to his right. "Well, he is kinda mumbling, Princess."

A wide grin broke out across Mae'Lee's soft, red cheeks as she knelt down. "I've never been so happy to hear such pitiful news."

"I don't know about *pitiful* news," Arlon replied while strolling off and staring at the cave opening. "But I do know about some *good* news."

"Yeah," Paymer said, nodding towards the immense carcass nearby. "The Mal'korr is dead."

Arlon bit his bottom lip. "I can't argue with you. That is good news. But I have even *better* news."

Trilyra kicked through a small pile of bones as she headed towards the creature's tail. "Please enlighten us."

Arlon stopped and pointed into the darkness. "The Mal'korr is proof…that somewhere…in there…is a Dragon. Or the remains of a Dragon."

"More relics!" Mae'Lee exclaimed.

"And if that cave is big enough to hold a freaky Mal'korr and a Dragon," Paymer noted, "then it will be big enough for all of us and our horses tonight. The sun will be setting soon."

Trilyra slid out her sword and held it high overhead. "Speaking of *big enough*…I think that this stinger will be big enough to make a handy little weapon." Her blade accelerated downward and cleanly severed the long, sharp point with a quick yet deep crunch.

"Careful," Mae'Lee cautioned. "It's probably still filled with dreadful poison."

Trilyra retrieved her prize and held it aloft proudly. "Actually, Princess…that was part of my intention."

"Oh," Mae'Lee shivered. "Well, keep it away from me."

Paymer looked impressed. "That thing is as big as a dagger!"

Trilyra sliced it through the air and spun it around. "And a dagger like no other. Anywhere."

"Just think," Arlon said, spreading his hands out. "From this moment onward, you will be known as Trilyra of Ammodis, the Mal'korr slayer."

"And you will have that freaky stinger to prove it," Paymer commented.

"You'll probably be celebrated as a great hero to the Kray," Arlon surmised. "I can hear it now…'*Behold! The Woman of the South who ended generations of fear and danger.*'"

"But, uh, also '*Behold! The girl who ruined one of our best children's stories,*'" Paymer said. "They, uh, the Kray might not be too happy about that."

"She didn't ruin it," Arlon protested. "She just…*added* to it."

Paymer's freckled face scrunched up. "Yeah, let's hope that's the way they see it."

Mae'Lee wasn't the least bit distracted by their teasing. "Why isn't Mogg waking up?" she asked. "He doesn't appear to be injured."

Paymer folded his arms. "I'm guessing he hit his head. Sometimes it takes a while for people to wake up." He paused. "If ever."

"Nonsense!" she retorted. "Don't talk like that. Don't even think like that."

"Sorry, Princess."

She cradled Mogg's head. "He's going to be fine."

Paymer nodded. "You're right, he's made it through a lot worse. He's the toughest Vish'tar I've ever met."

Arlon strolled back over to them. "Well, Paymer...why don't you and the Princess stay here with the toughest Vish'tar." He locked eyes with Trilyra. "And the two of us will explore the cave for a bit."

"You don't think there might be a *Mrs. Mal'korr* hiding in there somewhere do you?" Paymer inquired.

"If there is," Trilyra replied, fastening the stinger to her side and unsheathing her blade, "then we will help the pitiful beast to join her husband."

Arlon pulled out his own sword.

"We will be back soon."

They had explored dozens of caves.

But this was different.

It smelled different.

It *felt* different.

Arlon sensed his own heartbeat while they waited for their eyes to grow accustomed to the deep darkness of the cavern. A gentle stream of cool (almost cold) air greeted their skin and slick, damp rocks crunched below as they began trudging inward with extreme caution.

Trilyra raised her arm over her nose as her face contorted. "You told them that we would be back soon," she said, keeping her voice down. "I'm beginning to disagree with you. I think this smell is going to kill us both."

"Definitely worse than a wet horse," he mumbled.

"A *herd* of wet horses," she whispered. "In a cursed dung field. In the hot summer sun."

Arlon tried to breathe through his mouth. "Yeah...that, uh, that just about describes it."

The shifting layer of damp cave stones was soon replaced by a thick bed of crushed bones matted with stiff tufts of bloodied hair. Arlon spotted something glinting in the dim light and bent down.

"Looks like we're not the first ones to make it this far," he said, extracting a rusty helmet from the sickening debris. He held it aloft and admired it. "Looks pretty old."

She ignored him and pointed. "So are those."

Arlon looked above his ancient helmet and far beyond her fingers. An enormous, elongated pile of bleached-white bones rested against the dark, damp wall of the cavern.

"The Dragon," he muttered in awe.

"A big Dragon," she mumbled back.

The final amber radiance of the long-spent sun barely accented their tired faces as they relocated a yet-unconscious Mogg (and all their horses) well inside the depths of the cave.

The Princess looked increasingly sick as they crunched through the sea of jumbled bones.

"I am sorry," she complained, "but I don't think I can sleep here tonight. This odor is dreadful. Maybe the most dreadful odor I have ever smelled."

"I know," Arlon replied as he led a horse with Mogg flung on its back. "But it gets better farther in." He waved his torch from side to side. "I think we are in the area where the Mal'korr slept. Once we get past it, the fresh air from deeper in the cave pushes it out. You'll see."

"If I live to see."

"I'm dying right along with you, Princess," Paymer grumbled, his voice echoing off the stone walls. "I'm gonna sleep right next to the fire tonight. Maybe the smoke will smell better than this."

Mae'Lee nodded. "*Anything* smells better than this, thank you."

"That is true," Arlon replied. "But not much *looks* better than this."

The others drew closer as the shifting ground transitioned to a softer bed of sand and rounded gravel. Arlon dropped his reins and jogged ahead.

"Behold!" he called out with all the confidence of a proud showman. "Behold…the Kray legends are true." He took a few more steps and held his torch aloft. "I give you…the Dragon!"

"Oh, my," Mae'Lee gasped.

Paymer came alongside her. "By the Red Leaf!" he exclaimed. "That thing is huge. Freaky huge."

Arlon nodded. "It was probably two or three times as big as Terras Telos." He bent down and touched the remains. "And these are just the bones. Try to imagine the wings and muscle and all!"

"Suddenly the Mal'korr doesn't seem so scary," Mae'Lee replied.

"But which one is it?" Paymer asked. "Do we know which Dragon that is?"

"Not yet," Arlon said, picking his way back towards them. He fished something out of his pocket and held it up. "I've already taken this tooth. We can test it with one of the Rone pieces."

Paymer was stunned. "That's a tooth?! It looks like a talon!"

"Nope…it's a Dragon tooth." He glanced off to his left. "But let's set up camp right over there and get a fire started. We could all use some rest and hot food. And then we can test it."

"This whole trip could've been for nothing," Trilyra grumbled.

The Princess looked back at her. "What?"

"We, uh, we might already have a relic from this Dragon," Paymer explained softly. "Our shields. They could've been made from the remains of this Dragon."

"Oh."

"Hey, let's stay positive," Arlon retorted firmly. "We will all know soon enough."

Trilyra gestured towards Mogg. "He won't."

"Like I said," Arlon repeated slowly and clearly. "Let's stay *positive*. Remember, you're looking at a guy who survived a Dragon's bite. That isn't supposed to happen, right?"

"I'm not trying to be negative," Mae'Lee added. "But, has anyone thought about water? I'm pretty much out."

"When Arlon and I came in the first time," Trilyra answered, "we thought we heard some kind of running stream farther back. I'll do a little exploring once we're—"

She was interrupted by a haunting moan reverberating from far deeper in the cavern.

YEEAAAOOOWW!

Mae'Lee grabbed onto Paymer's arm. "What was that?! Is there another Mal'korr?!"

Trilyra grabbed her bow. "No…I…don't…think…so."

Arlon whirled around. "That sounded…almost….*human*."

WEE-HEE-AAOOOWWW!

Trilyra nodded. "That *is* human."

Paymer slid out his sword. "I've heard that sound before. Or something like it."

Arlon looked at him. "Stay with Mogg. Trilyra and I can check it out."

"Not a chance, pal," Paymer countered. "I'm going with you this time."

"I'll stay with Mogg," Mae'Lee called out. "And with the horses."

Trilyra passed by and patted her on the arm. "Start a fire. And keep your sword out."

"I will."

———————————————————————

The bizarre and strangely familiar moaning grew louder with each advance through the silty cave soil. The well-armed trio crossed a gurgling stream before lining up side-by-side to squeeze through a modest gap in the cave wall.

"Wee-ho-ho!" the voice continued to cry out.

"Look!" Arlon yelled, jabbing his finger out at something wiggling on the ground several feet away.

"I knew I knew that voice!" Paymer replied.

"You have got to be kidding me," Trilyra mumbled, lowering her bow.

"It's Sister!" Paymer whispered.

"Wee-ho-ho," the old woman muttered as she angled her head to take a look at them. "Tell Gorimarr I'll feed him to the dogs if he doesn't let me loose! Goose. Goosey loose."

"Umm…what is happening here, guys?" Trilyra asked. "Why is that crazy old lady here in the Mal'korr's cave?"

Arlon moved closer. "I don't know...but look. Her ankles and wrists are bound. With some kind of leather strap."

"Does any of this make any kind of sense to either of you?" Trilyra inquired.

"Not a freaky bit," Paymer mumbled. "But, uh, shouldn't we...be helping her?"

"Is it safe?" Trilyra asked with a fair amount of worry in her voice. "Maybe there's a reason she's bound up."

Arlon sheathed his sword and shook his head. "You just killed one of the most fearsome beasts in the history of the Five Kingdoms, and now you're frightened of a little old woman?!"

"*Frightened* is the wrong word," Trilyra countered. "Just...*concerned*."

"*LIAR!*" Sister exploded, making them all flinch. "She's a liar! Did you see that, Agailia? Company's here. And they brought that liar again!"

"We are not going to hurt you," Arlon explained calmly as he inched closer. He transferred his torch over to Paymer. "Now...I am going to undo those straps; if that's okay?"

"Strap. Slap. Wee-ho," she screeched. "And food. Agailia?! Where's my dinner?"

He studied her restraints. "So, are you hungry? You want food? We have plenty of food."

"Handfuls. Of appfuls."

He struggled to open the latch on the leather band that was immobilizing her wrinkled, bony ankles. "Well, we…uh…we don't have any apples. But…we…do…have…plenty of food. And…" He finally flung the latch open. "…we will have a warm fire."

Her wrist strap was a much simpler affair and it quickly fell to the ground. Arlon signaled for Trilyra to join him, and they gently lifted the shriveled babbler to her unsteady feet.

"Can you walk?" he inquired politely.

"Walk. Walk. Walk," she rambled. "All the day, wee-ho! Long journey. Long." The old woman waved her only good arm overhead. "Agailia! Get those birds out of my house!"

"We need you to follow us," Arlon said. "Just follow us, okay?"

"Follow. Hollow. Wee-ho. Hollow-ho. Yes."

Trilyra moved quickly to Arlon's side and leaned into his ear. "Are you sure this is a good idea? Taking a…*crazy* woman and bringing her into our little group?!"

"It will be alright."

"It would be alright if she was that other woman we met—"

"Shendollyn."

"Yes, Shendollyn," she repeated. "If it was her—"

"It *is* her."

Trilyra's whole face frowned. "Listen. You guys told me that you would explain that whole weird business with those two women —"

"With the *one woman*."

Trilyra took a deep breath and held it longer than normal. "Would you please just tell me what's —"

"It's almost sunset, right?"

Her face contorted. "Wait…what? What does that —"

"Paymer?" Arlon called out. "Is it almost sunset?"

"Uh, sure. Any minute now, pal."

Arlon retrieved his torch as he started walking. "I think that you will understand," he said before glancing back at Trilyra. "*Any minute now.*"

Paymer nodded at her with a curious smile and then followed right behind the old woman. "He's right. It should be interesting."

She sighed before shaking her head. "You two are impossible."

"Oh, no," Arlon called back over his shoulder. "The impossible? That is yet to come."

"Do my eyes deceive me?" Mae'Lee's voice echoed out through the deep red flames of a modest fire. Her silhouetted form rose up as the search party returned in single file. "Three left me. It looks like...*four* have returned?"

The old woman couldn't remain quiet. "Wee-hee-ho. Four. Floor. Door."

Mae'Lee folded her arms. "Uh...what?"

"It's a...long story," Arlon answered back.

"Which we still don't fully understand," Paymer added.

"And they won't tell me anything," Trilyra grumbled.

"Oh," Mae'Lee said. "Okay."

Arlon stepped to the side and gestured towards their new arrival. "Mae'Lee...do you remember Sister?"

"That's not Agailia!" the old woman squealed, looking around wildly. "And get these dogs away from me! They'll ruin this new dress!"

Mae'Lee scanned the area. "Um, dogs? Could someone—"

But that was as far as she got.

Something bizarre happened.

Paymer and Trilyra took off running.

Arlon seemed paralyzed with awe, but managed to scoot back.

It began with a brilliant flash of amber light that hovered around the tiny feet of their wrinkled visitor. The haunting, eerie glow was followed by one, then two, then ten, then dozens of sparkling points of light which started whirling around her crippled frame. They spun faster, then faster yet, soon becoming bright, blurry arcs in a frantic chase. Dozens of glowing pinpricks, perhaps hundreds more, joined in the rotating fanfare like a massive army of fireflies, cocooning her entire body in a fiery shell of white and orange light.

All watched in amazement as every crack and corner of the cave was bathed in the intense beams radiating out from the dazzling display. Arlon continued backing away until he found himself alongside Trilyra, more or less.

"What is happening?" she asked, quite out of breath.

He never took his wide eyes off of the show. "Shendollyn," he replied. "*Shendollyn* is happening."

"This is…impossible," she whispered.

The mesmerizing fireball of light encapsulating the old woman rose gradually and hung in the air several feet above the rocky cave soil. Instinctively, everyone retreated further yet (even the horses struggled to get away).

"This is absolutely freaky," Paymer whispered to Mae'Lee.

The Princess clung tightly to his arm with one hand and pointed with the other. "Look! Something's happening."

The luminescent shell had faded noticeably and the myriads of flaming streaks all eased to a glimmering standstill, revealing a regally dressed woman adorned with flowing blonde hair. The majestic figure floated back towards the ground and opened her kind eyes with a warm and growing smile.

"K'Kashmalon was right," Paymer muttered. "The two are one."

"She's…beautiful," Mae'Lee replied. "Beautiful beyond words."

Paymer leaned against the Princess, beaming with a satisfied grin. "And she's from *my* kingdom."

The swarm of lights carried Shendollyn gently back to the soil, with each bright burst vanishing upward the moment her dainty feet kissed the soil.

Trilyra inched closer to Arlon. "I…think I understand now." She smiled. "But I still don't believe it."

"Me, neither," he replied with a huge smile. "But here she is."

Shendollyn took the briefest of moments to study each of them in turn. She bowed slightly. "Once again, it is quite an honor to be in the presence of the Dunamai of so many kingdoms."

No one spoke. Trilyra nudged Arlon in the back, shoving him forward.

"Well, uh, yes," he said, his voice cracking. "Uh, thank you. *Shendollyn*. We are…happy to see you as well."

The tiniest of tears began to wind its way down her fair cheek. "And now…all of you have entered into that small company of those who now know...my *secret*."

Trilyra nudged him again.

"And, uh, your secret will be kept," Arlon said. "I promise you that we—"

"*Mogg!*" she exclaimed suddenly, rushing past all of them to kneel beside his fallen form. "What has befallen the Vish'tar of the Kla'aven Mage?!"

Mae'Lee joined her. "He went down, ma'am. Fighting the Mal'korr today."

Shendollyn examined him. "He appears to have no wounds. No swelling that I can see."

"No, ma'am. But we can't get him to wake up." Mae'Lee reached out and caressed his head. "Can you help him?"

Shendollyn brushed the tears from her face as the others gathered around. "Regardless of my *reputation*, young Dunamai," she began, swallowing hard. "A reputation that I have inadvertently cultivated...I am not a witch. I cannot perform magic healings, or any such thing."

"But you helped me," Mae'Lee implored. "I've been told that I was rescued from death itself."

Shendollyn grabbed her hand. "My child...I healed you with medicine, not *magic*. And it is truly a joy to see how far you have progressed in your recovery. You have been blessed by the Zho."

Arlon knelt beside them. "You said *medicine*. Do you know of any that might help him? Is there something we can find, or make, or—"

"But he must live," Shendollyn announced. "He…must…live. The final promise of the prophecy has yet to be fulfilled."

Mae'Lee squinted. "Prophecy?"

"'*This child shall rise, this child shall restore,*'" Arlon mumbled. "Wasn't that it?"

"That is correct, Arlon, Dunamai of the Kingdom of Soteria. A prophecy revealed to me near the time of his birth. The former has been fulfilled, this child has risen to be the Vish'tar of the Kla'aven Mage."

"So, what will he restore?" Mae'Lee inquired. "What does that even mean?"

"I do not know, child," Shendollyn admitted. "But it will surely fail if he does not recover. And a prophecy can never fail."

Mae'Lee looked up helplessly. "So, we do nothing?"

Shendollyn's face grew quite serious. "A prophecy gives us confidence, but it should never lead us to negligence."

Mae'Lee rubbed his forehead once again. "So, what do we do?"

"It is difficult to find a remedy, your Highness, when one does not understand the malady."

Paymer grinned and brought his hands together. "That is *well-spoken*."

"I see that you are learning the ways of the Kray, my fellow Oranian."

Paymer blushed. "Well, yes…and we are slowly bringing Mogg around to the ways of the Vice."

Shendollyn cocked her head with a skeptical stare. "And that is a difficult and noble challenge. In all of my long years, I have rarely seen such an accomplishment."

"He actually said *'yes'* the other day. I heard him."

"By the Red Leaf," she replied with a wink, "I'm impressed."

"I thought you would be."

Something stirred inside of Arlon.

Wait.

What did she say?

"Excuse me, ma'am," Arlon interjected. "What did you say?"

Shendollyn leaned back. "I said that was impressive."

"No, no…before that."

She blinked hard and looked away. "I believe I spoke something concerning a rare accomplishment."

"No, after that. You…spoke…about…the Red Leaf." He clapped his hands together. "*By the Red Leaf!*"

Shendollyn rose up. "Yes. I was referencing a common Kray expression."

Arlon stood as well and his mind raced. "And I am referencing a common *Sevasti* medicine."

"The Red Leaf," Shendollyn whispered. "Of course. It could aid in his recovery. But, my friends, I am sorry…I do not possess any leaves of the Cardidendron."

"You may not…but we do!" Paymer announced, scrambling over to search one of their satchels. "A whole pouch full of it."

"You possess leaves of the Cardidendron?"

Arlon nodded. "We do. A gift from the Sevasti."

"Quickly, then…heat some water," she commanded. "But not too hot."

"I'm on it," Arlon replied.

"And bring me some Cardidendron leaves."

"I'm already working on it," Paymer responded.

Mae'Lee glanced up. "Do you really think it will help him?"

Shendollyn folded her arms.

"By the will of the Zho, my child."

Arlon poured some water into a metal cup before suspending it over the fire. He tossed a few sticks into the blaze and stirred up the embers. Shendollyn glanced up from Mogg's unconscious form with a puzzled look on her face.

"Where is the other young man?" she asked. "The quiet boy." She touched just above her ears. "His head was shaved, on the sides."

Arlon swallowed hard. "That was, uh, Hort. From…Thilasson." His voice trailed off.

"Forgive me," she muttered, as a pained look washed across her face. "I can see it in your eyes. Has…misfortune fallen upon the young man?"

Arlon sighed as his throat tightened.

Shendollyn glanced over at Mae'Lee.

The Princess nodded and looked away.

"I am sorry," Shendollyn whispered. "May he rest to everlasting days in the dwelling of the Zho. And may the Zho comfort your hearts."

"It's been…hard," Arlon admitted. "Really hard."

Shendollyn patted his arm with tenderness. "I understand. I have also suffered loss. Many, many times."

"It happened, a short time after we first visited you," Mae'Lee explained.

"The Dragon?"

Mae'Lee nodded.

"Not to be insensitive and change the subject," Trilyra interjected, "but, just *how* did you get here?"

Shendollyn took a deep breath. "As you all can probably imagine, *Sister,* is not up to the task of traveling and navigating over large distances. Her physical frame and mental faculties are rather…*unstable.*"

"No offense," Trilyra added, "but, she talks to people who aren't really there. And she sees invisible dogs and birds and things."

"I am not offended, Trilyra of Ammodis. It is the sad effect of our prolonged years of life."

Arlon dipped his finger into the water. It was only beginning to get warm. "So, you are fully aware of the—*other*—part of you?" he asked. "Of Sister?"

"I am. And she is aware of me. But though we are one, we still are two. Mostly."

Paymer arrived with a handful of leaves. "No offense again, but that's kinda freaky."

"So," Shendollyn continued, "I had to travel only at night, after my regeneration. I was on horseback as much as possible. But each morning, before sunrise, I had to find a hiding place, usually a cave. And then I would eat and drink before I had to restrain myself. First my ankles, then my wrists. Finally, I had a pouch of Kray sleeping dust. Just before my transformation, I would inhale a small amount."

Arlon's eyes grew wide. "So that would keep Sister asleep through the day," he said.

"You are correct, young Dunamai. At least, she would be asleep for *most* of the day."

"That's brilliant!" Paymer noted.

"It worked most of the time," she replied. "And then, at sunset, I would untie my restraints and travel on. Trust me, this wasn't the first time I had to discover a way to travel with my rather unique limitations."

Arlon tested the water once again. "But how did you know about this place?"

"I was meditating a few weeks ago and I had a Rone vision." She looked around in obvious wonder. "I saw this place, and the remains of the Dragon...all of it. I floated high above the land

and the path was just revealed to me. I cannot explain it."

Arlon nodded. "I know how you feel."

Paymer squinted. "But how did you get past the Mal'korr?"

"I presume that you are speaking of the guardian of the cave? The beast with a scorpion's tail?"

"That's the one," Paymer replied.

She pointed farther in. "I discovered another entrance which connected with the rear of this cavern. I have been back there in waiting for four days. In all that time, I only ventured out once to see the beast. It was a most fearful sight."

"You will be happy to hear that it is a *dead* sight now," Paymer announced. "Trilyra killed it." He waved his finger towards her. "She even has the stinger from its tail."

"May the Zho be praised," Shendollyn said. "You are beginning to reclaim honor for your family."

Trilyra blushed. "Thank you."

"Hot water's ready," Arlon declared as he transported the cup over to Mogg's side.

Paymer deposited his crumpled leaves into Shendollyn's hands, and she crushed them even further before dumping them into the steaming metal container.

"We need to let those steep for a few minutes," she instructed.

Arlon glanced up at her. "Since we have the time...and, uh, since all of us here already know your *secret*...would you mind telling us how it all happened? You haven't always been like this—like two people—have you?"

Everyone sat down immediately and gazed up at her.

She smiled and took a long, deep breath. "No, no, no...heavens *no*. Not always...but it has been a long time. A very, very long time."

"Mogg once told me that you were older than the trees," Paymer added, his freckled face turning various shades of red. "No offense, ma'am."

"Oh, he did?" she responded. "Well, the Vish'tar of the Kla'aven Mage is right." She closed her beautiful eyes with a satisfied smile. "I am older than the trees. In fact, throughout the long years of my life, I have seen the rise and fall of entire forests of trees. Many times over." Her eyes remained shut.

Arlon waited for a few moments. "So, what happened?" he asked.

"I have not shared my story for generations," she replied, reopening her eyes and looking around at each of them. "I have not spoken of it since before any of you were born, or even your parents, or their parents, or their great, great grandparents."

"Freaky," Paymer whispered.

"The last time I was willing to recount the events surrounding my most unusual situation, it was not to such an honored gathering as sits before me today. It was an audience…of *one*."

"A handsome suitor?" Mae'Lee inquired with an excited smile. "A prince or a king?"

It was Shendollyn's turn to blush. "Handsome suitors, or even *any* suitors, are a wonderful luxury that has escaped my grasp, your Highness."

"So, who was it?" Arlon asked.

"I do not know his name," she replied, looking off into the distance. "Indeed, I never even had the pleasure of seeing his face."

Mae'Lee's face scrunched up. "You talked to him, but you didn't see him?"

"I did not see his *face*. He was…a Sevasti, my child."

"Oh," Mae'Lee whispered. "I get it. The mask."

Shendollyn gently pushed up her own flowing sleeve. "The only thing I can vividly remember, is that he had deep scars on one of his arms."

Arlon perked up.

Scars?

On his arm.

She met him hundreds and hundreds of years ago?

"We've met a great number of very old Sevasti," Arlon said. "After the Karaval, we were invited to visit Alaithia."

She seemed impressed. "That is a rare distinction reserved for a special few. It has long been my desire to behold that wondrous fortress...even from afar."

Trilyra's eyebrows shot up. "That pretty much sums up my experience," she grumbled.

"Your experience?"

"She didn't exactly go in," Paymer explained.

Arlon cleared his throat. "She was with us," he said. "But...for some reason, the Sevasti wouldn't let her into Alaithia. She didn't cross the Firebridge."

"Oh, I see." Shendollyn turned towards her. "Well, if it is any consolation, young lady...I have not even had the joy of being as close as you. And I have definitely never been invited."

"You're right...I was close," Trilyra replied. "I saw it day after day. But I wouldn't call it a joy."

A few seconds of strained silence followed, and Shendollyn cut it short with a nod coupled with a grim stare.

"I shall never forget the long and awful screams of that night," she began. Her already pale and sculpted face drained of all expression. "Heart-rending moans billowed among the hills.

Sleep…became an impossible goal. I finally saddled my strongest steed and raced across the countryside. I rode hard in the direction of those awful moans. I rode all night, and all the next day, and almost into the following night."

She struggled to continue while her tender eyes flooded with tears. "And…then I saw him. In a valley of rocks. He looked like an enormous statue…pitiful. Painted silver by moonslight." Her voice broke.

Mae'Lee reached out and touched her hand. "Who? Who did you see?"

"The Fifth Dread Guardian. The mighty Terras Phoenix." Shendollyn glared down at her. "And then…all four of his terrifying eyes stared into mine. I wanted to flee. And yet, I had a feeling, a compulsion, to draw near to him. And so…I did." She shook her head with a flat smile. "There was such strength in him…and yet, such need. Such weakness. And pain."

"What was wrong?" Mae'Lee whispered.

"The mighty Dragon was wounded." Shendollyn spun around and pointed along the edge of her own spine. "There was a sharp hook, lodged at the base of his wing. He couldn't reach it…with his forelegs, or his teeth. It wasn't easy, but I extracted it in a messy, bloody affair."

Mae'Lee looked beyond stunned. "The Dragon allowed you to…touch it?"

"He did. And somehow, in that moment, I had a knowing, an understanding of medicine and healing. Perhaps it was a blessing bestowed by Terras Phoenix. I remained with him, nursing his injury. For four days."

"Four days? Sounds dreadful."

"And yet, Princess…in all that time, I was not afraid." She glanced down at Mogg and then waved her hand. "Arlon? It is time to make him drink. Slowly."

"Yes, ma'am."

All watched in eager anticipation as he carefully poured a few sips between the lips of their unconscious friend. Mae'Lee caressed his head while gently dabbing the corners of his mouth with a soft scarf.

Paymer rolled a gold coin through his fingers. "How, uh, how soon will it work?"

Shendollyn took in a deep breath. "There are no guarantees of recovery," she began. "And certainly no guarantees of a recovery time. We must be patient…with the patient." She smiled.

Arlon dribbled in a few more sips and looked up. "And so…after four days with the Dragon, what happened?"

"Oh, yes, forgive me," she replied. "I did not finish my tale. It was at the close of the fourth day, right at last light…Terras Phoenix rose up, towering above me, wings unfurled. I had never seen him in his full height and majestic glory. It was beautifully terrifying." She paused as her eyes glistened with emerging tears. "Once again, he stared down at me…and then…he opened his tremendous jaws. His head snaked towards me."

"Oh!" Mae'Lee squinted. "Did you think he was going to eat you?"

"My dear Princess, I had so many thoughts running through my mind…I don't know what I thought! And then…I saw it. From deep within him, a radiant, glowing light that traveled up his long neck and into his gaping mouth. Followed by a rushing roar."

"Fire!" Paymer said.

"Yes…*fire*."

"Did you run?" Mae'Lee asked.

"There was nowhere to go, nowhere that I could hide. I remember turning my head to the side just as the final bit of the sun dipped below the horizon. A bright orange flash lit up the rocks all around, and I clamped my eyes shut, fearing the blast of painful heat that would surely turn my small body to ash."

Mae'Lee shut her own eyes and drew her knees up. "I can't watch!" she whispered.

"So, what happened next?" Arlon asked.

"What happened? Something…wonderful."

Paymer was hanging on her every word. "So, he didn't kill you?"

Trilyra rolled her eyes and popped him on the shoulder. "Paymer, really?" She pointed at Shendollyn. "She is standing right here, alive. So he obviously didn't kill her."

Paymer's eyes raced as an embarrassed smile spread across his freckled cheeks. "Oh, yeah. Sorry. Continue."

Shendollyn closed her eyes. "I stood there, with my eyes shut, for what seemed like hours. But I felt no heat...no pain. I was confused. Perhaps he had killed me so quickly that I felt no pain. Was I dead, was I alive? I didn't know. But, even through closed eyes I could perceive a brightness, all around." She paused again. "And then...I opened them."

"What did you see?" Paymer asked.

"I saw...*light*. Fire light. Spinning, swirling all around me. Covering me, yet not touching me. I couldn't see my surroundings, or even the Dragon. I felt light as a feather. And a tingling...on me, and through me. And then...the fire light faded away and I realized that I was floating, above the ground. I could begin to see the Dragon and I drifted back down. As the light vanished, I was standing before him, in this beautiful dress. I felt...fresh. And strong."

"Frea-ky," Paymer mumbled.

Mae'Lee cracked her eyes back open. "Is it safe?"

"It's safe," Arlon whispered through a smile.

Shendollyn spread her arms out and looked up. "And with a tremendous blast of wind and a victorious roar, Terras Phoenix bolted into the sky and vanished into the early night. I did not see his majestic form again for many, many years."

"But he had given you a gift," Arlon noted.

Her gaze and arms drifted back down slowly. "A gift. A gift that will remain as long as the Age of Dragons will endure."

Arlon gave Mogg another long sip. "And now, every day, right at sunset, you change into that same, young form, no matter how old you actually are?"

"That is correct, young Dunamai."

"And, let me guess," Paymer began, "right at *sunrise*, you change back to the, uh, the other person?"

"I change back to my *actual* age," she corrected. "With all of the ailments and frailties that brings."

"Sister," Paymer said.

"*Sister*," Shendollyn repeated back with a nod. "I will continue to age, and yet I will ever remain the same."

"So, you will live forever?" Paymer inquired.

"I shall live until the end of the Age of Dragons."

Mae'Lee looked up. "But some say that the Age of Dragons will never end. They say that the last Dragon is immortal."

"That is *one* interpretation of the prophecies, your Highness."

"But…if that isn't the right interpretation," Paymer said slowly, "then, when the last Dragon dies…*you* will…die?"

"That is correct."

"Oh."

One by one, they all traded uncomfortable glances.

She couldn't help but notice. "Why have your countenances fallen, my friends?"

Silence.

Shendollyn folded her arms. "You have had a thousand questions, but suddenly have nothing to speak of?" She looked around the cave. "Tell me, why are we here? What quest, what purpose brings us together?"

More silence.

"I have truthfully disclosed all that you have asked of me, and yet, now, you will not answer a single request?"

Arlon swallowed hard. "It…is a…*difficult* answer. Ma'am."

"And I made a most *difficult* journey to reach you," she retorted. "It would not be improper to say that you owe me some answers as well."

Trilyra rose up and stepped closer. "We have come to obtain a relic from the remains of the Dragon," she announced.

Shendollyn glanced in confusion over her shoulder at the dimly lit skeleton against the far wall. "To what purpose?" she asked, looking back at them. "To what end?"

"We are collecting one relic…from each of the dead Dragons," Paymer added, staring into his lap. "We've got three now. We think."

Their beautiful visitor slowly withdrew from them with horror in her reddening eyes. "And what explains this vile fascination with ancient relics? Have you…have *all of you* fallen into the madness of the Order?"

Arlon handed his cup to Mae'Lee and stood up in haste. "Oh, no, no," he countered, crunching through the gravel towards her. "No, we…we are not part of the Order. Actually, the Order is trying to kill us."

She glanced at Paymer.

"It's true," he said with a nod. "Trilyra had to kill two of them. She's really good with a bow and arrow. Shot one of them right through the head and—"

"*Paymer!*" Trilyra muttered. "That's enough details."

"Yeah. Sorry," he said. "No, we are not with them. The Order, that is. I'm gonna shut up now."

Shendollyn halted her retreat and locked eyes with Arlon. "Speak."

He bit his bottom lip. "The, uh, the last Dragon…Terras Telos…he is a vicious monster."

"I am well aware of his cruelty. All kingdoms are suffering under the indignation of his unrighteous rule."

"Yes, and well, there might be a…way to…*stop* him."

She squinted while folding her arms. "Stop the Dragon? What do you mean?"

"What he means," Trilyra said, trudging closer. "Is that there might be a way to *kill* it. And the sooner, the better."

Shendollyn began nodding. "I see." She looked at her. "So, it is *revenge* then. Sister of Pelias."

"My motivation has never been in doubt," Trilyra retorted.

"I am truly sorry. I cannot imagine your pain or your grief, my child."

"Nor my anger." Trilyra spun around and walked away. "But that beast will feel it."

Shendollyn hesitated. "And what of the rest of you? What leads the Dunamai to this desperate cause?"

Mae'Lee glanced over at her. "We feel…responsible, ma'am."

"You probably know about the terrible things that happened," Paymer added. "At the Karaval. During the Offering."

She nodded.

"Yeah," he continued. "Well, everyone kind of…blames us. Maybe they're right."

Shendollyn's eyebrows slid up. "History has been blackened by the evils and failures of many great people. The legacy of the final king of mankind, King Kyros the Cruel, is what we see before us today…a world of divided kingdoms, and an Age of Dragons. There was the greed of the Endochorians, and the bitterness of the Century War. And the Great Treachery that followed beyond the Treaty of the Five Kings." She paused. "But, my friends, if there is blame…perhaps it is blame…*misplaced*."

Arlon cleared his throat. "While we were at Alaithia…the Sevasti told us that there was a chance, a way, to stop the Dragon. To end him."

"The Sevasti, the keepers of the scriptures, spoke of *harming* a Dragon?" she inquired skeptically. "A most unusual claim."

"Well, not *all* of them," Paymer admitted. "A few of them. Two, actually."

"Fascinating," she whispered. "It seems that your story is beginning to rival my own. I traveled far to *save* a Dragon, and now you have journeyed far to *kill* one."

"It's not like that," Mae'Lee complained. "We don't want to. It's dreadful. But we feel like…we have to."

Shendollyn stepped closer. "And you hesitated to tell me, because if your quest is successful…"

"Then you will…die," Arlon declared.
Even more silence.

"My friends," she said, with fresh tears streaking down. "I have lived a hundred lifetimes, perhaps more. To ask, to seek another year or even another day, is but selfish greed. The Zho has blessed me greatly." She wiped her wet cheeks. "And if...my time in this world is drawing to a close, then how can I be anything but thankful? Especially in light of the possibility of an end to the suffering in this world."

Mae'Lee wiped her own tears. "That was...beautiful. Simply beautiful."

Shendollyn took a deep breath and strolled towards them. "So, tell me...what do the relics of six dead Dragons have to do with the killing of the seventh?"

"They, uh, the Sevasti, found a cryptic message," Arlon replied. "It seemed to say that the only way to kill a Dragon is to create a weapon, or a poison, from the remains of all the previous Dragons."

"'Dread against Dread, or suffer misery without end,'" she rehearsed under her breath. "Curious. That would seem to fulfill the prophecy. But yet a long-debated prophecy, for sure."

Paymer scrambled towards their supplies and dug out a shield. "The Sevasti gave us these. They are made from the remains of a Dragon. And then we found another Dragon, buried in the snow and ice in Orania. We got a claw from that one. It was Terras Kratos. So, we have two relics."

Shendollyn glanced back at the skeleton. "And this would be the third."

"A *possible* third," Arlon corrected, holding up the tooth he had just extracted.

"I don't understand."

Arlon pointed over at the shield. "The Sevasti aren't certain about where any of the Dragon's remains are. But they are certain that those shields are made from the remains of Terras Schema, the Fourth Dread Guardian." He gestured behind her. "Unfortunately, those bones over there could be what is left of the body of Terras Schema."

"Which would mean that we still only have two relics," Mae'Lee offered with a sigh. "Instead of three."

"And we need *six*," Paymer said.

"And...how would you know?" she asked.

Arlon walked over and picked up a pouch. "With these," he said, dumping the contents into his free palm.

"Rone fragments?"

"Rone fragments," he said. "Come just a little closer and I'll show you. Paymer? Could you bring me that shield?"

Paymer rushed over. "Just watch and listen...this is so freaky."

Arlon picked up a Rone fragment. "This is a piece of the Rone from Terras Kratos, the Second Dread Guardian." He pressed it against the Pyros and waited with a big smile.

A puzzled Shendollyn glanced up at him. "What? What was supposed to happen?"

"Nothing," Paymer said, beaming. "That's the point."

"I will freely admit...I don't understand."

"Nothing was supposed to happen," Arlon explained. "Because the shield was made from the fourth Dragon, but that Rone piece is from the *second* Dragon." He paused and traded pieces. "But now watch when I touch the shield with a Rone fragment from Terras Schema."

She leaned forward as the two materials made contact. Shendollyn flinched when the Rone began glowing and ringing out its sweet hum.

"Now that...that is...wonderful!" she said.

Arlon removed the stone and the show ended instantly. A bewildered Shendollyn took the fragment from his hand.

"Let me try," she said.

"Oh, yeah," he began, blushing a bit as her hand reached towards the shield. "You see, it won't do the same thing, because you're not—"

"*Look!*" Paymer yelled, almost jumping up and down. "*Look!*"

The fragment immediately lit up brightly.

Arlon stared over at her. "A Dunamai?!"

Shendollyn's conflicted face seemed to both smile and frown at the same time.

"I guess I didn't tell you my *whole* story."

"My life began in the year 5157," Shendollyn offered softly. "In Jireh, a fishing village along the southern plains of Orania."

"I've never heard of it," Paymer said.

"I'm not surprised," came the reply. "It has long since vanished. Too close to Skree lands, I suppose."

Can it be? Arlon thought.

Can she really be that old?

"5157?" he asked.

She nodded.

"And that is the year that Terras Schema died," he muttered. "The Fourth Dread Guardian."

"And I was born, not just the same year, or the same month. Or even the same week," she said. "But on the same *day*, he died." She faced away from them and lowered the edge of her dress, exposing the back of her pale right shoulder.

"The mark!" Paymer exclaimed.

"Indeed," she said, adjusting her dress and twirling back around. "I was born Shendollyn of Jireh, second daughter of Merklor. Dunamai of the Kingdom of Orania."

Paymer's face looked like it was about to burst open with pride. "Freaky! Absolutely freaky!"

"Oh, my," Mae'Lee said. "I just got the chills."

"What's wrong?" Arlon asked.

"Nothing really," the Princess replied. "But something just occurred to me. I just realized that every living Dunamai is together, in this cave. Right here. Right now."

"Perhaps," Shendollyn said. "Perhaps not, my child."

"Do you really think that there could be others?" Arlon asked. "Dunamai from long ago that are still somehow living?"

"It is possible," she said. "Look at me. Or it could be that some of the Sevasti elders may be Children of the Mark."

"Wow," Paymer whispered. "I never really thought about that. A Sevasti Dunamai."

"It just kills me to interrupt all these wonderful thoughts and ideas," Trilyra huffed sarcastically, "but are we ever going to find out if all our trouble to get here was worth it?!"

"Sorry, Trilyra," Arlon replied. "You're right. We need to settle this. Right now. There's no point in waiting." He retrieved the Dragon tooth and held it out. "Shendollyn? Would you please hold this?"

She nodded and he deposited it into her trembling, cupped hands.

"And now," he announced reverently, selecting a Rone fragment. "We do *NOT* want this to do anything special. This is from Terras Schema. And we already have remains from him." He lowered the stone until it touched the huge relic.

Everyone stood up and crowded in, especially Trilyra.

"Oh, no!" Mae'Lee mourned.

"You are kidding me," Paymer said.

"No. It's no joke," Arlon answered with a heavy sigh, staring at the glowing fragment. "The bones in this cave belong to the fourth Dragon…Terras Schema."

"*Curse it all!*" Trilyra screamed in rage. "All of this was for *NOTHING!*" She pivoted around, untethered her horse, and stormed off into the darkness.

Paymer started after her. Arlon lunged out and snagged his arm.

"Hey! Just, wait," he encouraged. "*Wait.* Let her cool off. She'll be back."

"I wouldn't blame her if she didn't," Paymer grumbled. "We came all this way, and that Mal'korr thing out there almost killed her, and who knows if Mogg will ever wake up. This is terrible!" He glared back at Arlon. "And this was all *your* idea!"

"Paymer!" Mae'Lee scolded. "Stop that right now! He just did what he thought was best. We all agreed, remember?"

"Trilyra didn't."

She took a deep breath. "But the rest of us did."

Paymer kicked a pile of rocks. "But it was still all for nothing!" He wagged a finger towards Arlon but glared at Mae'Lee. "And you're just defending *him* because you have feelings for him!"

"*Paymer!*" she yelled.

"Don't deny it, Princess!" he retorted. "We all know it."

"This isn't helping," Arlon protested. "Listen…if it matters…*I'll* take all the blame. There! It's my fault. But right now, we all need to calm down." He paused to catch his breath. "We knew this could happen. There was always the chance that this could happen. But this journey isn't over…this is just a setback."

"Sorry, Arlon, but I think this is quite a bit more than just a setback," Mae'Lee replied, kneeling down to administer another dose into Mogg's lips.

"What do you mean?"

"Well...this is it. This was our only lead, our only clue. And now we found it, and it turned out to be...*unnecessary*."

He plopped down beside her. "Unnecessary? I refuse to believe that this—*that any of this*—is unnecessary."

"You can believe whatever you want, pal," Paymer called out as he wandered around. "But that doesn't change what is actually true. Mae'Lee's right...we are at a dead end. It's hopeless. And we failed." He kicked another cluster of rocks. "Actually, this means that we've failed our kingdoms *twice* now. Wow."

Mae'Lee looked over at him. "Let me guess, the Oranians have a proverb about failing twice?"

"I'm working on it."

Shendollyn picked her way forward and sat beside Mogg. "You know...*hope*...it's like the stars in the heavens," she began. "When life is good, you don't think of it or feel it, but it is still there, like the stars in the middle of a summer day. You can't see them, but they are there...waiting." She lifted Arlon's right hand and rubbed it. "But it is in the night, in the darkness...that's when they shine forth. Hope is the same. Sometimes it takes the darkest of times to see and feel its power."

He stared up at the cave ceiling.

"I don't see any stars now."

"They are still there," she whispered. "But there's no need to look up." She took a moment to lock eyes with him. "*Hope*…is sitting right beside you."

His eyes shifted from Mogg, to Mae'Lee, and then back to her. "What do you mean?"

"Paymer?" Shendollyn called out. "Would you please join us, my fellow Oranian Dunamai?"

"I suppose," a weak voice came echoing back.

"As you can imagine, there are many, many more stories during the eons of my long life that I have not shared with you," she said. "But there is one more…one more that you need to know."

Paymer reached the group and dropped down into the gravel a bit closer to the fire.

"I know it's hard to believe…but I was there, at the Doro Drakon, over two thousand years ago," she said.

"Did the Dragon accept your Offering? The Offering from Orania?" Paymer asked.

"I'm sorry, Paymer." She gestured at Mae'Lee. "The Offering of Avdira was accepted on that day."

Paymer's head sank. "Oh."

Mae'Lee shook her head. "It's just so wonderful to think that you were there, actually there, in the same place we have been. Yet, so long ago."

"Yes, your Highness…I was there when the Fifth Dread Guardian, Terras Phoenix, was born. And, in a sense, I was there when the great Dragon died."

Paymer flicked a twig into the fire. "In a sense?"

Arlon frowned at her. "Wait…you know where the Dragon died?"

She squeezed her eyes shut again and tilted her head back. Her arms unfolded outward and upward like a waking flower. "I was meditating. Right after sunset. And I was clutching a piece of his Rone. I heard that cry…that mourning wail I had heard a thousand years before…echoing through my mind. And for the briefest of moments, I saw through his eyes…I heard through his ears. I felt what he felt. I felt his spirit leave. I felt his…death."

Arlon leaned towards her and spoke quite deliberately. "What did you see?"

Her eyes remained closed. "I saw…what looked like smoke. Smoke. Everywhere. Rising."

Mae'Lee squinted. "Smoke?"

"And I felt heat. And I saw…water…pools of water…as pure as aquamarine."

Mae'Lee glanced over.

"What else?" Arlon pressed.

Her eyelids trembled. "I saw…something gleaming. Rocks, rocks encrusted with golden yellow. All around the pools." Her dainty body twitched as a pained look washed across her face. "And then…then…*death*."

Shendollyn's unfurled arms buckled to the ground, and her body began to weaken and sway. Locks of blonde hair wrapped about her face as her head suddenly snapped forward, and she collapsed into Arlon's unprepared lap.

"*Shendollyn!*" he cried, scrambling to prop her back up. "Shendollyn!" Arlon clutched her shoulders and gently shook her. "Wake up! Shendollyn!"

Paymer raced to her side. "What happened?!"

"Is she breathing?!" a panicked Mae'Lee asked.

"I don't know…and I don't know," Arlon declared. He shook her again. "Shendollyn!"

The unresponsive woman's terrified eyes snapped open and everyone jumped. Shendollyn stared around in confusion, blinking several times just before her muscles tightened and she started to bolt.

"Whoa, whoa," Arlon offered softly in a low voice as he immediately restrained her. "It's okay. You are okay. You are with friends." He brought his face directly in front of hers, almost nose to nose. "Do you remember who I am?"

Shendollyn's trembling head rotated gradually from side to side before her bewildered eyes met with his. "Arlon," she whispered, carrying the last syllable out to the end of her breath.

"That's right," he offered through a reassuring smile. "And where are you?"

She hesitated and blinked.

And blinked.

"In a cave."

He nodded. "Right again."

"I...I am...sorry," she began, hardly above a whisper. "I am...alright. I'm alright." Shendollyn pulled away from his grasp and sat up straight.

"What happened?" Paymer asked.

"I don't know. I don't know. I was sitting there...remembering. And it all became...so...real. I could see and feel it all once again. And when the Dragon died...I...I—" Her body convulsed and tears raced down her face.

"Shhhhh, shhhhh," Mae'Lee whispered as she rubbed Shendollyn's arms. "It's okay. So, uh, tell me...what is...your...favorite flower?"

Arlon squinted and shot Mae'Lee a hard glance. "Flower?" he mouthed.

She returned his hard stare and then looked back at Shendollyn with a sweet smile. "Shendollyn? Do you have a favorite flower? I love the Willaby Double Rose. Do you have those where you live? They can be a lovely lavender, with just a hint of white at the tips."

Shendollyn finally looked at her. "Tealashes."

Mae'Lee's face lit up instantly. "Oh! I love Tealashes, too. They are so lovely. And their color! It's rather like your dress, don't you think?" She pulled in a deep breath. "And they smell absolutely delicious! Like honey bread, still in the oven."

Shendollyn nodded with a weak smile. "But that's not what they taste like."

Mae'Lee cocked her head. "Wait a minute...you mean...*you've* tried to eat them, too?! I thought I was the only one!"

They both laughed and hugged one another.

Shendollyn rubbed the hair out of her face. "Now that's a mistake, you only make once."

"Why?" Paymer inquired. "What do they taste like?"

The women looked at each other and then over at him. "Ashes," they replied in unison and laughed some more.

"I hadn't thought about that in a long time," Shendollyn remarked.

"And coming from you, that's saying something," Arlon teased. "Welcome back."

"Yeah," she said, pulling in a deep breath. "Sorry, about that. I'm fine."

Paymer suddenly erupted in a short-lived round of chuckling.

"You okay over there, Paymer?" the Princess asked.

"Oh, yeah," he said. "I, uh, I just got the name. *Tealashes*. Funny."

Shendollyn patted his shoulder. "The name really says it all."

Mae'Lee rose up and dusted herself off. "Paymer?" she said. "Would you mind keeping Shendollyn company for a moment? Arlon and I need to attend to something."

Arlon looked up. "We do?"

Mae'Lee kicked him discreetly.

"Oh, yeah....*that*," he said, standing up.

Paymer shrugged. "Uh, sure."

Mae'Lee held up a finger and smiled. "We will be right back."

"Yeah," Arlon added as they walked off. "As soon as we attend...to the thing...that needs attending to. Over there."

Mae'Lee pulled on his arm, and they moved out of earshot.

"What is going on?" he asked through gritted teeth.

She paused. "Hope."

Arlon blinked and furrowed his brow. "*Hope?* Am I missing something?"

"Think back...think back to our trip to the Karaval," she said with growing excitement.

"Uh, okay…let's see…I remember being on my back, mostly. And in pain, mostly. In a carriage. A nice carriage. Good food. A terrible nurse."

She slapped his good shoulder. "Listen! Do you remember where we stopped?"

"Stopped? We stopped a lot. Three or four times a day."

She shook her head. "Do you remember my favorite place?"

He paused. "Still…nothing."

"Water? Hot water?"

He concentrated. "Oh, wait…you mean that underground place…with the big pool of steaming water?"

She jumped up and down and grabbed his arm. "That's it."

"To-ber-something. To-ber-where?"

"*Tobermere*," she corrected.

"Okay, yeah…Tobermere. *You* went swimming, and *I* laid there thinking how horrible it would be to put my wounded back into that boiling bath."

"Listen," she urged. "Forget about all of that. Don't you get it?"

He bit his lip. "Um…still nothing."

"Shendollyn's vision!" she fairly squealed. "She saw pools of water—*hot water*. And steam…rising like smoke."

He nodded slowly. "And rocks with something yellow on them."

"Yes, yes! And I know that area. The whole region around Tobermere is filled with thermal pools. I've seen them from the road many times off to the east. I wanted to get closer, but my father wouldn't allow it. He said that it was dangerous. He told me that no one goes there. He said it's deadly."

"A dangerous, uninhabited place," Arlon muttered.

"A perfect place for a Dragon to die. The area is called the Steroth Swamp."

His mind raced.

"What do you think?" she asked expectantly.

"I think…that you were brilliant back there."

"What?"

"The whole '*favorite flower*' thing."

"Oh," she whispered. "That. Well, I knew that she needed to be distracted from that terrible memory. I changed the subject to something more lovely."

He looked at her. "It worked. Beautifully."

"Thank you."

Paymer's distant voice interrupted their moment. "Hey guys," he called out. "Mogg might be waking up."

Mae'Lee's face brightened. "We'll be right there!"

A smiling Arlon continued to stare at her for several seconds.

She blushed and looked down. "And just what are you looking at?"

"Hope."

He looks so lonely.

Reduced to little more than a dark shadow by the blaze of the young sunrise blinding their eyes, Mogg gently bounced along atop his horse as he led the pack. Arlon studied him.

I think he misses her.

Misses them both, actually.

It had been three days since they had departed from the cave.

Four days since they had bid a tearful farewell to Shendollyn.

And six days since anyone had seen or heard from Trilyra.

Her departure had been tough on all of them in so many ways. One less set of eyes for night watch meant that everyone enjoyed less sleep, and one less set of weapons meant that everything just got a lot more dangerous. Much (if not all) of the burden for both food and protection had now fallen upon Mogg's shoulders, and Arlon constantly worried that the quiet warrior would eventually break. It wasn't hard for him to imagine the scenario. The discouraged travelers were only a few day's ride from the lands of the Kla'aven Mage. The thought that they would awake one morning and discover that their hunter, navigator, and defender had simply vanished was a lurking suspicion, impossible to ignore.

But Trilyra's departure was not a suspicion.

A hundred scenarios crowded into Arlon's jumbled thoughts; things he could have done or things he wished he would've said. But, in the end, he couldn't blame her for giving up, for abandoning them…for being discouraged. He himself had tasted deeply from that dark well many times over of late.

She's probably almost home by now, he surmised. *And why not? We were practically on the border of Ammodis anyway.*

He looked off to the south.

The Eurus Pass isn't far.

I wish you well, Trilyra.

I really do.

In countless fireside conversations, everyone had agreed that she had every reason to leave and few real reasons to stay. Even Paymer had come around and admitted that it wasn't really Arlon's fault. And that helped a little.

But it still hurt.

His guilt tossed him around like a tiny leaf in the wind.

Not much of a leader, are you, Arlon?

First, you knew that Hort was in danger and you did nothing to stop it. And now, Trilyra gives up and you just let her go.

That's not leadership.

That's incompetence.

A new, softer voice invaded his troubled inner conversation. "Where are you, Arlon?"

He blinked hard and spun his head around.

"Hey! Over here."

He finally caught a glimpse of Mae'Lee riding just alongside him.

"Oh, sorry," he said. "I, uh, I was just a—"

"Just a thousand miles away is what you were," she declared. "Maybe *two* thousand." She paused. "Are you alright?"

"Yeah, sorry. Got a lot on my mind."

She put a hand on her chin. "Hmmm...let me guess...whatever you're thinking about has a blonde head and...a warrior's heart?"

He shrugged. "Well, yeah, but not just her." He pointed ahead. "And him, too."

"Mogg?"

He nodded.

"Oh, quit your worrying. He's fine. He's made a full and wonderful recovery."

"No…not just his body."

The Princess was silent for a while.

"So…you're worried about his heart," she muttered.

Arlon smiled (perhaps for the first time all day). "I'm fairly certain he has one beating somewhere inside that thick, muscled chest."

She chuckled with a subtle bow. "It is well-spoken."

"Doesn't he seem sad to you lately?"

Her dark eyebrows went up. "Well, he is a tough one to figure out…especially when it comes to emotions. But, to answer your question…*yes*, he is sad. I may not be an expert when it comes to males in Kray culture, but I can at least tell you that much."

"I think it's her."

"Who? Trilyra?"

He nodded again.

A sentimental look washed over her face. "My mother always says that '*teasing and flirting are the twin children of affection.*'"

"Sounds like she's been talking to the freckled King of Convenient Proverbs up ahead of us."

"Well, if my mother's right, then those two had quite an affection for each other."

"I saw it," he announced. "From the beginning. The very first day. Without a doubt."

She turned and admired him with a growing smile. "Oh, really?"

"It was that whole *'Woman of the South'* thing."

"Interesting."

Arlon tried to conceal a small laugh. "Every time he would say it, I would hear *'woman that I love'* instead."

"Well, listen to you!" she replied, taking a moment to study his face. "Who would have imagined that the renegade Dunamai of Soteria had such an *emotional* and tender side?"

"Oh…I've got a lot of sides."

She narrowed her big, brown eyes. "I'm beginning to see that."

Paymer moved the parchment a little closer to the campfire and angled it to catch better light. "Where are we at?" he asked, his voice echoing back quickly in the small, damp cave.

Arlon and Mogg leaned up against him from opposite sides and peered down. Mogg tapped his index finger on the map.

"At the eastern edge of the Woods of Ankath," he noted. "The borderlands of the Kla'aven Wins'orr. Not far from the borderlands of the Kla'aven Mage."

Mae'Lee looked concerned. "So, are we anywhere near that big, old abandoned city we found when we left the Karaval?"

"Tar'tain," Mogg asserted. "It is north. And we are not close."

She picked up a broken branch and examined it. "That's good. I was just thinking about those dreadful dreams we all had that one night. You said it was the wood and the smoke."

Mogg nodded. "Dreadwood." He picked up a stick as well and turned it over. "And this…is not Dreadwood."

"I had forgotten about that," Arlon mumbled. "Thanks a lot for bringing it all back, Mae'Lee," he teased.

"Sorry," she said, tossing her branch into the flames. "I just don't ever want to dream like that again. Ever."

"Dreadwood is not to fear," Mogg said. "But the Kray of these woods are to be much feared."

Arlon sighed. "That's what Trilyra told me. More than once."

"And we are being tracked," Mogg announced.

"Tracked?" Paymer repeated.

"It is well-spoken. For the last two days."

"Can you tell how many?" Arlon asked.

"It is an ill thought."

Arlon paused. "Is there anything we can do to avoid trouble?"

"We must leave the lands of Kla'aven Wins'orr."

"You've got no argument from me on that one," Arlon replied.

Paymer suddenly squinted down at the old map, pointing at a curving line. "And…what's this?"

Arlon hunkered closer and waved his hands to clear the crowding smoke that tickled his throat. "That is a river," he replied through a quick cough. "The Megalith. It comes down out of the Ploutonians." He traced a finger to the right. "And it flows northeast and meets up with the Grigory…right…here."

Mogg leaned back and sank his teeth into a sizable hunk of meat, ripping it from the bone. "By the will of the Zho," he said with his mouth mostly full, "we will reach the river by midday tomorrow."

Mae'Lee set her small plate down and carefully dabbed her mouth. "Should we follow the river as long as we can, or cross it at our first opportunity?"

"Like Mogg said, we need to get out of the Kray lands," Arlon said. "And the river is a natural boundary. There are several places close to us where the Megalith is wider and shallower. We should be able to cross on horseback without too much trouble."

Paymer glanced over at Mogg and studied him. "I don't think the depth of the water is going to be our biggest problem we have to cross, pal."

Arlon took a quick sip. "Then what is our *biggest* problem?"

Paymer reached up and touched the left side of Mogg's face. "This."

Arlon sighed. "Oh…his Dunamai birthmark."

"Once we leave these Kray lands, that famous little blemish ceases to bring us protection, and it starts inviting something…much less pleasant."

"Paymer's right," Mae'Lee piped up.

"Thank you, your Highness."

"It's such a rare thing," she replied with a wink. "So I like to point it out whenever it happens."

Paymer shot her a nasty but playful stare.

"What I wouldn't give for a Sevasti mask," Arlon mumbled.

Paymer pivoted towards him and grinned. "That's because you never had to wear one of those freaky things." He raised both hands and used them to completely cover his face. "They are horribly uncomfortable, and when you talk, it makes everything sound all hollow and creepy. And when you eat—"

"Not a mask for *me*," Arlon interjected. "For Mogg."

Paymer's eyes raced back and forth (if he blushed, it was impossible to tell in the warm glow of the fire), and he lowered his hands. "I knew that."

Arlon fidgeted with the hem of his cloak. "When I was injured by the Dragon bite, and you traveled up the river to Alaithia, how did you hide his mark then?"

"Bandage," Mae'Lee replied.

"The Princess is right," Paymer said.

"Thanks, Paymer."

He smiled with a nod. "Trilyra and Mae'Lee fixed a big bandage over it. We told the crew that the two of you had been attacked by a bear or something. "

Arlon scooted back and glanced over at Mogg. "Well, unless anyone has a better idea, we should probably go with that again. Is that alright with you?"

Mogg simply nodded and continued eating.

Arlon reached over. "Let me see that map," he said.

"It's all yours, pal."

"I think," he began, "that we need to stay in a southerly course." He spun the map a quarter turn and traced along with his finger. "Head just south of Lake Abyssinia…through the grasslands…and around the backside of Mt. Krysis…and then turn north…to Mae'Lee's favorite vacation spot. That route should help us avoid any sizable settlements."

Mae'Lee took a drink and stared above the fire. "Won't it be lovely?"

"What? The heated pools?" Arlon asked.

"No," she said. "*Settlements*. Won't it be lovely, once all this nastiness is over and behind us, to be able to move about freely? To enjoy people, and cities, and celebrations. I can't wait."

Arlon rolled the map up and took a deep breath. "Right now…that almost seems like a dream. An impossible dream."

"It will happen," she declared, growing wide-eyed. "And I will be back home in the capital. In the palace. With my dresses…and my daily fragrant baths…and my ocean view."

"I'd just be happy to be able to walk down a street without having to look over my shoulder in fear," Paymer said. "I don't need a fancy ocean view."

Arlon pinched his own nose. "But, um…you *do* need a fragrant bath."

They all laughed.

Even Mogg.

"How about you, Arlon?" Mae'Lee asked at the back end of a chuckle. "Tell us. What do you want to do?"

He bit his lip and pondered her interesting question. "Well, *when* this is over…I want…to bring Mogg to *my* capital. And show him the river front, and the Citadel. And present him to the

Trion. To start a new friendship…between our peoples."

Mogg brought his hands together. "I would be honored, my Soterian friend."

"And I would introduce you to my mother. And show her that the wild men of the west, aren't necessarily so…*wild*. She would love to hear—"

"It must be nice," Paymer muttered.

Arlon glanced up. "What?"

"To be able to dream about introducing someone to your mother. Must be nice."

Arlon's smile vanished instantly. "Yeah, Paymer. Sorry. We've talked about this before. You know I didn't—"

"I know." Paymer's eyes seemed to get lost as he stared at the flickering flames. "I know." He poked at the base of the fire with a pair of sticks. "But, none of these lovely and wonderful dreams matter anyway. If the Dragon has his way, none of us will have anything to return to. We've all seen what he can do. What he's already done. When was it? Maybe two days ago that we rode through miles and miles of charred forest. Dead trees. Dead animals. Nothing left."

He worked the sticks like makeshift tongs and managed to retrieve a bright red ember. A swirling ribbon of white streamed up from its shimmering surface. Paymer brought it closer and examined it. "Think about it," he said.

"Our homes could be nothing but smoking heaps of rocks and ashes right now."

Exhausting.

Yet exhilarating.

Eleven unbroken days of first-light to last-light treks across a mixed bag of geography and unpredictable weather had pushed the travelers and their horses to the very edge of endurance. Even though the threat of danger had subsided to a more tolerable level, the route hadn't been without incident.

Two days beyond the Megalith crossing, Mae'Lee's horse had stumbled into a mole's burrow (in the endless, waist-high grasslands spreading out southwest of Lake Abyssinia) and brutally snapped one of its forelegs. The Princess doubled up with Arlon until they bargained for a strong farm horse the next afternoon.

The jagged volcanic ridges forming the southeastern slopes of Mt. Krysis proved especially treacherous less than a week later. Mae'Lee almost fainted when Paymer returned with a sliced left elbow (instead of an armload of dry sticks for their fire) and rivers of blood gushing from his injured left knee.

The following morning, wave after wave of dense mountain fog, backlit by the rising sun, blinded the weary travelers. Arlon soon found himself separated from the others at the rear of the pack and hopelessly lost. Nearly half the day was wasted as they wandered the sharp crags and deep ravines before finally locating their disoriented friend.

Now, a few days later (and two straight days of miserable rain at that), the immense volcano was just a hazy peak shrinking behind them on the cloudy, southern horizon.

"Oh, great," Paymer grumbled. "Arlon! You might wanna stay close."

"Why? What's wrong?"

Mae'Lee leaned to the side and stared at him. "Is your leg bleeding again, Paymer?"

"No, my leg's fine. I mean, it still hurts mind you…but *look*." He waved his freckled hand forward. "Up ahead. Looks like more fog."

"Fog? Oh…that's not fog," Mae'Lee rebutted with an excited smile.

"You know what my mother says about fog?" Arlon asked.

"I don't know," Mae'Lee replied. "But I'm sure it's a wonderful thought."

He smiled. "She says that fog is *'just a cloud that forgot to get up in the morning'*."

A huge grin spread across Mae'Lee's face. "I knew it would be wonderful," she chuckled. "But after all the dreadful rain the last few days, I'd rather not think about clouds for a while, thank you."

Paymer squinted and shielded his eyes from the late morning sun. "So...what is that up there if it isn't fog? *Smoke?*"

Arlon shook his head. "Nope. *Steam.*"

"We're near the southern edge of Steroth Swamp," Mae'Lee announced. "That's steam rising from the hot pools. There are hundreds of them."

"Hundreds?" Paymer moaned. "How do we find the right one?"

"Shendollyn said that she saw rocks with a yellowish crust," Arlon answered. "We need to look for those."

"And what if they all have a yellow crust?"

Arlon's eyebrows shot up. "Then we will be checking *hundreds* of pools."

"Oh, I almost forgot!" Mae'Lee exclaimed, spreading her arms out nearly as wide as her radiant smile. "If I can have everyone's attention. As the daughter of King Leandros, I would like to be the first to welcome all of you to the Kingdom of Avdira."

"This is Avdira?" Paymer asked. "Really?"

"Really. The Steroth Swamps are the southern border of our lands."

Arlon cleared his throat. "And that little claim has been…*disputed* quite a bit over the years."

"Hmmm...do I detect a little jealousy there, my Soterian friend?" she asked playfully.

"*Jealousy?* I was just stating the historical facts, ma'am."

She sighed. "Well, it is a historical fact that Avdira maintains this small strip for access to Mt. Krysis."

"Which limits our access to decent seaports," he retorted.

Paymer pivoted his head around and took it all in. "I will let you two work that out, but I suppose that this is my first visit to Avdira."

"My *second*," Arlon muttered.

"Oh, that's right," Paymer replied. "Crazy story, huh?"

Arlon nodded. "Pretty crazy."

"I kinda forgot that you and the Princess met *before* the Karaval."

"I can still picture it like it was just yesterday," she recalled. "He was chained to a bench."

"And her eyes were chained to me," Arlon countered with a grin.

Nothing grew there.

Not a single tuft of dry grass

Even the gray rocks looked dead.

There was no doubt that life had forsaken the place long ago.

Arlon paused briefly in his search for the yellow crust to scan directly overhead. It seemed that the birds had abandoned the skies as well.

And then there was the heat.

And the smell.

"What is that?" Paymer complained, covering his nose with the edge of a wadded blanket.

"It smells like…burning…sulfur," Arlon responded.

"Not just *smells like*," Paymer said as he spat. "I can even taste it in my mouth. All of a sudden I'm not too impressed with Avdira."

"Burning is a good way to put it." Mae'Lee dabbed her reddened cheeks with a soft cloth. "Whatever it is, my eyes are stinging like they are on fire." She stared at the others while blinking rapidly. "Tell me, are they on fire?"

Paymer shook his head with a smile. "All my burning eyes see are two, big, beautiful, brown, royal eyes."

"Remind me to thank you when I can breathe properly. You're very sweet."

He coughed and brushed the sweat out of his eyes. "I wish the air was sweet."

She covered her mouth. "Do you think it's safe? Is the air poisonous?"

Arlon mulled that question over in his mind. "I don't really know, Princess."

"The horses will be our guide," Mogg called out over his shoulder. "If the air becomes too foul, they will not proceed."

Something caught Paymer's eye, and he pointed. "Uh, you sure about that?"

Mae'Lee gasped when she saw it as well. "Oh, disgusting!"

The grisly remains of a dead range wolf lay in the rocks off to their left, apparently mummified in its own shriveled and hairy hide. Arlon slowed his horse and hopped down for a closer inspection.

"What can you tell us?" Paymer inquired.

"It's...dead," he smirked.

"We can see that from up here, pal."

Arlon poked at it with his sword. "That's strange," he muttered. "There's no flies. No maggots. Nothing." He carefully flipped it over and waved away the steam that drifted over from a small, bubbling pool nearby. "And I don't see any wounds. Or blood."

"Then how did it die?" Mae'Lee asked.

"Probably the smell," Paymer joked.

Arlon stood up. "Maybe it was just...old."

Mogg shook his head. "It is an ill thought."

"Do you think we should go back?" Mae'Lee asked.

"That is also an ill thought," Mogg countered, pivoting around. "If the air is poisonous...we are already dead. We move forward."

An unhealthy dose of fear rose in Mae'Lee's trembling eyes.

"Well," Paymer began, "he's got a good point. In a...freaky sort of way, I guess."

Arlon stashed his sword before climbing back aboard his horse. "Since we left Alaithia, we've survived a Dragon, a Snow Serpent, and a Mal'korr. After all that, I don't think a little bad air is going to kill us."

Mae'Lee dabbed the trickles of sweat that rolled down her neck. "We also survived the cold and snow in the mountains of Orania, but this moist heat is just dreadful. I feel like we are traveling through an oven." She took a long drink from her water satchel.

"Wait a minute...I'm confused. I thought this was your favorite place for a vacation," Arlon teased.

She lowered the satchel. "*Tobermere* is at the northern end of the heated pools," she replied. "As you well remember, the temperature there is quite wonderful, and the air is as fresh as the sea breeze."

"I'd give anything for a nice sea breeze right now," Paymer noted.

Arlon shielded his eyes from the glaring sun as he studied the patches of pools that spread out in every direction. "You'd give *anything?*"

"That's what I said."

"How about your new sword?"

Paymer glared at him and slid out his blade. "Royal?"

"That's what *I* said."

Paymer pulled the shiny surface of the gorgeous weapon close to his face. "Don't listen to that terrible boy from Soteria," he whispered loud enough for everyone to hear. "He's just jealous. You know that I would never give you up."

Mae'Lee glanced down at her misty reflection as the exhausted group passed close to the edge of a particularly deep pool. "Doesn't it seem strange?" she said. "This water is so clear, and it is such a lovely color. But there are no fish. No frogs. No life at all."

"It is either too hot or too poisonous," Arlon replied.

"Or both," Paymer added.

Arlon nodded. "Or both. But you're right, Princess, the color is striking. Like a pure aquamarine. Just like Shendollyn said."

"*Hey! Hey!*" Paymer yelled as he began jutting his finger off to their right. "And there's something else just like Shendollyn said!"

"What is it?" Mae'Lee asked, straining to see through the curtains of steam.

"Yellow rocks! To the northeast!"

The Princess clapped for joy. "Do you see any Dragon bones?!"

"Oh, it's still too far off to see those," Paymer responded.

Mogg halted their forward motion and studied the horizon.

Arlon glanced up at the sun. "What do you think, Mogg? Do we have enough time?"

"What do you mean, pal?" Paymer asked.

"Well, there's no way we can spend the night anywhere around these heated pools," Arlon answered. "So whatever we do, we have to do it and then get out of here before nightfall."

"Oh, right. Good point."

"We should be able to reach better ground faster if we head due west," Mae'Lee said, drying her face off once again. "The Steroth Swamps are long, but narrow."

Arlon dug around and pulled out a map. He studied it quickly. "And...she's right."

"What about east?" Paymer asked.

"Nothing there but the sea," Mae'Lee replied. "I'm surprised that we haven't caught a glimpse of it yet. I blame all this dreadful steam."

A puzzled look overtook Paymer's freckled face. "I'm still trying to figure out where they got the word swamp for this place. Doesn't look too swampy to me."

"It is when you travel further west," Mae'Lee said. "The water is not so hot there, and there are whole forests that are growing right up out of the muddy ground. And a lot of bugs. Nasty ones. Oh, and snakes."

"I've seen enough snakes, thank you," Paymer said.

With a quick but firm kick, Arlon urged his horse ahead, and he drew alongside Mogg. "So, what do you think?"

Mogg continued to observe the sky. "By the will of the Zho, there is enough light."

"You don't sound too happy about it," Arlon replied.

Mogg scanned the horizon in all directions.

"You still worried about someone tracking us?" Arlon almost whispered.

"It is well-spoken. But…let us move forward, my friend. Our enemies will find it difficult to hide in these flatlands."

No one seemed to notice at first, but the awful stench began to subside, and the temperature sank as well. (In later conversations,

Mae'Lee attributed these pleasant changes to the influence of ocean breezes blowing inland. Paymer, however, insisted that they were probably just getting used to misery.)

The barren repetition of gray rocks and bluish-green pools across a fairly level landscape made judging distance a difficult affair. They traveled for over an hour with great anticipation yet their yellow-coated goal seemed always just beyond reach.

Paymer was the first to verbalize a frustrated explanation. "Do you think it's just a mirage?" he asked. "I've heard of thirsty people in the desert seeing huge lakes of water, but then they can't ever get to it. Or stories about sailors who see land, but can never sail there."

"Maybe we just wanted to see it so desperately, that we are imagining it," Mae'Lee added.

Arlon sighed. "Well, I don't think it's all in our heads. How could four people all have the exact same imagination at the same time?"

Paymer nodded. "Good point."

"You know, mirages or desperate imaginations are not my biggest concern," Arlon announced. He pointed all around. "Terras Phoenix died over a thousand years ago. Just think about how much the land could have changed in all that time. A thousand summers and winters…and thousands upon thousands of storms. This could look way different now than it did then."

"I hate to say it," Paymer mumbled. "But...*another* good point."

Arlon glanced down at the barren ground. "The yellow rocks that Shendollyn saw could have all eroded away hundreds of years ago. The yellow ones that we are chasing out there, those might be a new outcrop only a hundred years old. Who knows?"

"I wish you would quit making good points," Paymer complained.

"I'm just trying to be honest."

"Well, pal...could you be honest more silently?" He winked at him.

"Wait...Shendollyn said that she saw yellow rocks," Mae'Lee said. "She didn't say that they were close to her."

Paymer raised a finger. "*Another* good point."

"That is true," Arlon agreed. "Maybe we should start spreading out...now that we're getting closer to the yellow rocks. The Dragon's remains could be anywhere within sight of those."

"Kind of like what we did on the ice," Mae'Lee offered.

"Just like what we did on the ice," Arlon repeated.

Paymer patted his horse's neck. "Except now we have transportation and there is no cold or snow or ice. I like this way much better."

"It is well-spoken," Mogg said.

The group steadily fanned out in an erratic line stretching from Mogg in the northwest to Arlon deep in the southeast. The two boys could still see each other (when the steam allowed), but far enough apart that it was doubtful that they could actually hear one another.

The undistracted solitude of this new search arrangement allowed Arlon's active mind to drift. One name kept whispering through his thoughts.

Kash.

His imagination wandered back in time to an uncomfortable cage lumbering its way across Avdira many weeks before.

Why were you in that slave cart, Kash?
How did you even get there?

He peered down at his own perfect reflection in yet another steaming pool.

Was it all for me?
Why were you interested in helping me?

He clutched his necklace, rolling it side to side in his sweating palm.

And why did you give me this?
A piece of the Rone from the first Dragon.
The first Dragon.
Terras Adonis.

His thoughts bounced around…from Kash, to the Dragon, and then Alaithia.

Is there a connection between you and the Dragon, Kash? A connection? But that would be crazy.

That Dragon lived over six thousand years ago.

He took a deep breath and pictured the Sevasti elder as if he were simply riding alongside him.

Tell me something…just how old are you, Kash?

The smiling old man didn't so much as mutter a single word.

How long have you been at Alaithia?

Arlon thought he saw the very hint of a shrug.

And why do you know so much about life and history and Dragons…and everything?

Still nothing.

Why do you know so much about…me?

With that question, the silent Kash finally turned and locked eyes with the boy. He reached over and gently patted Arlon's hand. "There is something you need to know, my boy. About who you are."

Arlon's eyebrows shot up. "Tell me! What do I need to know?!"

"It is about your father, Arlon." A solemn expression rippled across Kash's kind face. "Or, more importantly…your grandfather."

"My grandfather?!"

Kash combed his fingers through his thick beard and started to say something.

But Arlon never heard it.

An enthusiastic female's voice from fifty yards away disturbed his daydream, and the imaginary conversation dissolved away with the playful wisps of steam rising all around him.

"*I found it!*" Mae'Lee screamed. "*I found it! Or him! And something else! Hurry! Hurry!*"

An exasperated Paymer was the last to arrive at the excited gathering perched along the brink of an enormous steaming pool.

"Let me see! Let me see!" he urged as he hopped down from his horse and roughly inserted himself between Arlon and Mogg.

"Slow down, pal," Arlon teased as he slapped him on the shoulder. "These bones have been here for over a thousand years. I don't think they're going anywhere anytime soon."

Paymer latched hold of Arlon's arm to anchor himself before leaning out over the edge and peering down. Sprawled out along the chalky bottom of the crystal clear pool was the unmistakable skeleton of a Dragon. The well-preserved remains were evenly coated with a soft layer of a pale yellow sediment.

"Wow. Oh, wow," Paymer muttered. "Now that's quite a sight."

But the dead Dragon wasn't the only occupant in the depths of the heated lake. Arlon pointed.

"Did you notice those?"

Paymer followed Arlon's hand and it guided his eyes to a pair of much smaller skeletons closer to the side of the pool.

"Oh, freaky," he said. "Two people." Paymer looked up. "What do you think happened? Do you think they attacked the Dragon, maybe they all died together?"

Arlon nodded. "A good thought. But, look what else Mae'Lee found." He led Paymer several feet away to a curious, brown pile that looked quite out of place. Arlon bent down and retrieved the eroded remains of what had once been a sword. He handed it to him and then pointed at another decaying object. "And that's probably what's left of a helmet. And Mogg found another sword. Or at least, the hilt. It's in pretty bad shape, like the rest of this stuff. We can't even tell which kingdom it's from."

Paymer glanced at the pool and then back at the rusty weapon in his hand. "So…a very long time ago…a *very* long time ago…a couple of soldiers found the Dragon remains." He paused and pointed. "Then, they took off their armor right here."

"I agree so far. Keep going," Arlon urged.

Paymer wandered back to the edge. "And then...they somehow...got in the water to...maybe...dive down to the remains?"

Arlon joined him. "And?"

"And...for some reason...they drowned." He glanced up at the others. "Maybe the heat...or uh, maybe the water was...poisonous?"

"That's what I said," Mae'Lee replied with a big smile. "Almost word for word."

Paymer rubbed his freckled chin. "But who would even think about getting into that water? It's gotta be almost boiling."

Arlon nodded. "That's the mystery, isn't it? The only thing I can think is that maybe—*a very long time ago*—this water wasn't as hot. Maybe they thought they could handle it. And then...they were wrong." Arlon hesitated. "What a terrible way to die."

"Dreadful," Mae'Lee shuddered. "I can't even think about it."

"But...why would they even try?" Paymer asked.

"Another good mystery," Arlon replied. "They obviously thought that getting to the Dragon bones was important. But there are other questions, like, was it just the two of them or were they part of a larger group? Were they ordered to get into the water or did they volunteer?"

"No...I don't think there were others, pal," Paymer countered. He raised the crumbling remains of the sword. "Why would they leave weapons and armor behind?"

"I've been thinking about that, too," Arlon responded. "They could have left them as a kind of memorial pile. In honor of their bravery. Like a grave marker."

"But that doesn't make sense either," Mae'Lee began. "If it was a bunch of soldiers, they probably would have devised a way to get to the remains down there. But it doesn't look like they are disturbed…in any way."

"She's got a good point," Paymer noted.

"It is well-spoken," Mogg muttered.

"How deep do you think that is?" Arlon wondered aloud. "I don't have too much experience with things like this. I lived above a river, but I only went there…once."

"Water is a tricky thing, pal." Paymer's eyebrows shot up. "A hundred feet of really clear water can look only waist deep. It's weird."

Mogg bent down. "There are ways to estimate." He selected a fist-sized chunk of rock and lobbed it in. Everyone watched as it sank lower and lower before finally coming to rest in a cloudy yet silent explosion of sand and silt. Mogg stood up.

"Forty, perhaps fifty feet," he announced.

Paymer whistled through his teeth. "Whoa. That's a good ways down. Those guys obviously didn't make it. How're we gonna get to it?"

"How long can you hold your breath?" Arlon asked with a smile.

"Very funny, pal." Paymer lowered his right palm a few inches above the pool's surface. He couldn't hold it there for long. "Wow. That water probably cooked those guys all the way through before either one of them even reached the bottom."

"Don't we have some rope?" Mae'Lee asked.

"Uh, yes. Yes, we do," Arlon answered as he jogged over to his horse. "But I don't think it's anywhere close to fifty feet." He returned with a large coil and picked up a rock. "Somebody attach this to the end to give it some weight."

Paymer located a wad of string and wrapped the stone securely several times. Arlon let out a little slack and swung the rope back like a pendulum before hurling it forward.

SPLAASSHHH!

Mae'Lee stepped closer to the rim. "Oh, no. Look!" she cried out. "The rock came loose."

Arlon slapped Paymer on the arm playfully. "Nice job."

"Sorry, pal."

"No," Mae'Lee mumbled. "It's not his fault. Pull it up. Now!"

Arlon yanked on the rope over and over until it finally flopped back up and onto the stony shore. The Princess knelt alongside the smoldering and frayed end and poked at it with a rock.

"It's…dissolving," she said. "That water must be corrosive."

A pained expression overtook Paymer's face. "Those poor guys. That had to be a terrible way to die."

"Well, that rules out using rope then," Arlon replied. "And obviously, we can't dive down to it. Any other ideas?"

"Is there a way to...maybe…*drain the water?*" Mae'Lee inquired.

Arlon folded his arms. "A nice idea. But probably an impossible one. Especially if all these pools share the same source."

Mogg stepped over to one of the horses and retrieved Mae'Lee's sword.

"What's he doing?" she asked, keeping her voice low.

Paymer shrugged. "Don't know, but I'm sure we're about to find out."

Mogg crept right up to the edge, squatted down and carefully dipped Mae'Lee's blade into the pool. He held it submerged for several seconds before sliding it back up and examining the weapon's surface.

"What was that all about?" Arlon asked.

"Cleaning my sword?" Mae'Lee asked.

Mogg stood up as a near smile began to dawn on his stoic face. "The metal…is unharmed."

Paymer squinted. "I don't get it...are we going to *fight* the water?"

Mogg laid the tip of the sword onto the rope. "We need to combine the two."

Paymer looked thoroughly confused. "A rope...made out of *swords?*"

"Of course!" Arlon exclaimed.

"Of course!" Mae'Lee clapped.

"Of course?!" Paymer repeated.

Arlon glanced over at Mogg. "We will have to find a town to buy one."

"A town with a capable blacksmith," Mae'Lee added.

"And he would have to fashion a hook or something on the end," Arlon said.

"First, we need to devise a way to mark this place and leave ourselves a trail," Mogg called out as he scurried back over to his horse.

Mae'Lee searched one of her satchels and yanked something out. "I have a mirror," she said. "Maybe we could use it to catch and reflect sunlight. As a marker."

Paymer stood there as the others scrambled into activity all around him. "Um...could someone tell me what is going on?"

Arlon hastily coiled up the rope and pressed it against his bewildered friend's chest.

"It's obvious, Paymer...we need to find someone to make us a long chain."

Two treks back and forth across the muddy swamp, four visits to three different villages, and dozens of hours of waiting. The entire ordeal cost them the better part of a few days, and far more than a few gold royals. Arlon was responsible for all the negotiating, while the others carefully kept out of sight, especially the Princess.

Paymer took a quick drink from his water satchel and stared at the coils of chain dangling and jingling from the side of Arlon's horse. "Do you think we have enough?" he asked.

"Mogg felt that it was about fifty feet down. That's why we purchased at least *eighty* feet. It'll be enough."

"But what if it is enough?"

Arlon looked over at him. "What?"

"I was just thinking. What if all this works? What then?"

"Then…we will have *three* relics, my friend."

Paymer rolled his eyes. "I know that…but what's our *next* move? We still need to find three more Dragons."

"I've been wondering the same thing, thank you," Mae'Lee called out. "Thought about it all night last night. Or, mostly all night."

"What about all the documents and maps that Kash and Gremlor gave us?" Paymer inquired. "Has anyone found any more clues in there, pal?"

Arlon stared out at the steamy horizon. "Nothing. Yet."

"I was afraid you were gonna say—"

"*There it is!*" Mae'Lee interrupted. "I can see it glinting in the sun!" She narrowed her eyes and jabbed her finger straight out. "A little bit to the right. See it? I knew that mirror would be useful."

Paymer glanced back at her. "Smart and beautiful. What more could this kingdom want in their future queen?"

"Thank you, Paymer."

"I've met our queen back in Orania several times," he smirked. "And trust me, she is *neither*.

She's not very intelligent, and she looks like an overweight buzzard."

"Paymer!" Mae'Lee scolded.

"If you only saw her, you'd understand."

"I did see her," she replied. "At the Karaval, remember?"

Paymer straightened up and looked away. "Well, then you know I'm right."

The midday sun played upon the links as the group spread the chain out along the edge of the pool. Arlon picked up the trio of jagged metal hooks that had been fastened at one end, while Mogg and Paymer secured the other around a sturdy boulder.

"Looks like a small boat anchor, pal," Paymer joked. "You think it'll actually work?"

Arlon allowed more slack and swung the hooks back and forth. "It'll work...I'm just not sure *how* to make it work."

"A big blob of meat on there might get a big fish," Paymer said. "But I don't think we can bait a dead Dragon."

Mae'Lee's face looked puzzled. "And if it lands on top of the bones, there's no way it can hook them, can it?"

Mogg trotted over and took the dangling chain from Arlon. He tossed the hooks far out across the ground and began sliding them back towards him. The sharp points bounced and clanked along the surface before lodging on the backside of a protruding rock several feet away. He yanked harder and broke a chunk of the stone free, then reeled it in.

"To capture a relic, we need to drag it along the bottom of the pool," Mogg explained.

"Oh, that makes sense," Paymer said.

Arlon folded his arms. "I like it."

Mae'Lee stared down into the pure, pale bluish-green waters. "But…if we get a relic, do we need to test it with a Rone?"

Arlon walked up beside her and studied the frightful ancient skeleton (which seemed to be only a few feet below the steamy surface, even though he knew it really wasn't). "*When* we get a relic," he corrected firmly, "we won't need to test it. We know for sure that those are the remains of Terras Phoenix."

Her eyes began glistening in an odd sort of way. "It's a really strange feeling, isn't it?" The Princess latched onto his arm and closed her eyes. "To think, that Shendollyn was alive, over a thousand years ago…and she saw the Dragon's last moments." Her eyes popped back open, and she gazed downward in wonder. "She saw that creature…right there…*die*."

Paymer joined them. "And hopefully, before long, *we* will all see another Dragon die."

Mae'Lee bit her bottom lip. "It's a dreadful thought…but I know it must be done."

"And by the Red Leaf," Mogg asserted, as he scooted closer to the water and gathered quite a bit of slack in the chain, "it will be done. Stand back."

After several gentle swings back and forth, Mogg hurled the hooks at least a stone's throw from the edge with a sizzling *WHOOSSSHHHH*, and the chain splashed down into the misty pool.

"Nice throw!" Paymer beamed.

They all huddled around Mogg and waited as the hooks plummeted into the depths.

"Oh, that…is…good," Arlon noted. "It looks like…it will land…on the far side of that…long wing bone."

He was right.

"But we don't want just any bone, right?" Paymer asked. "Don't we need a tooth or claw or something?"

"Considering how difficult this is going to be, I think we will take whatever we can get," Arlon replied. He studied the situation a bit further. "But…there's no way those hooks could pull that huge bone up anyway. And we have to be careful, we don't want to get our chain stuck."

"Good point," Paymer mumbled. "As usual."

"Speaking of stuck," Mae'Lee said, "I hope those remains aren't stuck to the bottom. They've been down there a long, long time."

"Only one way to find out," Arlon responded. "Start reeling it in."

With firm yet precise motions, Mogg began hauling the chain towards himself, hand over hand. The sliding hooks carved a cloudy, yellow trail along the bottom.

"Careful!" Paymer urged. "You're almost to that big bone."

The chain snapped taut. Mogg instantly let up.

"Are the hooks facing the right way?" Mae'Lee asked.

Arlon squatted down and squinted. "It's hard to tell, too much muddy water all around it." He waited for the yellowed sediment to disperse. "Hold on…It…uh…it looks like…*yes*. Yes, at least two of the hooks are towards the bone. I think."

"What do we do now?" Paymer asked.

"Only one thing we can do," Arlon answered. "We have to see if those remains can be moved. Start pulling…but not too hard."

Mogg strengthened his stance and began tugging on the chain once again. The muscles in his tanned arms flexed under the increasing strain.

"Anything?" Paymer asked.

"I haven't seen it move…yet," Arlon replied. "But that doesn't mean it's stuck. That bone could just be really heavy and—"

"*Look!*" Mae'Lee shouted.

The chain immediately slackened somewhat (forcing Mogg to almost stumble backward), and an eruption of muddy silt enveloped the entire length of the bone.

"It's moving!" Paymer yelled. "It's moving!"

An instant later, the chain went completely loose.

Mae'Lee leaned forward. "Wait…what happened?"

"It's alright," Arlon explained. "The hooks slipped right over the bone, and the bone moved. That's a good thing. We wanted that to happen." He paused. "I think."

She looked less than convinced. "If you say so."

Paymer knelt beside Arlon. "If we keep pulling, I don't think we will catch on anything else." He pointed. "The neck curves off too much. See?"

"That is true." Arlon stood up and motioned off to their right. "Mogg…I think you need to move that way as much as you can; otherwise, you'll miss hitting the rest of it." He popped Paymer on the back and motioned behind them. "Untie the other end of the chain, Mogg's gonna need lots more slack to get where he needs to be."

Paymer sprang into action. "I'm already on it!"

Mae'Lee and Arlon quickly ducked under the swaying chain as Mogg repositioned himself accordingly.

"Okay...that...should be...far enough," Arlon said. "Now...haul it in."

Once again, the trio of hooks plowed a murky path through the flat layers of fine sediment.

"Easy now," Arlon cautioned with a raised hand. "Easy...almost...there." His hand snapped flat. "Stop. You are there...I think. Right up against the neck bones."

Mae'Lee leaned in. "They're called *vertebrae*."

"Thank you, Princess *Anatomy*," Arlon smirked in a dignified voice. He glanced back and made a slow fist as if he were grabbing the chain. "Now, if the Vish'tar would apply consistent pressure, perhaps the *vertebrae* will cooperate."

"Wow," Paymer whispered. "That sounded so smart."

"Thanks."

Mogg nodded and inched back steadily, keeping both hands locked on to the chain as it grew taut.

"Come on," Paymer muttered under his breath. "Get it."

The strain on the chain increased as Mogg's muscles tensed up, but then collapsed without warning. Arlon tried to make sense of the murky mess down below.

"It…uh…moved," he announced. "Yes, it moved! And…pull some more…faster. Now. *Faster!*"

Mogg tugged it in dutifully as Arlon and Paymer's eyes grew wider. Then wider still.

"You got it!" Paymer yelled, dancing around. "You've got it!"

There was no doubt that the hooks had snagged a vertebra, and the bone rose slowly through a dirty wake of yellow silt and sand.

Arlon fought to stay calm. "Paymer's right…you do have it. It…is…coming…up. Yes. Coming up. Keep tension on it…so it doesn't bounce on the bottom again."

Mae'Lee clasped her hands together. "Wonderful! Just wonderful."

"Steady," Arlon encouraged. "Steady. You are doing…great. It…is…it…is…almost…almost…" Arlon's voice and expression suddenly sank.

"It is almost *what?*" Mae'Lee asked.

Arlon collapsed backward onto the ground and laid his arm over his disappointed face. "We…lost it," he said. "It came loose. And fell."

Mae'Lee stared over the edge. "Oh, my…Yes…he's right. I can see it. It's already back on the bottom. Just sitting out there away from all the rest."

Paymer clapped his hands. "That's alright…we've done it once, we can do it again. Back home we have a saying about this: '*If you don't get what you want the first time, keep doing it until you do get what you wan*t *and then stop.*'"

"Thank you, Paymer," Arlon announced as he rolled onto his side before pushing himself up into a seated position, hugging his knees. "That was both less-than-inspiring and more-than-obvious."

"Glad to help, pal."

Mae'Lee just smiled.

"Well, then, *pal*," Arlon began, stretching his right hand out towards him. "Why don't you *help* me stand back up and let's all try this again?"

And try they did.

For the better part of two hours.

The silty bottom of the pool became crisscrossed with the long scars of failed attempts and littered with the remnants of dislocated bones. (Arlon had an almost-successful snag of a small section of a rib, but the bone dislodged from the hooks just as the ancient relic began to break the surface.)

Paymer massaged his hand along the small of his back. "Wow. I am actually getting sore," he complained as the sweat rolled down his face. "And stiff. Who else wants to take another beating in this losing battle?"

"I do," Mae'Lee answered as she set her food down. The resolute Princess rose to her feet. "And the daughter of Leandros does not lose, thank you."

"Oh, really? Then what happened the last few times you tried?" he teased while transferring the chain over to her outstretched hands.

"That was simply...royal practice."

He bowed and gestured towards the steaming water. "Well, then please show us all how to *royally* fish for Dragon relics."

"Yes, please," Arlon shouted through a mouthful of bread, accidentally showering his lap and the ground with a spray of wet crumbs. "Fish away, your royal Highness."

"I don't *fish*," she replied while strolling a good distance away from them. "I *catch*."

"Are you going fishing or going for a walk?" Paymer called out through cupped hands.

She spun her head around and glanced back. "I need just a little more room."

"More room?" Arlon hollered with a smile. "For what? A dance?"

"No," she replied. "For *this*."

Mae'Lee laid the hooks on the ground and backed away in long, measured steps.

"What's she doing?" Paymer asked.

Arlon and Mogg simply shrugged.

Mae'Lee came to a stop and clutched the chain with both hands as she started twirling around. The chain tightened and the hooks first slid, then bounced, before finally lifting off the ground as her rotation increased, faster and faster. The metal links sliced through the moist air with a deep and mesmerizing hum.

WHIRRR! WHIIRRRR! WHIIIRRRRRR!

Arlon and Paymer flattened themselves on the ground and Mogg scrambled to take up shelter behind his startled horse.

"She's gonna lose the chain!" Arlon shouted, covering his head.

Paymer peeked through his fingers. "Or she's gonna hurt somebody!"

Mae'Lee pivoted around three more times before releasing the chain, which sizzled out over the pool in a long arc like a huge arrow bound to a thick string. The remaining slack raced through her dainty hands in a high-pitched, swift blur.

Paymer raised his head. *"Grab the—"*

"End!" Arlon screamed.

The final few feet of chain left the ground and shot through her grasp, but Mae'Lee clamped down hard and captured a handful of the last several links.

Arlon shook his head and collapsed. "Unbelievable!"

"She better get something," Paymer said, clutching his chest. "I don't think my heart can take another one of those."

The now-anchored hooks snapped to a stop several feet above the surface and plummeted straight down into the heated waters.

SPPLLAAASSSHHHHH!

Mogg emerged out of hiding and joined the other two boys rushing over to get a better view of the results.

"Furthest toss, that's for sure," Paymer whistled. "And *freakiest* toss. Great style."

Arlon pointed and squinted. "It looks like…it might land…by that leg. A hind leg. It's so hard to tell."

Paymer rubbed his chin. "That's about the only place we haven't hit yet."

"By the will of the Zho," Mogg whispered.

A small ring of murky clouds announced the hooks' impact.

"And so it begins," Paymer muttered. "Again."

"Nice shot, daughter of Leandros," Arlon called out.

"Thank you," echoed back.

Mae'Lee retreated a handful of steps until there was considerable tension on the chain.

"You're up against it," Arlon announced.

"You going for low and slow," Paymer asked, "or fast grab?"

"I'm…going," she said, "for…*this!*"

WHIIPPP!

With a violent lurch, Mae'Lee yanked on the chain with both arms and almost tumbled backwards.

"Whoa...you okay back there?" Arlon asked.

She recovered her footing. "Just fine, thank you."

Paymer hunkered forward, reviewing the progress at the bottom of the pool. "I don't know if you caught anything, your royal fisherness...but you sure stirred up a yellow storm down there."

"Excellent!" she remarked without hesitation. "That was my intent."

Arlon's face scrunched slightly. "Wait...test the chain. Is it loose or tight?"

She tugged. "Tight."

Paymer nodded. "Well, that looks promising."

"Yes," Arlon grinned. "Indeed it does. Pull harder."

Mae'Lee used her legs for added pulling power.

"That's it," Arlon said. "More."

"Go, go, go!" Paymer exclaimed.

The chain popped loose.

"Oh, no!" Mae'Lee said.

Arlon waved his hand frantically. "No is right! *No stopping*...don't stop. Keep going."

"What did I catch?"

"Something sharp," he responded. "Now faster! Paymer, why don't you help the Princess?"

Paymer scurried back. "I'm already on it!"

Mae'Lee pulled harder. "It doesn't feel very heavy. Are you sure I've got something?"

Mogg knelt along the edge. "It is well-spoken."

Arlon raised his hand. "Careful, you two…not too aggressive…keep it consistent."

"You got it, pal."

"So what is it?" she asked.

"Keep going," Arlon said. "Almost…there."

Mae'Lee frowned. "Is anyone going to tell me?"

"Just…a…few…more…feet."

"You're gonna like it," Paymer whispered into her ear.

Arlon waved his hand around and around. "Get…ting…clo…ser. I think…we…got it…this time."

"*Got what?!*" she demanded.

Arlon and Mogg simultaneously lunged for the edge as the trio of hooks gripping the artifact broke through the steamy surface.

"*Careful!*" Paymer yelled. "It's gonna be hot—"

"*YAAOOOWWW!*" Arlon shrieked as he painfully bobbled the blistering relic from hand to hand to hand again. The steaming remains tumbled out of his shaking palm, but Mogg intercepted it inches above the rocks.

"*By…the….Red….Leaf!*" he yelped before the scalding heat forced him to dump the cylindrical relic onto the ground like a gambler's token.

Mae'Lee dropped the chain and jogged up to them with Paymer not too far behind. "What is it?!" she asked.

Arlon bent low and utilized the loose edge of his shirt as a makeshift glove. He raised the bleached curiosity into everyone's view, and it glowed white in the blazing sunlight.

"Congratulations, royal Dragon relic hunter!" he said. "You did it!"

Mae'Lee's brown eyes glistened with awe and pure delight.

"A talon!" she squealed.

Dinner on the western fringes of the Steroth Swamps was a complicated blend of excitement mixed with despair. Enthusiasm seemed to rise and fall with the flickering flames of their late evening cooking fire. And beyond that, a quiet and jittery Mogg just couldn't seem to relax. He scrambled to his feet and scanned the area.

Again.

"Everything alright?" Paymer inquired. "That's gotta be the tenth time you've jumped up in the last half hour."

"I have seen movement," Mogg muttered. "To the north. And west."

Arlon took a small bite and swallowed. "Could be animals," he said.

With a grave stare, Mogg pivoted his head about as the crimson flames highlighted his sharp features with a hellish glow. "It is an ill thought. We are being tracked." He took a deep breath. "I have sensed it many times of late."

Mae'Lee's every word was laced with fear. "Who, uh, would it be?"

"Listen," Arlon interjected, shaking his head. "It could be *no one*."

"Or *someone*. Or *many someones*," Paymer offered in between bites. "Like the Order."

"There is no evidence for that," Arlon rebutted.

Paymer's hand shot straight out and pointed into the distance. "Mogg says that someone's out there. That's evidence."

"Yes," Arlon responded with a small sigh. "There are *lots* of people out there. It could be farmers, or travelers. Probably hunters…who knows?"

"Yeah, hunters. Like the Order," Paymer quipped. "Hunting *us*."

"Can we change the subject?" Mae'Lee asked.

"Yes, please," Arlon agreed.

Mogg took a final look around and returned to his seat beside the campfire. "It is an ill thought lodging out in the open," he said, keeping his voice low.

"Well, I'm sure that we would all love to be inside a huge cave right now," Arlon responded in kind. "But we haven't seen one in over four days. Once you go north of Mt. Krysis, this land gets too flat."

"And too populated," Mae'Lee added. "There are many Avdirian cities and towns once you begin to move north beyond the swamps."

"I can attest to that," Arlon said.

"We've already been south," Paymer noted. "And we're blocked by the ocean on the east, right?"

"That is correct," Mae'Lee answered.

"So, where do we go? What's the plan?"

Paymer's pressing question was met only with the irregular popping and smacking of the weakening fire. He glanced around at blank faces.

"Is there a plan?"

All eyes eventually landed on Arlon. He finally grabbed a stick and poked around at the base of the flames. "Well, Paymer…I've read everything that the Sevasti sent with us. Probably two or three times. But, uh, the only other clue I could find mentioned an island."

"An island?"

"Just an island. Nothing more."

"But there are hundreds of islands," Mae'Lee protested. "Or thousands of islands."

Arlon jabbed a red ember. "And that is why I almost didn't even mention it."

"So, we've got nothing," Paymer sighed.

"That's not true," Arlon replied. "We've done something that no one else, in all the history of the Five Civilized Kingdoms, has ever done. We have found the final remains of three Dragons. We've collected three different relics. That's not 'nothing'."

"But three is still a long way from six, pal."

"That's one way to look at it," Arlon began. "But I prefer to think of it as...we're halfway there."

"But half of impossible is still a lot," Paymer rebutted.

"It's not impossible!" Arlon exclaimed while tossing his stick into the fire. "Those Dragons are out there...somewhere. Which means that they can also be found...somewhere."

Paymer rolled his eyes. "Not if they're at the bottom of the sea."

"And you have no evidence of that."

"Maybe we won't have to find them," Mae'Lee said.

Paymer shot her a puzzled glance. "And...what does that mean exactly?"

"Well...what if someone else has already found them? Then we would just need to get them or buy them or—"

"Steal them?" Paymer said.

She seemed rather unsettled by his remark. "I didn't say that. But, if we had to? Then…yes."

"But who would have Dragon relics?" Paymer asked. "Except maybe…"

"The Order," Arlon mumbled.

"Yeah. Them."

Mae'Lee seemed even more unsettled. "But, hold on! That's…*unthinkable*. Having any type of dealings with those murderers is out of the question. Trilyra was right. The only way we should even consider it, is if we had no other options. *NO*…other…options."

"Look around, your Highness," Paymer smirked. "Do you see any other options just lying around? I sure don't."

She looked away and picked at the edge of her sleeve. "Just because you can't see something, doesn't mean it's not there."

"Hey, wait a minute," a stunned Paymer replied. "That sounds too close to an Oranian proverb. Did you borrow that one from—"

"There are…other options," Mogg interrupted.

Arlon's head was bobbing. "I agree."

Mogg stared above the fire and trails of smoke and into the night sky. "The Northern Elders. Perhaps they could tell us more of this island."

Paymer folded his arms. "So, now you want us to travel all the way back to Alaithia for our next clue? That'll take weeks."

Arlon grabbed a straight stick. "Not weeks," he replied while tracing a large circle over and over in the middle of the flames. "Just a few seconds."

"What?"

"Oh, yes," Mae'Lee said. "A Vision Fire."

"Oh, the freaky flaming blue circle thing."

Arlon chuckled. "That's what I'm talking about."

"Are you sure we still have the jar?" Paymer asked. "I thought we lost it on the boat."

Arlon's eyebrows raised as he took a deep breath. "Oh, that's right. The jar was with our two Sevasti here...right before they were arrested."

Mae'Lee looked horrified. "Really? So we don't have it?"

Arlon's head sank. "No. Captain Theele has it. Or he might've sold it by now. Probably thought it was worthless."

"So now we *do* have to travel all the way back to Alaithia," Mae'Lee mourned.

"No," Arlon answered. "Why would we do that? We'll just use a Vision Fire."

She shot him a hard glance. "But you just said—"

"I just said that Captain Theele has our jar." Arlon reached into his shirt. "And I...have...*this*."

"Your Rone necklace!" Mae'Lee whispered with delight.

"That's right." Arlon sandwiched the gem between his palms and twisted. "And Kash filled it up with more powder before we left Alaithia."

"You are full of surprises, Arlon, Dunamai of Soteria," Paymer declared with a growing grin.

"Thanks, Paymer."

"You really are, pal. You know, thinking back...Mogg and Trilyra and I get thrown in the brig, and you figure a way to bust us out. And then, when we hit a low spot in the Mal'korr's cave, you found a way to keep us going. Again."

"Hey, look, that was Mae'Lee and—"

"And now," Paymer continued, "now, we are at yet another hard place...and here you are, doing it once again." He paused. "With Arlon the Soterian...it's surprise. After surprise. After surprise."

The red light from the dying flames masked Arlon's blushing cheeks. "And where would I be," he countered, "if it weren't for all of you keeping me alive after the Dragon bite and getting me to Alaithia? I'd probably be buried in an unmarked grave somewhere along the banks of the Kordoni River right now."

"Don't say that," Mae'Lee protested. "Don't even think that."

"Well, it's true. I'd be nothing without all of you. And Mogg, I'm sure none of us would've made it one day in the lands of the Kla'aven Wins'orr."

Mogg bowed his head ever so slightly.

Paymer's eyes teared up, and he glanced back over at Arlon. "Anyway, listen, pal. I know that I've said some pretty harsh things. Things you didn't deserve. I, um, I just want to…you know…*I apologize*. It wasn't right. Bad things have happened, but none of them have been your fault."

Arlon blinked hard several times and cleared his throat. "Well, my Oranian friend, we have a saying about that back in Soteria."

"Really?"

"You bet. It goes something like: '*When someone apologizes to you, and it's awkward, and you don't know what to say…start a Vision Fire.*'"

Paymer laughed out loud with the others and slapped him on the arm. "I'll make you a deal. How about *I* get to stay in charge of all the wise proverbs, and *you* get to stay in charge of all the Vision Fires?"

Arlon squinted for a few moments. "Deal."

A very giddy Mae'Lee scooted closer. "Wait, can I sprinkle it?!"

He nodded while dumping a tiny bit of powder into her waiting palm. "Another *deal*."

"Alright," the Princess began. "Everyone get back. This is going to be spectacular." Mae'Lee took a deep breath, raised her hand close to her face and blasted the powder right into the flames with a quick exhale. A quick, bright shockwave exploded outward.

WHHOOOSSSSSHHHH!

"*Oh!*" a startled Mae'Lee cried out, scrambling back as the red and amber flames quickly altered into a dancing display of a hundred shades of radiant blue. Arlon chuckled at her reaction and handed her the stick.

"And now," he said, "please make a few royal circles, your Highness."

"And I would be honored, Arlon, Dunamai of Soteria." She raised the stick and began tracing a series of loops, over and over. The first of many tongues of bluish flame played all along her path. "Oh! Lovely!" she squealed. "Just lovely!" The excited princess pulled the stick away, and the ring of fire remained, and strengthened.

"Here comes the freaky part," Paymer mumbled through a nervous smile. "Let's hope Kash is in his chamber."

Arlon glanced up into the triple moonslight. "It's very late," he noted. "He should be in his room, asleep probably."

He wasn't wrong.

Mae'Lee covered her mouth. "Look!"

A dark, murky figure ambled into view.

"The freaky part," Paymer whispered.

Arlon cleared his throat. "Can you…can you hear us?"

Kash's unmistakable and kind voice rumbled back. "Hear and *see* you, my boy. All of you." The old man appeared to lean closer. "All…*four* of you?"

"Yes, sir, we…uh…lost one. Trilyra. Of Ammodis."

"*Lost?*"

"I mean, she's gone. Not here. She went back…home. It's a long story."

"How is your shoulder?"

Arlon rubbed it lightly. "Still pretty sore."

"It is to be expected." Kash leaned in again. "And you…daughter of Leandros. Has your hearing improved, your Highness?"

She smiled and nodded. "Much, much improved, sir. Thank you."

"Most interesting. Most interesting, indeed. Where are you at present?"

"We are…just west of the Steroth Swamps," Arlon replied.

"And have you had success in this endeavor?" Kash inquired. "Have you discovered the remains of any of the Dread Guardians?"

Paymer couldn't keep quiet any longer. "Three of them. Sir."

"*Three?!*" Kash rubbed his beard. "Three? Remarkable. This is nothing but the blessing of the Zho."

Paymer's eyes were wide. "The first was buried in the ice in the Valley of the Three Peaks, just like you thought. Mogg got it out with Dragon fire. The second one was in a cave, in the Woods of Ankath, guarded by a scorpion-wolf thing, which was really freaky. And we saw Shendollyn transform, right in front of us. And then, a few days ago, we found the third Dragon at the bottom of a heated pool with steam that looks like fog. Mae'Lee got it out with a chain and hooks."

Arlon smiled. "My Oranian friend is quite excited, as you can tell. Did you catch all that?"

"Most of it, my boy. And what I did gather is that all of you will have stories upon stories to share upon your return. Tales as great as any legend told in the Five Kingdoms, in any respect. Of that, there can be no doubt."

"Well, as great as our tales have been," Arlon began, "we need your help."

"Speak. If it is within my power, you shall have it."

"We, uh, we have run out of options," Arlon admitted. "We have no more clues to follow."

"Tell him about the island thing," Paymer whispered.

Kash cocked his head. "What's that?"

"We did find a small clue. Maybe. It said something about an island. But nothing more. I've read it over and over. Is there anything else you can tell us?"

"*Island?*" Kash repeated. "Island. Island. I am sorry. I must confess that I have no knowledge regarding the remains of a Dread Guardian and any island."

Mae'Lee sighed. "Then it is over?"

"Over?" Kash fairly chuckled, standing up. "My dear Princess, this quest is far from over." He started to walk away.

Arlon leaned in with a puzzled look as Kash completely vanished from sight. "Wait…where are you going?"

"To get help, young Dunamai," the old man's hollow, distant voice echoed back. "Be patient. And stay quiet."

"What does he mean by that?" Paymer whispered.

Arlon sat back and folded his arms. "I'm not sure."

"Whatever he means," Mae'Lee said, "he didn't sound too confident. I'm worried. What if he can't help us?"

"It's too soon for talk like that," Arlon replied, keeping his voice low. "Let's wait to see what he comes up with."

"What if it's nothing?" Paymer asked.

Arlon grabbed his shirt and jerked him closer. "Remember what you said, just a few minutes ago? Your apology and all?"

Paymer nodded.

Arlon pulled him closer yet. "If you keep talking like that, you might have to do it all over again."

Paymer's eyes raced back and forth. "Good point."

Mae'Lee tapped Arlon.

There was movement in the portal.

Not one, but two dark figures sat down.

Kash pointed. "You remember, Brother Gremlor?"

Arlon straightened up and nodded. "Yes, yes, of course. Greetings, sir."

"I cannot begin to convey the joy that fills my chest," Gremlor began. "To behold all of you. Safe and unharmed."

"Thank you, sir," Arlon replied with a small nod.

"Brother K'Kashmalon has relayed both your notable successes and your...most urgent need."

"So, what can you tell us?" Arlon pressed. "Do you know anything about an island? And Dragon remains?"

"Please say '*yes*'," Paymer mumbled. "It's a small word."

The pair of Sevasti elders traded quick but silent glances. Gremlor was the first to respond.

"This is a critical matter which may require considerable deliberation and research," he said.

"That wasn't much of a '*yes*'," Paymer whispered through a sigh.

"*Shhhh*," Mae'Lee urged.

Gremlor leaned in. "What is your present location?"

"We are near the Steroth Swamps. Sir."

"The thermal swamps encompass a considerable tract of Avdirian soil, young Dunamai," Gremlor said. "Could your description be more duly specific, my son?"

"Uh, sorry, sir. Perhaps Mae, I mean, perhaps the *Princess* could help you with that." Arlon nodded towards her.

Mae'Lee smiled and hunkered closer. "Yes, well…we are just south of Tallia, sir. Which is just south of—"

"Tobermere," Gremlor said.

She nodded. "Yes. Sir."

There was a pause.

Arlon frowned. "So, can you help us?"

Gremlor huddled close with Kash, and the elders exchanged a tense yet quiet conversation. Kash nodded and then stared back at the Dunamai.

"Grant us the space of at least two days," he said. "Two days in which to discover information which may be of further assistance in your journeys."

Arlon squinted. "You will be able to help us in two days?"

"In the will of the Zho," Kash affirmed with a noticeable degree of reservation. "But remember…when it comes to the location of the remains of Dread Guardians, who can speak with any certainty of such things?"

"We hope *you* can," Paymer piped up.

"Two days hence," Gremlor repeated as he rose from his seat and gathered his cloak.

"Remain where you are, young Dunamai…and establish contact with K'Kashmalon and myself about this same hour."

"I don't like waiting," Mae'Lee grumbled.

Arlon slid the sizzling pan out of their fire and sliced off a steaming rabbit's leg. "None of us do. But we were told to wait. And it's only been one day."

"And not even a full day," Paymer added. "We've got a long way to go. It's only sunset. If you think about—"

"*Eat your food*," Arlon urged coupled with a playful frown. "You're not helping." He looked back at Mae'Lee, instantly trading his scowl for a forced smile. "Plus, we've been on the run for so long. We need a break. To rest."

"I guess." She nibbled on her bread and gestured off to their left. "But he never gets any rest."

Arlon didn't need to look.

Mogg.

She's probably right.

"I've noticed," he said.

"Then have you also noticed how dreadfully quiet he's become?" she asked under her breath. "I mean, we all know that Mogg's never been a talker, but it's becoming really sad." She paused. "This is sorrow, sorrow borne of heartache."

"Careful," Paymer cautioned. "That started to sound almost…proverbial, like—"

"Eat your food," she said.

"I'm already on it."

Arlon set his meal down and jumped up.

"What's wrong?" Paymer asked.

"*Shhhh.*" Arlon closed his eyes and angled his head. "I hear…something. Like…singing."

"Singing?" Mae'Lee whispered.

"Yes. Singing. You know, saying words and changing your voice up and down. Don't they sing in Avdira?"

She stood beside him and cupped her ears. "We have wonderful songs in my kingdom. But I can't hear any right now. I realize that's not saying much."

"Wait…I hear it," Paymer said through a mouthful of meat. "I do hear it. It's coming from over—hey! Where'd Mogg go?"

Arlon opened his eyes and checked the area.

Mogg had vanished.

Mae'Lee pointed. "He was right there just a moment ago."

"I think I see the source of the singing," Arlon remarked. He jutted his finger out. "Over there. Looks like…a man…leading a horse."

"I still can't hear him," the Princess replied. "But…yes…yes, I see him now."

"And…it looks like he sees us," Paymer added. "And he is heading this way. Should I get my sword?"

"No, no," Arlon whispered. "Just…stay alert."

"You got it, pal."

"And quiet."

Paymer nodded.

"Mae'Lee…why don't you act like you're sleeping and keep your face turned away? And Paymer, keep those tattoos covered up."

"I'm already—"

"*On it*. I know."

Paymer winked. "Thanks, pal."

The traveler drew closer and his singing grew louder. Arlon didn't recognize the song, but it had a pleasant rhythm, and the deep voice was soothing.

"Hey there, friend," Arlon called out, stepping away from Mae'Lee. "Beautiful evening."

The old man took a few moments to finish his verse and looked up with a charming smile shrouded in a well-kept white beard that hung almost as low as his chest. "Yes. Yes. And...*yes*," he said.

Arlon squinted. "Excuse me?"

The gentleman adjusted his hat (which was rather flopped over) and brought himself and his white horse to a standstill. "*Yes*...I am a friend." He looked up. "*Yes*, it is beautiful. And *yes*, it is evening."

"Fair enough." Arlon gestured towards the fire. "Can I offer you a warm meal on your journey, or some fresh water for you or your horse?"

The visitor massaged his round belly. "One does not maintain a healthy midsection such as this by refusing the generosity of strangers, mind you. Especially when delicious smelling food is part and parcel of that generosity."

"Come," Arlon beckoned. "Join us."

The man tethered his steed and moseyed over to the camp. "I was raised by my grandmother on my father's side, and she taught me well that '*hospitality rejected is the greatest of all insults'*." He sat down and Arlon quickly gathered a cut of meat alongside a thick slice of bread and set it before him.

Arlon nodded. "Well, we certainly have plenty. It would be selfish to not at least offer something to a hungry traveler."

The old man devoured a few quick bites and glanced around. "Just the three of you? On four horses? Where are your parents?"

Arlon froze.

Parents?

What do I say?

What if Mogg returns?

"Uh…well, one of our party is out…hunting. And it's just us…no parents. We have left home."

The old man leaned in and dropped his voice way down. "Don't be afraid. Tell me…are the lot of you in some sort of trouble?"

"Oh, uh, no. No trouble. No."

The visitor swallowed again and took a fast drink. He pointed. "Truth be known, there's considerable lodging in Tallia, not a far stretch from where we now sit. Is there a reason you're avoiding town? Low on coin? It's nothing to be ashamed of, mind you. Times are difficult. But then again, you could get a respectable room for only a handful of clinks. Maybe a couple fractions at most."

Think, Arlon.

In his desperation, he reverted to the cover story they used aboard the *Graceful Galleon* several weeks before. "Oh, no. It's my wife...she was exhausted," Arlon rambled, pointing at Mae'Lee's blanket-wrapped form laying nearby. "So, we just stopped here."

"Wife? Goodness, such a young couple. Now, nothing wrong with that, mind you. Where are you folks headed?"

More questions.

"Tobermere," Arlon pretty much blurted out. "We are...visiting her family there."

"Tobermere?" the visitor repeated. *"Seeking family?"*

"Uh, yes. Sir."

The man paused. "Now, that's rather disappointing."

Arlon grasped his cup with trembling hands and sipped it. "Sorry, I don't understand—"

"Truth be known, I had hoped you were seeking something far more interesting than family."

What a strange statement, Arlon thought. *Think of something to say. And fast.*

"And...that's because you've never met my wife's family," Arlon managed to offer with the cover of a fake chuckle. "Pretty interesting people."

"That might be the case, young man...but I had sincerely hoped that your small company here was seeking...*Dragon relics.*"

A stunned Arlon nearly choked on his drink. He coughed into his hand and wiped his quivering mouth. "Um...excuse me?"

"I did not misspeak, mind you. Dragon relics. The remains of Dragon's long dead. This region is famous for it. At least to the right folk."

"Famous—?"

"There's a legend that one of the Dragons expired here many thousands of years past."

Arlon struggled to act surprised. "Really?"

"Truth be known, it wasn't actually *here.* It was more...*east* of here. Off the coast. Out in the sea."

Paymer shot a surprised glance over at Arlon.

"Out in the sea?" Arlon asked. "As in...*in* the water? *Under* the water?"

"No, no. Sorry," the man replied, ripping off another sizable chunk of meat. He dabbed his greasy lips on his broad sleeve. "It's reported to be on an island out in the sea."

"You don't say?" Arlon muttered as innocently as he could muster. "It's amazing the things you hear about as you travel."

"There is information, young man...and then, there is *valuable* information. The kind of information that leads people to desperate acts. Such as fighting. Or stealing. Or even killing."

A mixture of fear and uncertainty paralyzed Arlon for a few moments. He stared down in silence at his food. "So…how is the rabbit?" he finally asked. "Can I get you—"

"It's an odd thing, mind you," the visitor interrupted while staring coldly into the flames. "Sometimes the most valuable thing—the most precious thing—is not even a *thing* at all." He raised the empty palm of his left hand and studied it through squinting eyes shrouded by rows of deep wrinkles. "You can't hold it. Or see it. Or smell it. But it's worth more golden Royals than a caravan of the finest gems from the Ploutonian mines."

Arlon had not the slightest idea of how to respond, so he didn't. He forced a smile and then forced himself to take another bite of bread and then forced himself to swallow.

"So tell me, friend…are you interested?"
Even more questions.
This isn't going to end…well.
As Arlon glanced up, he realized that the old man's piercing and unwavering eyes were locked onto him. "Uh, sorry. Interested in what exactly?"

"Haven't you been paying attention, my boy?" their inquisitive visitor replied, obviously a bit disgusted. "I'm speaking of the most valuable of all commodities...*information*. Are you interested?"

"Well, see, I...am not entirely sure just—"

The old man tossed the remainder of his meal into the fire and quickly retrieved a small, rolled document from somewhere deep inside his cloak. He held it out. "If I were to tell you, that I was in possession of a map, a map which reveals the precise location of the remains of a Dread Guardian...would that be worth something to you, my young friends? Some have even said the remains of *two* Dread Guardians are there."

Arlon's eyebrows shot up.

The remains of two Dragons?

Parts of his first Rone vision flashed through his stunned mind. A pair of Dragons swirled into the sky engaged in a furious death battle.

Is that even possible? he wondered. *Could two Dragons have died at the same time? Was that a vision of the past?*

Just the very idea made his head hurt.

The man pressed him further. "Are you interested, my boy?"

Arlon froze (for what felt like the hundredth time). *What is happening here?* he wondered in a state of utter panic. *What do I do?*

What am I supposed to say?!

The stranger rose up in haste and began stashing the scroll back into his garment. "I suppose your silence is all the answer this traveler needs." With a few quick strokes of his hands, he brushed the scattered crumbs of bread from his cloak and nodded. "I thank you for the warm and delightful provisions, but now…I must take my leave. Tonight I lodge in Tallia."

He pivoted about and plodded towards his horse just as Mae'Lee discreetly spun her head around and glared up at Arlon.

"*What're you doing?*" she mouthed more than spoke. "*Get. That. Map.*" Paymer (donning a serious stare) wagged his head towards the departing visitor as well.

Arlon deposited his meal on the ground and started to stand up. "Hey. Uh, hold on there, please, sir."

If the man heard him, it didn't show in the least. With a quick snap, he loosed the tether and began leading his horse off to the north in tense silence.

"Excuse me," Arlon called out while chasing him down. "Excuse me, sir. We are interested. In the information. And the map."

The stranger kept moving and didn't even bother to look back. "Apparently not very interested," he replied before resuming his earlier song.

Arlon jogged past the man's horse and positioned himself directly in the stranger's path. He held up his hand. "Please stop. Sir. I would like to, uh, discuss your map."

The old man halted both his horse and his song. "*Discuss?* The hour is late. I regret that I certainly have no time for discussion."

"Sorry…*purchase*. We would like to *purchase* your map. Sir." Arlon reached into a satchel and pulled out five golden Royals. "Is this acceptable?"

The man's eyes squinted as he stared down at the coins. "*Acceptable?* Where I come from, that would be considered an *insult*." He stuck his arm out and lightly shoved against Arlon. "Now move aside, boy. I must be on my way."

Arlon refused to budge. He dug around inside the satchel and quickly doubled his original offer.

"*Ten* Royals?" the stranger muttered as he patted on his horse's neck. "That might purchase my old steed here, but truth be known, Chagrin isn't for sale today. Now, make way."

Arlon stood his ground and thrust the entire bag of coins into the man's hand. The stranger hefted it up and down with a satisfied grin.

"Hmmm…now things are beginning to feel…*acceptable*." He opened the satchel and studied the contents (as best he could in the shifting firelight). Arlon dumped the other ten coins back into the bag in a clinking cascade.

"There should be over fifty Royals in there," Arlon asserted as he withdrew his hand and folded his arms. "Plus several fractions." He paused and narrowed his eyes. "So tell me, friend…are you interested?"

The impatient visitor chuckled for several seconds. "Bailconn," he murmured.

Arlon leaned in with a puzzled look. "Sorry. *Bailconn?* I'm not familiar with that term."

"It's not a term, boy." The smiling stranger jabbed a stubby finger at his own chest. "It's my name. Bailconn." He reached into his cloak, fished out the scroll, and delivered it to Arlon.

"And, truth be known, I am presently the *former* owner of this map."

"I had almost forgotten how lovely a sunrise over the sea actually is," Mae'Lee offered with a sweet and satisfied smile. The Princess closed her eyes and leaned against the ship's rail as the early morning breezes toyed with her long, black hair. "And I love how it feels on my face."

Paymer shut his eyes and faced the brilliant sun as well. "Um…I don't really feel anything," he complained.

Arlon sneaked his hand over and flicked the tip of his friend's freckled nose.

"Yeow!" Paymer said, grabbing his face.

"Sorry, just making sure that your face could still feel things properly," Arlon replied with a wink.

Mae'Lee arched over the rail and watched the waves crash against the hull and churn into swirling rolls of broiling white foam. "Just think, we've all sailed on both oceans in less than several weeks! Isn't that wonderful?"

A whimsical smile broke out across Arlon's face. "And just think…until a few months ago, the only water I was ever allowed in, was in a bathtub."

"Nice, pal," Paymer replied.

"How far is the island?" Mae'Lee asked.

Arlon kept his voice down as the wind buffeted the main sail just overhead. "The captain said we should be there by tomorrow morning. He told me that they would drop us off and then leave. He said that they would pick us up in the same spot the next day."

"That seems odd," Mae'Lee noted, looking around. "Why wouldn't they wait? They don't have any other passengers on this boat, do they?"

"There are a few, but not too many that I've seen," Arlon answered.

"We certainly paid him enough," Paymer commented. "This little ocean voyage just about wiped us out. What if they don't come back?"

"Oh, they'll come back," Arlon responded. "I only gave him half of the fee."

Mae'Lee spun around and leaned her back against the wooden rails that had been rounded and polished from years of use. "But then why won't they wait?"

"The captain wouldn't say," Arlon replied. "But one of the crew admitted that this particular island has a...*bad reputation*. That's why we had so much trouble chartering a boat."

"Bad reputation?" Paymer repeated under his breath. "What does that mean, you think?"

"Apparently no one goes there, and no one has gone there for a long time. He said that there are legends about entire ships full of sailors harboring at the island, and then...they never return." He paused. "On most maps it's labeled as just one of the Breaker Islands. But the crewman said it has another name...a nickname. The sailors call it the Isle of Slaughter."

"Excuse me?" Paymer replied. "*Slaughter?* As in a terrible means of violent death?"

Arlon nodded.

Paymer grabbed his stomach. "Okay, pal. I think I'm going to be sick."

"And that's where we're going?" Mae'Lee asked, her voice trembling. "A dreadful island that no one ever returns from?"

Arlon nodded once more and lowered his voice even further. "We have to. That is...if we want more Dragon relics."

Paymer leaned closer to Arlon. "So, does the map say where the remains can be found on this terrible and dangerous island?"

Arlon nodded yet again. He motioned for Mae'Lee to scoot nearer before he retrieved the map and spread it out. He tapped his finger on the document. "This is the island...*here*."

Mae'Lee's face scrunched up. "That island...it...looks like a mountain, or a volcano."

"It *is* a volcano," Arlon countered. He pointed again. "The relics are supposed to be in it. At the top."

Paymer's eyebrows shot up. "Whoa, wait...we have to go *into* a volcano?"

"Relax, Paymer. It's a dead volcano."

"No lava and fire and smoke and all that?"

"Nothing but rocks and dirt. Supposedly."

"Well, then...that's not so bad, pal."

"Not bad?" Mae'Lee scoffed. "They call it the Isle of Slaughter."

Paymer nodded. "Oh yeah. Good point."

The large vessel rose up and slipped down in a gentle rhythm as they all enjoyed the salty spray which occasionally drifted over the sharp bow. A trio of playful sea birds flitted in the skies just above the mast.

"I'm glad that we got this map and all," Paymer said discreetly. "But I wish we would've talked again with Kash and Gremlor before we left. Like they told us to."

"You know there wasn't time," Arlon replied. "The captain said we had to sail before dark. We can make a Vision Fire once we're on the island. Hopefully we will have more relics by nightfall. Maybe even the relics from *two* Dragons."

Paymer couldn't hide his confusion. "I don't get it. How could the remains of two *different* Dragons be in one place? That doesn't make any sense…does it? Would they both choose the same place to die?"

Arlon shrugged. "There's so much that we just don't know." He paused and closed his eyes. "When I had that Rone vision at Mt. Krysis, I did see two Dragons fighting. And it was over a volcano."

"*You think they killed each other?!*" Paymer exclaimed in disbelief.

"Paymer!" Mae'Lee scolded under her breath. "Keep your voice down."

Arlon folded his arms and looked over at him. "If there are the remains of two Dragons on the island, at the top of a volcano…that would explain it."

"Freaky. Freaky."

"But, wait…I thought that Rone visions were always of the future," Mae'Lee halfway asked.

Arlon shrugged. "I don't know."

"There's a lot that we don't know," Paymer added.

Mae'Lee stepped back and scanned the area. "Where's Mogg?" she asked. "Still sleeping?"

"He is," Arlon replied.

"Last night he stood the last watch," Paymer reminded them. "Can't blame him for being tired. I'm tired, and I had the *first* watch."

"Exactly. So let him sleep," Arlon said. "And as much as he wants. I have a feeling that we will need his skills and strength once we land on the island."

"That's both comforting, and not at all comforting," Mae'Lee mourned.

Paymer gazed out at the bright horizon as a distant look washed over his face. "I wish she were here."

"Who's that?" Arlon asked.

"Trilyra."

That caught Arlon unprepared. "Oh, her. Yeah...me, too."

"Me, too, *too*," the Princess added.

The incessant rain that had pounded the ship all through the night had left the air clean and the modest deck thoroughly soaked. A still-sleepy Arlon was the first to wander topside, and he studied the angry line of gray clouds that hung like a dark blanket over the western horizon.

"Miserable storm last evening," one of the deckhands muttered as he passed by, hauling a thick coil of rope that was probably a bit too heavy for him.

"Sure sounded like it," Arlon replied with a yawn and a nod.

"We're gettin' close," the young man said, pointing. "Should have ya there before midday."

Arlon followed the deckhand's gesture to a cone-shaped island far off to their northeast. *There it is,* he thought. *The volcano!* A strained smile spread across his face.

Not as big as Mt. Krysis, that's for sure...but it is a volcano. But was that the volcano in my Rone vision?

Maybe.

After sloshing through two puddles and picking his way around a half-dozen out-of-place crates, the calm seas glistening back at him were certainly a pleasant surprise as Arlon approached the ship's edge.

And he desperately needed something pleasant.

His troubled thoughts (which had kept him up most of the night) danced between a nervous hope about finding relics and the nagging fear that he and his fellow Dunamai were headed to horrific deaths.

He gazed out across the ocean at the volcanic island rising and falling in the distance.

Another possibility haunted him.

It could all be a lie, he thought.

That Bailconn character might've taken our gold...and given us nothing. Nothing. Maybe the old man knew that the island was dangerous and that we would never come back. Between buying the map and chartering this boat, we're almost out of money.

What are we gonna do if we don't find anything?

His tired body collapsed against the rail.

Even if the relics are there, he sighed, *we might die before we find them. Or right after.*

A pair of busy crewmen rushed by lugging a heavy crate, laughing the entire way. A sudden suspicious chill shot up Arlon's spine.

Or, what if it's all a trap?

What if they drop us off, but then never come back?

A familiar voice interrupted his conflicted musings. "Is that the island?"

Arlon spun around as Mogg ambled up sporting a fresh face bandage. "Uh, yeah. That's it," he replied through a less-than-honest smile. "Good news…we should be there in a few hours."

Mogg turned to face him with a skeptical glance. "The words on your lips, do not match the fears on your face, my worried friend."

"Is it that obvious?"

Mogg scooted closer and lowered his voice. "The Kray have a saying about such things. *'The eyes are the twin traitors of the heart.'*"

Arlon looked away. "I can't hide it. You're right. I am worried."

Mogg nodded and also stared out at the sea. "And rightly so. Our fortunes are uncertain.

But a great leader must be the first to embrace danger, and yet the last to abandon hope." He took a deep breath and paused. "As our leader, it falls upon you to do both."

"*Leader?!*" Arlon chuckled in disbelief. "No, no, no. I don't see myself as a leader. *No way.* And certainly not a *great* one. Not even close."

Mogg laid a comforting hand on Arlon's arm. "And that, my friend, is precisely what qualifies you."

The two stood in shared silence for over a minute, enjoying the warm sunrise and the cool, salty breezes. Arlon spotted a tiny school of Silverfish jumping across the waves, and he watched them with only passing interest.

"I'm sorry," he finally said.

Mogg glanced over. "For what?"

"For…a lot of things."

"Perhaps one day, the Vice will learn to speak clearly," Mogg mumbled.

"Sorry. I guess…uh…I guess I was mainly thinking about…Trilyra."

Mogg's expression turned cold. "It was her decision. She abandoned us. You do not bear the burden of blame."

"I feel like I do."

Mogg squinted. "Feelings are not the same thing as truth."

"Well, listen to you," Arlon snickered. "You're just full of wisdom and proverbs this morning. If I didn't know better, I would've thought that someone with red hair and freckles was standing right next to me."

"It is an ill thought," Mogg muttered. "You did not cause her to leave...us."

Arlon hesitated, choosing his words with the utmost care. And respect. "So, tell me...was there something going on between the two of you?"

Mogg's brow wrinkled up. "The two of *me?*"

Arlon shook his head. "No, no...sorry. I meant, was there a certain...affection, or feelings between you and her? You and Trilyra?"

It was Mogg's turn to pause.

"The Kray, do not often...speak of such things," he muttered.

Arlon leaned closer with a smile. "So...is that a '*yes*'?" he asked (probably a bit louder than he meant to).

"Is what a '*yes*'?" a sweet voice rang out.

They both swiveled about and grinned at the Princess who had somehow managed to sneak up behind them. She struggled to keep the blowing hair out of her face, but finally surrendered.

"Good morning," Arlon said.

"Yes, it is a lovely morning," Mae'Lee replied, looking around. "Are we close?"

Arlon and Mogg both pointed. "Right over there," Arlon urged. "Only a few hours out."

"Oh, yes," she said. "I see the mountain now." Mae'Lee leaned against the rail while folding her arms. "I don't know whether to be excited. Or terrified."

"How about both?" Paymer offered, strolling up alongside all of them. "And don't forget broke. Excited. Terrified. And *broke*."

"Well...thank you for that uplifting and encouraging message this early morning," Arlon added sarcastically as he patted him on the shoulder. "Thank you very much." Arlon shivered and rubbed his own arms. "I bet we can all say that we feel the courage now rising up within us."

"Anytime, pal."

Everyone smiled.

But only briefly.

"Who's ready for a big breakfast?" Paymer asked with a clap as he scanned their faces. "I feel like I could eat two plates full of bacon, and at least four or five eggs."

Arlon nodded. "Sounds like a good meal."

"Let's hope it's not our *last* meal," Mae'Lee mourned.

"Oh, yeah, good point," Paymer noted. "And now...I'm not quite so hungry. How about...one plate of bacon. And...*three* eggs."

"Come on, now, folks," Arlon scolded with a playful grin. "We've made it this far. Let's, uh, let's enjoy a nice breakfast. Then pack up." He lowered his voice to just above a whisper. "And get ready for the Isle of *Relics*."

Mae'Lee frowned. "You mean the Isle of *Slaughter?*"

"Come on…that's just a legend," Arlon countered.

"Like the Mal'korr?" she replied with eyebrows raised. "You're starting to sound like a skeptical Ammodisian girl I once knew. And she was wrong, thank you."

Arlon shook his head and started to walk away. "You, are an *impossible* Princess," he whispered with a wink.

Paymer slid over to her. "But a cute one," he said, grabbing her arm. "A nice, cute one. Come on…let's go get something to eat." He pulled her along.

"Plus, I fight better on a full stomach."

Mae'Lee held onto the side of the small, creaking rowboat and leaned into Arlon's ear. "Why did the captain anchor the boat so far from the island?" she whispered. "It's going to take forever to reach the shore up ahead. Plus, it's making me feel a bit seasick."

Arlon glanced over her head and watched the main ship shrink behind them as the oars splashed back down into the water. None of the three crew members on the tender had said a word since the Dunamai had boarded. "I'm not sure," he replied. "Maybe...the water in this bay is too shallow," he answered discreetly. "Yeah, that's probably it."

"Or," she whispered harshly. "Or…he is so terrified of what's on that island, that he won't get the ship anywhere near it."

Arlon glanced over the side. "No, this bay is not deep enough," he replied firmly. "I can see the bottom."

"Their ship is not that big," she rebutted. "And you know it."

He glared at her and gestured with his arm. "Just take it all in and enjoy the ride."

The rugged, untouched scenery was breathtaking, as long as Arlon could ignore the troublesome prospect of either being stranded or slaughtered. He shielded his squinting eyes from the midday sun and glanced skyward. The ancient volcano, etched with deep, vertical gouges carved by eons of erosion, seemed to rise up right out of the shimmering blue waters of the bay. It looked to be almost as wide as Mt. Krysis at the base, but Arlon estimated that it was only half the height, perhaps even less.

Maybe it won't be too difficult an ascent, he said to himself.

In his nervous optimism, he imagined being the first to climb over the last few feet of the caldera's wide rim. Images of the bleached remains of two enormous Dragons scattered in a grass-covered plateau flashed through his mind. He looked around at the crew guiding the tender. The shore was now coming fast.

Let's just hope that they return to get us.

If not, we may have more relics, but we'll be trapped on the Isle of Slaughter.

For good.

"Tomorrow, right?" Arlon called out as the nose of the boat plowed into the dark sand in a grinding lurch a few minutes later. "You will be back to pick us up? Right here? Same time?"

"If that's what the captain said," one of the crew replied while he and the other two bent down to pick up their passenger's supplies. They seemed to be in a bothered rush.

Arlon stood up as the boat rocked and wobbled. "That is what he said. We have his word."

The ship's mate motioned towards the island. "Watch yer step. Let's move along."

In a sloppy, crunching mess, the Dunamai debarked single file over the bow, and the crew hastily tossed the remaining bags into their waiting arms. Moments later, after a fast shove on a long pole and a double splash of the oars, the boat slipped away against the steady pounding of the waves.

"Just to confirm...we *will* see you guys tomorrow, in this same spot?" Paymer yelled as he struggled to keep control of the three bags in his arms (while his feet continued to slip and sink into the gravely sand). "*Hello?*"

Arlon began climbing onto higher and dryer ground. "Don't let it bother you, pal. I don't think they were in a talkative mood." He waved his free hand as best he could. "Come on, let's get to a better vantage point, so we can find the best way to the top."

Mae'Lee looked up and studied the daunting cliffs jutting above them. "How about the *easiest* way to the top?"

Arlon smiled back at her. "Let's hope that it is both."

If the challenging ascent from the shoreline was any indication of what lay ahead, then Arlon knew that all such notions of best ways and easy ways would be quickly forgotten.

"Oh my," Mae'Lee mumbled as Arlon reached down and pulled her to the top of a dark, silty ravine. She scanned the bleak landscape sprawled out before her to the north and the west. The fairly level ground at the base of the mountain was a wasteland of jagged rocks interrupted only by the occasional tuft of dry, yellowed grass that somehow found a way to survive in the harsh conditions. She took a quick sip of water. "I was hoping that there would be more...you know—"

"*Life?*" Paymer asked.

She nodded.

Mogg scrambled to the top of a pile of large rocks and surveyed the flat terrain with keen eyes. "*Life* is what we do not want," he said.

"He's right," Arlon replied. "The less living things we run into, the better." He sheathed his sword and relaxed a bit. "I want this whole island to be as dead as the Dragon bones that are waiting for us way up there."

Paymer reclined against a boulder. "Maybe that's where this freaky place got its nickname."

The Princess looked up. "What do you mean?"

"*Death*. Think about it. There's no food. Probably very little fresh water. Maybe sailors that were low on supplies stopped here, only to find...nothing but death."

Arlon wandered around. "And over time, as the stories grew and were passed on as legends...death changed to *slaughter*. Makes sense."

Mae'Lee didn't seem convinced. "Or, the name means exactly what it means, thank you. There's someone, or some*thing* dreadful that lives here. Or under here." She pointed at the volcano. "Or up there. Something that slaughters people."

Mogg scrambled back down and jumped the last several feet, landing with a crunching thud. "It is well-spoken. We must assume that danger and death await at every moment."

"I sure am glad you agree with me," she said. "But I sure don't like the way you put it."

"Did you see any trees from up there?" Arlon inquired.

Mogg shook his head and spread his hands out. "It is…as you see, for as far as I could see."

"How much wood do we have left, Paymer?"

"Not much. Let me guess…cold meals until we leave this rock?"

Arlon paused. "Probably."

The Princess strolled off and gazed up at the mountain. "How long do you think it will take to reach the top there?"

Arlon joined her. He shaded his eyes. "Well, it's hard to say…I've never really climbed up the side of a volcano. But…if we can find a suitable path, maybe three or four hours?"

"What if it's not *suitable?*" Paymer asked.

"Well, then it could take all day, I guess."

"We must arrive before sundown," Mogg cautioned. "It would be both unwise and dangerous to remain on the side of the mountain through the night. Especially without enough wood for torches."

"He's got a good point," Paymer replied.

Arlon clutched a few satchels and gulped down a hurried drink. "Then, we need to get moving," he said. "We only have about five or six hours of sunlight. Carry only what we need. We can leave the rest here and pick it up on the way back." He pointed. "We can hide it under those boulders by Mogg."

Paymer nodded. "Good idea, pal."

"I'm sure the climb is going to be hard enough. No reason to make it any harder."

"Back home we've got a proverb about that. It goes—"

"Wait—I just thought of something," Mae'Lee ventured. "Do we all need to go? I mean, maybe it would be easier for only one of us to go get the relics and then come back."

"Whoa, whoa," Paymer replied quickly. "Split up? Are you serious? On Slaughter Island?"

Arlon stashed a couple of bags in a wide void between the rocks. "Paymer's right. We need to stay together." He started to take another drink when Mogg grabbed his wrist.

"Conserve water," he recommended. "It may be a long, hot climb."

Arlon nodded. "Good point."

"Hey, that's my line," Paymer protested.

"And if the boat doesn't return tomorrow," Mae'Lee added, "we may need our water to last a long…long time."

"And our food, too," Paymer noted. "Don't forget about that. Then, again…maybe we can eat grass. I don't think I've ever tried it. It might be—"

"No one's gonna have to eat grass," Arlon sighed with a frustrated smile. "And the ship will return."

Mae'Lee finished repacking her supplies. "But we can't count on that."

Arlon hooked a satchel over his shoulder. "And that's why we will *plan* for the worst, but we will also hope for the best."

Paymer grinned while rolling a coin through his fingers. "That reminds me of another saying back—"

"Let's go," Arlon urged. "We're wasting daylight."

———————————————

Paymer stared at the rock.

On any other day, he wouldn't have given it a second glance. But today wasn't like most other days.

So he stared at it.

And the one next to it.

He bent down and traced his trembling hand across its flat surface. "Um…guys," he called out. "*Hey, everybody*." He stood up. "I found something! Hurry! Come over here!"

An out-of-breath Arlon was the first to arrive. "Is it a tree?"

Paymer grinned. "We've been walking around this island for over an hour, pal. I think we've pretty well established that there aren't any trees."

Mae'Lee rushed over. "Is it relics?"

Paymer hesitated thoughtfully. "Well, in a manner of speaking…I guess so."

She squinted. "What?"

Mogg came up behind them. "By the Red Leaf," he muttered in awe. "Well done. Well done, my friend."

"What are you talking about?" Mae'Lee asked.

Paymer pointed proudly at the rock. And the one next to it. And a hundred more beyond that winding up the slope. "Stairs," he announced. "Stone stairs."

Arlon could hardly contain his excitement. "You found the best way!"

Mae'Lee giggled with joy. "And it looks like an easy way."

"Or at least an *easier* way," Arlon replied. He pivoted around and glanced over at Mogg. "This is good news."

Mogg's expression fell flat. "It is well-spoken."

"Oh really? *Well-spoken?* Well, I seem to remember an old Kray proverb…something about the eyes betraying the heart?" He sauntered right up to him. "And yours are telling a different story than your lips, my friend. What's wrong?"

Mogg pushed past them and ascended the first few steps. His heavy boot falls echoed across the slope. He swiveled around. "These stairs were built by someone."

"And a long time ago," Paymer noted. "By the looks of them. They look old. Very old."

"If these stones lead to the top of the mountain," Mogg continued, "then others will have had access to the relics as well."

"Gotcha," Arlon sighed. "And they might have taken them away. A very long time ago."

"I hate to even say this," Paymer began. "But maybe that old man makes his living selling those maps. He probably has a whole box just full of them. And right now, I bet that box is sitting next to a pouch. A pouch with over fifty Royals. *Our Royals.*"

With a quick heft and a firm resolve, Arlon adjusted his packs before bounding up the stone pathway. "Only one way to see if all this was worth it."

Paymer shifted his own satchels and matched his friend's aggressive pace. "Look out…I'm right behind you, pal."

Mae'Lee glanced back at Mogg. "I will take up the last position," he offered.

"Well, here I come, gentlemen," she called out in mid-stride. "Make sure you don't slow me down."

The western sky was a wall of fire.

And an exhausted Mae'Lee was determined to enjoy it. "Hold on," she cried out, completely winded.
"Can...we...take...a...break?"

The two boys slowed to a much-needed stop as Mogg eventually caught up. Arlon tried to wipe the waterfall of sweat that was almost blinding him and gestured up the mountain. "But...we are...almost there. Just...a little...further."

The Princess used one of her satchels as a temporary cushion and plopped down. "Listen," she huffed. "Those...bones...up there...have been there...a long time." After dabbing her cheeks and neck with a soft cloth, she jabbed a finger out towards the blazing sunset. "But...that...*that*... won't be."

Paymer sat as well. "Whoa," he gasped. "That's...just...wow."

Shifting crimson fingers of light rippled across the horizon as peach rays with lavender accents shot far overhead. A handful of stars were just beginning to pierce through the darkening haze.

"And I thought...that the sunsets...from the *Graceful Galleon*...were beautiful," Paymer said, still breathing hard.

"They were," Arlon replied. "But this...this is...something else." A huge grin broke out across his hot and wet face.

His thoughts began drifting a lot further west.

Mother…I wish you could be here with me to see this. Maybe I'll get the chance to describe it to you one day…but I'm not sure I can. Just imagine every incredible sunset you've ever seen…and then put them all together into one. That might come close.

Oh…I almost forgot. And then you have to see it after a very long climb to the top of a volcano. Sorry that I left that part out. It's important.

Mogg cleared his throat a few times. "Beauty is not the only thing…which is about to fade, my friends. If we delay…we will lose our light as well."

"Can't we have…just five more minutes?" Paymer begged. "We're just now…getting some freaky orange and purple…around those clouds there."

Arlon slapped him on the back. "Come on…let's go. Mogg is right."

"But the colors—"

Arlon hoisted him up by the armpit. "You forget that the rest of us…get to see this same color…all the time."

Paymer dusted himself off. "You what?"

Arlon messed up his friend's hair. "We see plenty of red…every day. Right here."

"Funny. Very funny."

"Time to go, your Highness," Arlon urged with his hand outstretched. She latched hold, and he gently pulled her to her feet. "Maybe one day…I'll hire the greatest artist in all the Five Kingdoms…to paint a picture of that," he said. "For you. As big as you want."

Her smile was priceless. "That's a lovely thought. I would love that!"

After a quick stretch, Paymer worked his way up the old path once again. "Just think. If we could get…our fifty Royals back, you could hire…a lot of artists, pal."

Arlon fell in close behind him. "I'll try to remember that…the next time I negotiate…for a map that could help…save the world."

"Good point. Let's hope ours…was worth the price. And worth…all of these steps." He glanced back down the steep slope. "Anyone…been keeping count?"

"I don't think…numbers go that high, Paymer," Mae'Lee called out.

"I've counted," Arlon said. "And it's…almost the same as the number…of your freckles."

"Really? First it's my hair…now it's my freckles," Paymer chuckled. "Anything else you want…to make fun of?"

"Uh, no," Arlon replied. "Not really. I would never…ever…make fun of…your *tattoos*."

"Don't listen to him," Mae'Lee quipped teasingly. "I think…they look…nice."

Paymer's eyebrows shot up as a proud smile broke out. "Well, well. I guess…that was a *royal* compliment. It's nice to see…that *someone* back there…appreciates handsome men."

Arlon passed by him and rolled his blue eyes. "Thanks, your Highness. Now his swelled head…is slowing him down. Keep moving."

"Hey…I slowed down on purpose," Paymer fired back. "This…is Slaughter Island. And we're almost at the top." He paused just long enough to almost catch his breath. "I bet that the first one there…is in the most danger. So…I'll stay back."

"Oh. Uh…*thanks?*"

"Anytime, pal. Anytime. You're our leader." Paymer whisked his hands forward a few times. "Now…keep going…*lead.*"

Arlon trudged along and sighed.

Sorry, Paymer.

Being out in front…doesn't make someone a leader.

"Weapons," Mogg called out. "The top is near. We do not know what may be waiting."

"Or *who*," Mae'Lee said.

"Or *both*," Paymer muttered.

Arlon swallowed hard and yanked his sword out. He heard Paymer do the same. The endless ancient stone stairs finally transitioned to a series of steep steps that appeared to lead through a wide gap in the eroding rim of the volcano. Arlon raised his left hand and silently cautioned everyone to wait. He hunkered low and crept up the stairs, peering over each of them until he ultimately gained a view of what lay beyond.

Paymer snuck up behind him. "What...do...you...see?" he whispered.

Arlon remained low and scanned the area.

"Any people? Or...slaughtering creatures?" Paymer murmured. "How about relics?"

Arlon ventured to lift his head higher and moments later, even higher yet. The steps before him led back down several feet before leveling off into an enormous plateau paved with a grid of gray stones. The seams between the carefully hewn rocks were remarkably straight, and he was struck by the lack of weeds invading the crisscrossing cracks. Dark blemishes of varying sizes randomly dotted the sculpted landscape. In the distance, perhaps a hundred yards further out, a pair of enormous stone platforms rose up, surrounded by wide steps.

Mogg jogged closer. "Is it safe, my friend?"

Arlon retreated carefully and pivoted around. "It's kinda like a huge courtyard. I didn't see anyone or anything, except for a couple of structures way out."

"No Dragon relics?" a disappointed Mae'Lee asked with a noticeable sigh.

"No Dragon relics...*yet*. But it's a big area."

With a few quick steps, Mogg stole past him and surveyed the area for himself. "Some of the stones have been blackened by fire," he relayed with obvious concern. "Fires for cooking, or heat, or light."

Paymer crawled up beside him but stayed low. "When? Yesterday? Or a hundred years ago?"

"The ashes and wood have gone," Mogg replied. "I cannot tell."

"Then I'm gonna say it was a hundred years ago," Paymer asserted. "That feels better. A lot better."

A timid Mae'Lee joined them as a puzzled look clouded her face. "Why would anyone go to all the effort to build something like this?" She looked back downhill. "Or all those stairs?"

Arlon stood up. "I have no idea." He looked around with a subtle nod. "But I'm glad they're not here."

The rugged rim of the volcano was already beginning to throw long and deepening shadows across the vast, empty plateau curiously nestled just below it.

Mogg motioned off to his left. "The light is failing. We must continue on."

At first, the group stayed in a tight cluster while descending into the mysterious plaza, but they gradually fanned out as they explored further.

Mae'Lee jutted her hand out at the stone structures up ahead. "What do you think those things are?"

"Platforms of some kind," Arlon replied.

"For what?"

"Speeches…or maybe performances of some kind," he said. "I really…don't…know." (Something on the ground caught his eye.) Arlon halted and knelt down suddenly. With a quick motion, he swept his hand across the flat stone, clearing off the thin layer of dark dust that seemed to coat everything and clog every crack. He lowered his face even further and blasted the area with a strong exhale. A tight pattern of similar engravings had been neatly carved into the pavement.

Four triangles.

Oh no.

A cold chill rippled across his flesh.

The Order.

"You find something, pal?" Paymer called out from several yards away.

A hundred concerns paralyzed him.

Should I tell them?

Mae'Lee would be terrified.

And we can't leave until tomorrow.

Arlon jumped up and moved on. "Oh, just some scratchings on a rock."

"Words?"

"No, just…scratchings."

Mae'Lee hugged her own arms and glanced around with an uneasy look as a cool wind swept across the hard pavement with a dull, eerie wail. "This place is so…empty. So quiet. It's creepy."

Mogg whirled about. "By the Red Leaf, I am thankful for empty and quiet. And it would be to our advantage if it remained so."

Paymer's right hand shot up. "I also vote for empty and quiet."

Arlon couldn't resist a little jab to break the tension. "I don't think it will ever be quiet with you around, Paymer."

"Hey, now! I can't help it that I'm a natural conversationalist."

Arlon smiled. "If you say so."

"It's true. I have the skills of a great orator. People used to sit and listen to me speak for hours and hours."

"I think you meant to say '*sleep*,'" Arlon teased. "People would listen to you and *sleep* for hours and hours."

(Mae'Lee tried not to chuckle, but it still slipped out).

They reached the base of the wide stairs leading up to one of the two platforms and Paymer hurried up them. "Now, hold on," he said. "Just wait right there down below and listen as I dazzle all of you with a glorious speech about a — *DRAGON?!*" Paymer began jumping up and down, pointing down wildly at something just out of their sight. "Dragon!" he yelled. "I found a Dragon!"

Arlon and Mogg instantly drew their swords and flew up the steps to reach him in a matter of seconds.

"Put your weapons down!" Paymer halfway yelled and halfway laughed. "I don't think you can kill it twice." The grinning redhead pointed down again. "See?"

"Oh, wow," Arlon muttered, lowering his blade.

"By the Red Leaf," Mogg whispered.

The circular stone pit sprawled out before them was roughly thirty feet from edge to edge, and several feet deep. The bottom contained two things: a fine, black gravel composed of crushed volcanic rock, and the well-preserved bones of a gigantic Dragon.

Mae'Lee scampered up the stairs and inserted herself between the three boys. The first thing she saw was the creature's massive skull glaring back at her. "Oh, my!" she exclaimed, retreating behind Arlon. She dared to peek back out. "Is it...dead?"

Mogg climbed down into the dark pit and cracked off an enormous tooth. "It is dead."

"The map was right, pal!" Paymer said, clapping his hands. "That old man didn't cheat us! I'd say those relics right there are worth every bit of fifty Royals. And maybe fifty more. And another fifty on top of that!"

Arlon looked up and squinted.

Wait a minute. The map. The old man. Bailconn.

He said something else.

"The other platform!" Arlon yelled as he swiveled to his right. He sheathed his sword and scrambled back down to the plateau before rushing up the other set of steps. He glanced down as he slid to a stop and felt like his heart would explode for joy. "*Get over here!*" he demanded. "You won't believe this!"

Paymer ran.

Mae'Lee jogged close on his heels.

"*TWO?!*" Paymer cried out. "*TWO DRAGONS?!*"

Mogg struggled to climb back up onto his platform. "What did you find?"

Paymer waved his arm wildly. "You need to get over here, Mogg! There's another round pit, just like that one by you, right here by us. And this one also has a Dragon!"

"A *dead* Dragon," Mae'Lee added. "I've never seen something so dreadful, that was also so lovely."

"A *second* Dread Guardian?!" Mogg exclaimed in disbelief as he finally began to make his way over to their platform.

"A second Dread Guardian," Arlon agreed. He hopped down into the pit with

Paymer's help. "It's a little bit smaller, but it's still a Dragon. So…what do you want?" he asked. "Tooth or claw?"

"A claw!" Paymer hollered with a nod. He pointed. "That big one, on the back leg over there."

Arlon took a few steps and jabbed his finger out. "This one?"

"That's it, pal."

Arlon knelt down beside the massive collection of bones and began working the talon loose.

Mother…if only you could see me right now. I am in the middle of the remains of a dead Dragon! And, believe it or not…I've seen four dead Dragons, and now we will have relics from five.

He paused and grinned.

Well, mother, actually maybe I have seen all five. But one of them was in the ice, in a vision. So, I kind of saw it. Just think about it…now we only need one more! And then, I will be…home.

Home.

His grin was replaced with a hearty smile.

I have so many stories to tell you, and so many things to show you. And so many new friends for you to meet!

"So, uh, do you think you'll have that claw out before we meet the boat tomorrow?" Paymer teased. "I can climb down there and give you some help if you need it."

"What claw?" Arlon asked. "You mean...*this one?*" In not much more than a blur, he rose up, spun around, and flung something through the air. Paymer scrambled and nearly fell down as he stretched out to catch the tumbling object.

"Did you get it?" Mae'Lee asked.

Paymer displayed the long relic with pride. "He might be a terrible thrower, but Paymer of Orania is a great catcher."

Arlon's feet crunched in the dark gravel as he picked his way back towards them. "Personally, I think that humility is your best quality."

Paymer nodded as he admired the fearsome claw. "I agree. Absolutely."

"I still just cannot believe it," Mae'Lee began. "Two Dragons. Right here. In one place."

"Believe it," Paymer replied, handing her the talon. "You're holding the royal evidence, your royal Highness."

She rolled it over in her palm. "But...what happened here? Did they die here? Or were those remains brought here from somewhere else? And why?"

Paymer and Mogg both reached down and hefted Arlon up and out of the pit. "All good questions, Princess," Arlon responded. He stood up and dusted himself off. "Because of my Rone vision...of the two Dragons and the volcano...I think they probably died here." He reached into his shirt and slipped out his Rone necklace. "And now…it's time to find out if either of these remains…belong to Terras Adonis. The first Dragon."

"Wouldn't that be simply lovely?" Mae'Lee said. "That would be just thrilling!"

"Paymer…if you would do the honor?" Arlon requested, gesturing towards his necklace.

The redhead reached out with the claw and lightly tapped the Rone fragment.

Nothing.

He touched it a second time. Then a third time.

Still nothing.

Arlon retrieved the relic and repeated the test.

"Not the first Dragon," Mae'Lee sighed.

"But still a Dragon," Paymer said with a bright smile.

"And now," Arlon began, motioning to Mogg. "Now…the tooth. Perhaps those remains in the other pit belong to the first Dragon."

"I think it is," Mae'Lee announced.

"It might be," Arlon replied. "The odds are pretty good."

"Anyone want to place any bets?" Paymer asked.

"Very funny, Paymer," Arlon groaned. "We are all pretty much broke."

"Yeah, good point, pal. Carry on."

Mogg grasped the tooth and lowered the edge of it onto the Rone. Everyone held their breath.

Nothing.

"Really?" Mae'Lee looked dejected. "So, we still haven't found the first Dragon."

"That's okay," Paymer responded. "But we've found five out of six. Only one to go!"

"Only one to go," Mae'Lee repeated slowly. "I like the sound of that."

Arlon couldn't hide his smile as he tucked his necklace down inside his shirt. "I like it, too."

Paymer surveyed the area once again. "So, what you do think? You think that someone found these remains up here, and then they built…all this?"

"It's almost like a shrine," Mae'Lee observed.

"But who would build a freaky shrine to dead Dragons?" Paymer asked. A moment later he shot her a quick glance before staring at the others. "You don't think…"

"The…Order," Mae'Lee muttered.

Arlon swallowed hard. "That, uh, that would explain some of the…scratchings I saw."

Mogg folded his arms. "And that would also explain the sailor's fear of this island."

"That's right!" Paymer exclaimed. "Maybe the Order has been killing anyone who comes to this place. And over hundreds of years, it got a reputation as Slaughter Island."

Mae'Lee looked around. "But, where are they?"

"By the looks of the place," Arlon said, "they might not have been here for years. Maybe even decades. Or more."

"I like the sound of that," Paymer quipped.

"But, just because you like the sound of it, doesn't mean that it's true, Paymer. They could come here often."

"I *don't like* the sound of that."

"I don't like the sound of any of it," Mae'Lee said. "We need to get off this island."

Arlon frowned. "No way to do that until midday tomorrow."

"And that's *if* they come back for us," Paymer countered.

Mae'Lee started back down the wide stairs. "I don't want to stay up here all night. This whole area is dreadful. I doubt I could sleep."

Mogg spread his hands out. "We cannot go down the mountain tonight. Dark is almost upon us."

"Mogg's right," Arlon added. "It would take at least a few hours to climb to the bottom. We wouldn't be able to make torches that would last the whole way. And those stairs are too dangerous in the dark."

Mae'Lee plopped down hard on the last step and rested her face in her hands. She looked like she was on the edge of tears. "So, we have to sleep here?" she huffed.

Mogg surveyed the area, which was quickly losing light. "It is well-spoken. But we have the high ground on the island. Any attack would require a long climb to reach us."

Paymer trotted down the steps and sat beside the Princess. "I agree with Mogg. There's absolutely no way anyone would climb all the way up here just to get us." He patted her arm. "Plus, no one really knows we're here. So we're safe."

He was wrong.
Wrong again.
And even more wrong.

It was like listening to a hundred wolves howling across a distant field.

And it went on and on and on.

Arlon bundled up his cloak a little tighter and turned his back to the cruel wind. It reminded him of the haunting gusts that had rolled off the snowy slopes in the mountains of Orania, yet without the bitter cold that had numbed his hands and feet.

He had volunteered to stand the first watch, so he couldn't complain, but Arlon doubted that any of them would get much real sleep. Even though they were nestled up against one of the platforms to shield them from the constant assault of the blustery wind, they couldn't escape its eerie wail.

He tried pacing to pass the time (sitting still always made him too sleepy), but he found it difficult to stay motivated since half the time the wind was slamming him in the back, and the other half it was slapping him in the face. There was a little moonslight, at least enough to get around, but he was concerned that he wouldn't be able to see any threats until they were almost upon them. And with the wailing winds, he was certain that he would never hear them.

So he did what he always did.

Arlon retreated into his thoughts.

He glanced over at stairs and pictured Kash sitting there, waiting for him. The imaginary old man beckoned towards him with his hand.

"Come. Rest by me, my boy. You appear beyond exhausted."

"I am tired," Arlon replied as he sauntered over. "The last few months have been…challenging. Very challenging."

Kash looked up and smiled warmly. "But this unlikely band has more than met the challenge. Do you remember what I said about that word *hopeless*?"

Arlon sat down. "You said a lot of things."

"I reminded you of the innumerable and insurmountable odds which you have both faced and mastered. An honest appraisal of your tremendous success leads one to see the blessing of the Zho."

Arlon stared down into his lap. "We haven't...*always* succeeded."

Kash folded his arms and sighed. "You are lamenting the loss of the young woman from Ammodis, are you not?"

A silent Arlon just nodded.

"And the loss of the Dunamai from Thilasson?"

More nodding.

Kash stared out into the surrounding darkness. "Every great victory involves sacrifice." He turned back towards the boy and their eyes met. "*Every...great...victory*. There are no exceptions. No battles are without losses, and no great accomplishments are without great toil and sometimes greater grief. But remember well, that every tear...every drop of sweat and blood, is softening the soil for a rich harvest of triumph yet to come."

"How do you always do that?"

Kash's wrinkled face wrinkled even further. "How do I do what, my boy?"

Arlon shook his head with a subtle laugh. "You always make things sound so...so big, and majestic, and inspiring."

Kash matched his laugh. "You are on a quest to defeat Terras Telos, the seventh Dread Guardian, who is besought with laying waste to the kingdoms of this world. In all the eons of my life, I have never witnessed something so big. So majestic. And so inspiring."

"You did it again."

"I am simply providing perspective."

Arlon reached into his cloak and pulled out a Dragon claw. He held it up and spun it around. "We've found the relics," he said. "Or, most of them. Five of them."

"Well done, my boy...that is the very definition of big, majestic, and inspiring."

"But, uh, we still have one more to find. And unless the Sevasti have some incredible wisdom that you're keeping secret, we are out of clues."

Kash hesitated while his warm smile dissolved. "Trust me when I say that Gremlor and I have exhausted our resources. If there are further clues to be found in Alaithia, they are unknown to us."

Arlon pulled the relic even closer. "And even if we did find the last one. What do we do with them? How does that work?"

Kash leaned in and squinted at the talon. "The document spoke of a lethal potion. '*Mortal poison for the immortal Dread.*' I would offer that they must be combined, perhaps ground into powder, and then placed on a sharp implement. But who can speak with certainty about such things?"

Arlon lowered the relic and pulled out his necklace. "Can you speak with certainty about this?"

Kash's eyes grew wide. "I can tell you that it is made from the Rone of Terras Adonis, the First Dread Guardian. I can tell you that it was my most precious possession."

"Tell me again about the visions it causes," Arlon began. "I thought they were always visions of the future?"

"Indeed, they are, my boy. Always the future."

"But, I saw—"

Kash held up his hand and rose up with a growing concern in his eyes. He stared off to the northwest. "Do you hear it?"

Arlon turned his head and listened intently. "Uh, just the wind. But it seems to be dying down somewhat."

"Listen. *Again.*"

Arlon stood up and closed his eyes.

The lessening gusts continued.

He strained to block them out.

Concentrate, he urged.

And then…he heard it.

Wait…what was that?

Something rhythmic.

Chanting?

Chanting.

"What do I do, Kash?"

He opened his eyes and whirled around. The old man had vanished back into the hidden corners of his memory. Arlon yanked out his sword and ran over to the others, kicking at their legs.

"Get up! Everyone!" he screamed. *"Hurry! We are in danger!"*

Mogg was the first to jump up, weapon in hand. "What is wrong?!"

"I—I don't know. I don't know. I can hear some kind of chanting. Sounds like voices." He pointed into the darkness as Paymer and Mae'Lee scrambled to their feet. "Over that way. Near the steps up the side of the volcano."

Mae'Lee looked terrified. "Who is it?!"

"I don't know. But it's something. Or someone."

"It's the Order!" she mourned.

"We don't know that," Arlon replied.

"But we think that," Paymer said.

"Stay together," Mogg ordered. "Take your weapons. And follow me."

The weakening wind still occasionally buffeted at their backs and wrapped their hair into their faces as they rushed off across the broad plateau. Mogg moved as fast as the deep darkness would allow, slowing only long enough to make sure that the group was still together.

"Oh…I can hear it now," Paymer muttered.

"I still can't," Mae'Lee complained.

"That's a good thing," he replied. "It sounds freaky."

Mogg held his finger to his lips. "Stay quiet. We are almost there. Weapons ready."

Everyone nodded (more or less), and he guided them the last several yards towards the broad steps leading back through the volcano's rim. It terrified Arlon to realize that their only possible escape route would lead them directly into the path of their unknown enemies. The disturbing echoes of the rhythmic chanting grew noticeably louder as he crept up the steps alongside Mogg. The tense pair crested the final slab and peeked down at the steep slope disappearing far below them.

Arlon hoped to spot only a few people.

Instead, he saw a few *hundred*.

An elongated train of flickering torches snaked its way along the dark mountainside like a thin and slow stream of fire. In an instant, the beautifully deadly sight paralyzed Arlon with a deep sense of justified fear. Paymer and Mae'Lee crawled on their bellies beside him to gawk at the foreboding view.

"*Oh, no!*" the Princess muttered on the verge of tears. "What do we do?!"

"Do we have the relics?" Mogg asked.

"Uh, yeah," Arlon replied. "I have them."

"What are we going to do?" Paymer asked frantically. "There's so many of them!"

"We cannot fight," Mogg said. "It is an ill thought. But we can hide. Come." The stealthy warrior kept low and retreated quickly, scrambling back down the stone steps before making a hard left. He led them along the ragged edge of the rim until they stumbled upon a craggy cavity large enough for them to huddle in.

"What's the plan?" Paymer asked.

Mogg positioned himself at the edge of the rock and kept a lookout. "Wait. Then escape," he answered.

"Do what?" Mae'Lee pressed.

Arlon slid up next to her. "If I'm understanding him right, I think Mogg wants to wait until they all get up here. And then, we can slip out in the darkness behind them and get back down the mountain."

She was trembling uncontrollably. "Wh— where d-did they all come f-from?"

Arlon shook his head. "I don't know, maybe their boat just landed." He rubbed her shoulder. "But listen…we are going to be okay. We've faced worse than this. A small crowd with torches can't even compare with the rage of a Dragon. Or a Mal'korr. And we made it through all that."

"Th-that was diff-fferent," she sobbed.

"You're right," Arlon agreed. "That was harder. And yet, here we—"

Mogg shot up his left hand and urged everyone to fall silent. The telltale soft orange glow of firelight began to spread out across the flat stones of the mountaintop courtyard. An instant later, the first of dozens and dozens of bright torches came into view, held aloft by an assortment of men and women, each carrying various bundles of wood or satchels undoubtedly stuffed with food and supplies.

"Only some of them have torches," Paymer whispered to Arlon as the chanting intensified. "That means there's a lot more people than we thought."

Arlon nodded before scurrying up beside Mogg. "It looks like they are headed for the Dragon pits," he whispered, pointing off to their left. "If they find what we've left behind over there, they will know that someone's here. And then look for us. We need to leave. Soon."

Mogg nodded.

The unusual procession continued to spill out onto the plateau for several minutes, as the devotees began pooling into a large, orderly mass before the pair of elevated stone platforms. Several of the congregation amassed piles of wood in various spots as others ignited them into roaring fires enriched by the fitful breezes.

"What are they saying out there?" Paymer asked.

"I can't tell," Arlon whispered back. "It sounds like a different language."

"Freaky."

The numbers of attendees pouring through the gap in the rim eventually dwindled to a mere trickle.

"Shouldn't we go now?" Arlon whispered. "There's only a few. And if they light any more of those big fires, they're gonna see us for sure."

Mogg shook his head and held up his hand once again. A frustrated Arlon glanced over at Mae'Lee hunkered in the corner with her head down. He couldn't tell if she was about to collapse from exhaustion or distress. He figured it was probably both.

"I…uh…I don't see anyone else over there," Paymer noted under his breath. "Gap looks clear."

Mogg glanced back. "The time is now. Get her royal Highness."

"You don't have to tell me twice," Paymer murmured as he slinked back, grabbing her arm. "Come on, Princess…we're getting out of here. Now."

In a silent and stealthy rush, Mogg led the frightened travelers as they hugged the edge of the rim in single file, doing their best to stay concealed under the unreliable cover of darkness. Off to their left, towering flames licked high into the night sky from the massive fires ignited by swaying worshipers whose long shadows now danced like dark demons along the cold stones of the plateau.

Arlon's heart throbbed.

Its pounding flooded his ears.

The chanting intensified.

With a raised fist, Mogg brought them to a standstill only a few feet away from the stairs ascending to the exit. He brandished a sword and stared at each of them. "Weapons ready." His eyes narrowed, and he nodded at them one by one. "We…go…*NOW!*"

In a furious bolt, they easily topped the short flight of steps without incident and began racing through the gap.

But their desperate escape ended there.

It all happened so fast.

It was a confusing blur of haste.

And yelling and strong arms.

And more yelling. And then ropes.

Lots of ropes.

And a net.

Arlon plowed into the back of Mae'Lee, who had slammed into the back of Mogg as Paymer crumpled to the ground and rolled sideways. Swords, now violently loosened from jolted hands, scraped and clinked and bounced across the stone as a swarm of dark figures encircled them.

There was torchlight.

A cloud of powder.

And everything went black.

There it is again.

Something irritated the back of his neck.

What is that? a very groggy Arlon wondered as he slowly regained consciousness.

At least it's warm.

He blinked several times and glanced down. Not only was he trapped inside of a crude net constructed of frayed ropes, but a pair of freckled arms were draped across his chest, and his back was plastered against something hard and quite uncomfortable. Arlon struggled to sit up when a snoring mop of red hair rolled onto his right shoulder.

Oh, it was Paymer's breath.

Well…that's nice.

Arlon elbowed his sleeping friend.

"Paymer!" he urged. "Wake up!"

A string of unintelligible babblings trickled out of the corner of Paymer's murmuring lips. Arlon elbowed him a second time (much harder), and his friend began to come around.

Arlon strained against the net to check on the whereabouts of the others. He was greatly relieved to catch a glimpse of Mogg passed out, face down, on the other side of Paymer's wiggling form. The Princess was a bit more jumbled up and laying across Mogg. Arlon was fairly certain he was sitting on at least one of her feet.

"Get them up," he whispered coarsely to Paymer. "They're on your right."

Paymer yawned and did his best to stretch (but the ropes converted that into an awkward and pointless exercise). "Do what?"

"I said, wake up the Princess and Mogg," Arlon repeated firmly. "And hurry. Someone's coming."

The huge fires in the distance silhouetted most of the crowd milling about aimlessly, but there was no doubt that one figure was approaching directly towards the netted captives. Arlon glanced off to his left and caught a glimpse of at least one guard and a few torches. As Paymer leaned to the side to rouse their friends, Arlon finally saw two more men standing watch on their right. Both with swords. There was a large sack laying at their feet, and Arlon spotted Paymer's sword and a few other of their personal belongings sticking out of it.

The lone figure drew closer, and the torchlight began to reveal his old and familiar face. "Truth be known, I didn't expect the lot of you folks to come around so quickly."

Bailconn! Arlon realized in horror. *I don't believe it…he set us up!*

Paymer leaned closer and whispered. "Hey! Isn't that the old guy that sold—"

Arlon elbowed him to stay quiet as Mae'Lee and Mogg struggled to find room to sit up.

Bailconn came to a stop before gesturing towards two of the guards and then looking back at the captives. "Are you hungry? We have plenty of provisions."

One of the guards deposited a plate of bread on the ground just beyond the net.

Bailconn smiled with a slight bow. "It's the least I could do, since you kindly offered this weary traveler a warm meal the last time we met." He picked up a hunk of bread and held it out. "Hungry?"

No one made a sound.

No one moved.

"Fair enough. Fair enough," he replied, bobbing his head. "But you know, my grandmother used to say that '*hospitality rejected is the greatest of all insults*.'" He set the food down and his expression grew dark. "And tonight is not the night to be insulting me, I can assure you of that." He moved closer and sat down. "It is most unfortunate, is it not? To be close, so close, to obtaining that which you think you need. And then…to have it all ripped from your very fingers." The old man chuckled as he reached into his cloak and pulled out a pair of relics. "A tooth…and a claw." He raised them up and inspected them. "And why would you have come all this way, to such an awful place, an island with a dangerous reputation, to gather a tooth and a claw? Why would you be seeking these?"

They all kept silent.

"Wait," he said, squinting. "Hold on. Tooth and claw. Where have I heard this before? Tooth? Claw?" His eyes flitted back and forth between the relics. "Oh, yes…now I remember. A poem. An old poem. Let's see…how does it go?" He cleared his throat and smiled.

> "'With tooth, with scale, with claw.
> Hallowed remnants of those long dead.
> Gather them each,
> Gather them all.
> Mortal poison for the immortal Dread.'"

Arlon was filled with horror as Bailconn and the three guards exploded into laughter.

"Did…did…did you know," Bailconn chuckled as he struggled to speak, "that…that it was one of my kin who invented that foolish little rhyme?" He glanced over at one of the guards as his belly continued to shake. "No, no, really," he replied with a wide smile. "I'm serious. The Apex told me that a distant ancestor of mine penned those wonderful words of false wisdom."

Arlon gasped.

False wisdom? Foolish rhyme?

Bailconn hunkered forward somewhat. "Oh, I can see a bit of concern on your faces, young Chosen Children. Truth be known, I guess it is to be expected. To have been so wickedly misled, to be…so terribly deceived. To have risked life and friends and comfort…in pursuit…of an ancient lie."

Arlon's mind raced.

It can't be. It cannot be.

Bailconn carefully set the relics on the flat stones of the plateau before him. "A Dragon cannot be killed by any mortal means, foolish children. Don't you believe the scriptures of truth?" He laughed again. "The remains of a Dread Guardian are worthless to people such as yourselves—they may be a curiosity or an interesting trinket for the market—but to you they are all but worthless. But to us, to the Order, they are beyond estimation."

A frightened chill went up Arlon's spine.

The Order.

Bailconn cleared his throat. "That little rhyme was contrived by our ancestors. My ancestors. And it was allowed to be found. And do you know why?" He turned to glare right at Arlon. "Because we wanted to multiply our resources, my boy. By creating legends and myths about what Dragon relics can do, we multiplied our search through people like you. And Kings. And other powerful and rich people. A genius enterprise, wouldn't you say?"

His question was only met with the sound of the flickering torches nearby.

"The idea of crafting a lethal poison to kill a Dragon was quite tempting," he continued with a self-satisfied grin, before pointing back towards the two platforms. "Many kings desired such a potion. And we used their coffers and lust for power to help us discover the remains you found in those pits behind me. We found the final resting places of those two Dread Guardians, and then had them relocated here for proper…respect." He paused. "But, truth be known, the promise of that little poem wasn't the most attractive benefit that Dragon relics could potentially bestow. We also spread other rumors…perhaps you have heard them? One of my favorites is the irresistible legend that Dragon bones can turn any metal into pure gold."

Paymer glanced over at Mae'Lee before looking down into his lap.

Bailconn motioned towards one of the guards, who quickly handed him a short blade. He lowered the tip and repeatedly tapped it against the Dragon tooth (and then the claw). He frowned and chuckled at the same time. "Oh, my…no gold. What a terrible shame!" He returned the weapon and locked eyes with Arlon once again. "But, to be fair…perhaps Dragon relics *do* lead to gold." Bailconn reached into his cloak and dug out a hefty pouch. "Look familiar? It should. This is *your* pouch." He jangled it right up against the net. "This is *your* gold."

Mae'Lee couldn't restrain her terrified and angry tongue any longer. "My father, King Leandros of Avdira, will hunt you down and kill you—*kill all of you*," she blurted out. "Don't you dare harm me or any of my friends! And, no matter what you say, we know that you are a liar!"

"My dear Princess," he muttered in the most condescending of tones. "I wouldn't dream of harming your precious little head. Or of harming any of you. At least, not until Terras Telos arrives." He scanned their faces. "Oh, yes…don't be surprised. The Dread Guardian is indeed coming. His majesty is presently on his way. We expect his glorious presence to arrive before sunrise." He took a long and deep breath. "And now, with the addition of your capture, we have all six of the Chosen Children."

"All six?!" Mae'Lee erupted. "Now we know that you are a bunch of murderous liars! The real Pelias died many years ago, thank you!

And the Dragon killed Hort after the Karaval! I was there."

Bailconn glanced up at all three of the guards. "A tragic contradiction, wouldn't you say? Such true beauty and yet such ugly ignorance." They all laughed. "*Greatly mistaken* daughter of Leandros, I can assure you that I have not uttered a single falsehood. All that I have spoken is true. Four of the Chosen Children sit before me, secured within a net, and far, far away…two more are secured within a cavern. And now, all six have been taken captive by the Order. A worthy gift for his majesty, Terras Telos. As you might recall, the Dread Guardian rejected all of you on the day of *your* offering." He smiled as the torchlight cast shifting shadows across his wrinkled face. "But, we have it on good authority, that he will not reject *our* offering."

"You are insane," Mae'Lee grumbled. "All of you! Insane and deluded."

"I am sorry, Princess…but if you believe there is hope." He shook his head. "If you believe that your father and all his armies can somehow rescue you from the clutches of Terras Telos…then it is *you* that suffers from a delusion. A delusion of the worst sort. But you will soon see the truth. Not that it really matters, though. Soon, armies will march. The final war will come. Kings will be overthrown. And the Order will rise." He squinted at them with a curious look. "It is almost a shame that none of you will live to see it. You have stirred up his majesty's wrath. And his wrath…is terrible beyond measure."

A pair of younger men rushed alongside Bailconn, and one of them knelt down before whispering in his ear. The elder gathered up the two relics and rose to his feet.

"And speaking of his majesty…I must beg your leave now." He dusted off the lower reaches of his cloak. "I must prepare for his arrival. But don't worry, I will send for you…at the proper time."

A few moments later, Bailconn and his escorts blended into the mass of silhouettes reveling in the distant firelight. The guard on their left picked up the plate of bread and joined the others on the opposite side. The three sat down and engaged in quiet conversation.

Arlon struggled to sort through Bailconn's troubling revelations. A mixture of hope and fear jumbled within. A tiny grin broke out on his tense face.

Hort…is alive?
The Dragon didn't kill him?
But then the smile vanished.
We have been chasing a lie.
The Order deceived us.
There is no way to kill the Dragon.

"He is lying," Mae'Lee whispered. She pushed forward against the net and looked at Arlon. "He is lying, isn't he?"

"He just said that Hort is still alive," Paymer replied excitedly. "But we saw the Dragon kill him."

Arlon looked down. "No. We didn't see the Dragon kill him. We saw…the Dragon…*take* him."

Paymer's face scrunched up. "But….but, we…uh…we—"

"We didn't see Hort die," Arlon repeated. "We saw the Dragon carry him away. Hort could be alive. Right now."

"I wouldn't trust anything that he says," Mae'Lee retorted. "It's all a dreadful lie. All that business about armies and war and all."

Paymer glanced over at her. "But…why would he lie? I mean…look around." He grabbed the net and shook it. "They have already captured us. Why lie to us now?"

"Paymer's right," Arlon responded. "It doesn't make sense that they would lie to us. They've got us. And the Dragon is coming. Lying would be pointless."

"It is well-spoken," Mogg declared quietly.

Mae'Lee's eyes looked all around. She finally pointed across the plateau. "But…but, he said that they brought those bones up here from somewhere else. That's not true." She stared at Arlon. "You saw it in a Rone vision. You saw those two Dragons fighting and dying above this volcano. Right?" She waited for him to reply.

He didn't.

"You did see it, didn't you?" she pressed. "I hope you weren't lying."

Paymer looked over. "Come on, pal...you saw it, right?"

Arlon raised his arm and patted his chest.

Oh no, he thought. *They took my necklace.*

Arlon clamped his eyes shut. He strained to remember, to hear Kash's comforting voice once again. Finally, the sound of Kash's wisdom echoed into his mind.

"My dear boy...Rone visions are always of the future."

Always?

"Always."

With a rush of emotion and dread, he forced himself to recall the fearful sight. Two Dragons, lashing out against each other in a furious conflict. Above a fuming and raging volcano. He played it over and over again in his mind, studying the beasts, as best he could.

A white Dragon.

And...a dark Dragon.

That dark Dragon...looks like...Terras Telos.

But how could that be?

His face contorted and shifted.

"Is he alright?" Mae'Lee asked. "*Arlon?*"

He couldn't hear her.

The horrifying visions continued to consume him. Again and again. Two Dragons. A volcano. *The future. The future?*

> *But how can there be TWO Dragons?*
> *The other six are all dead.*
> *We've found the bones of…five of them.*
> *Five.*
> *And I saw…two Dragons in my vision.*
> *Five. And two. That makes…seven.*
> *Can it be? But how?*

His mind raced, recalling as many scriptures as he could remember.

"Their power, none mortal shall vanquish. Dread against Dread, or suffer misery without end."

His excited eyes snapped open.

> *Dread against Dread.*
> *Dragon against Dragon?*

"I think he's back," Mae'Lee muttered. "Can you hear me now?"

"'Dread against Dread,'" Arlon whispered aloud. *"'Or suffer misery without end.'"*

"What is he saying?" the Princess asked.

"Something about a prophecy," Paymer muttered, keeping his voice down. "About Dragons. I think."

"'None mortal shall vanquish,'" Arlon murmured as he continued contemplating different scenarios. "We can't do it. Only Dragon can kill…Dragon. Only another Dragon can defeat…the last Dragon." He paused and stared

into the darkness. "But we've found five remains. And yet…none of them were the first Dragon. Terras Adonis. Rone visions. Always the future. Always."

"Are you going to share anything with us?" Mae'Lee urged, almost disgusted.

"Don't worry, Princess. He'll come around," Paymer replied. "He seems to be getting more…confident. He's working through something. Give him time."

"In case you haven't noticed," she began, shaking the net, "we probably don't have a lot of time!"

Arlon waved his hand, encouraging them all to get as close as possible.

"Here it comes," Paymer announced with a broad smile. "Told you."

"There…there is a reason that we haven't found any remains of the first Dragon," Arlon whispered.

"Is it because we haven't looked in the right places?" Mae'Lee asked.

"No," Arlon replied with a serious stare. "It's because there are no remains to be found. The first Dragon…*never died*."

"Whoa…*never died?!* What?!" Paymer erupted.

Mae'Lee slapped his shoulder. "Keep your voice down!"

"Sorry," Paymer whispered. "What are you talking about?"

"My vision. In my Rone vision, I saw two Dragons fighting to the death. One was Terras Telos. I'm sure of it now. The other was a white Dragon. I believe that I saw...Terras Adonis...the first Dragon."

Paymer started to speak. "But—"

"And Kash told me that Rone visions are always of the future. He said *always*."

Paymer nodded. "So, the bones in those two pits out there—"

"They are not the Dragons in my vision. They can't be," Arlon interrupted. "They died long ago. Bailconn was telling the truth. Those were brought here. By the Order."

"But that doesn't make any sense. How—"

"It doesn't matter, Paymer. A Rone vision is not a hope or a guess. Or a prediction. It *is* the future. The second Dragon in my vision, it must be Terras Adonis...the only Dread Guardian that could breathe Nightfire."

"Nightfire?" Paymer muttered. "You mean, fire at night?"

"Nightfire," Arlon reaffirmed. "It's a special Dragon fire. It is black as night. It gives off no light, and you can feel no heat...but it burns just the same. Very dangerous."

Mae'Lee glanced up as a strange look overtook her face. "Wait," she said. "Hold on. Night...fire." She continued staring for several seconds. "Nightfire."

"Oh, great," Paymer mumbled. "Now you've got the Princess doing that strange far-off look thing."

"Give her time," Arlon urged.

Her eyes squinted as her head bobbed subtly.

Arlon tapped her on the arm. "Tell us. What are you thinking?"

She blinked several times. "I, uh, I also had a Rone vision. While we were on the boat. Headed up-river to Alaithia. When I touched your necklace."

Arlon squinted as well. "And what did you see?"

A glistening line of tears began forming on her trembling eyelids. "Ter—terrible things," she sobbed under her breath.

"What terrible things?" Arlon asked in a low, soothing voice.

"I saw…soldiers. And blood. Soldiers killing people. Killing the Sevasti. I saw Alaithia. And the Firebridge."

"Wow," Paymer whispered. "Do you think that is what Bailconn was talking about? Armies and war?"

Arlon's eyes narrowed. "And what else did you see?"

"Fire," she replied coarsely as her voice broke. "Dark…fire."

"*Nightfire?*" Arlon asked.

She nodded with more tears. "I saw the shadow of a Dragon. And Nightfire. Nightfire raining down. It was…dreadful. Just dreadful." She collapsed against Paymer as her body heaved under the strain of her grief.

Arlon leaned back as Paymer sought to console the Princess. "Shhh. It's okay. It's okay. I'm sure it was awful."

"Nightfire," Arlon muttered. "Well…that settles it."

Paymer shot him a glance. "Excuse me? Huh? What settles what?"

"Nightfire," Arlon whispered once again.

"And why is this Nightfire business significant?"

"It is significant," Arlon began, "because, like I said, only one Dragon ever breathed Nightfire."

"The first Dragon?" Paymer asked.

Arlon nodded. "The first Dragon…Terras Adonis. Our two visions now confirm the truth."

"So, uh, what do we do?" Paymer inquired.

"The prophecy says '*Dread against Dread, or suffer misery without end.*'"

"Um, could you elaborate a bit on that, pal?"

Arlon paused, collecting his scattered thoughts. "It means, that we have to get him. We have to find the first Dragon. Only a Dragon can defeat a Dragon. The prophecy says '*or suffer misery without end*.' That means it might happen or it might not happen. It doesn't say '*will suffer*.' It says '*or suffer*.' Big difference."

"*We* have to find the first Dragon?!" Paymer exclaimed. "But why? You saw it in a vision. I thought visions always came true?"

"They do. But remember what Shendollyn said…it was something like '*prophecy makes us confident, but it should never make us negligent*.' Something like that."

"Well, that's a nice thought and all," Paymer began. "But, um, we seem to *not be* in the best position to go about hunting for this mysterious first Dragon. We are in fact…trapped. In a net. With no weapons." He paused. "And somehow they want to offer us to a Dragon."

Mogg took a deep breath and squinted.

"Unless the Zho intervenes…we will be dead before sunrise."

The elder Sevasti was beyond exhausted.

He had nearly nodded off to sleep when a familiar bluish glow and a deep rushing sound roused his head from his soft and comforting pillow.

"Lord Gremlor," a voice called out.

The tired sage rolled over just as a dark-headed figure materialized in the center of the Vision Fire's floating portal. He threw several layers of blankets back and strained to sit up. "Yes...yes, I am here," he called back.

"I do not see you," the murky visage said.

Gremlor grabbed a chair and slid it closer to the fire, before sitting down. "I am here, King

Leandros. But I must protest, the hour is late. What business—"

"Hold your tongue!" Leandros commanded. "My sources just informed me that my daughter was in Alaithia some weeks back. Why did you not contact me?!"

"Keep your voice down, you fool!" Gremlor scolded. He paused. "Your sources are correct. The young woman visited Alaithia."

"Why wasn't I contacted?!"

"We had planned to contact all of the kingdoms," Gremlor replied. "We had our swiftest riders prepared to bring word."

"You could have contacted me directly!" Leandros barked.

"Think before you speak, or I will end this pointless conversation!" Gremlor took a deep breath and tried to control his rage. "I could not contact you directly…for then our unique…*arrangement* would have been seriously jeopardized. How would the King of Avdira be able to account for the fact that he had received information long before the other kingdoms? Once again, this unforgivable degree of short-sightedness could invite tragic ruin on all of our plans!"

Leandros jumped up out of his chair and paced a bit. "Where is my daughter now?!"

"We do not know."

"What was her condition?"

"The Princess was in good health."

"Who was she traveling with?"

"She was accompanied by three other Dunamai, and a female from Ammodis."

Leandros leaned closer to the fire. "What was their business?"

"We...do not know. We are not sure if—"

"You *'don't know.'* You *'are not sure,'"* Leandros mocked with a condescending tone. "I am running out of patience for your incompetence and—"

"Choose the disposition of your next few words very carefully, Leandros of Avdira," Gremlor growled. "I am not a ward under your royal care, nor am I a feeble peasant scraping out a meager life in the far reaches of your bloated kingdom. You will address a Sevasti elder with the proper respect."

Leandros paced again. "Don't you mean, a *traitorous* Sevasti elder? Lord Gremlor forgets that I know of his wicked intentions."

"I will not subject the morality of my intentions to the opinion of the bloody and greedy Sovereign of Avdira!" Gremlor retorted. "For you forget that I also know of *your* less-than-righteous intentions, son of Thleggan."

Leandros chuckled. "And what of the intentions of Lo Ch'ar?"

Gremlor calmed somewhat and almost smiled. "I spoke at length with our counterpart in Ammodis less than a week past. His commitment is firm and unyielding. He remains ready to dispatch with Mandibar and to marshal his forces against Soteria."

Leandros sat back down. "Has your estimation of our timetable been altered?"

Gremlor leaned back.

"Everything is precisely on schedule."

The timing was perfect.

There was noise and confusion.

And darkness.

The two men standing guard at the stairs had rushed up and into the gap, torches in hand. No one remained to challenge the hooded figure stealing its way along the stone path up the side of the volcano.

No one witnessed the dark visitor scale the last few steps. No one saw the sword clasped firmly in its gloved hand. No one heard the gasp when the visitor caught sight of the throngs of worshipers silhouetted by firelight.

No one watched as the figure's eyes scanned the courtyard carefully, eventually coming to rest on the huddled mass of Dunamai enclosed tightly in a net.

No one noticed as the visitor shoved back her wide hood, revealing a mess of long blonde hair and a face full of resolve. She glared out at the crowds.

"The cursed beast that you adore may have killed my twin brother," she whispered, "but I will never let you harm my friends!"

The End of The Dragon Relics:
Book Three of the Arlon Prophecies

COMING SOON:

The Dragon King

Book Four of the Arlon Prophecies

For more information, visit:
www.MovingImagesPublications.com

ABOUT THE AUTHOR

As a science fiction movie fan and insatiable reader from his earliest memories in his birth state of California, Randy McWilson draws inspiration from a wide spectrum of interests and influences.

The reverberating echoes of Cold War espionage, explosions in scientific advancement, and strong, complex themes permeate his literary offerings. The historically-inclined reader finds a thrilling tale founded upon the rich fabric of both actual and alleged events.

He occupies his non-writing hours with a diverse range of hobbies: geology, theology, philosophy, history, and art.

McWilson currently lives in Jackson, Missouri, with his wife, Amanda, two children, a grandchild, and several pets.

Other books by Randy McWilson:

BACK TO NORMAL: SERIES ONE
Book One: Paradigm Rift
Book Two: Tradecraft
Book Three: Proximity
Book Four: Crossover

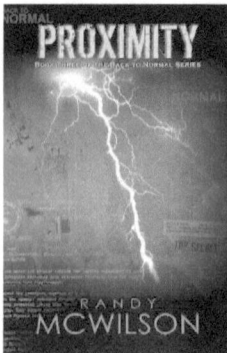 

www.ingramcontent.com/pod-product-compliance
Lightning Source LLC
Chambersburg PA
CBHW020456020726
47493CB00001B/51